PRAISE FOR THE PATH TO MISERY
Book I in the Hallowed Treasures Saga

"A sheltered princess's desire to travel before her arranged marriage places her at the center of a legendary quest in this YA novel....A page-turning fantasy set in a richly textured world, made all the more delightful by a thoughtful yet spirited heroine and her wonderfully oddball companions."
-Kirkus Review

PRAISE FOR IN LONELY EXILE
Book II in the Hallowed Treasures Saga

"The series continues to stand out for its foregrounding of friendship, diplomacy, and exploration over gory sword fights. A delightful reunion with old friends, sure to leave fans of strong female heroines craving the final installment."
-Kirkus Review

In Lonely Exile

Book II in the Hallowed Treasures Saga

IN LONELY EXILE

Book II in the Hallowed Treasures Saga

VICTORIA STEELE LOGUE

Victorialogue.com

Published in the United States by Ravenlore,
an imprint of Low Country Press

ISBN 978-0-9883044-8-2
eBook ISBN 978-0-9883044-9-9

Cover art copyright ©2016 by David Hayworth
Cover design, map and heraldic crests by David Hayworth

Printed in the United States of America

10 9 8 7 6 5 4 3 2 1

Dedication

To Frank, whose support made it possible for me
to bring the Hallowed Treasures Saga to life.

Western Kingdoms

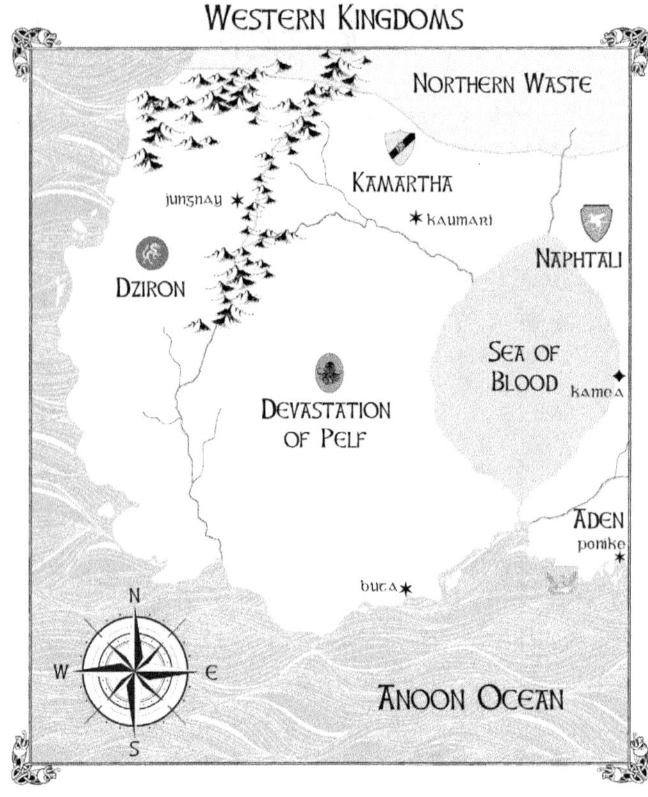

Eastern Kingdoms

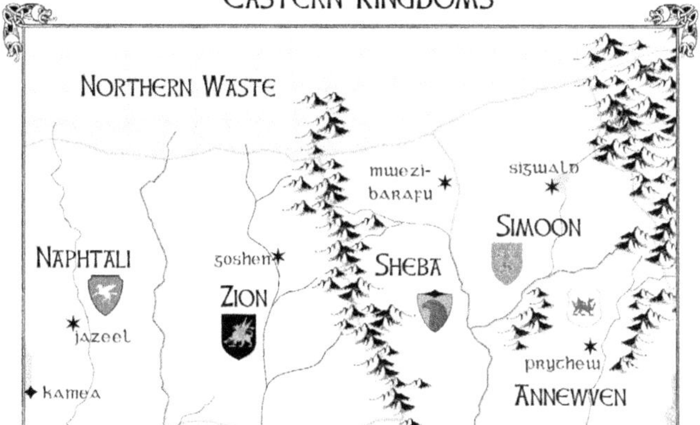

The Thirteen Hallowed Treasures

The quest central to this saga centers on recovering the Thirteen Treasures of the Thirteen Kingdoms. These hallowed treasures come from a Welsh tradition dating to the 15th-16th century, which lists these treasures as:

I. White Hilt: The Sword of Rhydderch the Generous
or *Dyrnwyn: Gleddyf Rhydderch Hael*
If a wellborn man drew it himself, it burst into flame from its hilt to its tip.

II. The Hamper of Gwyddno Long-Shank
or Mwys Gwyddno Garanir
It is said that one could put food for one man into the basket and when it opened, for one hundred men could be found within.

III. The Horn of Bran
or *Corn Bran Galed O'R Gogledd*
It was said that whatever drink one might wish for could found in this horn. It is also rumored that Merlin obtained the horn, which had been cut from the head of a satyr.

IV. The Chariot of Morgan the Wealthy
or *Car Morgan Mwynfawr*
Once in the chariot, a man could wish to be a certain place and
thus get there quickly.

V. The Halter of Clydno Eiddyn
or *Cebyster Clydno Eiddyn*
When attached to the foot of the bed, this halter would be
filled with whichever horse one wished for.

VI. The Knife of Llawfrodded the Horseman
or *Cyllel Llawfrodded Farchog*
This one knife would carve enough food to allow twenty-four
men to eat at table.

VII. The Cauldron of Dyrnwch the Giant
or *Pair Dyrnwch Gawr*
The cauldron would boil food for brave men only; never boil-
ing for cowards.

VIII. The Whetstone of Tudwal Tudglyd
or *Hogalen Tudwal Tudglydd*
If this stone was used by a brave man to sharpen his sword, and
he drew blood with it, that person would die. No harm would
come to the opponent from a coward's sharpened with it.

IX. The Coat of Padarn Red-Coat
or *Pais Padarn Beisrydd*
If worn by a well-born man, it would fit; if not, it would not
go in him.

X. The Crock and Dish of Rhyngenydd the Cleric
or *Gren A Desgyll Rhyngenydd Ysgolhaig*
Whatever food might be wished for would appear in the crock
and dish.

XI. Mantle of Arthur
or *Len Arthyr Yng Nghernyw*
The cloak has the ability to make the wearer invisible.

XII. The Chessboard of Gwenddolau, son of Ceidio
or *Gwyddbwyll Gwendolau ap Ceidio*
Made of silver and gold, the chessboard was said to possess mystical powers and would continue to play by itself once set up.

XIII. The Ring of Eluned
or *Eluned's Ring and Stone*
When it is placed on one's finger, with the stone inside the hand and closed upon the stone, the wearer is invisible.

Following the book, you will find information on each of the Thirteen Kingdoms, a pronunciation guide, as well as lists of the days of the week and months of the year.

In Lonely Exile
Book II in the Hallowed Treasures Saga

"What we call the beginning is often the end
And to make an end is to make a beginning.
The end is where we start from."

-T.S. Eliot
Little Gidding

Part Three Continued

> "Fire descends in the night,
> Lightning and thunder quicken the darkness,
> A dream takes root as I sleep."
>
> -Schlomo
> *The Divine Presence*

> "This is my Quest to follow that star,
> No matter how hopeless, no matter how far,
> To fight for the right without question or pause,
> To be willing to march into hell for a heavenly cause!"
>
> -Joe Darion
> *The Man of LaMancha*

12ᴛʜ Deer

As the first of the bells began to chime out the hour, Yona slipped out of her room and padded, as silently as she could, down the grand stairwell. She would have preferred to use one of the smaller stairways, but this one led directly to the foyer where the wicker basket was displayed in its glass case. 'You're a shadow,' she tried to convince herself, hugging the wall, 'no one can see you.' Fortunately, it was relatively dim with just a few flickering torches lighting the way.

When she reached the main entrance hall, she peered from the shadows of the staircase. Not only was the foyer blessedly empty, it was dark as well. She slipped a vial of oil, the glasscutter, her hairbrush, and a rag from the hamper. The oil, according to her research, made it easier to cut the glass; the rag would hopefully muffle the noise when she used the brush to tap the glass. She placed the rag and brush at her feet to keep her hands free for the oil and glasscutter.

Slowly, heart thundering in her chest, she opened the vial containing some olive oil, all she could lay her hands on, and smeared it in a circle around the ancient lock. She then anointed the cutting wheel, as well, just to be safe before pressing the wheel into the glass, defining, as best she could, a circle through the oil. She stopped, listening for the approach of the guards. Silence. She picked up the rag, and covering the lock with it, she rapped the end of the cutter against the circle. A faint crack, but the glass didn't move. She put the glasscutter on the floor and picked up the brush, which was wider and made of tortoise shell.

Biting her lip and taking a deep breath, she struck the glass forcefully. It was pretty thick. The glass tilted inward, lock still attached to the outside of the case. She returned the brush and glasscutter to the hamper, and using the rag, physically twisted the glass and lock until they snapped beneath the pressure.

Still no sound of guards. Were they taking advantage of the King's absence by making their rounds less often? Or not at all? She swung the door of the display case open and removed the Hamper, transferring, as quickly as possible, her belongings from the replacement hamper, which she then put in the display case.

She stood back to observe her handiwork. It was pretty damn obvious that it was a different hamper and that there was a gaping hole in the glass, but she didn't actually have much choice. She hoped the guards were sleeping it off somewhere and wouldn't reappear until morning. As added insurance, though, she removed the two nearest torches. There, she nodded to herself, the display case was now hidden in the shadows.

Grasping her treasure firmly by its wicker handle, she made her way to the servants' entrance. From there she would be allowed to leave the castle without much notice; just another nun leaving after praying with an ill child or dying parent.

Bowing her head, she made her way down the cobbled streets of Stonehelm. The city was silent but for the occasional skitter of a rat or yowl of a cat. Even the dogs seemed voiceless this morning.

Yona kept moving. Dawn was only a couple of hours away,

and she wanted to be as far from Stonehelm as possible when the sun rose.

5th DEER

As LUCK WOULD HAVE IT, stealing the Hamper, the treasure belonging to the Kingdom of Adamah, was turning out to be significantly more difficult than Yona had imagined. While she and her fiancé, King Hevel, had left Arberth on the coast of Annewven for Hevel's kingdom of Adamah before her friends had returned with King Arawn to his capital of Prythew, it had taken them more than four days by sea to get to Seagirt.

She had easily arranged to go with the king straight to his castle in Stonehelm using as her excuse the fact that she wanted to avoid her parents for a little longer. "They're so strict," she told him. "I'll be stuck in the house until I come visit you again. Despite my age, they treat me like a child. Please let me stay until Teeneh. That's not that much longer." As Hevel actually didn't care one way or another, he readily acquiesced.

But from Seagirt, it was more than a two-day trip by horseback to get to Stonehelm and Castle Lavieven. By then Yona had been so exhausted it had taken her an entire day to recuperate before she could start looking into the logistics of stealing the Hamper.

And, it didn't take her much time at all to ascertain the essential problem was something she'd never even considered. She had already suspected that the treasure, which was made even more special by the fact it was one of the Thirteen Hallowed Treasures, was not guarded twenty-four hours a day. Yona had quickly discovered that the King had it guarded during the day only when there were more of his subjects on the premises. At night, on the other hand, the regular guards checked it only during their rounds—a problem easy enough to maneuver around.

No, the real quandary was now that Castle Lavieven had its King back in residence, the number of people loitering about, day and night, was astounding. Servants, stewards, knights, pages, you name it—there were folks everywhere—all essential castle staff, but a preponderance of people nonetheless! Yona was truly flummoxed.

Perhaps things would calm down again once Hevel left for the Summer Solstice Masquerade in Annewven. She wasn't invited because she was still Hevel's fiancée, but once they were married she'd be expected to attend. Her new friend, the Princess Eluned felt sure the event included a religious ceremony involving human sacrifice, and Yona wasn't sure she was wrong. Eluned, along with her other friends were supposed to steal Annewven's two treasures while she stole the Hamper.

Like the rest of her friends, she would have to wait until Hevel (or, in their case, King Arawn) was otherwise occupied before she attempted to steal the treasure. Unfortunately, she scowled, that meant she could not even begin the journey to meet her friends in Favonia until they were on their way to Favonia.

She felt her stomach drop. It had just occurred to her if she had to travel after King Arawn's treasures had been stolen, her journey would become much more perilous. Hevel wouldn't have even suspected her of the theft (at least, at first), if she had been able to steal the Hamper before the chariot and chessboard were taken from Annewven.

Afterwards, though, both Annewven and Adamah would be on alert because they would know she had taken the treasure. How could they not? She had spent so much time with Eluned there wouldn't be any doubt. Even if Eluned, Chokhmah, Gwrhyr, and Jabberwock weren't successful, they would still search for her. They would also realize she had no intention of marrying Hevel.

Her father, who held command over Hevel's navy, would be patrolling the coast continuously. She had to come up with a new plan. There was no going back to Seagirt now, because, despite everything, she still intended to steal the Hamper and make it to Favonia.

Later in the afternoon, she made her way to Hevel's library to pore over his maps. She needed to know her options. There were so many things to take into account, but only one option seemed the most possible after she had considered everything. She would have to make her way along the trade route that twisted and curved beneath the mountains of Panavhadesh to the village of Markheshvan, which sat at the base of the mountains near the border between Adamah and Tarshish.

There she could hire a guide to lead her across the mountains through the Hatseetz Pass, which was the easiest gap to travel through, undetected, because it was the most difficult to reach. Should she reach Markheshvan and maneuver the Hatseetz Pass successfully, she could make her way to Smuggler's Bay on the coast of Tarshish, or, as her pirate lover, Libni, referred to it, "Abandon Hope". The horseshoe-shaped bay had a narrow entrance, which was easy to guard from the sea and sheer cliffs dropping straight into the bay that made it difficult to approach from behind.

But, smugglers are ingenious, even cunning, when it comes to protecting themselves and there was, naturally, a secret path down the cliffs. Libni had told her about it once when Yona was sixteen and they'd shared everything. Although that had been nearly five years ago, she was sure the path still existed.

The other obstacle was her appearance. She was a stunning young woman and she was betrothed to the King. Someone was sure to recognize her along some part of the journey to Tarshish. How could she change her appearance enough to make her unrecognizable to those she came in contact with? She needed to blend into background, so to speak. She needed to be someone who no one would give more than a passing glance.

Trying to disguise herself as a male was out of the question; her figure was just too feminine to pull it off. Besides, she'd missed her chance to pick up some male clothes while she was in Arberth because she'd opted to spend the day with Libni instead. There'd be too many questions if she tried to acquire trousers and a tunic in Stonehelm.

Her eyes brightened as the perfect answer dawned on her. Fortunately, no one else was in the library to catch her grinning like a fool. A Sister of Holy Supplication—that was the answer. No one yet knew she wouldn't be attending the masquerade nor did they know the theme of the celebration was the "supernatural". Of course, she couldn't help but snigger, considering their beliefs, the kings and their cronies would actually get a good laugh if she showed up in that particular costume!

Regardless, she could have one of the seamstresses create the nun's costume for her without any questions being asked. She hurried from the room. She had no time to waste.

A Sister could journey anywhere in Hevel's kingdom, she thought as she raced along the hallway to the staircase, and not only travel anywhere, but travel anywhere unmolested. She bit her lip, trying to hide her smile, as she dashed down the stairs to the first floor below ground where the seamstresses stitched away all day.

Theirs was a dreary life and she felt not a little guilt requesting the costume. The Princess had done wonders in opening her eyes to the plight of servants. Yet, hers was a much higher commission—bringing the treasures together once again for the benefit of humankind. Surely her God, Omni, would bless the woman who made her costume.

The seamstress promised Yona she would have the habit finished before she and the King left for Prythew the following week. King Arawn had been kind enough to offer to send Hevel the magic phaeton on Deethmarth with a servant in order that he and Chazak, his chancellor, could get there more quickly. So, while she hated being deceitful about the costume, she was also determined to remain single-minded in her goal of removing the Hamper from the Kingdom of Adamah.

Now to figure out just how she was going to remove that particular object from the glass case in which it was displayed. For example, where was the key to open the case? She was going to have to ask Hevel some pointed questions without it arousing his suspicions.

Fortunately, she was dining with him this evening. She'd make sure to tell his wine steward to bring out a bottle of the ancient vine as it was the most potent. She stopped by the wine cellar on the way back to her room. She needed to make sure she looked good this evening. Despite his indifference to her as a woman, he actually felt great pride when she played up her "attractiveness", which, she found herself smirking, was Hevel's way of saying cleavage.

Yona was brushing her hair out after her bath, long auburn waves tumbling half way down her back, when she realized she would have to cut it if she were going to play the part of a Sister of Holy Supplication. If for some reason she were caught with her veils off, she needed to look as close to the real thing as possible. She felt a brief stab of regret. Her hair was beautiful. Yet, there was also something a bit exciting, something nearly taboo about cutting it because while men often wore their hair long, she'd never known a woman to wear her hair short other than the nuns.

She pulled it away from her face. Not bad, she thought, I might actually like short hair. But she was getting distracted. She turned to the armoire where what few dresses she had with her were hanging. She chose the scarlet silk. It was cut the lowest and was snug across her ribs, as well, emphasizing her not insignificant cleavage. The things we do, she thought, shaking her head as she pulled it from the hanger.

"So," Yona said, as she poured Hevel some more wine, "I was looking at the Hamper today because I've never actually looked at it before. I know it's one of the thirteen treasures, but I am not really familiar with why it's a treasure, or rather, what its special magic is."

"It's a simple magic," he explained after taking a sip of wine, "one need only put within it a meal for one man, and a meal for one hundred men can be withdrawn from the Hamper."

"Nice," she said. "Very impressive. Do you use it often?"

"Use it? Heavens no!" Hevel looked shocked. "I don't think it has been removed from its case in more than a century. The key has long since been lost at any rate."

Yona nodded her head in understanding while thinking, 'Damn, now I'm going to have to break the glass. How do I do that quietly?' "Have you decided on your costume for the masquerade?" she asked, changing the subject.

The interrogation had gone much easier than she'd anticipated, but the news about the lost key left her nearly frantic. Originally, she thought it might take them a while to notice the hamper she had planned to replace the actual picnic basket with wasn't the authentic treasure. People were so used to it being there, after all. But, if she had to break the glass, they would notice right away—possibly the night she stole it. Too bad she'd never learned to pick locks.

She knew one or two people in Seagirt who could probably help her out that way, but not here in Stonehelm though doubtless the town boasted a lock picker or two. Unfortunately, she neither had the time to find one nor earn his or her trust. And though gold could open a lot of doors, she just couldn't take the risk that she would be discovered before she stole the Hamper. Why was nothing ever simple?

So, it was back to the library the following day. She had heard that diamonds cut glass, but after a bit of research browsing through books on everything from jewels to cut glass, she discovered that despite the fact she had a beautiful diamond sparkling on the ring finger of her left hand, she was going to need something a little more complicated. If she wanted to cut the glass on the display case, she would need a glasscutter. And that meant she would have to find one. Mentally she walked through Stonehelm and decided her best chance would be with someone who cut glass for windows and that type of thing. For small panes, they might just have a glasscutter around.

If she could get a glasscutter, the sound of the case breaking might not be as loud. She would just need a towel to mute the sound of her tapping (or hammering, if that's what it took) the scored line. Or what if she scored a circle around the lock itself? Could she tap the lock loose? Would that be less obvious? She would just have to try it and if it didn't work she'd go for the smash and grab. But that meant she would have to be ready to flee the palace as soon as she'd retrieved the Hamper from the case. And, she needed to keep in mind what Libni had told her more than once, "As long as you look like you know what you're doing, no one will bother you."

Now she had to come up with an excuse to visit a glass company. She was quite adept at pocketing small items, a skill she had honed when she first started hanging out on the docks with her pirate and smuggler pals. Once she had the glasscutter, she need only wait for Hevel to leave. She would bring very little with her, essentially what would fit in the Hamper, which should reduce her possessions to need rather than desire. Although, she thought, opening the slim volume that Eluned had bought for her in the market in Prythew, the poetry of Schlomo might be the exception.

WHILE ATTENDING MASS in the castle's small chapel on Deethseel, she had a flash of inspiration. She had given herself a headache trying to come up with a reason to need a sheet of glass. But, what if she didn't need glass but rather wanted to commission a piece of stained glass for the small chapel in memoriam of her grandmother? She had been very close to her mother's mother who had passed away two years ago. Obviously, it would have to be something from Scripture, but what? Perchance a representation of The Amma, the mother? That could work. Yes, she liked it.

On Deethyeen, she picked up her costume, no one yet the wiser to her plans, and stashed it in her room away from the prying eyes of her maidservants. She then told Hevel about her plans for a window dedicated to her grandmother, which, of course, he was fine with. It wasn't his religion anyway, and as far as Yona was concerned, the less he had to think about her the better. He was too busy immersed in last minute plans for the Summer Solstice.

The trip to the stained glass artist she had chosen happened without a hitch. It was easy to pick up one of the many glasscutters that littered the worktables. So, the following day, after saying her farewells to Hevel and his Chancellor, Chazak, she returned to her room, intending to hide out the remainder of her time in the castle. She feigned sickness and sent her ladies away after they had procured for her the bread, wine and cheese she would need to make it through the following day.

That night she chopped off her long hair using a pair of shears she'd slipped up her sleeve while in the quarters of the seamstresses. It looked a bit ragged, but she thought it quite becoming, nonetheless. She bundled the shorn hair into a sack and hid it in the back of her armoire. Hopefully, she would have a significant head start before they realized she was missing. And once they discovered the hair, she would have already "disappeared."

She packed what little she could bring into the faux hamper, including a couple of apples, a loaf of bread, a flask of wine and a flask of water, and a wedge of hard cheese. After all, she prayed, if Omni were good, this little bit of food would last her all the way to Smuggler's Bay, if necessary.

The sun eventually set on the appointed day, and she put on her costume, carefully arranging the veils to show as little of her face as possible. And then, she waited. Patiently, at first. But, as the hours slowly crept by (she was waiting for the bells to toll three o'clock in the morning), she found herself pacing her room in an attempt to keep her rising panic at bay.

Finally, the first of the bells began to ring the hour, and Yona began her journey.

9ᵗʰ Teeneh

Everything was perfect, paradisiacal, in fact. The Princess Eluned lounged on one of Seemu's white sand beaches, the light, frangipani-scented breeze gently tossing her dark curls. And exactly as she had imagined, Prince Irirangi was leaning forward to brush the hair out of her eyes. She had no doubt that if she leant toward him she would soon feel his lips pressed to hers. There was even a cool drink in her left hand and an umbrella blocking the worst of the sunlight from her face. Despite the umbrella, she could feel the heat of the sun on her cheeks, which were already beginning to deepen in tone from ivory to a well-creamed coffee. But if one more freckle peppered her nose, she wrinkled the aforementioned protuberance in irritation, she would be forced to wear a hat every time she was on the beach, as well.

So here she was in her self-imagined paradise, and yet something didn't feel right. This was everything she dreamed of when she left Zion behind, but she wasn't happy. Far from it.

First and foremost, Irirangi annoyed her to no end. It wasn't just that he was overly solicitous. She was enough of a princess to be accustomed to having her every need seen to. What really rankled her was the attitude that attended the honey-sweet devotion. It proved consistently that he thought her nothing but an empty-headed piece of chattel, albeit a royal and marriageable piece of chattel.

One day she had shown up at the stables in her leather breeches for a morning of horseback riding, and he refused to allow her to ride with him until she donned more appropriate attire. He seemed personally affronted that she had chosen to don pants for their outing. And if she tried to express her opinions too loudly, the withering look he gave her would cause her to clam up.

And now she was forced to sneak off to practice her swordplay. When he had discovered she'd asked one of Queen Miryam's captains to continue her training, he had been furious and had told her in no uncertain terms that no princess who wanted to keep his company would ever behave in such an unsuitable manner.

The truth was she had gone to her friend, Gwrhyr, first, but his big blue-green eyes looked both hurt and betrayed that she had even had the nerve to ask. And that wasn't the worst thing to have happened so far. Since she began her little romance with Irirangi, Gwrhyr had all but stopped speaking to her. He had even said that if Irirangi joined their quest, he would drop out. That had left her speechless. He was her compatriot. He had made her escape possible when King Arawn had attempted to offer her as a human sacrifice. And it wasn't just Gwrhyr, even her compatriots, Chokhmah and Bonpo, avoided her now.

True, Chokhmah stayed busy with Queen Miryam, her aunt, no doubt trying to talk her into relinquishing Favonia's treasure, the Coat of Padarn Red-Coat. And Bonpo, not surprisingly, stayed busy in the kitchens learning to prepare the native dishes. It was, perhaps, the new distance between herself and Jabberwock the Bandersnatch that caused her the most pain. He had been her mentor and teacher since she was a young girl. Now he just looked miffed whenever he saw her.

She felt the guilt of the postponed quest riding on her shoulders. And she had no one to blame but herself. She was the one who had been smitten with Irirangi. She was the one dragging her feet about continuing the journey.

But they had only been staying at Whanga Palace on the island of Favonia for less than a month. All in all, she scowled, that wasn't that long, especially considering what she'd been through before they arrived. Yet already the initial spark of her attraction to the Prince had quickly fizzled out. Gorgeous and exotic he might be, but the more she got to know him, the less she liked his chauvinism.

Meanwhile, they had yet to hear from Yona, and she just couldn't quite bring herself to continue the Quest without her. At the very least, she didn't want to continue their journey until they were apprised of her friend's whereabouts. She was supposed to be meeting them on Favonia with the Hamper of Gwyddno Garanir. On the other hand, she argued internally, wasn't it about time she talked to Chokhmah and see if their relationship could return to a somewhat normal state?

Although, she reminded herself, she wasn't completely sure they had ever experienced a completely "normal" time in their relationship. They'd had barely two days together after her tarot reading, before she and Gwrhyr had disappeared for a week on the faery isle.

And then they were at Castle Pwyll, and before she even had a chance to live like a "common" person, she was back to being a princess. And she still had to be a princess. Worse, she had to be a princess that was even more restricted in what she did and whom she saw than she had been with King Arawn.

She wanted to glare at Irirangi, but instead she stood abruptly and handed him her drink.

"What? What is it?" he asked, launching himself from his chair and staring at her in dismay.

"I need to talk to Chokhmah," she said, pulling the damned voluminous dress that Irirangi insisted she wear on the beach more tightly around her. She could barely walk in the thing. Oh, how she longed for her leather trousers even though they would, no doubt, be unbearably hot in this climate. Perhaps she could get some of the loose cotton pants that the natives wore here. To hell with Irirangi! At least her friends appreciated her for who she was. Or did until she foolishly fell for the misogynistic prince.

She stomped off, leaving Irirangi gaping at her in confusion.

BEFORE SHE FOUND CHOKHMAH, Eluned ran into Gwrhyr leaving the stables, short sword in hand. He was wearing only the loose cotton trousers she'd just been longing for, and his torso gleamed with the perspiration from recent training. She found she had a hard time tearing her eyes away from his chest. She hadn't realized that his torso was so muscular.

"Princess," he said, and his tone was icy.

She blushed and looked down at her feet, trying not to wriggle her bare toes in anxiety. She was wearing the thong sandals she wore to the beach.

"What the hell are you wearing?" he asked. "It looks like a tent."

That was too much. "Damn you," she launched herself at him, pounding his chest with her fists, "I was coming here to apologize, but you just cannot not be a jackass!"

He managed to quickly wrestle her to the ground, straddling her and pinning her arms to her sides. "Apologize?" he asked, face just inches from hers.

She glared at him, still struggling to release herself from his nearly vise-like grip. If he kissed her, she swore to herself, she'd bite his lip.

"Apologize." This time it was a command.

"Never," she hissed.

"Never?" His lips were nearly touching hers.

"Never," she whispered and then he was kissing her, and

Eluned was mortified to find herself responding. But, as she felt her wrists released, and her arms moving of their own accord to embrace him, Gwrhyr was suddenly pulled from her and flung roughly away from her. She scrambled to her feet just as Gwrhyr lunged for the short sword he had dropped when she had begun to hit him.

Irirangi charged him, bull like, but Gwrhyr quickly danced out of the way.

"Stop it!" the Princess screamed. "Just stop it!" Irirangi was already swinging at Gwrhyr, both fists tightly clenched. For the first time, Eluned realized just how big the Prince was. Even worse, he was making one of his, as far as she was concerned, stupid warrior faces—tongue extended, eyes bulging. If he didn't stop, Gwrhyr was going to be forced to use his sword.

So, she did the only thing she knew to do. She tackled his ankles, ramming her head into the back of his calves (by Omni, they were like rocks) before biting his Achilles' tendon. She didn't think she could actually do it damage but rather hoped the pain would cause him to pause. If not, well he'd just have to drag her around.

Irirangi stopped and looked down at her, eyes blazing. "What are you doing?" he asked. He looked like he wanted to pummel her as well.

"What are you doing?" she asked in return. "Why are you trying to hurt Gwrhyr?"

"Kill him, you mean?"

"Kill him! Are you insane?"

"He was kissing you."

"First of all," she said, refusing to relinquish her grip on his ankles, "it was an accident. It was as much my fault as his. Secondly, I don't belong to you. I can kiss whomever I damn well please."

"In that case, Princess, consider yourself no longer welcome in Favonia."

"Boo hoo. As if that's up to you to decide. I am sure your grandmother will have something to say about that."

"She'll agree once I tell her of your whorish ways."

"Now that's too much," Gwrhyr said, as he stepped up and placed the point of his sword against Irirangi's carotid. "You take that back. Eluned is right. It was an accident. Just because I lost control of myself doesn't make her a whore. Apologize." He prodded him with the sword and drew a drop of blood.

Irirangi swallowed hard, eyes and cheeks blazing. "I am sorry if I offended you Princess."

"It wouldn't be the first time," Eluned said, "but I accept your apology. The truth is I was on my way to tell Gwrhyr and Chokhmah that I think it's time we renew our quest. We'll be leaving Favonia soon, anyway."

Irirangi looked confounded. "I thought . . . I thought that we were a couple."

"What? I haven't even known you a month," she exclaimed. "I admit that I was infatuated with you at first because I had always believed in love at first sight and I thought for sure that's what it was. Now I realize that love isn't even possible until you get to know someone first. I mean, attraction is nice, essential even, but it means nothing if you don't even like the person."

"Are you saying you don't like me?" His expression wavered between hurt and anger.

"No, that sounds bad. I guess what I mean is that we're so fundamentally different. Different values, different goals. I could never be happy with you."

Irirangi nodded. "I guess it's true that you weren't living up to my expectations."

"Exactly," Eluned said, trying not to get angry, but thinking 'and why the hell should I have to live up to your expectations?' But she bit her tongue. At least he wasn't attacking Gwrhyr anymore.

"And you," the Prince said, turning to Gwrhyr, "I do not

know who you think you are but raising a weapon against a Prince of Favonia is considered treason."

"I was protecting myself, your highness," he said, voice as cold as the glaciers of Dziron. "And then I was protecting the honor of the Princess Eluned."

The Prince sneered as if still in doubt of the rectitude of Eluned's morals. "Well, as you'll be leaving soon anyway, I imagine we can just pretend this never happened." And he marched away from them not even deigning to look back.

They watched his exit from the stable yard before turning to each other. Now that the Prince was gone, they both seemed to be at a loss for words.

"I'm sorry, Eluned," Gwrhyr finally spoke. "I was angry and I let my anger take over."

"Well I've said it before and I imagine I will, no doubt, say it again countless times in the future, I probably deserved that."

"Kind of liked it too," he teased her, punching her lightly on the bicep.

"Very gentlemanly of you to remind me of that," she rolled her eyes.

"Don't you think it's time to change into something a little less dirty and awning-like?"

It was her turn to jab him in the arm. "Watch it, that's what started all this to begin with."

"I know," he smiled at her. "My thought exactly."

"Oh you're incorrigible!" she said, taking his arm. "But I agree. It's an outfit I won't be caught dead in ever again. Can you find Chokhmah and the others while I change? I think it's time we got together and discussed our next steps."

13ᵀᴴ Deer

Yona surveyed the sky with trepidation. A storm was clearly building to the east and it wouldn't be long before the trade road she travelled at the base of the mountains (Adam's Way, it was called) would be drenched in its downpour. She needed to be on the lookout for some sort of shelter. She was between villages, but there might be a barn, or if she were lucky, one of the three-sided shelters scattered along the route for journeyers.

Soon she saw her first flash of lightning, and jumped at the thunderous clap that followed shortly thereafter. There was nothing on either side of the road but row after row of grape vines, fruit slowly swelling to maturity. She guessed that she could shelter beneath their leaves as a last resort, but picked up her pace anyway despite the fact she would never be able to outrun the approaching storm.

Less than a quarter of a mile away the road seemed to curve back towards the Panavhadesh Mountains, which still towered over her to her right. Maybe she would find shelter around the curve? Her pace quickened to a slow jog. A couple of minutes later she rounded the bend in the road and nearly cried when she saw a crumbling shack about one hundred yards away. The first drops of rain were spattering the road as she sprinted to the safety of the building.

It turned out to be more ruin than shelter, but she no longer had a choice. She clambered over half-burned timbers, and made her way to a dark corner where the roof still seemed somewhat intact. Yona guessed it must be the remains of a viticulturist's or other caretaker's cottage. It had been relatively spacious at some point, but now smelled only of rot and ash and mildew.

She huddled in the corner wincing every time lightning flashed. The split second of light transformed the deterioration around her into a gruesome display of loss and decay. In her imagination, she could almost hear the screams of the dying.

Yona took a deep, shuddering breath of relief as the sky began to lighten again and the rain slowed to a drizzle before passing on. Soon there was only the sound of dripping from the rafters and other exposed sections of the roof. This time she made her way cautiously over the fallen beams and rotting remains of the cottage. She was just about to step out into the open when she heard voices on the road.

Drawing back into the ruin, and peering through a smaller hole in the wall, she searched for the source of the voices. Friend or foe? She was certain Hevel had his men out searching for her at this point, but how did they catch up with her so quickly? And then, below the constant dripping, she heard the soft clip clop of hooves on the muddy road. The horses rounded the bend, and she watched as the men reined them in as they caught sight of the ruined cottage.

The larger man, his attire suggested he was a knight, pointed and said something she couldn't make out. The other man laughed, derisively, and she realized he was naught but a boy, probably the man's squire. The knight cuffed him on the ear and he quickly scrabbled off his horse, handing the older man his reins.

Damn, she thought, looking around wildly. He was going

to search the place. Where could she hide? Even the corner where she'd waited out the storm was no longer dark. He would spot her immediately. She would have to see what was behind the cottage.

She scurried to the nearest gap in the back wall, squeezed through, and quickly scanned her surroundings. There were several piles of damp and moldering refuse pulled from the bungalow following the fire, no doubt. None of it of any worth, which is why it remained. But the piles were too small to hide her. There was a privy about twenty yards away, undamaged by the fire, but fallen into disrepair. She might chance hiding behind it as she could not risk getting trapped within. She just prayed there weren't any gaps in the back wall of the latrine large enough to spy her through.

Luck, or Omni, was with her. The back of the latrine was still solid. Apparently, most of the storms approached from the east. She could already hear the youth searching through the house, and she had no doubt he'd check the privy as well after the clout he'd just received from his knight.

She waited, heart pounding painfully against her ribs, breath caught in her throat, as she heard him finally leave the cottage and approach the out house. She listened as he opened the door, which shrieked in protest. She guessed it had been awhile since anyone had entered it. The sound of the door being opened was quickly replaced by a groan of disgust, and she clapped her hand over her nose and mouth as she caught a whiff of the scent that the boy released. No one had bothered to clean it in ages either, and the hot summer sun had done its work.

The squire gagged loudly and turned and scampered back to the road.

Praise Omni for small favors, Yona thought. The odor had been enough of a deterrent to prevent him from checking behind the privy or in the vineyard behind it. Her knees buckled as she breathed a sigh of relief. She would have hated to be discovered less than two days into her flight from Lavieven. As it was she was going to have to wait a good half hour before she could follow behind her searchers, and then she'd really have to remain on the lookout. Fortunately they were on horseback, which meant they could travel significantly faster than she could.

How long would it be before they gave up and turned back? From Hashirim, the previous village, the road led south-eastward to Seagirt. But surely that was already being searched as well. She wasn't sure but she thought she remembered that the next hamlet, Tobermory, was more of a way station along Adam's Way than a destination—more of shantytown for the grape harvesters in season. They might travel as far as the town of Hagafen, where another sizeable trade road led to Seagirt. Would they head to the port town, remain on Adam's Way, return to Stonehelm? She had no way of knowing.

There was so much of which she could not be certain. Did they know she was on foot? Had the seamstress discovered she'd been lied to about the costume? Probably. Gossip travelled fast around the castle. The real question was whether or not she had said anything to anyone. She suspected that the seamstress had not said anything knowing the way the folk felt about Hevel. Yona had made it a habit to go out of her way to be kind to those the King referred to as "the little people", an attitude that had always irked her.

The scent of the privy was soon strong enough to rouse her from her thoughts. She stood up, brushed off her under-skirts and tunic, and looked for a sunnier, if not drier spot in which to wait to return to the road. On the southern side of the cottage, beneath an ancient olive tree she had yet to notice, was an old stone bench. It wasn't completely in the sun and it probably wasn't completely dry either, but it was long enough that she could recline on it. Hopefully, she would hear any travellers before they rounded the bend on the north side, or cleared the vines on south exposing her to their view. She had heard the knight and squire before they appeared and hoped that would hold true for anyone else as well.

She lay down upon the cold, damp stone after removing her outer veil to use as a pillow. The whispering leaves on the olive tree's branches, and the dappled sunlight on her face soon lulled her to sleep.

Yona was startled awake twenty-five minutes later by the sound of loudly creaking wheels. She rolled off the bench, grabbing her veil and her basket before fleeing to the relative safety at the back of the cottage. She made her way back to her spy hole and waited for the vehicle to come into view. It sounded, now that it was closer, more like a horse-drawn cart than a carriage.

Sure enough, it was a pedlar of some sort. And there was a woman, probably his wife, carrying a baby, and what appeared to be three more children—two were toddlers, the third still very young—balanced atop whatever was being hauled in the cart.

Yona made a split second decision. They might be Omnisent, and she couldn't risk losing the opportunity to travel with someone on this open road.

She hurried from the cottage, calling out to the family.

"Sister," the woman and man mumbled, bowing in respect.

Yona explained that she had been called to Hagafen to sit at the side of a wealthy matron on her deathbed. "The call came so suddenly that I was forced to travel by myself," she lied. "I really don't like being all alone on the road. You never know whom you will run into and whether or not they will respect the habit. Would you mind if I walk with you for a while?"

Of course not, they assured her.

"If I could put my basket in the cart," Yona said, "I would be happy to carry the babe. I am sure you could use a rest." The woman, who surely couldn't yet be thirty, looked closer to fifty.

"Are ye sure ye dunna mind?" The woman asked, eyes lighting with relief.

"Absolutely not," Yona replied. "But first, I have apples. Does anyone want one?" She smiled at the children.

A chorus of "me's" filled the air. Yona reached into her basket and handed round apples knowing that should she need more the Hamper would supply them for her. "I'm Sister," she began before realizing she hadn't come up with a name. She could hardly use her own. "Miryam," she said, thinking of Favonia where she hoped Eluned was waiting for her.

A COUPLE OF HOURS LATER they reached Tobermory. The knight and his squire were nowhere in sight. They had probably continued on to Hagafen, Yona thought, or was she praying? Clearly, Tobermory offered little in the way of lodging, food, or any other type of hospitality.

It had turned out that the man, Simon, wasn't technically a pedlar at all but more of a merchant. A year-round resident of Tobermory, he kept the seasonal workers supplied with necessary items like food. At this point, his cart was filled with food and other supplies for his family—rice, potatoes, flour and the like. They grew their own vegetables, his wife Leah had explained to her, as well as keeping a cow, a few sheep, and some chickens for milk, wool, eggs, and the occasional ability to supplement their meals with meat.

Knowing how desperately close to the bone they lived, Yona couldn't bring herself to ask for accommodation. She imagined their home was small and already cramped by their growing family. Instead, she asked if they knew somewhere she could lodge for the night. Dusk was quickly approaching and she realized she didn't want to be out on the road come nightfall. She was already thinking that when she got to Hagafen she should find some sort of weapon for self-protection. She couldn't believe she hadn't thought of that before she'd left Castle Lavieven where weapons of all sorts abounded.

Simon explained to her how to get to the traveller's hostel at the far end of town where she could bunk for the night.

"It ain't purty," he said, "but it be shelter. It be free, as well. Ther' be no food, tho'. We could fix ye somethin' to take wit' ye."

"Thank you," she said, "but I have enough in the Hamper." She handed the baby, Tombo they called him, back to his mother. He'd been a lot heavier than she'd reckoned on. Clearly she had done the woman a great favor by carrying him. She hugged the other three children, hefted her basket, and waved goodbye, thanking them again for allowing her to walk with them.

"Thank'ee," Leah said, "fer the apples, and fer carryin' li'l Tombo."

"You're more than welcome," she replied graciously before continuing along Adam's Way. She prayed that the horses that carried the men looking for her wouldn't be at the hostel.

Fortunately, the run down building seemed to be empty. It was still weeks before the grape harvest so she would probably have the place to herself that evening. Omni was surely looking out for her. She settled onto the cleanest bunk she could find, retrieving some bread, cheese, and her volume of Schlomo from the Hamper. It wouldn't be long before it was too dark for her to see.

Candles, she thought. A weapon and candles. Or a lantern. So many items she hadn't thought of needing before leaving Stonehelm. But, she was sure she could pick them up in Hagafen.

2ND TEENEH

Even with the shutters across the open windows, Eluned could still feel the wind from the late afternoon storm finagling its way into the room to toss her hair into her face. She finally pulled it back, wound it into a bun and secured it with the porcupine quill that had yet to do its duty as a pen. It had pushed buttons, held her hair off her face, even occasionally marked her place in a book, and she had no idea what she might use it for next. She just knew it had become so handy, she hated to destroy it by carving it into an ink quill.

"Princess?" Chokhmah was saying.

"What?" She looked around. They were all looking at her expectantly. The fellows along with Chokhmah and Eluned were reunited in her room at Whanga Palace. She wasn't sure why it was her bedroom that became the de facto place to gather, and she didn't actually mind, it just struck her as somehow amusing.

"I'm sorry," she apologized. "My mind was wandering. I seem to slip off easily whenever Arawn's name is mentioned." She could still feel the way her sword, Dyrnwyn, had sliced through his wrist. Just like butter, she had thought at the time, but it seemed somehow wrong to contrast something so violent with food. She didn't even want to think about having killed Matraqua and Hywel.

"You're doing it again," Gwrhyr said, snapping his fingers in front of her eyes. She and Gwrhyr and Chokhmah had squeezed themselves onto the small sofa. Even more amazingly, Bonpo had somehow managed to wedge his giant frame into an armchair, although the Princess admitted to herself, it was a pretty big armchair. Everything seemed somewhat larger than life here in Favonia. Perhaps it was because its people, other than Chokhmah's aunt, Queen Miryam, tended to be quite large, if not actually obese. It was apparently a sign of prosperity to be large.

Jabberwock sat in the other armchair. "I apologize, Eluned," he said, "but we have to talk about the King. Quite obviously, he was not amused by the turn of events."

"Has anyone heard anything?" she asked.

"Not much," Gwrhyr said. "We know that Hevel returned almost immediately to Adamah, and that Yona has disappeared with the Hamper. We know that King Hamartia returned to Simoon. Are they lying low while formulating what to do next? Do they know where we are? We don't know."

"We no know who else die, eidah," said Bonpo.

"I imagine they are trying to keep us knowing as little as possible," Chokhmah said. "I believe stealing the treasures has come as quite a shock on top of the deaths of Matraqua and Hywel, not to mention Arawn's injury."

Gwrhyr chuckled. "Either he is going to have to learn to wield a weapon in his left hand or remain well behind the battle lines should we ever come to war."

Eluned slapped his thigh. "Shame on you! That's hardly our biggest worry at this point. I just hope we haven't put Favonia in danger."

"Sorry," Gwrhyr said. "You're right, of course. The sooner we leave for another allied country, the better."

"But what about the treasures?" Eluned asked. "Which do we take with us? It would seem risky, for example, to bring the Phaeton or the Chessboard. I would hate to have them stolen from us."

"Can we trust Queen Miryam to hide them here?" Jabberwock asked Chokhmah.

"We have discussed this, and both of us think it would be wiser to hide them on one of the smaller islands," she replied.

"Hemamoku?" Eluned wondered.

"No, even smaller," Chokhmah said. "Perhaps Paliaina? It is the furthest east in the Favonian chain, and inhabited only by a few fishermen as it is mostly cliffs."

"Is there somewhere to hide the treasures there where they'll be safe?" Gwrhyr asked.

"Supposedly there is a hidden grotto that the fishermen know about, but have never trusted Miryam with the location," Chokhmah explained.

"Why dey trust us?" Bonpo asked.

Chokhmah grimaced. "Therein lies the rub."

"Oh great," moaned Eluned. "Nothing is ever simple."

"Perhaps the Princesses?" Jabberwock ventured.

"Leleua and Talei?" Eluned asked.

"Actually, I was thinking Leleua, Talei, and Eluned," he said.

"Charm them into giving the location away?" Gwrhyr seemed appalled.

The Bandersnatch snorted. "Of course not! I just think they would make a kinder, gentler deputation. The Favonian Princesses could translate for Eluned, who can put all her dramatic flair into the part of desperately needing a place to safely store the treasures. Favonia may have its warrior stock, but the fisher folk have always been a peaceful sort. How could they refuse to rescue a lovely princess who has only the welfare of the world in mind?"

"It just might work," Gwrhyr admitted.

"It's definitely worth a try," Eluned said. "I just hope that Irirangi hasn't turned his sisters against me."

"Actually, I imagine he would do whatever he needs to do to get you far, far away from here," Gwrhyr said. "If he's poisoned them against you, he'd probably still talk them into helping you."

"It is true," said Chokhmah. "He has quite the ego and you have wounded him deeply."

The Princess blushed. "I didn't mean to hurt him. Isn't it better that I realized sooner rather than later that we aren't suited for each other? It's not like I have a lot of experience as far as romance is concerned."

"Don't angst over it too much, Eluned," Jabberwock said. "We are all happy to have you back, so to speak."

"Yeah," Bonpo chuckled. "We all tink you gone ova to da dark side."

"Great," she groaned. "Looks like I've managed to wound more than just Irirangi."

"Fortunately," Gwrhyr squeezed her hand, "they are all wounds that will heal."

Eluned squeezed back, leaning her head against his shoulder. "Good," she said. "Because I feel like I've come home again."

THE PRINCESS BEGAN HER ASSAULT ON THE AFFECTIONS of Irirangi's sisters that very evening at dinner. She wished fervently she had the effervescent Yona by her side. Charm was definitely one of her friend's super powers, and had never been her forte. But, she would do the best she could.

Queen Miryam's family, along with Chokhmah and her companions, were gathered in the big dining room eating shredded pork that had been steamed in an underground oven, mashed taro root (not Eluned's favorite but she was getting used to it), and a variety of tropical fruit—pineapple, papaya, mangos, and coconut. There was, as usual, plenty of the intoxicating kava drink at hand, but Eluned sipped on water, preferring to keep her wits about her.

The twin princesses were sixteen and Eluned could see very little of their grandmother's blood in their beautiful, but clearly islander faces. They had long and thick wavy brown hair, huge dark brown eyes and full lips. They would have been impossible to tell apart but Talei had a small scar on her chin from when her older brother had inadvertently, so he said, hit her while learning a stick game as children.

The Princess had made sure she sat between Leleua and Talei, explaining that she was embarrassed that she hadn't spent the time to get to know them better sooner.

"Irirangi tends to have that affect on women," Leleua slid a not completely kind glance his way.

"They seem to get over it pretty quickly, though," Talei added with a smirk.

As the Prince was glowering at the three of them, Eluned wisely chose not to respond, but rather asked the Princesses what they did to entertain themselves. She noted that Gwrhyr was deep in conversation with Prince Mauri and his wife, Elili, and that Jabberwock and Bonpo were conspiring while Chokhmah talked to her aunt. That left Irirangi pretty much at loose ends, but she decided to ignore him, and it wasn't long before he excused himself and left the table.

Eluned managed to keep Leleua and Talei engaged throughout the entire meal, and even refrained from mentioning the treasures, or the need to hide them on Paliaina, although she would have to broach that subject soon.

Returning to her room later that evening, Eluned felt pretty good about her progress. It was fortunate, though not completely surprising, that Irirangi had alienated his sisters to some degree. It would make it easier for her to spend time with them and get to know them better. Sadly, she didn't have much time to spend with them. She had promised Irirangi they would be leaving as quickly as possible. On the plus side, this new plan allowed her a little more time to wait for Yona to arrive.

Now that they were no longer in Annewven, Chokhmah was no longer waiting on her. So, Eluned, once again (she feared she was the reason for the initial distance between herself and her older companion; having been so absorbed in Irirangi, she'd pushed all her friends away), readied herself for bed. The room was eerily quiet and she had to admit that she was feeling rather lonely. Having gone from having too many people around while living in Castle Mykerinos, she had longed for solitude of the upcoming journey with Jabberwock. But they had quickly added Bonpo to their troupe, and then Gwrhyr had joined them, then Chokhmah, then Yona. And now, she was the most alone she had ever been in her life.

She wasn't sure how to take it. Part of her wanted to weep because it made her heart ache. Another part of her wanted to be defiant and say, 'The hell with it. I don't need anyone but myself.' And yet she knew, rationally, that she couldn't do it all by herself. They were a team for a reason. Damn, it was so difficult to be human. Sometimes she wished she could just be a cat, she thought, climbing into her bed and curling up beneath the light covers. The breeze from the ocean was fragrant and gentle again now that the storm had passed. Cats didn't seem to care about anything but their own needs and desires—a little affection (when they wanted it), food, water and sleep. Lots of naps. Yes, sleep. That's all she needed to worry about now. She could worry about the plan tomorrow.

ELUNED WANDERED INTO BREAKFAST HALF ASLEEP as per usual. It had been a while since Chokhmah had brought her coffee in bed. And she probably deserved that. Today, despite her grogginess, she realized that the Princesses were present. Had they been there for the past few weeks? The Princess was horrified at herself. Had she seriously been that oblivious? She greeted them warmly and sat down next to them, thoroughly creamed coffee in hand.

"Isn't it too early for us to be here?" she asked but there was a mischievous light in her eyes. After all she was only eighteen and it didn't take her that long to wake up in the morning.

They giggled, and Leleua complained, "I don't understand why our lessons can't start an hour later. I would gladly give another hour in the afternoon not to have to get up so early."

"If you didn't stay up so late reading," Talei teased her, "then you wouldn't have a problem getting up on time. She's addicted to romance novels," she mock whispered to Eluned.

"I'll have to admit," she confided to Leleua, "that I've read quite a few myself."

Leleua gave her sister an I-told-you-I-wasn't-that-weird look. "At least I like to read," she said. "Talei would rather just talk about boys. It's much more fun to read about romantic adventures even though I will probably never get to have any."

"You never know," Eluned said. She had certainly not counted on the adventures she'd already experienced in such a relatively short period of time, some of which she would gladly forfeit.

Chokhmah and soon thereafter, Mauri and Elili, dragged themselves in and Eluned was even more thankful that she was young. They looked bleary eyed. It would probably take a cup of coffee or two before they were fully awake. Yes, she nodded to herself, there were definitely some advantages to being young. She'd better enjoy it while she had the chance.

Before the twins excused themselves, Eluned arranged to meet them later that afternoon for a beach walk. "After four o'clock would be best for me," she said, pointing to her pale skin. "I burn easily."

"Goodness!" exclaimed Talei, "that would never have occurred to me." Her own skin was a deep, coppery brown.

"Yes," Eluned explained, "unfortunately, I have to be very

careful. When I was in Zion, which is quite cold much of the year, I longed for the beaches of Favonia. Gwrhyr tried to warn me that I would have to protect my skin, but I guess I've been in denial about that. I had only to burn once before I changed my mind."

"We can ask for an early supper and take a sunset walk," Leleua suggested. "Or shall we make it a picnic on the beach? I adore picnics."

"So do I!" Eluned agreed. "Let's make it a picnic. Just the three of us."

"It will be fun," said Talei, hugging Eluned. "I look forward to it." The Princesses exited the room and the remaining Princess turned to face Chokhmah who was having a difficult time hiding her amusement.

"What?" Eluned asked, sitting down next to her.

"It is nothing, my dear," her glance toward Mauri and Elili told her otherwise. "It sounds like a wonderful way to get to know the twins better."

"So, what were you smiling about?" The Princess asked as she and Chokhmah walked along the beach following breakfast.

"Oh," Chokhmah replied as she bent down to pick up a lovely, peach-toned cowrie shell, and wipe away the fine white sand that coated it, "I was amused at how quickly you set about gaining the favor of Talei and Leleua. They seem enchanted by you."

"The older, wiser young woman." Eluned had the grace to laugh at herself.

"Doubtless," Chokhmah chuckled. "I would think you seem as exotic to them as they seem to you."

"Imagine not having to worry about your skin burning," Eluned sighed glancing at the sun, which was already higher in the sky than she might have liked. She had neglected to bring her hat or parasol. "Actually I hate to admit it, but I really am anxious to have the treasures hidden and us gone from this island as soon as possible. The fact that there is absolutely no information filtering out of Annewven, Simoon or Adamah is truly troubling."

Chokhmah shuddered. "I agree. When children play so quietly, they are usually up to no good."

The Princess linked arms with her as they turned and walked back toward the palace. It was good to have her friends back. She prayed to Omni that she wouldn't do anything so foolish again.

"I am happy that you have returned to your senses," Chokhmah murmured as if reading her mind.

14ᵀᴴ Deer

Yona resumed her journey at dawn following a restless night in Tobermory. Until she had something with which to protect herself, she knew she was going to continue to jump at the slightest noise.

The previous evening she had fallen pretty quickly into a deep and dreamless sleep once darkness had descended. But, as soon as she had slept off the exhaustion and stress, the skittering of mice against the floorboards woke her. They were heading for her basket, no doubt for the cheese and bread contained therein.

She pulled the Hamper onto her bunk, hugging it to her like a child, and closed her eyes in an attempt to return to sleep. But, she soon found her mind racing ahead to her return to Adam's Way the following morning. Would she run into the two men she'd avoided at the ruined cottage? Would she be faced with others searching for her? If she could just make it to Hagafen unmolested, she'd easily be able to disappear in that busy, bigger city.

Because of her ties to Seagirt, she was pretty sure they would be searching all the routes that led to the port town rather than those leading to Tarshish, and more particularly to the Hatseetz Pass and Smuggler's Bay. Once past Hagafen, Adam's Way became little more than a rutted track. The few villages that sat alongside it grew smaller and smaller the closer they were to the mountainous border with Tarshish. She only needed to make it to Markheshvan, but that would all depend on whether or not she was spotted before she reached Hagafen or, she grimaced, while she was there.

The pitter-patter of little mice feet had faded away as soon as the creatures realized the source of food had been removed from their reach. But now that she was awake, Yona's hearing seemed extraordinarily acute in the quiet of the empty building. Every creak as the building settled, every brush of a branch against a window, even the occasional call of an owl or other night bird set her heart racing once again.

Part of her just wanted to give up, drag herself out of bed, and start walking, but she knew that she might run into something far more dangerous in the dark be it human, animal or supernatural. There were all manner of dangerous things abroad at night. Besides, she rationalized, it couldn't be but a few hours 'til dawn and there was always the chance she would get a little more sleep before then.

Yona closed her eyes again because straining to see into the darkness was rather pointless, and took one deep breath after another, smiling when she remembered all the times Eluned had used the same tactic to calm herself. By Omni, she truly missed her new friends. Tears of loneliness welled in her eyes. It's not that she minded having agreed to acquire the Hamper, but she wished she had at least one person sharing this adventure with her.

Not for the first time she wondered if the others had made it to Favonia. It was so distressing knowing absolutely nothing. She'd been so busy avoiding people that she'd heard nothing, and of course, she had no way to get word to them about how she was faring.

Damn it, she was worrying again. Taking another deep breath, she smiled. She knew exactly what to do. She would just pretend that she was back in Castle Pwyll with Eluned before they left for Arberth, before Arawn had started being so controlling of the Princess. They had had those few glorious days when they were first becoming friends that had been so relaxing and full of promise. It seemed a lifetime ago now, but had only been less than three months. How much had changed in that short time!

Taking another deep breath, she remembered the large, canopied bed that had taken up most of a wall in Eluned's rooms in Castle Pwyll, and recalled how they would draw out the lavender curtains so the morning light wouldn't wake them. They had snuggled beneath the down-filled, lavender hued duvet, and giggled like schoolgirls before drifting off to sleep. What would she have thought if someone had told her that she'd better enjoy herself because life as she knew it would soon change? She probably would not have believed them.

Concentrate on the good, she reprimanded herself. So, she pictured once again nestling against Eluned's back for the warmth it provided during those last chill days before spring. It had been heaven. A short-lived heaven, but heaven nonetheless. She felt herself relaxing, the activity in her brain finally grinding to a halt, and soon she was once again asleep.

The grey light of dawn, and the shout of someone in the village awakened her. It was time to hit the road, she thought, as she sat up yawning. Tired or not, she was still thankful for the last hour or so of sleep.

Grabbing the Hamper, she hurried outside to splash some cold water on her face before reaffixing the veils on her head. She could eat an apple while walking, but what she wouldn't do for a cup of coffee, much less a hot bath, clean clothes and something to eat besides bread, apples and cheese.

She glanced around as she approached Adam's Way but

didn't see a soul. She didn't know whose yell had awakened her, and she'd been asleep so it could have been someone scolding a child or a dog or livestock or even a called greeting. It didn't actually matter. What mattered was that she remain vigilant, keeping a constant lookout for somewhere to hide should she hear or see someone approaching.

She had only had to scurry beneath the ever-present grapevines three times before she decided to make her way off the road at noonday. Two of those times had been false alarms—once she'd mistaken the voice of a shepherd (there were now open pastures on the south side of the road) chiding his sheep for that of someone actually on the road; the other time, the first time, it had been the sheep themselves she had been unable to identify immediately. She had hidden both times and felt completely foolish reemerging from the vines. One time though, she had actually seen the dust of a rider approaching. He had galloped past her soon after she'd hidden behind a vine loaded with not-quite-ripe grapes.

A messenger, she wondered. Who else would ride so quickly? Her stomach grumbled as she contemplated the grapes. Too soon, she told herself, they'll be sour. But, she was hungry. She needed to find someplace she could rest and eat, somewhere far enough off the road that she could hide comfortably but close enough that she could see if anyone else should come along.

Another quarter of a mile down the road she spied an olive grove on the south side of Adam's Way. If she could get far enough into the grove she could easily hide herself behind one of the ancient trunks, which were wider than she was.

The day had warmed considerably, and the first thing she did once she was hidden from view, was remove her veils. Yes, they hid her face, but Omni, they made movement difficult. She was glad it was only temporary.

Reaching into the Hamper, Yona pulled out one of the two

flasks she kept within. One was filled with water, the other, wine. She took a long drink of the water before sliding it back into the Hamper so that it could refill. As long as she didn't empty it, she would have water at hand whenever she needed it.

She nibbled on the bread and cheese with less enthusiasm, promising herself a decent meal when she arrived in Hagafen. Then settling back against the wide trunk of the olive tree, she took a moment to relax completely. But she soon found that between the warmth of the sun and the quiet buzzing of the insects, it became increasingly difficult to keep her eyes open.

"Just a short nap," she mumbled before dozing off.

The sound of a dog barking awakened her about half an hour later, setting her heart to racing. It took every bit of self-control she possessed not to jump up, but as low as she was to the ground her chances of being seen from the road or elsewhere were greatly reduced. The barking was coming from the far end of the grove and not from the road, which was good. It was more than likely a sheep dog doing his job, she thought, pressing her hand against her chest as if it might still her wildly beating heart.

She peeked around the tree to survey Adam's Way. It was empty. She replaced her veils and purposefully strode back to the road. She would prefer to avoid as much human contact as possible at this point so it was better to head away from the sound of the dog, which probably meant there was a shepherd nearby, and toward the road.

Once back on Adam's Way, she resumed her practice of keeping an eye out for emergency shelter while listening for approaching humans, animals and conveyances. But until she was on the outskirts of Hagafen, with dusk fast approaching, she saw no one. Apparently, it wasn't a time of year when Adam's Way got a lot of the traffic. On the other hand, the road that led to Seagirt held considerably more traffic as traders and travellers made their way to the city gates, seeking the safety of the town before they closed for the evening.

She fell in behind a tinker, the dust of the road heavy in her nostrils. She walked slowly and deliberately trying to hide behind the cart, but she found that those who passed her by usually nodded or bowed to her, respectfully, which heartened her.

I guess I must really pass for a sister, she thought, feeling as if she'd been released from a heavy burden. She felt her heart lifting and wanted to skip, but that was hardly appropriate and would draw unwanted attention.

As the line of traffic reached the gates of the city, it crept to a halt. She realized people were being questioned before they were being allowed to enter the town, and her heart filled with dread. Were they looking for her? But she had to persevere. If she ducked out of line now, she would definitely be noticed in a bad way. She prayed to Omni that they would not make her lift her veils. The Sisters, unfortunately, tended to be a haven for the unattractive or unmarriageable. She clearly didn't fit the first category and because of that had she been destitute, she was still a prime match for even the poorest of paupers.

Heart thumping, head bowed, she continued to move at a snail's pace along with her fellow travellers, the gates of the city growing larger and more forbidding the closer she got.

By the time it was her turn, she felt as if she might pass out from the fear. And when the gatekeeper said, "Oh, Sister, we been on ther' lookout fer yee," she felt the ground shift beneath her feet.

"I'm sorry it took me so long," she said, unsure of what she was apologizing for.

"The Lord Mayor will be relieved," said another man, dressed like a city official. She bowed her head and for one terrifying second thought she might vomit all over the man's bejeweled slippers. She gritted her teeth, swallowed hard, and murmured something incoherent. "This way," said the man, taking her elbow. "We thought his wife might die before you could be there to pray for her."

"There are no Sisters in the city?" Yona found herself responding in a tone of disbelief.

He looked at her oddly, but said, "They're all at the annual convocation in Seagirt."

She shook her head and quickly apologized, "I'm sorry, I had forgotten all about that. I've spent the past few weeks in Hashirim with a dying alderman, and completely lost track of time. The pigeon saying I was needed in Hagafen arrived Deethmerker evening and I set out the next day."

"You left the alderman?"

"Oh, no!" she quickly reassured him. "He died Deethmarth morning. I just remained an extra day to help his wife with arrangements. She seemed so lost."

"Ah," he nodded as they wended their way through the crowded streets. "The house is not far. It's up here on the right."

Yona's mind was racing. It was as if she had prophesied her own future. Did Omni have a sense of humor? Was this Its way of helping her maintain her cover or would the real Sister of Holy Supplication find her way there before the "wealthy matron" passed on? What had she gotten herself into?

10ᵗʜ Teeneh

The sun was hanging low in the west when the three princesses ventured out onto the beach. After removing their sandals, they walked down to the water's edge before turning east to keep the sun at their backs.

"There is nothing worse than walking with the setting sun directly in your eyes," Lelelua noted. "We can spread the blanket beneath that cluster of palm trees." She pointed down the beach to where half a dozen palm trees about a hundred yards away promised a bit of shade.

"Perfect," Eluned agreed.

Now she wouldn't have to wear the massive sun hat she had brought along. It itched her scalp unmercifully. She was thankful when they reached the trees, and not just because of the hat. Having spent half of that day practicing her swordplay with Dyrnwyn, she was extremely exhausted. Gwrhyr had taken it upon himself to give her an extra lesson in addition to her regular training. She'd been sweating in a most unseemly way (for a princess) by the time he called it quits. The Princess realized that she probably could have stopped the lesson sooner, but her pride forced her to continue as long as Gwrhyr wished to continue. The grueling practice was, she suspected, a bit of revenge for abandoning him for so long, and she had to admit, yet again, that she probably deserved it.

But the training session was now taking its toll—she could already feel the muscles in her left arm beginning to scream at the abuse. She probably wouldn't be able to use it tomorrow. And her legs felt rubbery. It was with great relief that she collapsed onto the blanket, which Talei had spread on the sand once she kicked a few dry and crackly palm fronds out of the way.

"Are you all right?" Leleua asked, as Eluned let out a low moan.

"I'm fine," she assured her, "just very sore."

"Sore?" she asked.

"Eluned was playing with her sword again," Talei said, but it was clear she was teasing the Princess.

"I wish it was just playing," Eluned said, retrieving the cold pork sandwiches from the hamper. "If I hadn't already been forced to use Dyrnwyn to protect myself, I wouldn't take the training so seriously."

"So, you all are serious about going after the rest of the treasures?" Lelelua asked.

The Princess had just taken a bite of her sandwich, and had to swallow before she could answer. "It's very clear that this is something we have to do," she explained. "Everything keeps falling into place. Well, almost everything."

"Almost?" Talei's brow creased in puzzlement.

"There are a couple of things we need to solve before we can leave Favonia. Most importantly, we need to figure out where we can hide the treasures we can't bring with us. We can't risk them being stolen or lost while we're looking for the remaining treasures."

"Which treasures do you intend to hide?" Talei asked. "I'm guessing the sword isn't one of them."

"I definitely plan to keep the sword with me," Eluned affirmed. "It's already saved my life once. At this point, we want to hide the Phaeton and the chessboard despite the fact the Phaeton could come in really handy."

"True," Talei said, "without it you might not have escaped Annewven."

Eluned nodded, remembering. She and Gwrhyr had come very close to not making it to the carriage, which transported them magically to Favonia in seconds. But, if Bonpo were to continue the Quest with them, he wouldn't fit in the conveyance. No, they had to leave it behind and take their chances. "I want to keep the Ring with me, as well." She continued, "And the Cloak is still safely in Aden."

"Where do you intend to hide them?" Leleua wanted to know.

"To be completely honest, we are hoping that we can get the people of Paliaina to hide them in the mysterious cave that no one seems to know the location of."

The Princesses nodded in appreciation. "I agree that makes sense," Talei said, "but they won't even let us know where it is."

"Yes," Eluned sighed, "I understand that they aren't too pleased about the gypsy queen."

"I don't think it's that so much," Talei said. "They're worried that if the knowledge of its location somehow becomes known to her people, even unintentionally, it will lose its sacredness."

"Even if they can keep it a secret," Leleua added. "It's a very holy place. I think they still hold some of their rituals there."

"I can understand their desire to keep it secret," Eluned said. "I guess I just wonder if there's some way they could hide the treasures for us there. We wouldn't even have to know the location. As a matter of fact, I like the idea of not knowing where they're hidden. That way, if anything should happen to any of us, we can genuinely say we don't know."

"That might make it more likely," Leleua nodded.

"Do you think it's possible that if the three of us formally asked them, they might seriously consider it?" Eluned ventured.

"The three of us?" Talei asked.

"I just don't think I can ask on my own," Eluned explained. "I may be a princess, and I may even be from a kingdom allied to Favonia, but I'm still a stranger, a foreigner. If you could go along with me, at least you have the advantage of being mostly Favonian and royal. Not to mention the fact that you speak the language. Or am I grasping at straws here?"

"No, it makes sense," Leleua said. "Let me talk to my parents about it."

"Would you? I'd be eternally grateful. If they don't think it's a good idea, then I will take their word for it and look for another option."

"So, what's the other thing?" Talei asked, removing a coconut confection from the hamper and passing it around.

"Other?" Eluned looked confused for a second, and then remembered. "Oh, yes, I was hoping Yona would arrive with the Hamper before we have to leave."

"You mean King Hevel's fiancée?" Leleua asked.

"Yes. We became friends this spring while in Annewven. It turns out she wasn't really thrilled about being betrothed to Hevel, nor about becoming part of his religion so she was happy to join us on our quest."

"Why wouldn't she want to marry a king?" Talei wanted to know. "She isn't even royalty."

"The truth is," Eluned paused. Should she tell them the truth? Would it make a difference to them? What if it endangered their hiding the treasures on Paliaina? Should she risk it?

"Yes?" Talei prodded.

"She's trying to decide whether or not to tell us that Yona prefers women to men," Leleua told her sister.

"Oh that," Talei said. "I thought they'd worked out some arrangement. Everybody knows that Hevel is a homosexual. At least in the Triquetra Alliance, they do."

"I'm pretty sure he wouldn't be allowed in the Awen Alliance if King Hamartia knew," Leleua said.

"Why is that?" Eluned asked.

"Because he hates just about everyone who isn't what he considers normal," Talei explained. "At least that's what Grandmother says."

Eluned groaned and rolled her eyes, "Apparently my parents protected me a hell of a lot more than I realized. What little I knew when I left Zion came from what I read in my great-grandmother's romance novels and from my minstrel friend in Zion. Since then, Chokhmah has been bringing me up to date on the goings on in all the kingdoms. She and Gwrhyr. And the Bandersnatch, a bit, since we began this journey. It has been truly embarrassing at times."

"That's awful," Leleua commiserated. "It seems like they would expect you to know as much as possible, particularly if you are going to be the Queen of Aden some day."

"And eventually of Aden and Zion," Talei added.

"Well, as you seem to know all about that," Eluned sighed, "I guess you need only know that she felt it wasn't worth remaining with Hevel once she found out that she could lead whatever life she wanted to lead if she came with us."

"I wish I could come with you," Leleua said.

"It's not as romantic as it sounds," Eluned reminded her. "Remember, I was almost sacrificed. Both Gwrhyr and I could have died. And what's really awful is a lot of the treasures are still in non-allied kingdoms. Also, and this is the worst of all, one of the treasures is in The Devastation of Pelf."

"The Devastation!" Talei's eyes widened. "No one survives there."

"Exactly. Hopefully, we'll save that one for last."

"You're really going to venture into The Devastation of Pelf?" Leleua asked, finally realizing the dangers inherent in the Quest.

Eluned nodded. "I don't take what we're doing lightly. We are all risking our lives. But, if we succeed, we may be able to stop a world war. If only we can find them all in time."

Talei was packing the uneaten food back into the basket. The sun was now a fiery red ball on the horizon and they needed to begin the return trip to the castle.

"Which is why it's important to keep the treasures safe and hidden," Leleua said.

"I'm glad you understand," Eluned said, groaning as she stood. She picked up the blanket and walked a short distance away to shake it out into the wind before folding it.

"I'll talk to father tonight," Leleua promised when she returned.

"Thank you," Eluned said, linking arms with her. "As I said, I will be eternally grateful."

"WELL, THAT WAS SUCCESSFUL," the Princess said, sitting down on the sofa between Chokhmah and Gwrhyr.

"How so?" Gwrhyr asked.

"The princesses agreed to ask their parents about approaching the people of Paliaina to make our request," Eluned explained.

"Another step closer to getting away from this island," Gwrhyr sighed, happily.

"It's not that bad, is it?" Eluned asked, concern creasing her forehead.

"No, no," Gwrhyr assured her. "But, admittedly, I'd just like to get on with this thing."

"Well, I'll take as much training as I can get before we leave," she said. "Not that I'm going to be fit to do anything tomorrow." She glared at him.

"Hey, you could have stopped any time you wanted," Gwrhyr objected.

"And have you think me a poltroon?" Eluned exclaimed.

"Poltroon! Nice, Princess. Is that from one of your romance novels?" Eluned blushed, guiltily. "Don't worry, I wouldn't have thought you craven. And your muscles may be sore tomorrow, but if you work them, anyway, they'll actually feel a lot better and begin to grow stronger."

Eluned groaned at the thought of another workout .

"Don't worry," Gwrhyr assured her, "We'll keep it to one practice tomorrow. I'll let the captain have it."

"Nice of you," she said.

"You're welcome," he said, without a trace of sarcasm.

"So," Jabberwock jumped in as the Princess was opening her mouth to respond to Gwrhyr, "now that we've established that you're working hard on your swordplay, how do we intend to get the Phaeton and Chessboard to Paliaina?"

"That shouldn't be too difficult," Chokhmah replied. "They can go via the Phaeton and return by boat."

"What 'bout horse?" Bonpo asked.

"True." Chokhmah didn't relish the idea of subjecting Halelu to a sea voyage in order to transport the Phaeton. "Perhaps we can gift them with a horse or mule."

"Mule," Eluned said, tone mournful. A day hadn't gone by that she didn't think of poor Hayduke, her beloved mule, left behind in Annewven when they escaped to Favonia. "He probably had him killed," she worried, eyes filling with tears.

Chokhmah took her hand and squeezed it. If they had been thinking more clearly, she would have harnessed Hayduke to the Phaeton, as well. The truth was, and she hated to admit it, it hadn't occurred to her. Hayduke had pretty much been out of sight the entire time they were in Annewven. He had been left behind with Halelu and Honeysuckle when they left Prythew for Arberth, and they had been so busy trying to establish a routine with the horses when they returned, that they had completely neglected Hayduke. The quiet that descended on the group when Eluned spoke her fear about the mule's demise, meant that everyone else suspected the same. It would not be in the least surprising for the Crimson King to kill an innocent animal in retaliation, if for no other reason than his own satisfaction. "I am so sorry, my dear," she murmured.

Eluned took a deep breath. "I'm as much at fault as any one. I was so panicky there at the end that I didn't even think about him. Out of sight, out of mind. And, I'm not sure I can forgive myself for that."

"Of course you can forgive your self," Chokhmah admonished the Princess. "You did nothing maliciously and you are not to be blamed for worrying about your own life. You should blame us for not taking your fears seriously. It certainly never occurred to me that Arawn would do something as foolish as murder another king's daughter. What on earth was he thinking? Surely he was not prepared to go to war already?"

"I wouldn't have said so," Gwrhyr agreed. He had been out recruiting and training with the king's soldiers. He didn't know how far along King Hevel and King Hamartia were in their preparations, but his best guess for Arawn would have been another few years, two minimum.

"I agree," said Jabberwock. "There was never a time in our discussions that he spoke as if war was imminent."

"Which only means," Eluned chimed in, "that he actually believed my story about running away, and assumed, correctly no doubt, that it would be a long time before my father discovered what had happened to me. After all, it's still more than two and a half years before I have to be back in Zion. That would give him ample time to finish his preparations."

Bonpo's skin paled as a realization dawned, "And he would prolly send yo fadda something to prove you kirred."

Mulling over the possibilities made the Princess queasy. The idea of her father and mother opening a package from King

Arawn to find what? A lock of her hair and a finger, perhaps? And, he would have, in all likelihood, put the Ring of Eluned on that finger as even more proof, not even realizing he was sending one of the treasures back to the king. That made her smile a little. At least he wouldn't have that particular treasure. By Omni, what was she thinking! None of that had happened thanks to Gwrhyr's quick thinking. She suddenly sobbed, and turned to hug him, tightly. "Thank you," she said, choking back another sob. "Thank you for saving my life. I might be nothing but a finger and hair."

"What?" he asked, returning her hug before tilting her chin with his finger so that her green eyes gazed into his, which were looking greyish at the moment because of the pewter-toned tunic he was wearing. "A finger and hair?" He wiped away a slowly descending tear with his thumb.

Eluned sniffed. "I just imagined my father receiving a package from Arawn," she began, before choking up again.

"With your finger and a lock of your hair within?" he asked.

"Y-y-yes," she whimpered. She wanted to wail but Gwrhyr's eyes held hers, and she saw only concern in them. Concern and, perhaps, something more. Fondness, maybe?

He pulled her close again, and stroked her black curls. "Don't worry Princess. There is no way in heaven or on earth that I will ever allow anything to happen to you."

"Amen," Chokhmah kissed her cheek. Bonpo murmured his assent, as well. But Jabberwock was silent. Divinely inspired or not, he knew that it wasn't a guarantee of safety. Sometimes great sacrifice was required, and he sensed that they wouldn't end this quest unscathed.

But Eluned, with her left cheek pressed firmly into Gwrhyr's chest, felt very safe indeed. Once again she thanked Omni for helping to bring together this wonderful group of friends.

14ᵗʜ Deer

Yona's heart rate was finally beginning to slow as they turned down a tree-lined boulevard. The homes were much larger here, and it wasn't hard to guess which one they were heading toward. Two men in ceremonial garb, hands firmly planted on swords, stood in front of a gate that had to be more than a dozen feet tall.

When they were seen hurrying toward them, the taller man called out something, and the gate slowly cranked open. The guards stepped aside, lowering their eyes and bowing in respect as she passed through the gate. Once again, Yona found herself grateful for the light veils that covered her face. Most people barely glanced at a sister's face, choosing to lower their eyes and bow in respect instead.

But, she knew that she wouldn't be able to keep her face covered indefinitely, and if any one actually looked at her, it would be hard to hide her beauty. She would need to come up with a reason for having joined the order despite her looks. Now, though, there were more serious issues at stake. Could she actually pull off playing the part of a sister? On the bright side, she had spent a lot of time in church during the past month. Surely Omni would give her the right words to say.

She followed the mayor's assistant, Eli, up a short flight of steps where another guard waited outside a heavy oaken door. The guard rapped on the door, in what was clearly a code, with the hilt of his sword, and the door swung open.

Yona's brow furrowed at the intensity of the security. Was it really that dangerous being Lord Mayor of Hagafen? She must have voiced her astonishment because Eli was quick to explain. "We've been instructed by the King to tighten our security."

"I'm sorry," she said, "has something happened of which I am unaware?"

"You haven't heard?"

"Apparently not."

"Not only has the King's fiancée gone missing, with the kingdom's treasured hamper, no less, but King Arawn was attacked and both his Lord High Steward and King Hamartia's Chancellor were murdered."

"Omni have mercy," she breathed as her stomach dropped and her heart started beating wildly again. "Did they catch the culprits?"

"No, they managed to escape with two of Annewven's treasures."

Yona clutched the handle of the basket more firmly in her right hand praying her relief wasn't obvious. Eluned was safe. They had made it to Favonia, but this meant that she was going to have to be even more careful.

"I will pray about this," she murmured, "but first . . ."

"Yes, Lady Naomi," he said, and she followed him up yet another staircase, although this was broad with ornately carved bannisters and steps covered in a crimson carpet. As they began to ascend, an older, heavy-set man rushed down the stairs toward them.

"Praise Omni," he nearly cried, "I was worried you wouldn't make it in time."

"I apologize, Lord Mayor," Yona said, "I got here as quickly as I could."

"Come, come," he said, turning around and heading back up the stairs, "Naomi will be so happy to see you."

They followed the mayor's broad back as he mounted the steps, turning right at the top of the staircase and heading down a short hallway, also carpeted in the same shade as the stairs. At the end of the hallway, which overlooked the foyer to the right, a door stood open.

"Is she here, Avi?" a weak voice called out.

"Yes, my love, she is here."

Yona entered the room and bowed to Lady Naomi, who was propped up with numerous pillows in a large bed. Yona counted at least three cats curled up beside her. Unlike her husband, the Lady Naomi was small and frail, her long gray hair barely hidden by a night bonnet.

"Come here, Sister," Naomi extended a skeletal hand. Yona hurried to her side, taking the frail hand, knotted with large purplish veins, into her own. "Just shoo Gabi aside," she indicated a large white cat curled up next to her. Gabi had raised his head when he heard his name spoken. He regarded Yona with large sapphire eyes, before slowly jumping from the bed and exiting the room, tail upraised and twitching.

"I don't think he's happy about my taking his place," Yona said, sitting on the bed.

"He'll be back," Naomi said with a twinkle in her faded blue eyes. "He's just a grumpy old man."

Yona found herself smiling at Lady Naomi but her mind was racing. She felt sure this woman would want to see her face. "Do you need me to do anything for you or would you like to pray first?" she asked.

The Lord Mayor cleared his throat and Yona turned to look at him. "I will be down the hall in the room adjacent to the staircase if you need me," he said. "Just ring that bell on the bedside table. I'll hear that."

"Thank you, darling," Naomi said, and he left the room with Eli tagging along behind him. Yona turned back to Lady Naomi.

"Can I get you anything?" Yona asked, setting her basket down on the floor at her feet. With the Lord Mayor and his assistant gone, she felt a tad safer.

"You could remove your veil," Naomi said. "I feel like I am talking to a ghost."

"Certainly. It is only for modesty's sake we wear them." She removed the grey, nearly translucent veil that covered her face, choosing to keep her head and throat covered with the second veil.

Naomi exhaled loudly. "You're quite lovely for a Sister," she noted.

Yona blushed, ignoring the compliment. "I grew up in the order. The sisters found me on their doorstep when I was just a child. I was wrapped in blankets and curled up in a basket."

"The basket you carried in here?"

"As a matter of fact," Yona smiled knowing the Hamper was safe for the moment. "It's the only thing I have to tie me to my past. It's a sentimentality, no doubt, but I feel it is a harmless one."

Naomi nodded in understanding. "I thought it looked old. So, you chose to remain with the order, then?"

"I suppose a husband could have been found for me, someone who didn't need any sort of dowry, but the Sisters are my family, my home." And she prayed silently to Omni that Lady Naomi wasn't familiar with any of them.

"I have to confess," Naomi said, "that I never attended church very often when I was growing up, and probably less so as an adult. I was the only daughter of a wealthy textile merchant and most of my time was spent learning the etiquette and occupations of a lady."

"Dancing, embroidery, polite conversation . . ."

"Playing the harpsichord, reading the philosophers, endless card games, chess, and the ways to keep a man interested in me."

"It looks like it worked."

"Yes, Avram has been a good husband and father, but now that it's too late, I wish that I had done something more significant with my life."

"I'm not so sure that being a loving wife and mother isn't a ministry of its own," Yona took her hand again. "If I felt I had been called to that sort of life, I think I would have easily fallen into it, but that's not what my heart wanted." No, what her heart wanted was to be with her friends again so that they could continue their quest. And, hopefully someday, a lover she could settle down with.

The Lady Naomi's eyelids fluttered and Yona realized the elderly woman was beginning to drift off. "Let me pray with you as you fall asleep," she said, squeezing the woman's hand and beginning to murmur, "Blessed art thou, O Omni, King of the universe, who makest the bands of sleep to fall upon thine eyes, and slumber upon thine eyelids . . ."

"Lovely," Naomi sighed, relaxing into the pillows.

"May it be thy will," she continued, "to suffer Lady Naomi to lie down in peace and to let her rise up again in peace. Let not her thoughts trouble her, nor evil dreams, nor evil fancies, but let her rest be perfect before thee. Blessed art thou, O Omni, who givest light to the whole world in thy glory." By the time she finished, Naomi's breathing had slowed and she was clearly fast asleep. Rather than chance waking her up with the ringing of the bell, she replaced her veil and rose slowly from the bed. As she arose, Gabi jumped back on the bed to reclaim his spot next to Naomi. She hadn't noticed that he'd been waiting.

Picking up her basket, she tiptoed out the door and stepped lightly down the hallway looking for the Lord Mayor. He had said he would be in the room adjacent to the staircase and as she walked that way she soon heard a susurration of voices coming from the room to her right. She knocked lightly on the door and the voices ceased. Within a second Eli was at the door.

"Yes?"

"The Lady is napping," she said. "Is there somewhere I could freshen up before she awakes? I've been on the road for two days." Three actually, but they didn't need to know that.

The Lord Mayor appeared at the door. "Show her the maid's closet."

"Yes, M'Lord," Eli said. "This way, Sister." He led her back down the hallway toward Lady Naomi's bedroom, and paused next to a brass sconce mounted on the wall. Now that she was feeling a little more confident, Yona noticed that the hallway was papered in a cream-colored silk that was textured by velvet fleur de lis of metallic gold. Eli pressed on the wall and a door sprang open.

Yona gasped, and Eli chuckled in response, "It's quite dramatic, isn't it?"

"I'll say! I hadn't even realized there was a door there."

"It does blend in, doesn't it?" He led her into the narrow room, which featured a small bath, a single bed, a small table and a few hooks on the wall. A screen separated the bath from the bed, and to the immediate right, once she stepped through the doorway, another doorway led to a short and dark corridor.

"That leads to Lady Naomi's room," Eli explained. "If you hear the bell while you are in here, you can take that corridor to reach her room quickly. Normally, her lady's maid would stay here, but she's beyond that now."

Yona nodded. "Thank you. This is perfect. What would you have me do about meals?"

"Her maid will see to the Lady's meals. You may go down to the kitchen when you have the time, and ask them to provide you with what you need."

"Thank you," she said again, as Eli bowed and retreated from the room. She would have to be careful about what she requested. She was a Sister and therefore her fare must be humble. Still, some plain chicken or even a couple of eggs or soup would be a welcome respite at the moment.

Setting her hamper on the floor beneath the small table, she removed her veils, scapular and tunic so that she could take a quick hand bath. Her stomach had begun to grumble as she thought about food. She could bathe more thoroughly later.

Once more ensconced in her costume, Yona found her way downstairs to the foyer where a servant directed her to the kitchen. Much to her continued delight, she was greeted warmly, seated at a table off to the side, and soon a bowl of beef stew was sitting before her. It was going to take a concentrated effort to eat slowly. A slice of bread for sopping up the broth was placed next the bowl—hot from the oven and smelling heavenly.

"Anythin' else, I can do fer ye, Sister . . . ?" the cook, a matronly woman with pink cheeks that belied her somber grey eyes, asked.

"Sister Miryam," Yona quickly supplied. "No, this is perfect. It's a feast compared to what I was eating on the road."

The cook smiled. "Sister Miryam. I'm Marta, should ye need anythin.'"

Yona laughed in delight. "Miryam and Marta! And do you need anything, Marta? Prayers, perhaps?"

"If'n ye dern't mind, Sister, I would have ye pray fer me daughter. She be due any day now, an' it's her first. I would have ye pray fer a safe delivery."

"Absolutely!" Yona agreed. "What's her name?"

"Ester. Thank ye, Sister, It would mean much ter me."

"Ester and her child will remain in my prayers," she said, "but please let me know when she gives birth. Hopefully, I will still be here. Lady Naomi is weak, but I don't believe it's yet time."

"She be a strong one," Marta said warmly. A pot on the stove started bubbling loudly, and Marta bustled away. Glad for the distraction, Yona smoothed back her veil over her head and took her first spoonful of stew. At some point, she realized, she would once more have to explain why she had chosen the Sisterhood. It seemed rude to continue to speak to Marta through her veil.

BACK IN HER ROOM, YONA DOZED as she waited for the bell to signal Lady Naomi's waking. She imagined that she'd either be up with her off and on all night, or, alternately, be up with her for an hour or so before she slept through the night. Obviously, she preferred the latter, but she'd made her bed, so to speak, and was willing to do whatever she had to do to keep up the ruse while she was here. And, while she really didn't want Lady Naomi to die, it made her anxious to be putting off her trip. All she wanted was to get to Markheshvan. If she could make it there, and find a guide, she would finally allow herself to hope that she might make it to Favonia.

She was so deep in her thoughts that she startled when the bell began to ring. It was actually more of a tinkling as it was a small crystal bell, but the sound was distinct enough to rouse her. Straightening her tunic and pulling her veil down over her face, she hurried down the corridor. She would be happy to remove the veil for Lady Naomi, but she preferred that none of the men saw her face, if possible, and she wasn't positive Avi wouldn't be hurrying to the room, as well.

Entering Naomi's bedroom, she found her to be alone. "Good evening," she said, hastening to her bedside. "Did you have a restful sleep, my Lady?"

Naomi patted the bed, which was cat-free at the moment, and Yona sat down while removing her veil. "Did Avi take care of you while I was asleep?" she asked.

"Oh yes. He had Eli show me my room and after I freshened up, Marta made sure I was well fed."

"She's a good one," Naomi smiled. "It's always nice to find servants you can trust."

Yona winced inwardly. Would it not have been just as fair to say that Marta had found an employer she could trust? Why had humans decided that inequality was the norm? Somehow she doubted that it was a condition that could be righted. If only humans could somehow derive pleasure from their differences rather than feeling the need to make each other disparate.

"What are you thinking, my dear? You're a thousand miles away."

"I'm sorry," Yona apologized. "I was suddenly just very thankful that Omni created us each to be unique."

"And how was that prompted?"

"I was realizing that I have never met any one like you nor like Marta, for example. And I thought how lucky I am to have the chance to meet so many different people during what is often a deeply reflective time."

"I suppose that's true," Naomi said. "It is only when you realize that you have very little time left that you start to ruminate on whether or not you have accomplished anything in your life. Or, at the very least, that you have lived a life that you feel worthwhile."

"You said earlier that you wished you had done something more significant with your life. Is there something you wished to accomplish?"

"No, dear, the truth is I was always very content. I'm not sure why I feel guilty admitting that. So many people have lives of such tragedy, and I am one of those fortunate few who had every thing she wished for. My last child was stillborn, but I had three healthy children prior to that—two boys and a girl. What more could a woman ask for?"

"A rare blessing indeed. And one you need not feel

guilty for. Why shouldn't there be some people who live their dreams, particularly if the dream is a relatively simple one. So many people are not content with their lives—they want more whether the more is fame or fortune, love or power. And they may have these things already in sufficient quantity, but spend their entire lives thirsting for more and thus end their lives regretting that they didn't appreciate what they had."

"And that is the reason you chose the Sisterhood? Because you were content with what you have?"

"Yes," Yona lied. "I didn't want more, but it would have seemed greedy had I wanted more." How awkward, she thought, I actually believe what I'm saying, and yet I don't want to be queen. I want to live a different dream. Was that wrong? Was she being foolish?

14ᵀᴴ Teeneh

The Phaeton, as ever, arrived on the shores of Paliaina silently. Eluned, Leleua and Talei had directed the Phaeton to a beach near the village of Vailima where they were to meet with the island council. Eluned had warned them that they might experience the nausea and disorientation that often followed a "ride" in the carriage, and they were prepared to recuperate at the beach, if necessary.

Though it had been nearly a month since she had last ridden in the Phaeton, Eluned felt only a mild queasiness upon landing. Leleua and Talei, on the other hand, were going to need a short nap before they could proceed into Vailima. So, while the twins stretched out on their palm mats beneath the shade of a few trees, Eluned made herself comfortable in the former chariot. She opened a book, intending to read, but kept finding her eyes drawn to the cliffs that towered above the beach. Chokhmah had not been joking when she said Paliaina was mostly cliffs.

They were truly breathtaking, and she could easily see why this island had remained mostly uninhabited except for the small fishing village of Vailima and a few huts scattered here and there along the island's shores. She had a strong compulsion to go exploring. She wanted to see this hidden grotto where they were going to ask to hide the Phaeton and Chessboard. Would they be truly safe there? Would it be possible to keep them from being damaged by the ocean? The truth was she didn't know what type of grotto it was, which meant she really didn't have the first idea where to begin looking.

She glanced up at the fluted cliffs again which soared to razor sharp ridges and plummeted to narrow valleys. She wasn't sure she wanted to venture into the jungle that flourished on its slopes. Not without a guide, anyway. No, she decided, she'd save the adventuring for the upcoming quest. Why risk endangering herself until necessary?

THE THREE PRINCESSES LED THE MULE harnessed to the Phaeton down the beach toward the village. A black sand road switchbacked up a short ridge to a small plateau beneath the towering cliffs. Here a small village crowded the shore and several farms pushed back against the cliffside. It was clear that the village had grown outward and backwards, and that it had involved heavy labor as it was clearly terraced by the people who had lived here for millennia.

Eluned was well aware that this planet was ancient, but sometimes it took seeing something like Paliaina, where the people had lived in one place for eons with next to no modernization, for her to truly understand just how old it was. Because the island could only be reached by boat (or the Phaeton, she smiled to herself), and because it was largely uninhabitable, it had seen very little outside traffic since the volcano it had once been had begun to erode. She had no doubt that its leadership, as well as the kings and queens of Favonia, had turned down countless offers to allow its wealthier inhabitants and outsiders to build second homes in this mini paradise. They had been wise to let it remain mostly hidden away from the world. No greed here. She hoped that lack of greed would work in her favor.

Once in the village, they made their way down the main street toward a large, thatched-roof pavilion. Here the village's council awaited them. And, as is true in any polite society, the princesses were honored first and treated to a simple feast of various types of seafood ranging from mahi-mahi and shark steaks to opihi and squid, plenty of poi and fruits, as well as the ubiquitous kava.

Having eaten and then enjoyed an hour's entertainment—music with some traditional dances—the leadership seemed ready to get down to business. Prince Mauri had offered to write the prolocutor of Vailima's council to introduce his daughters and the Princess Eluned and request a meeting. But while he had explained that the women had a request to make, he felt it wise to keep them uninformed of the request, itself.

"I have a feeling they'll find it more difficult to refuse you in person, particularly if you arrive with the Phaeton and Chessboard," he said.

And now it was time. Eluned felt it best that Leleua and Talei speak first. The Princess was nervous but Leleua and Talei stood up, confidently, and faced the three men who sat on the opposite side of the head table with them.

"I know my father explained that we have a request to make of you," Leleua began.

"This is true," said Ailani, the prolocutor, "but he gave us no idea of what that might be."

"That is because what we are going to ask will be a very huge favor," Talei said.

Ailani raised his thick black brows, but it was the old man to his right that spoke. "This is all certainly intriguing, but please just go ahead and ask." Kaimana was rather gruff.

"We are actually here to support the Princess Eluned in her request," Leleua said.

As the Princess stood, she was glad for her long wrap skirt as it hid the fact her knees were shaking. She had faced a crowd of people who wished to kill her, but for some reason the thought of asking these strangers for a favor was unnerving to her. She curtsied and cleared her throat.

"I think it's best to start at the beginning," she began. And with Leleua translating as the Princess spoke very little Favonian, she continued: "On my birthday, I set out with my mentor on what I thought would be a three-year journey to do nothing but experience the world outside my father's kingdom. It quickly became apparent as the number of my companions continued to grow that it was more than a journey, that we were, in fact, on a quest." She paused to take a breath.

"A quest?" asked Palani, the other member of the council.

"My birthday gift from my father was a ring and a moonstone," she explained, "but it wasn't until I found a book called *The Thirteen Royal Treasures of the Thirteen Kingdoms* that I discovered my ring is one of those treasures. I was then led by an animal spirit to another treasure," she touched the sword at her side, "Dyrnwyn."

"The sword of Rhydderch the Generous?" Kaimana's voice was hoarse with awe. Apparently he spoke the Common Tongue as he interjected this before Leleua had time to translate.

Eluned pulled the sword from its scabbard and the blue light raced along her arm as those watching gasped and began to murmur to each other. Once they had quieted, she continued. "By this time, I was also aware that my fiancé owned the Mantle of Arthur. Finding the sword seemed to confirm that our journey was actually a quest. We were on our way to Annewven at the time, and that is when we met the Queen's niece, Chokhmah, and she joined the Quest. We hoped once we arrived we would find a way to leave with all three of Annewven's treasures, which would mean that we had a total of six in hand, nearly half of the them."

"I do not know much about these treasures," Ailani said, "but I know enough that the legend says if all the treasures are gathered together a good man (or woman, Eluned thought) can bring about world peace."

"That's our hope," she said, "particularly in the light of the fact that Annewven, Simoon and Adamah are currently working towards war."

"You know this for a fact?" Kaimana asked.

"Yes, regrettably," she said. "While in Annewven, Gwrhyr who works for King Uriel in some capacity . . ."

"Some capacity?" Palani repeated.

"He has never quite admitted what he does for the King, but I'm convinced he's some sort of spy. Regardless, he trained with the army while we were there and learned first hand of their plans. We also learned that the Halter of Clydno Eiddyn had disappeared from Annewven when the King's great-great-grandmother tried to capture a unicorn by sliding the Halter over its head. The unicorn escaped, and no one knows where it is now. But King Arawn still possessed two other treasures—the Chessboard of Gwenddolau and the Chariot of Morgan the Wealthy—and we were determined to gain possession of them. It was our plan to use the chariot to escape, which is why Bonpo had to come to Favonia early."

"Bonpo?" Kaimana asked.

"The giant," Ailani explained.

Kaimana nodded. News of the yeti's arrival in Seemu had reached the furthest island in the chain.

"Anyway," Eluned took a deep breath, "it wasn't as easy to escape as we thought it would be. King Arawn had hoped to use me as a human sacrifice. If it hadn't been for Gwrhyr and Dyrnwyn, I might have died. But we managed to escape with the treasures and here we are."

"So you are in possession of five of them?" Ailani asked.

"We've since learned that our friend, Yona, has managed to run away with the Hamper of Gwyddno Garanir, the treasure that belongs to Adamah."

"She stole it from her fiancé, King Hevel," Leleua explained.

"And she is supposed to be making her way to Favonia," Talei added, "but there has been no word of her in nearly a month."

"If she does arrive," Eluned said, "and I pray to Omni that she does, we will have six of the treasures. And if Queen Miryam will allow us access to the Coat of Padarn when the time comes, we will have seven. More than half."

"I imagine the reason you are here has something to do with the treasures?" Ailani stated more than asked.

"Yes," Eluned admitted. "We understand you have a hidden grotto, and hoped that you might be able to hide the Phaeton and Chessboard within it. Obviously, I know nothing about it. It might not even be possible even if you were willing to do so."

"How big is this phaeton?" Kaimana asked.

Eluned turned around and pointed to where the mule, still attached to the carriage, cropped at the grass that grew on the pavilion's lawn. The men stood and walked out of the pavilion, the girls trailing behind followed by the remainder of the islanders who were attending.

Eluned hated that so many people now knew of the Phaeton and where it might be hidden. All it would take is one bad seed to find Arawn and tell him of its location. But the Queen and her advisors all swore that the people of Paliaina were above reproach because they avoided contact with the outside world as much as possible.

The men studied the Phaeton for a moment before excusing themselves to discuss the matter. The princesses talked to the islanders while they were gone, but Eluned was so nervous she found herself pacing back and forth along the road, attempting to take deep breaths to ward off her panic. If they refused, they would have to begin the process again. There were still Hemamoku and Hakinaipo, but she really, really hoped that Omni was with them and that they wouldn't have to resort to asking.

Eluned had only to pace for ten minutes or so. That, she thought, when they were asked to return to the pavilion, could either be good or bad news as it had been decided so quickly. At least, she surmised, as she returned to the table, they hadn't needed to argue about it. She would have hated to think that one of the three men was opposed to whatever choice had been made.

When they were seated once again, Ailani began to speak, "It is to our advantage for this world to be a peaceful place. Because we are so close to Annewven, Favonia would no doubt be among the first kingdoms to be challenged to go to war. We will be happy to hide these two treasures, but would ask how long we might have to keep them hidden?"

"I have to return to Zion by my twenty-first birthday," Eluned explained, "because that is when I will be married to King Uriel. If we haven't gathered all the treasures by then, I imagine we will keep what we have gathered in Aden."

"Less than three years then." Kaimana said.

"Yes, unless it turns out we need the chariot to complete the Quest," she explained. "And I would add that none of us want to know where this hidden grotto is, or if that is even where you end up hiding them. We can't be compelled to tell something we don't know."

"Understood," Ailani said.

Tears suddenly filled Eluned's eyes. "I'm sorry," she said, "I can't even begin to tell you how much this means to me."

"We are happy to be of service to Zion and Aden, and most importantly, to our own kingdom, Favonia."

Eluned raised her cup of kava, "To the good people of Paliaina," she said, "may Omni bless you and keep you."

"Manuia!" the islanders responded loudly.

Eluned took a thankful sip. Now they only had to get back to Seemu. The plan was to send a boat for them if they didn't return by way of the Phaeton that evening. But the council had known they would probably spend the night and arrangements had been made. She took another sip of kava. Now she could just sit back and enjoy herself.

21ˢᵗ Deer

It took a week before the Lady Naomi finally slipped into the next world, and Yona spent much of that time by her side. To be perfectly honest, Yona was glad she had been granted the chance to spend time with Naomi during her final days.

When her grandmother died, it was following nearly two years of predominantly being confined to a bed. Lady Naomi, on the other hand, had told Yona that she'd only been in bed for a week before she'd arrived.

"I just couldn't seem to stand up for any length of time without getting really dizzy and weak," she'd said. "And it wasn't something I could hide from Avi. When he saw how long it was taking me just to get up the stairs, he made me confess to not feeling as well as I ought. I never told him that the exertion also made my heart feel as if it might explode in my chest. I went from toddling about this floor to creeping around my room and then finally I ended up here. I have to admit that I find it deeply embarrassing to be reduced to using a chamber pot that someone else must empty."

This contrasted with the two-year confinement that changed Yona's grandmother. The woman she had once shared secrets with, laughed with, and travelled with had grown bitter and distrustful, and worse, often downright cruel. Every time Yona had visited her was a practice in patience. She often clenched her jaw so tightly to prevent herself from saying words she might later regret that the muscles would be sore for days afterwards. How could this be the same woman that had often brought tears of laughter to her eyes? How many times had they collapsed in each other's arms guffawing over something they had seen or overheard? Watching her beloved grandmother slowly die had been a deeply painful experience for her. Even today she sometimes questioned whether it had actually been the same woman at the end.

When news reached her that her grandmother didn't have much longer to live, she arrived just in time to say goodbye but no more than that. On that final night, the old woman shooed them away in obvious annoyance, insisting she was just fine and only wanted to sleep.

And sleep she had, never to awaken again. By the time the Sister had notified them, her grandmother's skin was already cooling. Everyone, including the Sister, had believed her when she had said she was fine. The Sister had retired, promising to monitor her occasionally during the night, but apparently had fallen asleep. When she finally got up to check on her about four o'clock, she noticed that she was no longer breathing.

They had prayed over her dead body and Yona had been left feeling as if something had been left unsaid between them.

And although Lady Naomi was not her grandmother, and had grandchildren of her own that visited her each day along with their parents, Yona felt as if she had been granted a truly wonderful gift in being allowed to share some special time with Lady Naomi as she lay dying. She was consistently upbeat and gracious with her family, but when she was alone with Yona she became reflective and was able to ask questions that might have been misunderstood by or hurtful to her family.

Their discussions were helpful to Yona, as well. As they

discussed what defined a life well lived or what might occur in the after life and whether or not an after life was important or necessary, Yona began to make decisions about what those particular concepts meant to her.

Yona's faith actually grew stronger after their talks because it made her more firmly convinced that her time with Lady Naomi was not mere chance but Omnincidence, as Eluned called it—all a part of some greater plan. Yes, she itched to get back on the road, but she also understood that her time in Hagafen was necessary for her growth. Oh how she wished that she had Eluned to talk to about all of this. She should probably be keeping a journal so she didn't forget anything. Actually, that was a good idea—she'd ask Eli if they had a note-book or notepaper that she could use. She could catch up on her journey since her return to Adamah during one of Lady Naomi's frequent naps.

AND SO THE FINAL WEEK GLIDED BY with nary a boulder to cause the occasional ripple of disturbance. Lady Naomi slept more and more and by her last day, she awakened only long enough to feebly ring the bell—the bell's crystal tinkling barely making enough sound to wake the cats.

But Yona heard it. It was that strangely dark hour just be-fore dawn on Deethsadoorn morning. Yona had often imag-ined the sun pulling the covers over its head and begging to sleep just a little longer. And, honestly, that's what she wanted at that moment, as well. But, she pulled her habit on as quickly as possible and rushed to Lady Naomi's room. When she reached her bedside, Yona rang the bell again, loudly, and Avram was soon by his wife's side, as well. Yona had been veil-less for sev-eral days now and Avram and the children no longer remarked upon it.

For a little over half an hour they each held one of the Lady Naomi's hands while Yona prayed and Avram and Naomi whispered their farewells. And then her grip on their hands tightened briefly as she exhaled before her grip loosened completely. Her chest did not rise again.

Avram held himself together long enough to send Eli for the children. As soon as the front door could be heard closing behind his assistant, he fell to his knees, a great sob erupting from his throat. "It's not that it's unexpected," he wept. "I've been dreading this day for weeks. I just couldn't bring myself to imagine life without her."

The tears were sliding down Yona's cheeks as she took his hand and pulled him to his feet, leading him to a nearby armchair.

"Perhaps that's one reason I chose the Sisterhood," she mused aloud. "Marriage always ends in tragedy—if not death then distancing. I've seen so many people grief-stricken and there is absolutely nothing I can do to help assuage your pain."

Avram looked at her with swollen, reddened eyes. "It's true," he said, "and yet it is much better that it is I and not her that remain. She was so dependent on me."

Yona had no doubt that there was some truth to that statement but she knew that Lady Naomi had been a lot stronger than she had ever allowed Avram or her children to realize. The discussions they had had during the past two weeks were proof of that. She had played the role of adoring wife and mother because it was the life she had chosen. She had questioned that choice at the end but had come to the decision that she had nothing to regret.

"One makes one's choices, dear," she told Yona one evening. "I could have chosen differently, but once I made the decision to live life as a Lady there was no going back as far as I was concerned. Could I have accomplished something more significant in my life? Undoubtedly. But, what I chose wasn't insignificant, and I have no doubt that those I leave behind will grieve my absence whether I wish them to do so or not. And if Avi chooses to think that it was better that I died first, let him have that peace. I love him, dearly, but I also know that he is the type of man who needs to be cared for and there will doubtless be a second wife once the appropriate mourning period has passed."

Yona had not argued with her. Lady Naomi may have been frail, but her mind was as sharp as a dagger. Yona sighed, returning to the present moment, and asked Avram the obligatory question, "Would you like me to stay and help with the funeral preparations?" She was hoping against hope that he would say it was unnecessary as his sons and daughter would assist him that way.

"We would be eternally grateful if you helped us," he said, "but more importantly, I am sure that Naomi would want you to be a part of her service."

"I agree," a voice from the doorway added, and Yona looked up to see Lady Naomi's daughter, Sarah, standing there. "Mother spoke very highly of you. She said the talks you had each night meant a lot to her."

Sarah walked closer to the bed and looked down at her mother's still body. Her eyes reflected both grief and resignation. She turned to her father and bent to give him a brief kiss on the cheek. "How are you, father?"

Avram took a deep, but shaky breath. "I'll be fine, darling. When your brothers arrive we can plan the shemira. Hopefully, we can pull the funeral together by Deethyeen." He shook his head as he thought. "Unfortunately, it is going to have to be a big funeral. Your mother was much loved. But, I'm hoping we can have a private burial service."

"That would be nice," Sarah said. "I like the idea of saying our final goodbyes as a family."

"I know that Lady Naomi wasn't particularly religious," Yona interjected, "but we did discuss a few things about her service, and she thought it would be nice if we had the traditional Eucharist ceremony when she is buried."

Avram grunted in surprise. "That is a change of heart," he

said. "I like the idea of that, as well. It seems an appropriate way of saying goodbye."

Yitzak and Yaakov, Naomi and Avram's sons, arrived together.

"We left the children with Michael, Ruth and Hannah," Yitzak, the elder son, said. "We thought later we could come individually by family."

"Thank you, son," Avram said.

The men walked solemnly over to the bed to kiss their mother goodbye, and Yona moved toward the door.

"If you don't mind, do you think it would it be okay if I ventured to the market? They will be closed tomorrow and I have some items I need to pick up before I begin the trek back to Stonehelm on Deethmarth."

Avram seemed startled for a second, before saying, "How thoughtless. Of course, you must return. I'm sure there is someone else in need and we can't assume all your time. You're welcome to anything we have here, of course."

Yona paused and he quickly assured her, "I understand. Would you like an escort?"

Yona had only paused because she was trying to come up with an excuse for why she needed a weapon, but apparently he had jumped to the conclusion she needed items of a personal nature. She felt her cheeks reddening despite herself though that was no doubt an appropriate response for a sister. Although, she realized, she didn't know how much longer her journey would be and that probably wasn't such a bad idea.

"Thank you," she said warmly. "I realize the timing is awkward, but it shouldn't take me more than a couple of hours. I should be back well before lunch and perhaps then we can make some more definite plans. Would you like me to send the priest while I am out?"

"That's quite all right," Avram said. "I am sure Eli is taking care of that while we speak."

And indeed he had. A light tap at the door alerted them to the priest's presence.

"That was eerie timing," the priest said. "A certain idiom comes to mind but I'll refrain from using it."

Yona smiled and said, "My gr, uh, Mother Superior preferred to say, 'Speak of the sun and it doth shine.'"

"Infinitely preferable," the priest agreed, and Yona suddenly realized that she wasn't wearing her veil.

Avram standing and extending his hand saved her from further scrutiny, "Father, thank you for coming."

"Of course," the priest replied, taking his hand. He then turned to the children. "I'm Father Mordecai."

While everyone was introducing themselves, Yona slipped from the room and returned to her chamber. She dashed some cold water on her face. Her cheeks were still flushed and her heart pounding. She hoped Father Mordecai would forget her face quickly. Grabbing her veils, she quickly covered her head and face before picking up her basket, and making her way to the kitchen. Once there, she pulled her veil away from her face.

Marta was already there and preparing breakfast for the family. She poured a mug of coffee and handed it to Yona who accepted it gratefully. They looked at each other sadly.

"I hate ter say it," Marta wiped a tear from her eye, "but I be glad it's finally over. Ther's been a pall hangin' over ther house fer a coupler weeks now."

Yona hugged the cook in commiseration. "It's true," she sighed, taking a seat at the table. "There were times it almost felt like the buzzards were gathering. I only hope that Lady Naomi didn't feel that."

"If'n she did, she would ne'er had said a word."

Yona nodded. That was undoubtedly true. Despite their numerous conversations, Lady Naomi was painstakingly careful about what she said to whom. If she felt like they were just waiting for her to die so that they could get on with their lives, she would never have admitted it.

"Are ye goin' somewheres?" Marta nodded at the basket.

"Just to the market," Yona explained. "I need to pick up a few items before I begin the journey back to Stonehelm."

"Would ye care ter break yer fast, first?"

"I'd love to," she said, and her stomach grumbled loudly in response.

"Yer stomach agrees," Marta tittered, turning back to the stove and cracking a couple of eggs into the frying pan.

Stomach pleasantly full of fried eggs, bacon, cheese toast and coffee, Yona found her way to the market. It was still early enough that there were few shoppers, which made finding the stalls she needed much easier. She opted for a small oil-burning lantern because she realized that if she burned olive oil, she would have a constant supply because it was technically a food.

Yona found herself walking away from that booth thanking Omni for her veils because once again she was grinning like a fool at her own cleverness. Now she just needed a knife or some other form of protection.

She was looking for a stall that sold weapons when she passed a small booth selling jewelry and was immediately reminded of Eluned and the poor man who had paid the price for selling her a pair of earrings that had once belonged to King Arawn. She stopped abruptly, overcome by memories, and finally the attendant had to prompt her.

"Excuse me, Sister, may I help thee?"

Yona jumped, startled, and turned to look at the seller. His accent was strange. He was definitely not from Adamah or Annewven, for that matter. "I'm sorry," she apologized, "your stall brought back memories."

"Most hopefully they were pleasant ones," he said.

"Yes, and no," she admitted. "And, obviously," she indicated her habit, "I am no longer in need of jewelry. But, you wouldn't happen to know where I could find a stall in which to buy a knife or dagger, would you?"

"A dagger, you say? Why would a Sister be in need of a weapon?"

She just couldn't place his accent. "I realize it seems odd, but as I was travelling here from Hashirim, I realized how vulnerable I was while alone on Adam's Way when I didn't have someone with whom to travel. Not so much during the day, but at night."

He nodded in understanding. He had a pleasant face in which serious brown eyes regarded her almost solemnly. "Actually," he said, reaching into a large leather bag and pulling out a roll of felt, I happen to have some small daggers." He unrolled the felt and showed her the half dozen daggers that glittered on midnight blue fabric.

One of the daggers caught her eye immediately as its cross guard and hilt glittered with jewels. Eluned would have chosen that little dagger in a flash. It was smaller than the others and looked as if it would fit perfectly in her hand. She picked it up and tried it. She saw the look in his eyes and said, "It reminds me of a sword that belongs to a friend of mine."

He raised his eyebrows. "It's said to be modeled after Dyrnwyn."

"Dyrnwyn?" she asked although she knew to which sword he referred.

"It has also been called White Hilt or Excalibur."

"I think I've heard of Excalibur," she admitted. "How interesting."

"So, your friend's sword looks like this?"

"Oh no! It just reminds me of it. It's probably just the jewels. She's a pirate," she lied. "She likes sparkling things. I tease her that she's more like a raven then a pirate."

"A pirate, huh?" He said, insinuating that perhaps a pirate wasn't the best company for a Sister.

"I was in Seagirt," she continued her fabrication, "to care for an innkeeper who was dying, and she came in with a serious injury and I couldn't not help her."

He nodded as if that made sense.

"I can't quite place your accent," she continued. "I can tell you're not from Adamah."

"Naphtali."

"Oh, um," she hesitated. She couldn't act as if she knew too much. "Is that Queen Njima?"

"Yes," he admitted, mouth twisting in a moue of disgust, "which is one of the reasons I am here."

"I don't understand," she lied, trying to keep the anger from her voice.

"She doesn't like men," he said, "if you understand my meaning."

"Ah." she said. "Yes, I have heard that." Did he not know about Hevel? She found that rather ironic—to leave one kingdom ruled by a homosexual for another. If she didn't need a weapon, and to get back to the Lord Mayor's house, she would have continued searching for a dagger. And if he hadn't been so homophobic, she would have loved to find out more about Queen Njima. Instead, she told him she would take the dagger and quickly bargained on a price, explaining that she seriously needed to get back to the Lord Mayor's house as his wife had just passed away. She suddenly, desperately wanted to get out of there. The man was just too inquisitive. She hoped the fact she was staying with Avram would douse his curiosity.

14ᵀᴴ Teeneh

In fact, the Princesses soon figured out that they'd be required to remain on Paliaina for two nights before they were able to return to Seemu, setting sail on the morning of the third day.

Eluned came to that particular realization that evening as they were escorted to their lodgings—clearly a guesthouse for the occasional visitor to the island.

"It's the only thing that makes sense," she told Leleua and Talei. "After all, they couldn't send the ship to pick us up until they were absolutely sure the Phaeton wasn't coming back."

"I hadn't thought of that," Leleua said, "and just how long will they wait before they come to that decision?"

"Certainly they'll wait long enough, past sunset anyway, and then they can't possibly send a boat out tonight," Talei said. "I mean, I know it's possible to sail at night, but why do so if we're safe on Paliaina?"

That meant the ship wouldn't leave until the morning, and the island being so far east meant that it could easily take the entire day for the sailboat to make the trip, which, in turn, meant they would not be able to set off for Seemu until the following morning. Eluned sighed, inwardly. She hoped they could find something to do that wouldn't involve the islanders feeling it necessary to entertain them. They had already extended them more than the usual hospitality.

Once again the Princess wondered if she could somehow manage to finagle her way into seeing the goods stowed away in the secret cave. But then she thought better of it. Yes, it was tempting, but it might be detrimental for her to know the location. She couldn't be tortured into revealing something she didn't know, right?

Her thoughts were interrupted as Leleua stopped abruptly in front of her. The woman who was showing them to their rooms opened a door to Eluned's left and indicated that it was her room. She handed her a lantern that smelled faintly of some coconut-based oil, and the Princess thanked her and said goodnight to Leleua and Talei.

The woman said something in Favonian, and Talei quickly translated. Although by that point Eluned had picked up enough of the language to understand she was pointing out where the bathroom was located.

"Maururu," Eluned thanked her in Favonian and entered her room. The bedroom was small, but the furniture was exquisitely made, though unpretentious. Except for her bed. Though clearly meant for a single person, it was ornately carved and inlaid with iridescent nacre that nearly throbbed in its opalescence. Although, on second thought, she mused, the flickering of the lantern light perhaps caused the pulsation?

She pulled back the intricately painted tapa cloth coverlet, sat on the cotton sheet beneath and surveyed the rest of the room. Curtains fluttered at the open window allowing the salty sea breeze to cool the room. A small ebony dresser, a straight-backed chair, and a few hooks on the wall beside the dresser completed the room's furnishings. If it weren't for the bed, it would be an incredibly austere space, but it was definitely more than adequate for her needs.

She imagined she wouldn't be spending a lot of time here despite the fact they were required to spend an additional day on Paliaina. She chafed at losing yet another day of sword practice, but assuring that the Phaeton and Chessboard remained safe was definitely more important.

Her tapestry travelling bag had been placed on the dresser for her, but before she prepared herself for bed she had a little furniture arranging to accomplish. She stood up and moved the chair from where it was placed beside the dresser and sat it next to the bed to act as a bedside table. She then placed the lantern on the chair seat so she wouldn't have to hold it any longer. Yawning hugely, she retrieved her nightgown from the bag, and headed to the bathroom to brush her teeth and wash her face before returning to her room. The kava and the day of festivities were beginning to take their toll—she fell asleep almost as soon as her head hit the pillow.

A QUIET TAPPING ON HER DOOR awoke Eluned the following morning. She was briefly disoriented by her inability to see before she realized that she must have pulled the sheet over her head at some point. No doubt to shelter her eyes from the growing light, she realized as she sat up. It was full daylight! How long had she been asleep?

There was another quiet rap against the door.

"Yes?" she called out.

"Eluned?" It was Leleua. "Are you all right?"

"Come in," she invited. "I'm fine," she explained as they stepped into the room. "I must have really needed the sleep, or more specifically, I probably should have napped after the ride here. I forgot that Chokhmah always made me one of her magic teas after a phaeton trip, and it took more out of me than I realized."

"Well, it's a beautiful day," Talei said, "and we were thinking of hiking up to this waterfall that Anuhea was telling us about. Hokulani Falls. She said it drops more than one hundred feet over the edge of a cliff and into a beautiful pool that you can swim in."

"Anuhea? Swim?" The Princess was still trying to shake the cobwebs of sleep from her head.

"The woman who showed us to our rooms last night," Leleua enlightened her. "And no, we probably won't swim because we didn't bring anything to swim in," she turned to punch Talei lightly on the upper arm.

"Ow," she slapped her sister's hand away. "Definitely forgot to plan for an extra day, but we could always bring a picnic lunch and dip our feet in the pool."

"Do I have time to grab some coffee and breakfast first? Fruit would be fine. I just need a little something before hiking."

"Sure," said Talei. "Get dressed and meet us in the kitchen. It's just past the bathroom on the right. We'll go see what we can gather for a picnic."

Eluned slid out of bed and grabbed the sarong she'd worn the previous day. The sea green fabric had been embroidered with dozens of deep pink plumeria with lemon yellow centers. She debated wearing it again, but decided to save it for the boat trip back to Seemu, and pulled her loose cotton trousers, which had been dyed a robin's egg blue, from the bag along with a pale grey sleeveless blouse. Her cold weather clothes had done her little good here, but she knew they'd be travelling on and that they would be needed once again. Meanwhile, she would continue to wear the cotton trousers (damn Irirangi for not allowing her to get some sooner) and sarong as much as possible.

Her feet weren't nearly as tough as those of the twins, and she hoped her leather sandals would suffice for a hike. She looked forward to being able to wear her boots again. After pulling her hair back into a ponytail, and a quick stop in the bathroom, she joined the other princesses in the kitchen where Anuhea was pouring her a mug of coffee.

"Leleua say you like cream," she said in the common

tongue, and placed it on the table next to a plate of fruit. "Dat okay?" she asked, indicating the plate.

"It's wonderful," Eluned assured her, sitting down on the bench that ran the length of the table. "How far is it to the falls?" She asked Talei.

"About three miles, right?" she confirmed with Anuhea, who nodded.

Three miles, Eluned thought, picking up a slice of mango, that didn't sound too bad. Unless, of course, the path was rocky. "Will I be able to hike in these," she stuck out her sandaled foot.

Anuhea said something in Favonian and Leleua translated. "She says that most of the way has been trod flat over the years, but it gets a little rocky and rooty nearer to the falls. You should be all right, though."

BLESSEDLY, FOR ELUNED AT LEAST, they reached the shelter of the trees within a quarter of a mile. The Favonian sun could be merciless at times and this day in mid Teeneh was particularly steamy as far as she was concerned. Leleua and Talei naturally seemed to take it all in stride, but she was thankful for the branches of the koa trees that dappled the sunlight for her.

The plant growth thickened and the temperature dropped a bit as they climbed toward the falls, and when the first rocks and roots appeared, Eluned made a point to tread more carefully. A twisted ankle was the last thing she needed. Hopefully, Yona would arrive soon and they could leave for cooler climes, but they would be starting from scratch and who knew how long it might take them to acquire horses, if indeed they could do so. She couldn't even begin to imagine what the travel situation might be like wherever they went next. And that was something they definitely needed to discuss. Where were they going next?

Eluned's thoughts were interrupted by a gentle roaring

sound that she soon identified as the falls. It wasn't long before the roar of the falls grew louder with each step and soon they were standing at the edge of a crystal clear pool. About 50 yards away, the stream that formed Hokulani Falls tumbled over the side of the fern-covered cliff to the pool below, sunlight caused the spray to sparkle and shimmer, and the foam and mist where the falls met the pool glowed incandescently. Ginger, plumeria and other flowers bloomed along the far edge of the pool, and it took a moment for Eluned to realize that she'd been holding her breath while she gazed in wonder at the beauty of the setting.

"Breathtaking." Leleua said.

"Literally!" Eluned laughed as she bent down to remove her sandals and dipped a toe into the placid water farthest from the falls. She removed it quickly with a gasp. "I wasn't expecting it to be that cold."

"That would take some getting used to," Talei agreed, as she dipped her foot into the pool.

"Although I imagine some of these boulders would be warm enough to lie on after you got out," Leleua pointed to a particularly flat stone fully exposed to the sun.

"True," Eluned said, "but I'm going to stick to the shade." She settled herself on a rock, but soon grew bored and got up to wander around the edge of the pool. It was too early to eat lunch so there was plenty of time for a bit of exploring. The Princess wondered how close she could get to the falls without soaking herself.

As she was slowly picking her way across some tumbled boulders, Eluned noticed some movement out of the corner of her eye. Stopping, she surveyed the area around the falls for a moment. Was it just the water cascading down over the cliff? A breeze ruffling the leaves? It had struck her as very human, though. She continued to edge closer to the falls and soon reached the cliff face to the left of the waterfall. From there, she could see behind the fall itself although it was somewhat obscured by the brume thrown up by the water hitting the pool. Still, it was pretty obvious that there was nothing or, more importantly, no one there.

Strange, she thought, I must be seeing things. A fine mist of spray was starting to collect in her hair and on her clothes. Eluned was turning to make her way back to where the princesses were lounging when she was distracted by motion again, this time behind the falls. Turning back toward the falls, she found herself staring into a pair of huge brown eyes that probably looked just as surprised as her own.

Where had this woman come from? She hadn't been there a second ago. They stared at each other for a moment before the woman clearly reached a decision and beckoned her. Eluned glanced at the Leleua and Talei to see if they were watching her, but they were now sitting with their feet in the pool and seemed engrossed in conversation.

The Princess tread carefully over the boulders toward the back of the falls. Because of the dampness, many were slippery with moss or algae. She found herself leaning toward the cliff face so that if she fell it would be away from the water. The mist from the falls was getting her wetter by the second, but her curiosity was stronger than her distaste at getting soaked.

Once behind the falls, Eluned could see that the woman, while young, was definitely older than she was, maybe nearer to thirty. She turned and led Eluned to an entrance in the cliff, itself. There, she set down the basket she had been carrying that contained dead flowers. Eluned was puzzled but followed her down a narrow tunnel for about a dozen feet before turning left. Here the tunnel opened up into a small, concave room, which was lit by candles set in niches carved into the curved rock wall. In the glittering light, Eluned could see an altar, clearly recently replenished with fresh flowers, on the opposite side of the room. That explained the basket.

"May I?" the Princess whispered, indicating that she wanted to approach the altar.

The young woman nodded and Eluned wondered if she were a priestess of the goddess venerated here or simply an acolyte. Because it was clearly a goddess, Eluned mused. The islanders were too traditional to allow a female to serve a masculine god.

You wouldn't know it by the carved figure that held a place of honor in the center of the altar because the male and female deities all seemed to look alike to Eluned, but the tiki was surrounded by feminine objects. The most striking being an abalone shell, the inside of which had been polished until it practically glowed. Inside this striking shell sat a large black pearl surrounded by dozens of smaller pearls ranging from white and cream to rose, lavender, blue and black. They glimmered in the candlelight and were clearly a favorite offering to the goddess.

Eluned glanced at the woman standing next her. "Eluned," she said, pointing to herself.

The woman nodded, and replied, "Kiha," pointing to herself, and "Namaka," pointing to the goddess on the altar.

The sound of Talei and Leleua calling out for the Princess interrupted them. They turned together toward the tunnel's entrance into the room.

"Oh," Leleua gasped as she entered the cave.

"It is home to Namaka," Eluned explained simply, summing up the little she knew. "And this is Kiha."

Talei said something in Favonian and soon the three women were conversing. They spoke for so long that Eluned began to wonder what they could possibly be discussing.

Suddenly, Talei turned to Eluned and asked, "Can we tell her why we are here? She seems to have the feeling that you were led here for a reason. It would be good to have the Goddess of the Sea on our side as we journey back to Seemu."

"And whenever you must travel by sea in your quest," Leleua added.

"Yona could probably use some prayers as well," Eluned noted.

Taking that as a "yes," Talei turned back to Kiha and began speaking rapidly in Favonian again.

Soon Kiha was smiling broadly and taking Eluned by the hand, she led her back toward the altar. This might be an Omni-inspired quest, Eluned thought, but she would not refuse the help of any god or goddess that might pass her way. Hadn't the necklace given to her by Cuhvetena on the faery isle helped to enchant Arawn and the other men that night? And Yona, too, she couldn't help but smile. But, if she hadn't had that necklace to help charm them, she and her friends might have met with trouble a lot sooner.

No, she would not turn down anything that seemed to fall in her path, especially if it seemed to be divine intervention when it happened. Or Omninspired, as Chokhmah liked to say.

Talei and Kiha were speaking again, and then they turned to her and Talei explained that Kiha wanted her to choose one of the pearls in the abalone shell to carry with her as a sign of the presence of Namaka.

Eluned looked at the pearls again. They were all so exquisite! Yet, as she was already carrying the pearl white moonstone in her pouch, the opposite called to her and she removed one of the black pearls from the shell. It glowed in the palm of her hand, and she suddenly wished she had something with which to reciprocate. Unfortunately, knowing they were about to go on a hike, she hadn't even bothered to put on any jewelry that morning.

"What's wrong?" Leleua asked, noticing that Eluned's brow was furrowed and that she appeared distraught.

"I don't have anything to give Namaka," she said.

"I'm sure it's fine," said Leleua and said something to Kiha who smiled and patted Eluned on the arm.

Then Eluned suddenly brightened. "Kiha could join us for lunch," she suggested. "I assume that we have more than enough. Picnic lunches always seem plentiful."

"There is definitely more than enough to share," Talei agreed. "Anuhea thought you'd probably be hungry after having only eaten fruit for breakfast."

Leleua spoke to Kiha, who said, yes, she would be delighted to join them. Eluned could decipher that much, anyway, so she turned and led the women out of the cave and back to where the picnic lunch waited.

"Jus' one ting," Kiha said, and blushed clearly not comfortable with her knowledge of the common tongue.

"Yes?" Eluned urged. During their meal, she had been forced to either converse with Leleua or Talei and leave Kiha in the dark or remain silent. She had chosen to keep quiet as much as possible while the other three women talked to each other.

"Da . . ." she struggled for the word, and pointed to the pearl necklace she wore around her neck.

"The pearl?"

"Yes. Pearl." With an apologetic look at Eluned, she turned to Talei and spoke rapidly in Favonian.

"Kiha says it is important that you hold the pearl when you need Namaka's help because it has been blessed by the goddess, herself. Can she see the pearl?"

The Princess removed the pearl from the leather pouch she always wore around her neck. The Ring of Eluned's moonstone already resided there along with her heart-shaped piece of amethyst and the betrothal ring from King Uriel. She handed it to Kiha who placed it in the palm of her left hand, which she then covered with her right.

"Hold it like that?" Eluned asked.

"Yes, like dis. Den . . . ," she paused again and spoke to Talei.

"Hold it like that," Talei translated, "and then tell Namaka specifically what it is you want or need."

"As far as the ocean is concerned, I assume?" Eluned asked.

Talei checked with Kiha, and Kiha nodded, emphatically.

"Yes, Namaka is ocean goddess," she said.

Eluned was feeling somewhat overwhelmed. Could she really just hold the pearl in the palm of her hand and ask Namaka to calm a roiling sea, for instance? That seemed nearly miraculous, but then again so had her time on the faery isle not to mention the way she'd found her sword, Dyrnwyn, when the Pwca, Aeron, had led her to the lake in the middle of the desert. She seemed to have lived the miraculous since she began her journey. So, why not a magic pearl?

Kalei said something and Leleua added, "She says that obviously it has to be something important, and something that is for the welfare of all concerned."

Eluned thought about that for a moment. "For example, if we were being chased, I could ask for a wind to help us to sail away faster but I couldn't ask for someone's ship to sink? Like that?"

Leleua repeated what the Princess had said to Kiha, who once again nodded, and returned the pearl to Eluned, who promptly deposited it her suede pouch. Yet another item she couldn't risk losing. She glanced at the elaborately engraved gold band that graced her right ring finger. At the rate she was gaining Treasures and "treasures," she would soon have to get something to cart them around in, she thought with a smile. Which, of course, is why she was glad they'd be able to leave behind the Phaeton and Chessboard on Paliaina.

It was now well past noon and the twins were cleaning up the remainder of their feast and putting it back in the basket.

Eluned groaned inwardly. She was suddenly incredibly anxious to get back to Seemu, and not only would they probably not arrive there until the following evening, but she still had the rest of the day to waste. A nap would be nice but it might prevent her from sleeping that night, and she didn't relish the idea of staring into space for countless hours.

Well, they still had the trek back to Vailima, she thought. Perhaps, she could come up with something to do by the time they arrived. They said their goodbyes and thank yous to Kiha and were soon on their way.

23RD DEER

Yona managed to beg off attending the funeral service for Lady Naomi at the church claiming she required time to pray and to prepare herself for the graveside rite. In truth, she was terrified that she would be recognized. So far, other than the overly inquisitive vendor at the market, she had managed not to arouse anyone's curiosity. Even Father Mordecai seemed to take her at her word, working with her to plan Naomi's service at the cemetery.

The burial liturgy was to be for family only, but even so she still intended to wear her veils. Gathered at the family plot, they stood in silence around the grave as Father Mordecai consecrated the Sacraments and the ceremony began.

As each family member, beginning with Avram and proceeding to the children and grandchildren, received the bread, they gave thanks and then crumbled it into the grave. The chalice of wine was then passed round, each person spilling a drop onto the casket.

Finally, each person picked up a handful of dirt. As it was tossed onto the coffin, Yona prayed, "Forasmuch as it hath pleased thou, O Omni, of Its great mercy to take unto Itself the soul of our dear Naomi, here departed, we therefore commit her body to the ground; earth to earth, ashes to ashes, dust to dust; in sure and certain hope of the Resurrection to eternal life in You, O Omni, according to Your mighty workings, whereby You are able to subdue all things to Yourself."

The family responded with "amens" of varying degrees of strength from Avram's grief-choked sob to Sarah's strong and loving exclamation of faith and the mumbled and half-whispered exhalations of the grandchildren.

The long, hot days of summer had settled in, and an almost unseemly cloudless azure sky was beginning to fade against the ever strengthening rays of the sun as the star moved toward its apex. Naomi would have been happy, no doubt, to be buried on such a cheerful day, but Yona had long been of the opinion that funerals should go hand-in-hand with gloomy, grey days.

Yona joined Avram and Father Mordecai in the carriage that had carried them to the graveyard along with the polished oaken casket that contained Naomi's remains. They rode in silence back to the house where the staff and some close friends waited to celebrate the traditional post funeral wake.

Starving because she'd been too nervous to eat breakfast, Yona prepared herself a plate as soon as it was seemly, and with a large goblet of wine, hurried upstairs to her room to eat in seclusion. Still so far, so good, but she was itching to leave. The anxiety just to be on the road again was nearly more than she could bear.

It had occurred to her after she'd returned from the market on Deethsadoorn that she might have done well to have purchased some trousers, a sweater or flannel shirt and a leather jacket or jerkin for when she reached Markheshvan. Certainly by then, she mused, she would no longer need the Sister's rather hampering costume. It seemed as if it might make it much more difficult to traverse the path to the Hatseetz Pass.

Now she hesitated to return to the market for fear of seeing the vendor from Naphtali. She hated to do it, but she wondered if she could pilfer anything from Eli, Avram or one of the male servants? The time seemed right to look with everyone else preoccupied with the wake.

Eli seemed to be somewhat of a dandy but he was closest to her size. She would try his room first. It was located down the hallway to the left of the broad staircase. She just hoped that if anyone was in the foyer when she ventured down the corridor that they wouldn't notice her.

But, Omni was with her once again, and she made it unseen to Eli's door and knocked quietly on it, praying fervently that he was not within. After waiting a half a minute, she unlatched the door and stepped inside.

She wasn't surprised to find a well-appointed room with a rather large armoire taking up most of one wall. She opened it to find it stuffed full of clothing. Apparently, Eli didn't throw anything away. She was looking for something that would've been squeezed into a far corner, clothing that might take a while for him to notice that it was missing.

Sure enough, she found a fearfully outmoded leather pants and jacket ensemble to the far right in the armoire. The unstylish outfit would just have to do. Whomever she found to guide her would just be welcome to his laugh. That's all there was to it, she decided.

She bundled the clothing up and shoved it into her basket. Who knew that the Hamper would have become an indispensable part of her habiliment?

She quietly left Eli's room after making sure no one was wandering around the upstairs hallway, and hurried back to her room. After tucking the clothes beneath the pillow on her bed, she hurried down the private corridor to Naomi's and Avram's room.

He hadn't been staying there for quite a while, having moved to a room near Eli's when Naomi's health became too fragile, but she was sure she could find some of his older, unworn, clothing in his armoire. And she found just what she needed on the shelf located above the hanging clothing—an

     In Lonely Exile

old, flannel shirt worn smooth by repeated washings. The red and blue plaid had greatly faded, it was slightly moth eaten, and like Avram, slightly on the large side, but with the leather jacket, she would have no trouble keeping warm at nights and when they were in the upper elevations of the mountains.

She heard steps ascending the stairs, and stowing the shirt in her basket and shutting the armoire door, she scurried back to her room. And just in time. She had no sooner settled herself on her bed and picked up the sandwich she hadn't yet finished, when there came a gentle knock at her door.

Putting the sandwich back down despite the fact her belly grumbled in protest, she hurried to the door. Her stomach fell when she saw that it was Father Mordecai.

"Father?" She tried hard not to gulp the question. She could think of absolutely no reason why he might need to see her, although, she supposed, there might be some formalities of which she was unaware.

"Sister," he replied, and she was sure she heard a peculiar emphasis on that. "Can we talk? Privately."

She swallowed, hard, and ushered him into her small room, trying hard not to panic. She had come so close to getting out of this town without being spotted. Was it all to come crumbling down around her now?

"I'm sorry," he said, noticing the barely nibbled sandwich on the bed, "I've interrupted your meal. Please continue. We can talk while you eat."

"I'm afraid I don't have much appetite," she lied, although at the moment that was true, although she took a fortifying gulp of wine from her goblet.

"Then let me put your mind at ease, Yona. I'm not here to foil your plans. I'm here to offer my service."

She shook her head in disbelief, mind whirling. He knew who she was. "I don't understand."

"Please sit, and I'll explain."

She sat on the edge of the bed, gratefully, as her knees still felt weak with the panic she was experiencing.

"There are many of us," he began.

"Us?"

"In this case, mostly priests, but others as well, who have become aware that, how shall I say this, something's afoot."

"Afoot?" Yona felt it best to play dumb as long as possible.

"No need to play dumb."

Was he reading her mind? She cleared her throat and said, "Please tell me what you mean. Specifically."

"We know that your friend, the Princess Eluned, is on a divinely-inspired quest to bring together the Thirteen Hallowed Treasures."

"Who?"

"Please save yourself some time and drop the act. I am here to tell you that we want to do everything we can to help you in the Quest knowing that we can't actually search for the treasures ourselves."

"Is this Omninspired knowledge?"

Father Mordecai smiled. "Nice. I like that. Omninspired. Yes, to some degree it is. That, along with the fact that we've heard things, and we know that certain Kingdoms have been preparing for war."

Yona supposed she would have to trust him. It would have been easier to quietly kill her and slip out of the house than spend this much time talking. "And when you heard that Eluned and her friends had disappeared with a couple of treasures and that I had disappeared with another, you put two and one together and made three?"

"Exactly."

Picking up her sandwich, Yona took a bite. She was, after all, very hungry. "And how do you propose to help me?" she asked after she had chewed and swallowed.

"First, let me say that my name is not Mordecai, and I am not from here."

Yona's eyes widened in surprise. "I'm pretty good with accents and you fooled me. You could've been born and raised here."

"Thank you. It's a gift. The truth is my name is Olcan, and I am from Dyfed."

"What? They are an enemy of Adamah. Why would you choose to . . . oh. Spy."

"I hate to think of it that way, but yes. It was important that the allied Kingdoms keep an eye on what our enemies are up to. I have no doubt they do the same."

Yona nodded. Unfortunately, that was probably true, which meant they should have been and should be more careful in the future.

"If it's any consolation, I think that your disguise is definitely Omninspired. If I hadn't known what to look for, I would never have noticed. But, we figured you'd be working your way toward Tarshish or Dyfed and so we have scouts looking out for you."

"The allied and neutral countries that border Adamah. What about Sheba and Zion and Aden?"

"Well, we were pretty sure the Princess would not have retreated to Zion, and Sheba borders Annewven, and we had calculated, considering your acquaintances, that you'd most likely be heading to a country with a coast."

"Dyfed or Tarshish."

"Yes, and that's where most of our spies are located."

She shook her head in wonder. "This is so much bigger than I had realized."

"The tension between good and evil grows stronger daily. It is of crucial importance evil doesn't triumph. Should it do so, it will, essentially, mean the end of the world."

Yona sat in stunned silence. She had realized the Quest was divinely inspired—too many things had fallen into place for it not to be so—but she had not, and she was sure neither had the others, been aware of just how important their quest was to the future of the world.

"I'm speechless," she admitted. "I've been on my own for so long, or it feels like I have, anyway, that knowing there are people out there looking out for me, for us . . . well, it's nearly incomprehensible."

"We had intended to keep our presence a secret," Olcan said, "but we decided that it was in our best interests to help you get where you are going. May I ask where that might be?"

"I'm heading to Markheshvan where I hope to hire a guide to take me over the Hatseetz Pass and from there, down into Smuggler's Bay."

"Will your friends pick you up once you arrive there?"

"Hopefully. Unfortunately, I had no way to get a message to Libni or anyone else before I set out. I imagine I will have to wait until someone arrives and then I pray that they will either take me to Favonia, or somewhere where I can find another ship heading that way."

"Ah, Favonia," he exclaimed. "That makes sense. We have no one there because we haven't come up with a valid reason to be there. It's pretty small so strangers stand out more."

"Chokhmah's aunt is the Queen of Favonia."

Olcan nodded again. "Making it even easier to stay hidden."

"I imagine they are fretting about my whereabouts. Surely by now, they know that I've disappeared with the Hamper."

"Doubtless. When do you leave for Markheshvan?"

"Tomorrow," she said taking the last bite of her sandwich. She retrieved the clothes from under the pillow and pulled the shirt out of the basket. "I was just borrowing some clothes from Avram and Eli when you arrived. I realized that I wouldn't be able to hike up to the pass in this outfit."

Olcan grimaced.

"I know," she agreed, "the outfit's horribly outdated, but I thought by the time I was leaving Markheshvan with a guide, I wouldn't stand out as much."

"I have no doubt that's true, but we can pull something together for you that will both fit you better and look a little more up-to-date."

"We?"

"My brother and I. I will have Faolan meet you just outside of town tomorrow. He will travel with you to Markheshvan and then lead you up to the Hatseetz Pass."

"Is he going to agree to that?" Yona asked.

"He is as fully committed as I am, perhaps more so, and you will stand out less travelling with someone else."

"But as a Sister won't that seem a little odd?"

"You can change into some travelling clothes."

"There's just one small problem." She pulled the veil from her head.

He considered her shorn locks for a moment mentally going through the options before offering, "How about a head scarf?"

"That could work."

"It will work because it has to," he smiled. "Well, I'd best be going. I've got some shopping to do and some arrangements to make."

"And where am I to meet Faolan? About what time?"

"There is a traveller's shelter about a mile past the city gates for those who can't make it to town before the gates shut for the night. If you leave soon after first light, you should arrive after anyone who is staying there has left for the day. Faolan will be there when you arrive. There you can change into travelling clothes and leave your habit behind. Someone, probably my self, will pick it up later so that it's not discovered."

Yona felt a tremendous sense of relief wash over her as she shook Olcan's hand and ushered him out the door. It was going to happen. It was now only a matter of time before she was safely ensconced on Favonia, and once more with her companions. She felt tears of happiness well in her eyes, and as she turned to face the bed, a little sob escaped her throat.

Yona had not realized just how anxious she had become with this delay. Picking up the leather suit and flannel shirt, she stuffed them beneath the mattress. She felt sure they would eventually be discovered but by that time she would be long gone. But to make sure, she would remove the sheets from her bed before she left in the morning. It would probably be a while before there was a reason to make it up again. Yona couldn't imagine Avram returning to the room he once shared with Naomi unless he was on his deathbed himself.

24ᵀᴴ Deer

Faolan had to admit to himself that he was nervous. As he paced the already trampled area in front of the traveller's shelter, he tried to quiet his mind before Yona's arrival. It was amusing, really. He wasn't in the least bit nervous about escorting Yona to the village of Markheshvan, and then up and over the Panavhadesh mountains through the Hatseetz Pass. That would be a piece of cake, so to speak. He wasn't even worried about her discovering his true identity. He planned on informing her about that as soon as possible.

No, what really worried him was that he would fail to ingratiate himself enough with Yona, that she would find his service dispensable. He desperately wanted to become a part of this quest. Ever since their network of informants had figured out that the Treasures were being gathered again, Faolan had felt a strong urge to help find them. But, to do so, he would have to be invited to join the band that was seeking the treasures. That gave him about two weeks or so to convince Yona to, at the very least, introduce him to her companions once they arrived in Favonia.

He was sure he could get to Favonia. Not only would whoever picked them up at Smuggler's Bay (he hoped that it would be Libni as that would be a coup in his favor) not force him to walk back to Hagafen if he requested to continue the journey, but he would also claim that he promised to see the Treasure safely there. That was the plan, anyway. And, if he were on good terms with Yona, again hopefully, he could convince the others as well. Still, it was only a hope and not a certainty, and hope can be a very fragile thing.

Faolan continued to pace and mentally prepare for Yona's arrival. He had waited about twenty minutes when he saw a woman dressed like a Sister of Holy Supplication heading his way. The chance that the woman approaching him was any one but Yona was less than zero, but he waited to say anything or even greet her until she arrived at the shelter.

"Faolan?" She asked when she got within speaking distance.

He extended a long-fingered hand, and she reached out to clasp it. They shook, and Yona marveled at how warm his hand seemed. Yes, it was late in the month of Deer, but the mornings here were still on the cool side until the sun had risen enough to warm the landscape.

"Are you well?" she queried, concern in her voice. Perhaps having spent the past week with a sick and dying woman had attuned her to illness although he certainly appeared well enough. His grey-blue eyes were bright though his forehead was creased with worry.

"I'm fine," he assured her, turning toward the shelter to retrieve a parcel sitting on the wooden platform out front. "I tend to run a little hot, that's all." It was his standard line. It was neither the time nor the place to inform her of the family 'curse'. "Here are your traveling clothes," he said, handing her the package. "I'll get the horses while you change."

Yona's eyes lit up, and she removed her veil, smiling. "Thank Omni and thank you," she replied. "I am so grateful that we won't have to walk to Markheshvan. That should cut the time it will take us to get there nearly in half, correct?"

"Yes," he smiled back, and Yona suddenly realized just how attractive this Faolan was. "Depending on the weather, about a week."

"Wonderful," she exclaimed, climbing into the shelter. She opened the parcel and was pleased to find a split leg riding skirt of light tweed and a full-sleeved blouse of apricot-hued cotton. The headscarf was also cotton woven in tones of brown and orange. She was actually thankful for it, as well. It would protect her head from the hot summer sun.

"You look nothing like your brother," she said, once they were mounted, and heading south along Adam's Way.

He chuckled in assent. Where Olcan was olive-skinned with dark eyes and thick, wavy black hair, Faolan was much paler with nearly baby soft light brown hair, which he kept cut short. "We are a contrast as are our parents."

"And who do you favor?"

"My father," and nearly continued with 'but the curse is patrilineal so Olcan is affected as well,' but checked himself in time. Instead he said, "I imagine you are glad to be rid of the habit."

"You have no idea," she laughed, "but I am enjoying the shorter hair. I wish I didn't have to conceal it. Although as long as we're out in the sun I don't really mind the extra bit of protection that the scarf provides."

"Well, it should only be while we're on Adam's Way," he assured her. "Once we begin the climb to the pass, you're more than welcome to remove the scarf. We just need to stand out as little as possible."

"Have you done this trek?"

"No," he admitted, "but I've been given explicit instructions."

"And you're sure they'll suffice?" She eyed him warily.

"Absolutely," he assured her. "I may not have climbed this

particular trail, but I have extensive experience in the outdoors. You could even go so far as to say that I cut my teeth in the woods." He smiled, inwardly, at his wordplay. Or, at least, he thought he had.

"What's so funny?" Yona asked.

He chuckled and shook his head. "Nothing, really. Sometimes I just amuse myself. So, tell me how you managed to appropriate the Hamper," he nodded at the basket securely attached to her horse's saddle.

"Appropriate," she smiled. "Thank you. I like that. Well, it was both easy and complicated," and she launched into the tale of what would eventually become known as the 'Great Deception' because Yona was already being vilified around the Kingdom as a traitor no better than her pirate friends.

Faolan nodded appreciatively as she finished. "Well, I have to say we've all been impressed by how you've managed this, and we would love to hear how your friends managed to get away with the Chariot of Morgan and the chessboard."

"I'm looking forward to hearing that tale, myself," she said. "And, I wasn't as successful as I might have thought. I was discovered."

"It wasn't because you were disguised as a Sister, though," Faolan said. "It was sheer coincidence . . ."

"Omnincidence," Yona interrupted.

"Indeed. Omnincidence," he conceded, "that you ended up at the home of the Lord Mayor, and that it was Olcan who performed the funeral. He just put it all together."

"I wasn't wearing my veils," Yona informed him. "At that point I was so accustomed to not wearing them around the family, and Mordecai, I mean Olcan, surprised us when he arrived so soon after Lady Naomi's death. We remarked on it at the time. I left soon thereafter for the market, but naturally he would have noted my appearance."

"It is true that he noticed. I just arrived in town a couple of days ago in order to relieve Olcan. He'll be returning home to take care of our horse farm. Anyway, he said something when we met that night about the unusually attractive Sister who had been in attendance at Lady Naomi's deathbed. It was then that we began to wonder. It seemed farfetched, but it didn't take us long to convince ourselves that it had to be true. Although," he added, "it makes one wonder had it not been Olcan would another priest have focused on that at the time?"

"I guess we'll never know. Once again, thank Omni, and that's why you can't help but realize that this is all meant to happen."

They subsided into silence—Faolan wondering whether his teaming up with Yona and her friends was 'meant to happen,' and Yona musing on just how blessed she had been at every turn of this adventure.

"Honestly," Yona confided to Faolan half an hour later, "I won't feel safe until I am well away from Hagafen. I swear there was a spy for Hevel in the marketplace and I may have aroused his suspicions."

She told him about looking for a weapon and how he had seemed inordinately interested in why a Sister might be purchasing such an item.

"He was from Naphtali," she added, "but spoke poorly of Queen Njima."

"Very likely a spy," agreed Faolan.

"That's why I chose not to attend the funeral," she explained. "I was terrified he would seek me out there. Other than the graveside service, I tried to remain out of sight until I left. It is my hope that he thinks I headed south to Seagirt as I mentioned that I've been there."

Faolan considered this, brow furrowed as he thought it through, before shaking his head. "No, I am sure we are not being followed. Other than Olcan, I saw no one this morning. I left before dawn and when I arrived at the shelter no one was there. I'm pretty sure no one even stayed at the shelter last night. I understand that south of Hagafen Adam's Way gets very little traffic, so unless this man really second guesses us, I imagine he's stationed on the road to Seagirt if he actually suspects you."

Yona breathed a sigh of relief. That was her hope, as well. There really was no reason why anyone would suspect her of heading to Tarshish.

THEY HAPPENED ON A THREE-SIDED travellers' shelter shortly after sunset, and in the dark tethered their horses where they could nibble at the grass and slake their thirst at the spring-fed trough. Yona loosened their saddles and fed them some oats while Faolan went about scrounging up a quick supper of dried mutton and cold potatoes.

Both Yona and Faolan were too tired to do more than the bare minimum of chores in the light of two lanterns. Other than a couple of brief stops for lunch and later to relieve them-selves-taking turns while the other held the horses—they had ridden hard that day. They weren't the only ones who were tired. Their mounts were in desperate need of rest, as well.

It was easier to gulp down some food, cold and unappetiz-ing as it might be, and fall into an exhausted sleep than to make a pretense at conversation.

Within half an hour, they were snuggled into their blan-kets and even the hard wooden floor of the shelter didn't pre-vent them from quickly falling into a dreamless sleep.

YONA WAS AWAKENED JUST BEFORE DAWN by the sound of Faolan starting a small fire to make some coffee. While she waited, she packed away their blankets and checked on the horses.

They broke their fast with hard-boiled eggs and cheese,

and were on the road again as the sun crested on the horizon to their left. Vineyards, olive groves and pastureland for sheep had given way to a never ending panorama of wheat fields at this point and the grain glowed rose gold in the early morning sunlight.

"Beautiful," Yona murmured. Other than the clip clop of their horses' hooves and early morning bird song, it was quiet.

"It's almost as if we're the only humans remaining," Faolan remarked.

It certainly felt that way at the moment, but Yona had no doubt they would be passing a farmstead or two before the morning ended. At least she hoped so. It would be great if they could purchase some fresh meat for dinner that evening. As anxious as she was to get to Smuggler's Bay, she would gladly sacrifice an hour for a decent meal that evening.

She guessed she had more of an appetite travelling with Faolan than she had on her own because she didn't fear being discovered with every step she took. In some ways, she ought to feel somewhat ashamed of herself, she realized. She had so willingly entrusted herself into Faolan's care that she was actually enjoying the journey, as exhausting as it might be.

And yet, she felt intuitively she could trust him. Yes, there was something he wasn't telling her, that was true, but it didn't concern the Quest, she was sure of that.

"Yona," Faolan said again, and she realized he'd been trying to get her attention.

"I'm sorry," she lightly slapped her face as if to wake herself up, "just woolgathering."

"I was just saying that if we pass a farm house, we might want to stop and pick up some provisions for the next couple of days."

"That would be wonderful," she said. "I have an infinite supply of bread, cheese and apples, wine, water and olive oil in my basket, but I can say from experience that one will soon grow awfully tired of that fare."

"And it's not exactly protein heavy, is it?"

"Are you one of those 'have to have meat with every meal' men?"

He surveyed her with some discomfort.

"What is it? I have the feeling there's something you're not telling me," she said.

He took a deep breath. The sooner he got this out of the way, the sooner she could grow comfortable with what he had to say and, hopefully, forget about it. He cleared his throat. "The truth is that while I'm in this form, I do need protein at almost every meal to keep my strength up."

"This form?" Yona's forehead creased this time.

"Don't be worried or alarmed. It is something that has been passed down in my family since time out of mind, and we have long since learned to control it."

"I'm waiting," Yona said, reining her horse to a standstill.

"We are Shapeshifters," he admitted.

"And what shape do you shift into? Or is there more than one?"

He removed his hat and ruffled his short hair with his left hand vying for time. He was accustomed to people reacting with fear when he named the creature he shifted to despite the fact that his people were known to be guardians and protectors of children, wounded men and lost persons. They were more like the creatures they shifted into than the monsters that shared their name. "Wolf," he said but it was more of a whisper.

"A werewolf?" Yona felt herself involuntarily leaning away from him.

"No!" he barked before collecting himself. "No," he continued more quietly. "Werewolves are monsters completely at the beck and call of the full moon. They would as soon rip apart a human as a sheep. We are as old as time and more like the canines we shift into. We would rather die than hurt a member of our family or someone we love or care about. And we can tell the difference once we have shifted."

"So why shift at all?"

"Therein lies the rub. It's complicated, but essentially we cannot survive unless we occasionally shift. It would be as if one half of ourselves is starving out the other half."

"Are you stronger when you are a wolf?"

"Considerably, and a much better hunter."

Yona clucked to her horse and started moving again. "Very interesting. I have a deep respect for wolves. My friend, Merari, has a wolf that he tamed and it's very loyal to him. And if you're really like a wolf when you've shifted then I have little to fear. I do know that wolves are really averse to harming humans. Besides, the fantastical just seems to be a part of this quest. Somehow, I am just not that surprised."

Faolan grinned and set his horse at a trot. Maybe he had a chance after all. "How do you mean, fantastical?" he asked, and Yona proceeded to tell him all about the Quest so far from the strange little creature that called itself Jabberwock the Bandersnatch to Eluned's experience with the Barrow Wight and meeting the yeti, Bonpo, up to that very moment.

"The only thing I don't know is what happened when Eluned returned to Prythew," Yona finished her tale. "I know they escaped with the treasures, but I haven't heard anything else."

Faolan nodded grimly. "We know very little, but we do know that King Hamartia's Chancellor, Matraqua, was killed as was King Arawn's Lord High Steward . . ."

"Hywel?" she interrupted. A beautiful man, she remembered, and so enamored of Eluned. They'd spent many hours in his company both in Prythew and Arberth. Despite whom he worked for, he had always seemed like a decent man. "Who killed them?"

"We're not positive, but we are fairly certain it was either the Princess Eluned, Gwrhyr, or both of them together. Also, King Arawn lost his right hand in whatever skirmish took the lives of the other two."

Yona's head was whirling. What had gone so horribly wrong? She now felt completely sure that Eluned had been right. It would take attempting to sacrifice the Princess for her and Gwrhyr to kill. Self-defense was the only thing that made sense.

"What is it?" Faolan asked when he saw the pained expression on Yona's face.

"It's just that when Hevel and I left for Adamah, Eluned was afraid to return to Prythew," Yona's voice quavered with guilt. "She was convinced that it was Arawn's intention to sacrifice her to his gods. We all thought that she was over-reacting. We just couldn't believe that a king would risk killing another king's daughter. It just didn't seem possible. But somehow that must be what happened because I can think of no other reason for Eluned and Gwrhyr to attack and kill anyone unless their lives were threatened."

Faolan asked why Eluned might have thought she would be sacrificed and Yona explained to him all the eerie coincidences from the earrings to the death of the man who sold them and their meeting with the woodcutter in the forest, among other things.

"Still interested in joining the Quest?" she asked when she was finished.

Faolan colored, and stammered a response, "What makes you think that's my interest?"

Yona guffawed. "You're an open book, Wolfman. That's something you might want to work on. As you can see this isn't just a jaunt. It is truly dangerous."

"And yet here you are."

"Exactly. Fortunately, you have some time to think about it. Not that it'll be up to me, anyway."

They rode in silence until they reached the first farmhouse.

THAT EVENING, THEY DECIDED to stop an hour before sunset rather than push on to the next shelter. They had left wheat and corn fields behind for lemon orchards and situated themselves in a grassy area between two rows of trees.

They scavenged amongst the trees for downed wood with which to build a fire. They had picked up a chicken and some corn at the first farmhouse in exchange for currency as they had nothing to barter with, and their intention was to roast it all and save half for the following day with Faolan eating the lion's share to assuage his need for protein. This would become their pattern for the next week—purchasing food every other day and, unless a shelter presented itself a good hour before sunset, finding a likely spot to camp for the night—before arriving in Markheshvan the following Deethmarth, a week and a day after they had set forth from Hagafen. They decided they didn't want to risk carrying fresh meat in the basket for days, magical or not, although chances were that it might work and when they began the hike to the pass, it might become necessary.

The week passed with little of incidence occurring. They were caught by a late afternoon thunderstorm one afternoon, and stopped two hours earlier than planned because a shelter was available for them to spread out and get things dried before they moved on, but mostly the travel pattern remained the same.

That slight delay, though, had them riding into Markheshvan at dusk on Deethmarth evening. The tiny village didn't boast an inn, but the local trading post offered a bunkroom in addition to providing meals for the rare traveller to the town.

After a deeply satisfying bowl of mutton stew and mug of spiced wine, Yona and Faolan purchased the few supplies they would need for the trip up to the Hatseetz Pass. Of course, they couldn't admit that was the route they were taking. Instead, they professed to be taking the main road, which led westward over the mountains and down the other side, skirting the desert on its way to the capital of Tarshish, Tartessos, a more likely destination than Smuggler's Bay.

But the pathway over the mountains could only be traversed on foot, and Faolan, after speaking with the owner of the trading post, set out to see if he could find someone or some ones, for that matter, to purchase their horses. He returned to the bunkroom about nine o'clock and Yona handed him a mug of wine. They discussed a few last minute details before turning in for the night half an hour later. It was their plan to get up at daybreak and hit the trail.

16ᵀᴴ Teeneh

Abrilliant white light followed nearly simultaneously by a great peal of thunder jolted Eluned from a deep sleep. She jumped from her bed and slammed the shutters closed on the guestroom window just ahead of the torrential downpour that lashed the island.

Staring into darkness illuminated intermittently by the flashes of lightning that pulsed through the shutters, Eluned tried to guess the time. If it were closer to midnight, they might still be able to sail back to Seemu in the morning. Otherwise, it would mean another entire day spent on the island. Unless, she mused, she convinced them to set sail anyway with the promise of calling on Namaka. But why in Omni's name should they believe her? She wasn't completely sure she believed it herself. It was just a black pearl, after all. Maybe if they were already at sea and a storm struck—then she wouldn't have to convince anyone; she would only have to retrieve the pearl from its hiding place.

Pulling the sheet over her head in an effort to drown out the cacophonic thunder, the Princess attempted to keep her frustration at bay. The problem was that she couldn't let on just how desperate she was to begin the Quest again. Leleua and

Talei, the entire royal family, in fact, with maybe the exception of Irirangi, had gone out of their way as far as hospitality was concerned. And now the Paliainans had thrown in their lot, as well.

She owed them a great deal and, she admitted to herself reluctantly, one more day on the island would not destroy the Quest. It simply wouldn't. In fact, it would force her to be more gracious and to devote more time to getting to know the two young women who had willingly embraced helping her hide the treasures. And yet she still chafed at the thought of delaying the Quest any longer. Also, remaining on Paliaina would mean yet another day away from her friends and from Dyrnwyn, and she had just reacquainted herself with both.

The fury of the storm soon passed, and Eluned was lulled back to sleep as the rain slackened to a gentle murmur against the thatched roof of the hut. When she awoke a few hours later, it was to another sunny day. It was with a smile of gratitude that she flung open the shutters, silently thanking Omni for delivering them from the storm. Touching the suede pouch that lay against her chest, she smiled again. It looked like they would be sailing to Seemu, and she probably wouldn't have to call on Namaka, after all.

Yawning and stretching in the grey light of dawn, Eluned pulled up the cotton sheet, followed by the comforter, leaving her bed somewhat made. She took her sarong off the hook and picked up the cropped top constructed of a light fabric adorned with hundreds of bird feathers in varying shades of greens, pinks and yellows. It was exquisite and she hadn't minded wearing it on the brief trip to Paliaina aboard the Phaeton as the outfit was appropriate for the ceremony that followed their arrival. But, she worried that it would get ruined on the ocean voyage back to Seemu.

Yet, after the hike to and from the waterfall yesterday, the slacks and shirt she had worn were looking a little worse for the wear. Decisions, decisions. Compromise, she finally decided. She would wear the trousers and sleeveless blouse until they were in sight of Seemu, and then change into the more formal wear. They were returning home conquering heroes, so to speak. She needed to look the part.

She metaphorically patted herself on the back before turning to make sure the room looked neat enough to leave. Then she quickly dressed, packed her long-suffering tapestry bag (oh what it had been through in the past four months!) and headed for the kitchen and some much needed coffee.

When the princesses joined her there a few minutes later, they were dressed in their formal garb. They eyed Eluned askance until she offered that she intended to change once in sight of Seemu.

"I've never actually sailed on a ship," she admitted. "Zion is a land- and ice-locked kingdom. And until Neeon, I had never been outside the walls of my father's castle. "

Talei and Leleua shifted uncomfortably.

"Considering all that you've been through since you left Castle Mykerinos," Leleua said. "It's always difficult for me to remember just how sheltered you were while living there."

"I'm sure your parents had their reasons," Talei said, "but it just seems unusual for a princess, that's all."

"I may never understand although I imagine it probably had something to do with my mother's fears that I might end up like my great grandmother, Queen Fuchsia, who ran away from the castle shortly after giving birth to my grandfather. Anyway," she continued, "I honestly don't know what it will be like for me on the ship. I don't tend to motion sickness. That is, I've been fine on horses, in small boats and even on the Phaeton, but this is all new to me. I didn't know if I'd get wet or sick or what might happen once we set sail, so I opted to start out this way."

"I would guess," Talei ventured, "that you're probably going to be fine, but I do understand why you didn't want to take the risk. And there should be no problem with changing before we get there."

Leleua nodded her head in agreement, and patted Eluned's arm. "I'm sure you're worrying unnecessarily."

As it turned out the Favonian princesses were right. Eluned was exhilarated by sea travel. Slicing through the ocean, with the wind in her face, left her feeling energized. Her only regret was that she was forced to keep the sun at bay by clasping a hat to her head with one hand while the other gripped the railing of the ship to keep her steady on her feet.

Leleua and Talei lounged in deck chairs, and napped for most of the trip. Other than a quick lunch around a table near the galley—fresh fruit and crab salad—Eluned spent the remainder of her time on deck. It was a perfect day for sailing. The storm had washed the haze from the air and she could see for miles, and with the wind at their backs they were making good time as they skirted past the islands of Hakanaipo and Hemamoku.

As the shores of Favonia came into view, Eluned was thrilled to see dolphins frolicking alongside the ship and watched them for the next half hour until they turned away from the vessel and disappeared behind them.

When the dolphins were no longer in sight, Eluned borrowed the Captain's cabin to change into her formal clothes, and then she returned to the deck to watch their approach to Seemu.

They were coasting into the capitol's small harbor when she suddenly emitted a near shriek not dissimilar to the one that had erupted from Yona's throat nearly three months previously in Arberth. And for the same reason—it was Libni's sloop docked on the other side of the wharf.

"Queen of the May!" Eluned sang doing an impromptu jig. "Queen of the May!"

Leleua and Talei had rushed to her side when she'd squealed, and were now watching her with bemusement.

"I don't understand," Leleua said as Eluned threw her arms around the princess, tears of happiness welling in her eyes.

"The Queen of the May!" Eluned cried, pointing to the ship on the opposite side of the dock. "It's Libni's ship! Don't you understand? It means that Yona's here!"

"So by the time we got to Markheshvan," Yona explained, "it was a pretty easy trek up to the Hatseetz Pass and then down to Smuggler's Bay."

"If by easy, you mean uneventful," Faolan interjected.

The Questers were once again gathered in Eluned's room although this time Faolan and Gwrhyr flanked Chokhmah on the sofa, and Yona and Eluned were sitting together on her bed.

"True," Yona giggled. "Physically, that was a really tough ascent although I imagine it would have been easier on four legs rather than two."

Faolan's pale skin turned rosy, and Chokhmah turned to him with a knowing glint in her eye.

"I thought you felt a little warm." With two males sitting on the couch, she was snugly wedged between them. Eluned's small frame had left her a little more room. "What do you shift to?"

"Shift?" Eluned and Gwrhyr blurted simultaneously.

"Jinx!" Eluned called out, laughing. "No, seriously Gwrhyr, there's something you don't know? I'm used to not knowing things, but this may be a first," she teased him.

"Very funny, Princess," he scowled at her.

"Faolan's a Shapeshifter," Yona explained. "He can shift into a wolf."

"Really?" Eluned was intrigued. "I take it since Yona's still alive that you don't eat people?'

"Wolves don't attack humans unless threatened or starving," Faolan said.

"Of course, they do not," Chokhmah patted his thigh, smiling. Faolan thought he could drown in her thick-lashed amber eyes. He swallowed hard. It took an effort to pull his eyes away and when he did, he found Jabberwock watching him.

"Don't mind Jabb," Eluned said. "He may be telepathic, but he doesn't embarrass us by revealing what we're thinking."

"Unless you're alone with him," Gwrhyr groused.

"Anyway," Eluned turned back to Yona, "was Libni waiting in Smuggler's Bay when you got there?"

"No. We were there a couple of days before she showed up," Yona said. "But, she would have arrived a lot later if it hadn't been for Olcan and Faolan. Olcan was able to get to Seagirt to get a message to her."

"We were incredibly lucky," Faolan added. "Libni was already on her way into port when Olcan arrived. All she had to do was restock her ship and set sail again."

"I'm not sure that 'luck' is the word." Eluned interrupted, "This entire journey has been more than luck. For example, if I hadn't of been attacked by that barrow wight, we wouldn't have stopped early that day, which means that we wouldn't have met Bonpo. I could name more examples concerning myself, but what about Yona? If she hadn't decided to disguise herself as a Sister of Holy Supplication, she wouldn't have ended up with the Lady Naomi, which means she wouldn't have met Olcan and then Faolan. She might not even be here right now or ever. I say we've been guided the entire way whether consciously or not. I would even go so far as to say that there was probably a reason that I was nearly sacrificed, or at the very least, some good came out of that happening. I'm not saying any of us are death proof, but I imagine that if we do die while on this quest, it will be because it was necessary to the gathering of the treasures."

"Leened right," Bonpo added. "Dis quest vely impoltant."

"I concur," said Jabberwock, "but it's also very dangerous. Most of the remaining treasures are in Kingdoms that won't want us to take their treasures if they are aware of their existence. One treasure is in the Devastation of Pelf. Before we go any further, we each need to decide whether we want to continue. I imagine our retinue is growing for a reason, and at some point, we will probably be required to split up into smaller groups. I assume there are no objections to Faolan joining us if he so desires?"

Faolan was extremely aware that every pair of eyes in the room were watching him, and his heart beat in trepidation that someone, he worried most about Gwrhyr, would turn him down.

But Gwrhyr had already sensed Chokhmah's interest in the Shapeshifter, and actually felt a sense of relief. He'd been feeling a slight sense of guilt about his near lapse in the gypsy camp for months. Because of his jealousy and anger at the Princess, not to mention the fact he'd had a lot to drink, he had almost made love to the beautiful gypsy that night. Faolan's involvement would completely remove that temptation although he seriously doubted that it would arise again.

"So, no one seems to have any objections," Chokhmah patted his thigh again. "What about you, my dear? Do you want to continue with us?"

Faolan wondered if he'd regret not being able to say no to the intriguing woman at his side. Though it was difficult to guess her age, she was probably his senior by as much as ten years. Yet he felt drawn to her like a hummingbird to nectar. If for no other reason than wanting to get to know Chokhmah better, he couldn't say no. But being part of the Quest was what he wanted, no matter the dangers he might face. "I'm in," he responded simply.

"Great!" Yona said. She'd grown fond of him in the past

couple of weeks, and he definitely would be an asset to their entourage. "Obviously, I'm in too. And, it's not like I can go back to Adamah, right?"

"Me three," laughed Eluned, hugging Yona.

"Myself as well," Chokhmah agreed. Eluned noted that she was practically glowing. Everyone being together again had brought them a newfound energy.

"You can't get rid of me," Gwrhyr winked at Eluned.

"Me eidah," Bonpo seconded.

"Well then," the Bandersnatch said. "Then there's just one more question. Where do we go next?"

"Can I make a suggestion?" Faolan ventured.

"Absolutely," Eluned affirmed.

"We're pretty sure that the unicorn is in Dyfed now, and..."

"Nyx!" Eluned launched herself off the bed. "Yes, that's perfect! Besides, Dyfed is allied. It seems like the best place to start. Not to mention the fact that I'm still currently capable of drawing a unicorn to me. If Arawn had had his way that might not be true."

"Don't remind me," Gwrhyr scowled. "The bastard."

"I think he decided to sacrifice me just because I wouldn't willingly fall into his arms," Eluned explained to Faolan.

"That was no doubt one of his considerations," Chokhmah agreed.

"So, are we all agreed?" Eluned asked, and was treated to a round of 'here heres'. "Dyfed it is," she beamed at her compatriots.

Part IV

"When life itself seems lunatic, who knows where madness lies?
Perhaps to be too practical is madness. To surrender dreams —
this may be madness. Too much sanity may be madness — and
maddest of all: to see life as it is, and not as it should be!"
— Miguel de Cervantes Saavedra
Don Quixote

"Deep into that darkness peering,
long I stood there, wondering, fearing,
doubting, dreaming dreams no mortal
ever dared to dream before."
—Edgar Allan Poe
The Raven

2ND COLTH

The Queen of the May sailed into the harbor of Thírnagall in Dyfed just thirteen days after she left Seemu. It had been smooth sailing the entire trip as if the breath of Omni Itself had pushed them northwards toward the tip of Tarshish before driving them along it's southern coast to Dyfed. Eluned wasn't sure whether she should be chagrinned that she had once again not been able to test her pearl.

Because there were now seven confederates on the Quest, including the very large Bonpo, plus Olcan who needed to return to Dyfed, Libni had been required to leave a portion of her crew in Favonia. Not only would she have to return to Seemu to pick them up, but also she would lose more than a month's wages. To compensate her, Eluned wrote a letter of introduction to be taken to her father with a request that he remunerate Libni for having helped them out, an expense Jabberwock had not foreseen to budget.

The Princess also instructed two of Libni's crew members, Noahdiah and Mehetabel, on the story they would tell her father about the Quest. Needless to say, it was a much watered down version of what had actually happened. The plan was for

Noahdiah and Mehetabel to travel as a couple from Seemu to the port of Baharimto on the Sheban side of the River Mab. From there, they would make their way northeast to Mjijangwa and then take the trade road to Goshen and Castle Mykerinos. That way, they reasoned, they would only travel in allied kingdoms, and greatly reduce any risk of being associated with the Princess and her friends.

Should they be caught with the letter, they would not only risk their own lives but the lives of Libni and the remainder of her crew. Unfortunately, it would probably take Noahdiah and Mehetabel as long to get to Baharimto as it would take the Queen of the May to get to Thírnagall, and then they would have to make the two week or so trip to Castle Mykerinos. At least, Eluned consoled herself, they won't have to worry about the Snow of Misery when crossing the Mountains of Misericord as it would be midsummer when they arrived there.

The group had seriously considered sending a pigeon to King Seraphim as it would reach him much sooner, but that would require adding logistics to the note that were probably better left unwritten.

Instead, they opted for the plan of sending Noahdiah and Mehetabel. Once they had been in touch with King Seraphim, he, in turn, could acquire horses so that they might return to Baharimto sooner. From there, they could catch another ship back to Favonia. Libni would have plenty of time to return to Seemu and pick them up there.

The only problem was that they had no idea where they would be in two weeks and thus had no way of discovering whether everything had worked out. It was finally decided that word should be left with Queen Miryam, and at some point they could be in touch with her via pigeon or letter.

Now, as they approached the docks in the quaint harbor town of Thírnagall, Eluned was looking forward to getting her land legs back and going in search of Nyx.

The sun was setting in a brilliant display of oranges, pinks and yellows as they made their way to The Lion and the Unicorn to arrange lodging for the night. Yona was spending one last evening on board the Queen of the May with Libni so she'd be rooming with Chokhmah, alone, that evening. Although if Chokhmah had her way, Eluned found herself grinning, she'd be sharing a room with Faolan. The two of them had become very cozy on the two-week voyage when the Questers weren't busy helping out with crew responsibilities.

Bonpo had gladly taken over the galley so she'd seen little of him. And, she'd had to share Yona with Libni during that time, as well. But, it had allowed her to spend some quality time with Jabberwock, her size and skills allowing her to do little more than some basic cleaning. It was actually a pleasure being with him again. After having spent a lot of time together during the eleven years he was her mentor and tutor, she'd had little time with him once they reached Annewven, and later Favonia.

They had easily fallen back into the friendly bantering they had shared for more than eleven years, discussing everything from his history—from Vulpecula and the aftermath of crossing the Devastation of Pelf to her great grandmother Queen Fuchsia to the current quest. And, when Faolan and Chokhmah were off getting to know each other better, Gwrhyr and Olcan would join their conversations.

While walking down the cobbled street lined with homes and businesses on their way to the inn, Eluned reflected that perhaps the reason they had experienced such a halcyon voyage was so they would have time to bond with each other again. Things had moved so quickly once the Princess had returned to the fold, so to speak, that they hadn't spent much time together.

Eluned was actually a little disappointed that Olcan wouldn't be joining them until he confessed that he was married and hadn't been home to his wife and children in nearly six months.

"While I feel called to give of my time to help with this quest," he explained, "neither do I want to miss my children growing up. And, of course, I really miss my wife, Beibhinn."

"Basically," Faolan added, "we take on six-month assignments and then return to normal life for six months."

"And what is your normal life?" Eluned wanted to know.

"We have a horse farm in Bogaine," Olcan said.

"Interesting," Eluned said. "Will we get to go there?" As it turned out, they would. The plan was to secure mounts for everyone but Chokhmah, who had Halelu, and Bonpo and Jabberwock, before travelling around Dyfed's numerous forests to see if there had been any Nyx sightings or see if they could find her themselves.

"Yes," Faolan answered her. "It's only a day's walk from here, and I would prefer to use our horses for this."

Eluned chuckled at the thought of a wolf riding a horse although she knew that wasn't what would actually happen. "So we'll get to meet your wife and children, Olcan. I look forward to that. How old are they?"

"Fianna, my daughter, is twelve, and Conall, my son, is ten." Olcan told her.

"Are they also Shapeshifters?" Eluned asked before realizing it might be a sensitive subject. "Or is that rude to ask?"

"They know," Faolan told his brother.

"Well, the curse is patrilineal," Olcan continued, "although both parents can have it. Both our mother and father are Shapeshifters, but Beibhinn isn't," he started to explain.

"It seems a shame to call it a curse," Eluned interjected.

"Thank you," Olcan replied. "I agree, but as the curse is patrilineal both my children are shifters. It was a bargain Beibhinn was willing to make."

"Is that why you're not married?" Eluned asked Faolan.

"One of the reasons," he agreed. "That, and I have never found a woman that I loved enough to not only tell her what I am, but also explain that our children would be as well. I'm still in shock that you guys have taken it all in stride."

Chokhmah took his hand and squeezed it. "This little coterie is already such a mélange that you fit right in."

Faolan squeezed her hand back and thanked her. They were about the same height so it was impossible for him not to gaze into those dark lashed eyes and see the affection there. And he shared that affection, and he was beginning to hope that he would continue to do so for a long time. He had never met anyone like Chokhmah.

CHOKHMAH AND FAOLAN HAD WALKED to the inn holding hands, and Eluned felt a twinge of jealousy as they reluctantly let go to head to their separate rooms. She wanted to feel that way too, and Chokhmah was getting to enjoy romance for the second time when the Princess hadn't even truly experienced it once. Irirangi didn't count—she'd just been in love with the idea of being in love. She'd never actually felt anything for him, after the first physical attraction, other than annoyance.

Of course, Chokhmah deserved to find someone new having lost her husband while still young. The Princess was just ready for her time in love's embrace. She pouted silently as she climbed the stairs.

"You really like him, don't you?" Eluned asked once they were safely in their room.

"Yes, my dear. I really do. Not only do I find him attractive, but he is also kind and strong. He can speak seriously, or have fun like a little boy. I have yet to find anything I do not like."

"And the shape shifting doesn't bother you?" Eluned prodded.

"Does it you?"

"Of course not!" Eluned walked over to the window, and turned away, disappointed. She could only see the wall of the building on the other side of the back alley.

"Exactly," Chokhmah smiled. "And why should it?"

"Have you seen him shift yet?" Eluned asked sitting down in the room's only chair.

"Yes, I have. He thought it important that I see that side of him as soon as possible."

"Was it scary?"

"Honestly, it was rather exciting," Chokhmah uncharacteristically giggled. "He is a beautiful wolf, and I know that he would protect us, his pack, with his very life."

"That's good to know," Eluned reflected. "I imagine most of us feel that way about this, what did you call it, coterie? And it is true that in all likelihood we'll face dangers again. Particularly when we have to find treasures in the non-allied kingdoms." She stood up. "I'm not sure I want to unpack until I know how long we'll be staying here. I'm ready for some wine and dinner."

"As am I," Chokhmah agreed. "We must also figure out what supplies we need to gather tomorrow. I am very low on some of the herbs I use for my teas, for example."

"And I'm sure Yona would like to find some more clothing. At this point she has only that tweed riding skirt and blouse." The sarong and cotton pants she'd acquired on the island weren't warm enough for Dyfed's climate.

"I have to admit," Chokhmah said, indicating the purple skirt she was wearing, "that I am inclined to find myself some leather trousers, as well. They make much more sense if one is going to be riding a lot, and as I no longer have to pretend that I am your lady-in waiting . . ."

"Yes!" Eluned exclaimed. "That's true. You'll love them. I promise. Besides," she said, playfully punching her companion lightly on her arm, "I imagine Faolan will like them as well."

The gypsy threw back her head and laughed. "If that is true then I must get two pairs!"

They were still giggling when they walked into the dining room.

"WHAT ARE YOU LAUGHING ABOUT?" Gwrhyr asked as they sat down at the long trestle table nestled in a corner of the dining room.

"Not you, if that's what you're thinking." Eluned kicked his foot. He was sitting across the table from her.

Gwrhyr's cheeks flamed briefly. That was exactly what he'd been thinking. He was still having trouble coming to terms with the new and improved Princess Eluned. The antagonism of the early days had been replaced with acceptance and affection. It wasn't love, but it was an improvement.

Chokhmah, who was sitting between Eluned and Faolan clarified. "We were discussing only that we needed some appropriate travelling clothes."

Faolan looked confused. "And why is that humorous?"

"We were just wondering what you'd think of seeing Chokhmah in trousers," Eluned interjected. "She's never worn them and we thought it would be amusing for her to try out, that's all."

"I have to admit I'd enjoy that." Faolan nudged the gypsy's shoulder with his.

"That's exactly what I said," Eluned laughed.

"And why I said that I must find two pairs," Chokhmah said, taking his left hand in hers.

"Ah," Gwrhyr said, understanding. "It all makes sense. I remember the first time I saw Eluned in pants. It was quite a treat."

Eluned remembered, as well, and her cheeks colored. Somehow it was different. Chokhmah liked Faolan, but that morning in Mjijangwa she had definitely been distrustful of Gwrhyr. How things changed! She now valued his friendship, even liked him as a person, but she still didn't want him to feel that way about her.

Fortunately, before she could say something she might later regret, Bonpo entered the room carrying a cauldron of coddle, which he placed on the table. As they began serving themselves, he disappeared into the kitchen again and soon returned with soda bread, butter and a large pitcher of stout beer.

"Delicious!" Eluned told Bonpo when he joined them at the table. "Did you get the recipe?"

"O'course, Plincess," the giant smiled. "It made from reftovers so good traver food."

"Excellent!" she said, passing him the pitcher of stout.

AFTER THE DISHES WERE CLEARED AWAY, planning began— most specifically, what they would need to purchase before they left for Bogaine. It was a day's walk from Thírnagall and if they didn't get what they needed before noon, they would have to leave the following day.

Jabberwock delegated tasks for the morning urging everyone to be up early and out as soon as the shops opened. Sunset was later this time of year so if they could leave by ten o'clock, they might make it to Bogaine before dark. But, Olcan couldn't send a pigeon to warn Beibhinn of their arrival until they were actually on the road.

Once that was settled, talk turned to where they might first begin their quest for the unicorn.

"My gut feeling," Faolan said, "is that Nyx might be in Hardaigh Forest."

"Why is that?" Chokhmah asked, as she believed gut feelings should not be ignored.

"It is the most isolated forest in the country," Olcan said.

"It's not easy to get to, for one," Faolan explained. "You have to cross the Seven Sisters to reach it."

"Seven Sisters?" Gwrhyr asked.

"It's a mountain chain," Olcan said.

"The mountains aren't that high, but the terrain is really rugged and exposed. They're known for their bad weather,"

Faolan continued. "Strong winds, often foggy and rainy and occasionally there's even unexpected snow."

"And the forest, itself?" Eluned queried.

"It's supposed to be very wild," Faolan said.

Olcan chuckled, "All manner of creatures are reputed to live there—faeries, elves, imps . . ."

"Shapeshifters," Eluned interjected with a giggle. It was Gwrhyr's turn to kick her. "Ow! I didn't kick you that hard!"

"All I meant to say is if magical creatures exist there then why not a unicorn?" Olcan finished.

Eluned sobered. "Having already been in contact with faeries, an ancient goddess, and a pwca, not to mention the Janawar, Jabberwock the Bandersnatch, Bonpo and you and Faolan, I wouldn't be surprised to find more interesting and fantastical creatures in Hardaigh Forest or elsewhere on this journey, for that matter."

"I agree," said Jabberwock, "Hardaigh seems a very likely place to start, and as we must begin somewhere, why not with the most likely place?"

A shadow passed over Eluned's face and she suddenly shivered.

"What is it, my dear?" Chokhmah asked.

"A ghul breathed on my neck," Eluned said, remembering King Hamartia's saying for an unexpected chill.

"What?" Gwrhyr asked.

Eluned shook her head as if trying to clear her thoughts. "It's just that we are all talking so blithely about trekking over the Seven Sisters and exploring Hardaigh Forest, but the truth is that the unicorn won't come to anyone but me. Right?"

Everyone stared at her guiltily. The men were ruled out because they were male. Chokhmah had been married and was clearly no longer a virgin. There was Yona, but Eluned somehow suspected that her longtime affair with Libni, even though Libni was female, would discount her as well.

Other than a couple of kisses from Gwrhyr, both totally unexpected and unasked for, she was as chaste as the driven snow. She was also the most innocent, perhaps even naïve, of the troop. Yes, she had learned a lot in the past five months, but she suspected there was so much more she had yet to comprehend.

"And because of that," she continued, "doesn't that mean that I will have to be alone in the forest?"

Gwrhyr was shaking his head. "No, not at first. We can check the forest's relative safety first, right Faolan? Surely you can shift and explore it that way. Would a unicorn be aware that you are more than a wolf?"

"That's an excellent idea," Faolan admitted. "I am as clueless as you about how Nyx might react, but it's certainly worth trying. If nothing else, I can see if there are any dangerous creatures abroad, particularly if I explore at night when most wild things are out."

Eluned leaned forward to look at Jabberwock at the other end of the table. "Nocturnal," they said, simultaneously, and laughed. It had been Eluned's favorite word when she met the Bandersnatch at the age of seven. She shivered again.

"It's funny," she told Jabberwock. "I had no idea eleven years ago when we were discussing whether or not faeries are nocturnal that one day I would spend a week dancing with them."

"Omni clearly has a sense of humor," Jabberwock agreed.

"And I can now say with confidence that faeries are indeed nocturnal," she grinned.

"So," the Bandersnatch said. "Are we all clear? Up and out early so that we can leave for Bogaine tomorrow?"

"Does Yona know?" Eluned asked.

"I'm about to send a messenger to the Queen of the May," Gwrhyr said.

"I'm sure she'll be the first to arrive here in the morning,"

Olcan stood up. "She put a lot on the line to be a part of this quest."

"True," Faolan agreed. "Not only figuring out how to steal the Hamper, but doing it entirely on her own. And, I never heard a single word of complaint from her once we left Hagafen."

"She truly deserves a final night with Libni," Eluned said, sliding off the bench she shared with Chokhmah, Faolan and Jabberwock. "They've been close for a long time, and Libni has also sacrificed a lot for this mission."

Jabberwock jumped down from the bench as Gwrhyr and Bonpo stood.

"I go terr cook to have someting we can carry for runch ready by ten o'crock, jus' in case," Bonpo said, heading for the kitchen. "Bleakfast at seven, ev'rybody."

"Goodnight, Bonpo!" Eluned called after him.

"Goodnight Plincess!" he turned, and blew her a kiss, which she caught and planted against her cheek.

Gwrhyr looked at her awkwardly. Clearly he wanted to give her an actual good night's kiss. Instead, he hugged her, wished her sweet dreams and turned to go in search of a messenger.

Eluned glanced at Chokhmah who was still sitting on the bench with Faolan.

"We still need to say our goodnights," Chokhmah explained.

Eluned arched an eyebrow, "Oh, is that what we're calling it now?"

Chokhmah and Faolan had the grace to blush.

"I'll see you upstairs in a little while," Eluned said, chuckling as she departed the room.

"I'll leave you two alone," Olcan said. "See you upstairs, Faolan. You going up?" he asked Jabberwock.

"Yes," the Bandersnatch affirmed. "Hopefully sleep will

keep the floor from rolling when I walk. I still feel like I'm on the Queen of the May."

"Well," Olcan said as they left the room, "if sleep doesn't cure it, the walk to Bogaine will."

Chokhmah and Faolan watched them depart.

"I thought they'd never leave," Faolan sighed once they were alone, and pulled Chokhmah into his arms.

She caressed his face, traced his lips with a slender finger. "Omni willing, we will be at Bogaine tomorrow night."

"And then we can truly be alone," he promised before kissing her. He had his own cottage there.

The sound of the kitchen door opening made them jump apart.

"Don't mind me," Bonpo said as he passed through the room on the way to the staircase. The couple wished him a good night, waiting as the giant thudded up the stairs. It was nearly impossible for Bonpo to move quietly.

As he leaned in for another kiss, the front door to the inn opened, and Gwrhyr entered. He waved to the couple as he headed for the stairs, which unlike Bonpo he ascended quietly and rapidly.

"Is that everybody?" Faolan asked. He was beginning to feel frustrated by the fact that there was consistently someone in their vicinity since the day they'd first met.

"Be patient, my love," Chokhmah soothed, leaning her head against his shoulder. "We have plenty of time."

"I hope so," he said, tilting her head toward his with his hand so he might kiss her again. "I really hope so."

She pulled away after a moment and gazed into his eyes. When Yitzak died, she had mourned for the required year coming to terms with the fact that she would probably never love again. He had been a good man and a good husband.

She had nearly made the mistake of following through with the seduction of Gwrhyr on the night of her Pomona, the celebration freeing her from a year of grieving. It truly would have been only a passing fling—she was lonely, but she was also a passionate woman and it had been a very long time since she'd been with a man. Years, in fact, as Yitzak had been sick for so very long before he died.

Fortunately, Jabberwock and Omni, no doubt, had managed to prevent that for now she saw very clearly that it was Gwrhyr and Eluned who were meant to bond for life. Not that she would tell the Princess that. That was something Eluned would have to discover on her own.

And then Faolan entered her life. She had known the moment she met him. He filled her with a passion that not even Yitzak could compare with. And now she had another chance, and he also had the chance for a love that he thought was denied to him.

"What are you thinking?" he whispered.

"I am thinking that I am so thankful that Omni found a way to place you in my life." She felt tears of happiness rise in her eyes, and one escaped and slid down her cheek.

Faolan brushed it away. "I feel the same way," he agreed, kissing her again.

3ʳᵈ Colth

Everyone was fully outfitted by ten o'clock, and Olcan was able to send a pigeon to his wife to warn her of their impending arrival before they hit the road for the brothers' horse farm. A hired donkey and Halelu carried the bulk of their gear. And Eluned, feeling nostalgic for her mule, Hayduke, was happy to take the donkey's lead and guide it during the hike to Bogaine.

Naturally, the first thing she wanted to know was whether or not the donkey had a name, and she was pleased to discover that Olcan had asked.

"Derry," he told her. "It means 'like an oak', which is what you want your pack animals to be like, right?"

Eluned nodded. She supposed that was true, but she still didn't like to see her beasts of burden overburdened. She ruffled Derry's forelock and promised him that she'd take care of him. *I surely won't consign you to Hayduke's likely fate,* she thought.

The path to Bogaine was a pleasant trek through rolling, rock-studded hills carpeted in emerald green grass interrupted by the occasional brook. They walked in companionable silence most of the morning, each consumed by their own thoughts.

Olcan led the way, anticipating seeing his family again. He also wondered what repair work he'd need to catch up on once home. There was always something major to do whenever he was gone this long.

Jabberwock, as per usual, was fretting over how to go about seeking the remainder of the treasures. Should he split this company of Questers up? And if so, how? And who would go where? The possibilities were endless.

Eluned was consumed, though she hated to admit it, by jealousy. In order to not think about the fact that Chokhmah was apparently head-over-heels in love with Faolan and she had no one, she tried to imagine what she would do once she found Nyx because she was confident the unicorn would come to her.

Bonpo, naturally, was running over menus and the like in his head. He needed to keep food supplies as simple as possible, but make sure he had enough to keep the seven of them relatively well fed.

Gwrhyr, keeping his pace slow by treading behind Yona and Eluned, pondered ways to keep the Princess safe in Hardaigh Forest without risking scaring away the unicorn. He, too, was trying not to think about the lovebirds behind him, and how desperate he was to gain Eluned's affection. No, he had her affection. He wanted her love. That's what he really wanted.

Yona reflected on the time she had just spent with Libni because while it had been enjoyable, she wasn't sure it was a future she wanted to seek. Yona the Pirate? No, it just wasn't her. She'd found it exciting at sixteen, but five years later, she wasn't so sure. And would this quest change what she wanted from life? She had no way of knowing, but considering how much had transpired already, she felt more transitions in her thinking were sure to come.

Faolan and Chokhmah held hands, trailing behind the others and speaking quietly so as not to disturb the group. Halelu trailed behind them from a lead that Faolan had secured to his belt. They, too, were wondering about the future, and if being a couple might affect the group's dynamics.

Shortly before noon, they arrived at a small farm populated with numerous goats that surveyed the small party with interest behind the stone fences that contained them.

"I know Jarlath," Olcan told them. "I'm sure he won't mind, but I'll ask if we might stop here to eat our lunch."

The group settled themselves down in a small grove of birch trees, and waited for Olcan. The leaves on the trees whispered in the soft breeze, and protected the group from the worst of the noonday sun. Fortunately, it wasn't long before Olcan returned, a pitcher of fresh goat's milk in his hand.

"Compliments of Jarlath's wife, Roisin," Olcan said. So, instead of the water they carried, they washed down their smoked salmon and barley bread with creamy goat's milk.

"Much more satisfying," Yona noted. "Please give her our thanks," she told Olcan when he left to return the pitcher.

They retraced their steps to the track with renewed energy, and reached the rock walls that enclosed Bogaine about half an hour before sunset. Before Olcan had a chance to unlatch the gate, several dogs came bounding up, barking excitedly. As he closed the gate behind the travellers, the dogs launched themselves at Olcan and Faolan as they vied for attention.

"Have you kept my family safe?" Olcan asked as he patted their heads.

The farm was picturesque to say the least. The rolling grass-covered hills were dotted with grazing horses. Situated at the end of a short carriageway were numerous white washed stone buildings—a two-story home with smoke wafting from the chimneys at either end, a large stable, a quaint cottage with a thatched roof and a profusion of roses lining the path that led to its cheery red door. There were also several out buildings being used for the storage of everything from grain to garden implements and tack for the horses.

"This is quite a spread." Gwrhyr's voice was fraught with admiration.

The shamrock green door of the farmhouse opened, and Olcan's children came bounding out followed by Beibhinn. Unlike their swarthy father, the children, Fianna and Conall, favored their mother with fair skin, wheat blonde hair and eyes of cornflower blue.

"Daddy!" they called as they ran the few yards that separated them. "Daddy's home!" They hugged him, and then their uncle, before finally studying the crew that had arrived with him, mouths dropping at the sight of Bonpo who stood at the back of the group.

Beibhinn had arrived and was receiving a hearty kiss and embrace from her husband.

"Let me introduce everyone," Olcan said. "I'm sure Faolan is anxious to show Chokhmah his cottage."

This last remark elicited a titter from Eluned, who apologized before collapsing in laughter, which forced her to apologize again. "I'm so sorry. I can be such a twelve-year-old sometimes." She immediately realized what she'd said, and continued. "Not that all twelve-year-olds are immature, Fianna. I just happened to be when I was twelve."

"Nice save," Gwrhyr whispered in her ear.

"The Princess Eluned of Zion," Olcan chuckled. "Never a dull moment in her presence."

"You're a real princess?" Fianna's eyes were filled with awe.

"Absolutely," Eluned extended her hand. Fianna took it, eyes shining, a broad smile on her face. "I'm pleased to make your acquaintance."

"This is Chokhmah," Faolan introduced the woman whose hand he was holding. "And, Olcan is correct about my house."

"Yes, he is," Chokhmah agreed. "Faolan has been telling

me all about his little rose cottage, and I am looking forward to seeing it."

"Will you be joining us for dinner?" Beibhinn asked.

"Of course," Faolan said. "How much, I mean, when should we be there?"

"The meal should be ready in about an hour," she replied. She watched with amusement as Faolan led Chokhmah away, and turned to Olcan with arched eyebrow. "Will wonders never cease?"

"I believe it was love at first sight," Yona laughed. "Right, Eluned?"

Nodding her agreement, Eluned replied, "This is Yona, the former fiancée of King Hevel of Adamah."

"Former?" Beibhinn asked.

"I'll explain later," said Olcan. "Meanwhile, this is Gwrhyr, King Uriel of Aden's man."

"That's one way of putting it," Eluned said under her breath to Yona, who snickered.

"The giant is Bonpo although I think officially he is one of the dzu-tch of Dziron," Olcan continued his introductions.

"Yeah, dat collect," he extended a hand that dwarfed Beibhinn's.

She took it tentatively, but Bonpo's shake was very gentle. The children still eyed him warily, stepping behind their father when the giant stepped forward to shake their mother's hand.

"And finally, Jabberwock," Olcan introduced what Beibhinn had thought was a little dog or grey fox at his feet. "Jabb is one of, or maybe the only, Janawar remaining."

"Pleased to make your acquaintance," Jabberwock said, and the children gasped. He turned to them, crooked teeth bared in a smile. "I've known the Princess since she was seven years old," he told them.

"I met him in the forest when I was attempting to be a naughty little girl," Eluned explained, "and we've been best friends ever since."

"Why were you naughty?" Conall asked.

"I thought I was escaping from my ladies-in-waiting," Eluned confessed.

"What's that?" the young boy queried.

"Silly," Fianna said. "That's something princesses have. They are women who make sure she has what she needs, and that she's never alone."

"Exactly, Fianna." Eluned said. "And I hated never being alone."

"Oh," Conall replied in a tone that said that they were now just talking boring girl stuff. "What's a Janawar?"

"Jabberwock's real name is Hiurau," Eluned explained, "and he lived with the other Janawar in the Vale Vixen, which is a valley in the Peaks of Vulpecula in Dziron. The Janawar can talk, and they also live forever, and they are telepathic, too. But, it was thought that they were witches, and they were hunted down and killed off. Jabb escaped. We just don't know if anyone else did."

"Wow." Conall's eyes were round with wonder. "What am I thinking now?"

"That you don't believe I can read your thoughts," the Bandersnatch replied.

Conall blushed.

"Don't worry, I don't make a habit of listening in," the Bandersnatch assured him. "It can get quite chaotic if I do. I've learned to tune out the thoughts of others unless I need to listen."

Conall seemed greatly relieved.

"Shall we go inside?" Olcan offered. "I'm sure we could all use some wine."

"Definitely," Gwrhyr agreed. "It has been a long day."

FAOLAN AND CHOKHMAH JOINED THEM about ten minutes later, Faolan doing his best not to look put out. Clearly

Chokhmah had advised him to rein in his desires for a while longer, Gwrhyr judged.

"Wise woman," Jabberwock agreed quietly. "They need a night not an hour."

Gwrhyr nodded. The sexual tension between the couple was leaning towards being extremely uncomfortable for the others. It would actually be nice to have some relief from that.

In order to give Bonpo a break before the next segment of the journey had him preparing all the meals, the women joined Beibhinn in the kitchen. While Yona peeled and sliced potatoes before putting them on the stove to boil, Chokhmah sliced and then boiled the cabbage that would complete the dish that combined mashed potatoes and shredded cabbage. Eluned set out plates and silverware for eleven. Because of the size of their group, not all of them could fit at the dining room table, she realized. Some of them would have to seat themselves in the living room or kitchen.

With the extra hands in the kitchen, the meal was ready to be served in no time, and soon everyone was piling their plates with corned beef and the mashed potato concoction. Gwrhyr, Yona and Eluned returned to the living room with their plates while Faolan and Chokhmah found a quiet corner in which to dine alone, which left plenty of room in the dining room for the others.

It was when they were cleaning up afterwards that it was noticed that Chokhmah and Faolan had managed to sneak away unobserved.

"They must have worked out a plan," Eluned smirked.

"It might have been better to be obvious about it," Yona noted.

"It's going to make it very difficult not to tease them in the morning," Gwrhyr added, although he might have found himself doing the same thing if Eluned felt that way about him.

CHOKHMAH AND FAOLAN ACCEPTED Eluned's gentle ribbing the following day with good nature. The gypsy had already explained to him that the Princess was desperate to fall in love within the next two-and-a-half years because otherwise she would have to marry King Uriel.

"And it aggrieves her to no end that she has no choice, has never had any choice in the matter," she told him.

"So there's a wee bit of jealousy behind the badgering?"

Chokhmah nodded. "And Omni have mercy, I am just too happy for it not to show."

Faolan grinned and hugged her. "I wouldn't have it any other way."

THE BLESSING WAS THAT WITH THE TENSION RELIEVED, the couple was able to once again fully participate in the preparations for the next step of the Quest.

After breakfast, Faolan and Olcan headed out with Gwrhyr to choose horses for the travellers, stopping near the stable to discuss options. Once again, Bonpo would walk and Jabberwock would sit in a basket secured to the donkey.

"We could reduce the number of mounts we need to care for by sharing," Faolan offered. "Obviously, I don't mind riding with Chokhmah, but do you think Eluned would share with either you or Yona?" he asked Gwrhyr.

"I'm pretty sure that she'd balk at sharing a horse with me," he replied, "but honestly I think we'd do better to each ride separately. We've got a lot of gear and we have to carry Bonpo's as well. On the other hand, I have no problem with some tent sharing."

Faolan brightened at that, and Gwrhyr was forced to add, "I have no problem with your sharing a tent with Chokhmah, but I would advise you not to do anything that would make the rest of us uncomfortable. You know what I mean." He gave Faolan a stern look.

Faolan blushed, but nodded.

"I'm serious," Gwrhyr continued. "This quest is all important, and if you and Chokhmah aren't fully invested; that is, if you and Chokhmah feel the need to spend all of your time together, and can't give your fair share and undivided attention to what might happen (and you are aware of what might happen) then my advice would be to remain here."

Faolan swallowed hard. All he had wanted for the past month or so was to be a part of this quest. He hadn't reckoned on meeting Chokhmah and falling in love with her. But, neither did he want to give up this mission. He was pretty sure Chokhmah wouldn't want to do so either. She'd been a part of the search for the treasures almost as long as Gwrhyr.

As long as they were together, he was more than happy to put that aspect of their relationship on hold. At least they'd have another night in his cottage. That said, the sooner they collected the rest of the treasures, the better, he thought. Then maybe he could bring Chokhmah back to Rose Cottage for good. Besides, while at Whanga Palace, Jabberwock had indicated that they might have to split up into smaller groups to search for the treasures that remained in non-allied countries. Perhaps he and Chokhmah could partner for one of those assignments.

"Faolan," Olcan was saying, repeatedly. "Faolan."

"Oh, sorry," he said, lightly slapping his face.

"You were playing with the pixies, brother." Olcan said. "We need to focus."

"Sorry, yes. Yes, we do," he responded.

"I was asking if Chokhmah would be riding Halelu?" Olcan continued.

"Yes, she definitely would prefer that," Faolan said. "And I'll ride Fiachdubh, of course."

"Fiachdubh?" Gwrhyr wondered aloud.

"My black stallion." Faolan said, pointing to the raven

black horse that grazed nearby. "He's comfortable around me if I should need to shift."

"That means we need mounts for Gwrhyr, Yona and Eluned. I was going to suggest Ruari for Gwrhyr," Olcan said.

"That sounds reasonable," Faolan agreed. "Ruari is a chestnut stallion—strong, dependable and most importantly, sure-footed," he informed Gwrhyr.

"Sounds fine by me," Gwrhyr said. "I rode a chestnut stallion to Prythew."

"What about the Princess?" Faolan wanted to know. "What kind of rider is she? I know that Yona is accomplished."

"The Princess as well," he answered. "She rode a gentle mare when we were travelling to Annewven, but had no problem riding the pwca bareback. Whichever horse can handle crossing the Seven Sisters will do."

"What about Ronan?" Olcan suggested.

Faolan nodded. Ronan was a seal brown gelding, thus its name. "How about Aine for Yona?"

It was Olcan's turn to nod. He pointed to a dappled grey mare a few feet away from Ronan.

"I trust your judgment," Gwrhyr said.

"We can get their tack ready now so that we'll be ready to saddle them up first thing in the morning." Faolan turned, and walked into the stable followed by Gwrhyr and Olcan.

5ᵗʰ Colth

Hardaigh Forest was located on the western coast of Dyfed bounded by the Anoon Ocean on one side and The Seven Sisters on the other. Faolan estimated it would take them four to five days of riding almost nonstop from dawn until dusk to get there.

The Questers were chatting animatedly as they departed Bogaine that morning. Everyone except the Princess, that is. The truth was she was feeling a little more than a "wee" bit jealous. There was nothing like having two people giddily in love by your side to dampen your spirits. Particularly when love had been your main objective when setting out on a great journey beyond the walls of a castle you'd been trapped inside of for eighteen years.

And the more Eluned thought about the unfairness of it all, the gloomier she got. Responses to questions posed to her during that first day's ride spiraled downward from full sentences to one word to mere grunts. It wasn't long before the group wisely decided to leave her alone, and their excited chatter was muted by her glowering presence.

Chokhmah's emotions ran the gamut from feeling guilty at her happiness to being angry with the Princess for acting like a child, though child she still was in some aspects. Only Chokhmah and Jabberwock understood the source of Eluned's depression—Eluned had more than once confided to the gypsy that she longed to experience love, and of course, Eluned had asked Chokhmah whether she would meet the 'love of her life' while on this journey when she had given her a Tarot card reading not long after they met.

The Bandersnatch, too, having known Eluned since she was a child, also knew how much she longed for 'true love.' But how do you explain to an eighteen-year-old that love arrives in many forms and not always how one expects, or even wants, it to arrive.

And while he called Kamali his wife, in truth the Janawar didn't marry. They were actually arranged partnerships, but the alliances weren't political and didn't involve money or power. They were carefully orchestrated couplings that united a pair of Janawar to the one best suited to the other. So, had there been love between Hiurau and Kamali? Yes, their love had been extraordinary. Had they fallen in love before they were matched? Honestly, he hadn't even noticed her prior to that.

The royalty often found themselves betrothed to one another for political reasons. Sometimes it ended well as it had for both Eluned's and Uriel's parents, which is why it had been easy for them to make a similar alliance for their children. But Jabberwock also knew it could end badly, as it had for Eluned's great grandmother, Queen Fuchsia. Unfortunately, being royal came with certain responsibilities. And while he felt sure that the Princess would grow into that, it didn't help her at the moment. Today, she was eighteen and lovelorn.

Tomorrow, he knew, would be better if she could just make it through the day. The next time Chokhmah glanced back to see how Eluned was doing, Jabberwock shook his head, and telepathized to the gypsy: Give her time. Chokhmah sighed deeply, but she rode face forwards for the remainder of the day.

Eluned, on the other hand trailed behind everyone except Gwrhyr. He didn't know what was wrong with her, but he'd be damned if he let her fall behind. He would try to talk to her that evening, but meanwhile Ronan attempted to keep pace with the rest of the horses with Ruari right on his tail.

THEY STOPPED FOR THE NIGHT IN AN OAK GROVE that was just off the road and atop the summit of a hill. Gwrhyr thought it would be a good spot from which to watch the road, and the trees offered them some protection from the elements. The plan was to make a circle of the tents and tether the horses within. Although, Gwrhyr smiled to himself, they had both a wolf and a giant to battle any predators they might face. Even humans, for that matter. Eluned made a powerful adversary with Dyrnwyn. The way the blue light raced along her arm when she held it in her hand was enough to scare off most people.

Chokhmah and Yona were the wild cards when it came to fighting skills. He might have to teach them some basic techniques. Chokhmah was still valuable for her proficiency with healing, but now that Yona had secured the Hamper he needed to find out what else she could offer.

Looking around at the settled camp, Gwrhyr noticed that the Princess was missing. Rather than risk stumbling upon her in a possibly embarrassing position, he opted to seek out Jabberwock for a little telepathic guidance.

"Try the boulders on the far side of the grove," the Bandersnatch directed him.

She sat alone on top of a large flat boulder staring moodily out over the valley on the north side of the hill. To the west, the orange and pink sky was rapidly darkening, but you could still make out that the lumpy shapes scattered here and there were sheep. Well, so much for predators, Gwrhyr couldn't help but think. They'd go for the sheep before they went after horses or humans.

He sat down next to her, and when she didn't say anything or jump up and stomp off to be alone again, he said, "Can I ask what's wrong?"

She looked up at him mournfully. Even sitting, the top of her head reached only to his shoulder. "I hate myself."

He shook his head. "Why? I don't understand."

"I'm so jealous of Chokhmah, and I hate myself for feeling that way."

Honestly, he was a bit jealous too, but he didn't want to make this about him. He knew the Princess well enough to know what this was about. "And you're afraid that you won't get to experience the same love before you have to go back to Zion and marry King Uriel."

"That," she said, "and it just occurred to me today. What if I do fall in love with someone? I still have to go back to Zion and marry Uriel. We've been betrothed since we were children."

"I wouldn't worry about that," Gwrhyr drew her closer to him, it was getting chilly as the sun set, and she was starting to shiver. "If he's like most men, he will not want to be wed to a woman whose heart belongs to another man."

"Do you really think so?" She tried to take in this new development. Was it possible she could break the betrothal if she admitted to Uriel she was in love with someone else? The day's pent up tears began to well up in her eyes as a whole new world suddenly opened up before her. Perhaps circumstances were not as dire as she thought. Once again she found herself releasing her sorrows in Gwrhyr's arms.

He just hugged her closer and waited for the flood to cease.

"Why is it that I always end up crying against your chest?" she sniffled once the tears had abated.

He handed her a handkerchief. "I don't know, but I'm honored that you feel comfortable enough to do so."

"Yeah?" she said.

"Yeah." He stood, pulling her to her feet. "Now, let's get you a sweater and a glass of wine."

Eluned didn't let go of his hand once they were standing. "If by glass you mean a tankard," she smiled up at him. "Thank you for being so understanding, Gwrhyr. We've come a long way since the Trade Route Inn, haven't we?"

"Yes," he chuckled. "I guess we have."

Twining her fingers in his, they started to make their way back to the camp, and only Jabberwock noticed that they were still holding hands when they arrived. Gwrhyr allowed himself a glimmer of hope as she disappeared into the tent she was sharing with Yona. Maybe, just maybe, he could eventually win her love.

Eluned reappeared with her grey cotton sweater pulled on over the rough-spun blouse she'd been wearing with her new leather pants. She'd invested in another pair while both Yona and Chokhmah had been purchasing trousers for themselves. She didn't have a coat, but the chill worried her. She had hoped she wouldn't have to buy something heavier until late Meen or early Gort, but here it was getting cool at night, still early in the month of Colth. She'd become so accustomed to the heat of Favonia that she'd forgotten many countries became cooler earlier in the year. She would, she realized, be wearing a coat by now if she were still in Zion.

She and Gwrhyr joined the others around the campfire, and she was glad he had chosen to sit next to Jabberwock. While she was somewhat ashamed of having been so morose during the day, she still didn't feel quite up to chitchatting with the others. She mostly listened, occasionally spoke to either Jabb or Gwrhyr, and by the time they headed off to their respective tents for the evening, she was able to be civil to Yona.

"I'm sorry you had a bad day," Yona said as they prepared for bed. "That time of the month?"

"No, just feeling down. I'm sure I'll be back to my old self by morning."

"So you weren't upset with me?"

"No!" Eluned exclaimed, "Not at all! I'm happy that you're here with us. I was so worried that you wouldn't make it to Favonia."

"Good," Yona said, pulling the blanket up around her shoulders. "And if I ever do anything to make you angry, just tell me. I can take it. I'd rather have it out in the open."

"I will," Eluned promised. "Sweet dreams, Yona."

"Oh so sweet," Yona murmured, closing her eyes.

THE FOLLOWING MORNING they were up and on the road again not long after sunrise. Eluned was feeling much better.

"I think it is finally sinking in that we've begun the Quest again," she told Gwrhyr who was riding next to her on the left side.

"It hasn't even been two months since we escaped to Favonia," Gwrhyr reminded her. "In the scheme of things that really isn't that long. And, don't forget that we already have more than half of the treasures."

"More than half? Oh, by Omni, how did I forget? Chokhmah talked her aunt out of the Coat of Padarn Red-Coat?"

"Yes, she did. I believe she brought it with her."

"I'm not really sure what its magic power is," Eluned said.

"It will only fit a well-born man," he said.

"Or woman, no doubt." She remembered being led to Dyrnwyn, and Morgan, the snake-haired woman piloting the Chariot in King Arawn's tapestry. Plus, the Hamper had not failed to provide Yona with food just because she was a female. The treasures didn't seem to be gender biased. "Anyway," she continued, "I still don't see how that matters."

"I'm not sure if or even how we'll use it," Gwrhyr said, "but Omni has guided us so far, and I imagine It will continue to do so."

"That is true," Eluned said. "I found Dyrnwyn before I later had to use it to save my life." And, she thought, my meager training sufficed. She was very thankful she'd been able to get some lessons in the use of a sword since then.

"And we've already used the Phaeton and the Hamper," Gwrhyr added.

And now they sought the Halter of Clydno Eiddyn with its ability to produce whatever horse was wished for, Eluned mused, surveying the road ahead of them. It wound through the rolling, rock-strewn hills on its way to the Seven Sisters although at this point she could only see that it curved to the right at the bottom of the hill they were descending. Would all the treasures demonstrate their worth before this quest was finished, she wondered.

THE NEXT TWO NIGHTS were spent in camps similar to the first camp—in a grove of trees atop a hill so that they might simultaneously keep the horses protected and keep a watch for any approaching travellers.

They arrived each evening exhausted from a long day of riding, and more often than not, crashed shortly after Bonpo had prepared the evening meal, and everyone had finished their assigned chores. These varied from the gathering of wood for the fire, to helping Bonpo clean up, to setting up the tents, to seeing that the horses and Derry were settled for the evening.

By the morning of the fourth day of riding, Eluned was beginning to think they would never reach The Seven Sisters. But by that evening they left the rolling hills behind and entered the thick pine forest that covered the plain from which The Seven Sisters rose.

It was dark under the pines although they managed to find a clearing in which they could build a campfire without risking setting the fragrant trees alight.

Following dinner and clean up, Eluned took her turn in the woods. She was just about to head back to camp—she could see the glimmer of the campfire about fifty yards away—when a flickering light caught her eye. It was about a man's height off the ground, she estimated, and maybe twice that to her left.

It was too far away for her to make out what it was, so she moved a few feet closer, stopping only when she realized it was approaching her. It was too big to be a firefly. Heart in her throat, and left hand on Dyrnwyn's hilt, she waited to see what it would do.

It moved a little higher, definitely out of her reach, until it was nearly directly above her.

"What are you?" Eluned barely managed to squeak. She cleared her throat and tried again. "What are you?"

"Are you going to hurt me?" a voice tinkled.

"Not if your intentions toward me are honorable."

The glittery object rang with laughter that reminded the Princess of a small crystal bell. "You are so much larger than me," it said. "I could only misguide you, perhaps, if you were asking for directions. Or give you the wrong information."

"Good to know!" Eluned laughed. "No, of course I'm not going to hurt you. I still don't know what you are. I can only see light."

"Take a seat," the voice ordered.

The Princess sat down, legs crossed, on the pine straw.

The creature of light floated downwards until it was about a foot away from Eluned's face, just slightly above eye level. Eluned gasped for now she could see it was a very small human with pointed ears, and glowing wings that moved constantly in order to keep it in place.

"Isn't that tiring?" Eluned asked. "Constantly flapping your wings like that?" It reminded her of treading water or a hummingbird sipping nectar from a flower.

The creature nodded, and Eluned held out her hand, palm up. "Please sit. I promise not to hurt you."

"Thank you." It landed on her palm and sat, legs crossed like Eluned's. It was quite light, like holding a small bird in her hand. She'd had a canary when she was young that hadn't weighed much more than this creature. Because of the luminosity of its wings, Eluned couldn't quite see what it was wearing, but it looked silvery and glittered as well.

"Are you a faery? Because this is how I always pictured faeries would look, but the faeries I met on the island near Ruisidho were the same size as me."

"Ah, you have met the sí? We, too, are descended from the aos sí. How did you manage to escape them? It is my understanding that when Cuhvetena allows humans to visit her island, they don't leave."

"If I hadn't been so worried about our quest, and my friends and family, we might be there still," Eluned admitted.

"Quest?"

"I . . ." Eluned trailed off.

"You are wondering whether you can trust me?"

The Princess nodded. "I don't even know your name yet."

"Just call me Ziza. That's closest to how it's pronounced. And you are?"

"Eluned."

"Eluned," Ziza continued, "I know that we have a reputation for being troublemakers, but as soon as I saw you I sensed that I was meant to meet you."

"Which is why you didn't fly away?"

Ziza nodded.

"We are on a quest for the Thirteen Hallowed Treasures," Eluned conceded, touching the sword at her side.

Ziza's eyes widened. "Is that . . .?"

The Princess was nodding. "We've already gathered seven of them."

It was Ziza's turn to nod. "It is no wonder I sensed something. You must be here for the Halter."

"You know about it?" Eluned's voice squeaked again, this time with elation.

"Nyx has exiled herself to Hardaigh Forest. At least, that is the rumor."

Eluned's heart was hammering with excitement. Faolan's instincts had been correct. Nyx was mostly likely in Hardaigh.

"I know how you can find out for sure, though. Before you go to the trouble of crossing The Seven Sisters, anyway," Ziza continued.

"Yes?" Eluned breathed.

"I know someone who is very likely to know. He is a sionnach síth."

Eluned shook her head. "I'm not familiar with what that is."

"It is an animal sí. I believe you call it a fox?"

"A faery fox?" There was so much she didn't know.

"He is called Rua."

"Eluned!" she heard several voices shouting her name, and Ziza stood in alarm.

"It's my fellow Questers," Eluned explained. "I've probably been gone awhile. Please, before you go, how do I find Rua?"

"I will send a message by my raven friend to tell him to be on the lookout for you," Ziza said.

"Does he speak?"

Ziza groaned. "Not a language you can understand, but Mérimée can."

"Eluned!" Gwrhyr's voice was closer.

"The raven?"

"Yes, I will explain everything to him. Now go!" And Ziza quickly disappeared into the darkness of the pine forest.

"I'm here, Gwrhyr," Eluned called as she stood. "I'm on my way."

"Where have you been?" Gwrhyr pulled Eluned into a bear hug. "We've been worried sick."

"I can't breathe," she gasped, and he loosened his grip. "How long have I been gone? I lost track of time."

"I don't know. By the time we noticed you hadn't returned, it had been at least half an hour. Speaking of which, cover your ears." Eluned did as requested, and Gwrhyr bellowed, "Found her!"

There were shouts of relief, and Eluned inwardly rolled her eyes. Omni have mercy, she thought, I was never lost. "I was never lost," she grumbled to Gwrhyr.

"We didn't know that," he slung a protective arm around her shoulders, and guided her back to camp.

Everyone hugged her when she returned, even Faolan. The Bandersnatch couldn't hug, but he nuzzled her face when she took a seat by the fire. "I think some of us were just remembering the time you disappeared in the Desert of Serket," he explained.

"And what happened then?" she arched an eyebrow.

"You not get 'nudda tleasure?" Bonpo's voice was filled with awe.

The Princess shook her head. "That would have taken longer, I'm sure. No. No treasure, but I do know that Faolan is probably correct in assuming that Nyx can be found in Hardaigh Forest." She gave him a thumbs up, and he grinned, glad to have been able to offer something productive to the Quest. Chokhmah kissed his cheek in appreciation.

"How do you know this Princess?" Jabberwock asked.

"I met a different kind of faery," she said and you could hear a hint of delayed shock and wonder in her voice. Would she ever cease to be amazed by the magic that continually materialized around her?

"More faeries?" Gwrhyr asked, clearly dubious. The last time they happened on faeries the Quest had nearly come to a halt.

"A different kind of faery, one descended from the aos sí," Eluned explained. "She, at least I think it was a she, was so tiny she could sit in the palm of my hand. Her name was Ziza." And she proceeded to tell them everything—from the moment they met until her disappearance into the forest.

A log cracked when she finished her tale and several of the group jumped.

"We're definitely heading into a place of magic and enchantment." Yona's eyes were wide with wonder. "I hope I get to meet Rua. I'd love to see a fox with wings." She glanced at Faolan then at Jabberwock. "Sorry, Faolan and Jabb. Shapeshifting wolves and Janawar are amazing, but a fox with wings? I can't even imagine."

"We don't know that he'll have wings, Yona," Eluned cautioned her. "The faeries on the island just looked like beautiful humans. They didn't have wings."

"But what else would distinguish it as a faery fox?" was her rejoinder.

"She's got a point," Faolan said in her defense.

Chokhmah agreed. "Otherwise it could be just any fox. Especially as it cannot speak to us."

"True," Eluned agreed. "It is kind of freaky that a raven is going to be a fox's interpreter."

"I may be able to provide some help there as well," the Bandersnatch noted.

"How so?" Eluned queried.

"He is telepathic," Gwrhyr reminded her.

"I know, but don't we think in the thoughts of our own language?" she asked.

"Yes," Jabberwock explained, patiently. "But the fact we both have canine ancestry will change that."

Eluned's eyes widened in understanding. "Well that's good. Now we can double check what the raven tells us."

"Exactly." Jabberwock got up and shook himself. "Now it is off to bed for everyone. I suspect tomorrow is going to be an interesting day."

10TH COLTH

The road through the forest was mostly straight, and carpeted in pine needles, which contributed to an almost ethereal hush beneath the towering trees. The preternatural silence caused the group of Questers to speak in low tones as they made their way toward The Seven Sisters. And yet there was also a growing sense of anticipation that caused them to fidget in their saddles as if any sort of movement would get them to their destination more quickly.

The hours dragged by, but the day eventually waned toward sunset, the light beneath the trees fading as the sun began to edge toward the western horizon, and there was still no end in sight.

Eluned was trying not to get frantic. She had hoped to search for Rua that evening, but she felt confident that Jabberwock and Faolan and even Gwrhyr—no, she admitted to herself, everyone but herself—would advise waiting until the following morning no matter where they ended up for the night. Faolan had cautioned them about the unpredictable weather and the brutal terrain of The Seven Sisters, and there was no possibility of her doing any searching in the rapidly approaching darkness.

If they could only reach a point in which they could see the forest end. Then she might have the patience to wait. As it was, she had nearly convinced herself that they would be in this forest forever. Why was not knowing something always so difficult? If someone had said to her, 'don't worry, Eluned, within half an hour or an hour or first thing tomorrow morning the forest will end and the rocky plain from which The Seven Sisters rise will begin,' she could relax. It was the not knowing that was making her anxious.

Her tutor, Brother Columcille, would have insisted she put her trust in Omni, and think more productive thoughts, that what was meant to happen would happen.
He had constantly urged her to live in the present moment.

"You are not in control," he'd remind her. "Omni is. Stop pining for what might happen and enjoy what is happening. You can't force the future, and you can't mold it to your desires."

And while she knew that was probably true, right now it was hard to live by that philosophy.

Hearing Faolan call out something she missed snapped her out of her reverie. She had been so absorbed by her thoughts that she hadn't noticed she had dropped back, nor that Faolan had cantered ahead to see the lay of the land and search for a possible campsite.

"What is it?" she asked Yona, who was just slightly ahead of her.

"I couldn't quite make out what he said, but it sounds like he's found something."

The wide path they were following curved ahead, and Faolan was still out of sight. "Let's go!" Eluned urged her horse into a trot. The others followed suit, and even Bonpo picked up his pace, forcing poor little Derry into a trot as well. Jabberwock bounced around in his basket and finally begged Bonpo to remove him.

As they rounded the bend, they saw Fiachdubh and Faolan

trotting back their way. They also saw what Faolan had seen—the forest was finally opening up, the trees more widely spaced and the ground getting rockier.

"We should probably stop before it gets too stony," he suggested.

They pulled up short. Eluned desperately wanted to continue, but wisdom prevailed. She dismounted. "Then we better get camp set up and gather wood before the sun sets completely." They set to work.

THE PRINCESS RUSHED THROUGH HER CHORES the following morning urging the others to do likewise.

"Foxes don't like being out in the middle of the day," she said. "What if we miss him? Ziza made it sound like we had to see him before we travelled over The Seven Sisters."

"Stop fretting, my dear." Chokhmah's voice was soothing. "I feel confident that if Ziza sent, what was its name? Mérrimée? If she sent Mérrimée to warn Rua of our approach, then he will be watching out for us."

"I wouldn't be surprised if he's waiting for us to come out of the forest," Faolan answered.

"I agree," Jabberwock said. "If he has information for us then he will be waiting. Faeries can be mischievous, but why send the seven of us plus the horses and a donkey over treacherous mountains if what we seek is not there? They're not that cruel."

Eluned took a deep breath. "All right, I believe you." She closed her eyes and stroked Ronan's velvet-soft muzzle. "Omni is in control. Omni is in control," she breathed it like a mantra under her breath. "Always remember that Omni is in control." But by Omni, she thought as she waited for the others to get ready, there were times when that was really difficult to remember. The letting go and allowing the moment to happen was a difficult skill to master. It might take her the remainder of her life. Assuming, that was, that she still had a long time to live.

A moment later, Yona joined her, then Chokhmah, Gwrhyr and Faolan.

"Jus' haf ta put Jabb in basket," Bonpo called to them. "Den we finarry leady."

It took a good half hour for them to leave the dwindling trees behind and start across the barren, rocky plain that caused the seven-peak range to look higher than it actually was. The path they were on would take them through the pass that was second highest in elevation as the lowest pass was far too rocky and steep for the horses.

Another half hour brought them to the crossroads where the trail over the mountains, much smaller than the path they'd been on, continued straight ahead. To the left, the path continued southwards to the coast of Dyfed and northwards to the Kingdom of Aden.

They continued straight ahead, Faolan and Eluned both insisting on leading the way. The Princess was relegated to second in line.

"I am fully capable of taking care of myself." Her tone was steely. Both Gwrhyr and the Bandersnatch maintained that their first duty was to keep her safe, and it annoyed her to no end that they refused to acknowledge how capable she was at swordplay. "Besides, my safety didn't seem to concern you when we left Castle Mykerinos," Eluned told the Bandersnatch.

"I had things under control," Jabberwock reminded her. "Did I not rescue you from the barrow wight?"

"Well, yes . . ."

"And did not Omni put Bonpo in our path that very night?"

Eluned was forced to concede that was true. And they'd made it through the snowstorm in the Mountains of Misericord and to the town of Mjijangwa where Gwrhyr had joined them. And it was Gwrhyr who had rescued her from King Arawn. Damn, why were they always right? Regardless, she still thought she could defend herself if necessary.

They began switch-backing their way up to the pass, horse feet clomping loudly on the gravel path. Eluned kept her eyes peeled for Rua. Surely she couldn't miss a red fox with wings? But, Faolan spotted him first—probably some canine senses at play there, the Princess thought.

Faolan reined in his stallion, and the others stopped as well. A raven, as black as Fiachdubh, who'd been named for the bird, landed next to Rua, who was sitting on a large boulder that overlooked the trail.

"Greetings!" Faolan said.

The fox bowed its head and extended its wings. Rua was quite lovely—a beautiful specimen of a red fox in every aspect except he had the added glory of the iridescent wings that rose from his back. He folded his wings again and looked at Mérimée.

"Seek ye Nyx?" the raven cawed.

"Yes," Eluned said. "I do." Rua turned to look at her, and that is when Jabberwock pattered up. The Janawar and the si-onnach síth regarded each other for a couple of minutes. Then Rua made a yipping bark and nodded his head to the Bander-snatch.

"He said," Jabberwock informed the group, which had now pulled as closely together as possible, "that Nyx has exiled herself to Hardaigh."

"That's what Ziza said," Eluned frowned. "What do they mean by exiled?"

"They use the word exile," Jabberwock explained, "because the unicorn was so embarrassed that she'd allowed herself to be caught that she finally fled to a place where she might not have to risk that again. The halter she wears puts her in more danger of being caught easily."

Rua barked again, and Jabberwock listened for a minute before continuing. "He says that Hardaigh Forest is so isolated that Nyx felt that there was no risk of running into a virgin there."

"Because . . . what was it Leonardo da Vinci said?" Eluned ventured. "I wrote it down in my journal—something about having no self-control when approached by 'fair maidens'?"

Jabberwock repeated this to Rua who yipped his approval and nodded his head.

"But we don't want to capture her," Eluned said. "We just want the Halter."

"Seek ye must, and find," cawed Mérimée, "but ye must be patient."

"Did you hear that Princess?" Gwrhyr teased her. "You must be patient."

Eluned scowled at him. "I can be patient if I know what I am being patient for."

Gwrhyr chuckled. She almost never failed to take the bait, he just wished he didn't find it so compelling to taunt her. Sometimes Eluned brought out the adolescent in him. "Well, it looks like we're going to find out."

"Is the forest dangerous?" Faolan asking Rua a question interrupted Gwrhyr's sparring with Eluned.

"Dense, but not impenetrable," Jabberwock relayed the information. "There are also some boggy areas to be aware of because of its proximity to the ocean."

"Ye must tread carefully," the raven warned.

"Looks like you're going to be the point man, or wolf, rather, Faolan," Gwrhyr noted. "Surely a wolf can sense dangerous terrain more easily than a man."

Faolan nodded. "That I can, particularly if it's only the ground I need to be wary of and not predators."

"Rua says there are no predators for wolves and humans—just owls, foxes, that type of thing." Jabberwock assured Faolan.

"Ye may see will o' the wisps in the bogs," Mérimée said.

"Ignore them, and ye won't be led astray. I'll get word to the pixies to leave ye in peace, as well."

Rua barked again, and once again the Bandersnatch listened for a few minutes. "He says that it is very important that we find all the treasures," Jabberwock translated. "It's not just the safety of humans that is at risk. If King Arawn comes into power with Kings Hamartia and Hevel, and whoever else supports them, then all creatures are at risk, particularly those of us who are different. If they don't use us to strengthen their own powers then we will surely be killed when we are discovered."

That sobered the group up—of the seven of them, three were not strictly human. Eluned thought of all the magical creatures, not including those she travelled with, that she'd encountered on this trip from Aeron the Pwca to the winged fox, Rua, sitting on the boulder in front of her. Too many to count, and impossible to estimate how many more she would meet. Her hand touched the pouch that hung from her neck before falling to the sword scabbarded by her side. Gwrhyr had been thoughtful enough to have one made for her while she was stuck in Arberth.

And while the search for Nyx didn't seem inherently dangerous, the remainder of the treasures were in either neutral or enemy kingdoms, and they would definitely reach a point in which their very presence in those places was life threatening.

Rua barked, and Mérimée said, "We see ye understand the gravity of the situation. Go in Peace, and may Omni be with you."

"Thank you so much Rua and Mérimée," Eluned's voice was full of emotion. "We are forever indebted to you."

Mérimée cawed, "Ye be most welcome." Then he flapped his wings and was soon soaring eastward back toward the pine forest and Ziza.

"Can I touch him?" Eluned asked Jabberwock, who soon nodded the affirmative. Eluned edged her horse closer to the rock, and reached up. Rua sniffed her hand before bowing his head, and she scratched him behind his soft, furry ears. Thank you so much, her eyes said. Rua's eyes were nearly the same reddish brown as his fur. He yipped a response, and spread his large wings, which glimmered in the sunlight, before launching himself from the boulder and flying northward toward the peak that towered over them.

The group began moving again. In all likelihood they would be spending the night on the boulder-strewn slopes of the mountain, but at least they knew they were heading in the right direction. And that was a good thing because as they continued to ascend toward the pass, they climbed into a thick cloud. Eluned could barely see Faolan in front of her or Gwrhyr behind her, and the rest of the group just disappeared in the fog. The temperature was dropping as well, and she scrabbled in her saddlebag for her sweater. She was deeply regretting leaving her cloak and wool sweater in Castle Pwyll. The vagaries of weather, she mused. This was definitely a journey in which she needed to be prepared for all manner of weather and situations.

It was probably a good hour past noon when they reached the crest of the pass. The only reason she knew this was because Faolan shouted that he was stopping, and everyone reined in their horses.

"There should be a shelter here," he explained. "We can eat lunch in it before we continue. Otherwise, we probably won't find a place to stop until a much lower elevation."

He dismounted, and disappeared into the fog. A moment later he returned. "It's here to the right. You'd probably be better off leading your mounts." He had Fiachdubh's reins in his hand.

Following him a short distance ahead on the path, then down another trail to the right, they soon found themselves in front of a stone cabin with a much weathered hitching post in front of a spring-filled trough. They tethered their horses and entered the cabin. It was windowless. Added protection in foul weather, Eluned guessed. Bonpo left and soon returned with several lanterns.

"Omni have mercy!" Eluned gasped after hers had been lit. "Look at this stonework." Every stone on the cabin's walls had initials or names or dates carved into it, some of which were quite old.

"I guess there's not much else to do if you find yourself trapped in here until bad weather passes," Gwrhyr noted.

"But look at these dates," she marveled. "Some of them go as far back as the Great Demesne." She pointed out the archaic lettering, a sure sign of the presence of travellers in the cabin prior to the massive changes wrought on the planet by climate change and the wars that followed.

"We still have some signs with lettering like this in Aden," Gwrhyr noted.

"So do we," Eluned agreed, but you have to admit they're very rare."

"Runch!" Bonpo called.

If it can be called that, Eluned thought—crackers, hard cheese, pickles. They were definitely travelling rations. There were drawbacks to trekking with seven mouths to feed for an indeterminate amount of time. Hopefully, Bonpo would be able to add to their diet once they reached Hardaigh. He and Chokhmah were adept at finding berries, fungi and greens. Despite the chill, it was still summer. Surely plants would be plentiful, she thought, as she bit into her pickle, which was good but a salad would have been better.

Then another thought occurred to her, "Hey, Faolan!" Naturally, he and Chokhmah were cozied up in a corner of the cabin. She experienced another brief sting of jealousy before pushing it away.

"Yes?" he answered.

"Is there a river or even a large stream that runs through Hardaigh Forest?"

"I believe so, yes." He closed his eyes, picturing the lay of the land in his head. "I think it's the River Leprican."

"I'm thinking," Eluned informed the group, "that we should find this River Leprican and set up a base camp there."

Jabberwock was nodding. "She's right, of course."

"Obviously you two know something we don't." Yona leaned toward the Princess, nudging her shoulder.

"Fish!" Eluned and Jabberwock cheered simultaneously.

Bonpo clapped his hands in appreciation, and the others joined in.

"Brilliant idea, Princess," Gwrhyr's eyes shone with approval. "Fresh meat is definitely in order. And I imagine Faolan can help us out that way, as well, right? Surely it wouldn't be too difficult to chase down a few rabbits?"

"Not a problem," Faolan agreed. "But why a base camp?"

"Mérimée said that I'd have to be patient," Eluned explained. "I'm presuming that means that I am going to be doing a lot of sitting and waiting. From the little I've read, I think Nyx has to come to me. That means I have to find a spot in which to wait."

"Ah," he nodded in understanding. "And it needs to be close enough to camp for you to return each evening?"

"Exactly." She'd been doing a lot of thinking, and she had come to the realization that if she tried moving around the forest, finding a different place to sit each day, she might continually miss Nyx if the unicorn was also moving around the forest. But, if she chose a likely spot, and sat and waited, then eventually Nyx would sense her and be drawn to her. At least, that's what she hoped. How long that might take, she had no idea.

SHORTLY AFTER LEAVING THE CABIN, they began to descend again, and within a few hours they left the cloud line behind. As the terrain was still steep and rocky, they decided to push on until it was absolutely necessary to stop. But luck, or Omni, was with them and by nightfall they reached the transition zone between mountain and forest. It was still boulder strewn, but they were able to set up camp, albeit a little more haphazardly than usual. Because it was nearing dark, they were forced to get their tents set up in the last of the light. It was dark when they finished, which made gathering wood troublesome. Instead, Bonpo prepared a quick, cold meal by lantern light—olives and cheese and bread again, and dried dates.

"Highly unsatisfactory," she grumbled to Yona as they crawled into their tent. "I can't wait to set up a more permanent camp just so we can eat better."

"I'm jealous of Faolan," Yona admitted. "He can shift and go catch something in the forest tonight."

"True, but it will be raw." Eluned wrinkled her nose.

"But as a wolf he won't care. Also, as a Shapeshifter he doesn't really have a choice. He needs lots of protein."

"Does that mean he'll go back to Chokhmah with raw meat on his breath?" the Princess giggled. "The whole shapeshifting thing was hard for her to get her mind around.

Yona laughed, "I'm sure she makes him brush his teeth first! At least, I would."

"Did you see him shift while you were travelling with him?" Eluned wanted to know.

"No, he was always very careful. If it happened, which I'm sure it did, it was when I was asleep." Yona paused. "I'm pretty sure that he has to be naked to shift."

"I guess that makes sense." Eluned pondered human to animal transformation. It would be awkward to make that transition with clothes on, but it would also mean that you would have to be careful about when and where you shifted. "Well," she noted finally as they settled beneath their blankets, "he definitely found the right woman in Chokhmah. She doesn't seem to have a problem with anything but evil, and Faolan is definitely not that."

"No, he isn't," Yona agreed, "and he absolutely adores her.

I imagine we're all a little jealous of their love." She paused. "Except maybe for Bonpo. He seems fine with just being loved and appreciated by all of us."

"I agree," Eluned yawned, "and that is exactly why I would never complain about what we are eating in front of him. He's taken on the burden of feeding us willingly. I sure wouldn't want that responsibility."

"Amen," Yona yawned in response, "but I'll help him gather fresh food once we establish a camp."

Eluned didn't answer as she was already drifting off to sleep.

IN THE MORNING, they quickly packed up and headed north to find the river, Leprican, which was fed by streams flowing down from The Seven Sisters, before winding its way southwestward through Hardaigh Forest. The forest was too dense and too unknown for them to risk riding through it so they took the path that skirted the edge of the forest, confident that at some point they would have to reach the river.

They reached the Leprican shortly before noon, and decided to ford it as most of the forest lay on its northern side. The river was wide and relatively shallow at this point, and if the terrain on the opposite side wasn't too rocky, it would probably make a good camping spot.

While Bonpo prepared the group a quick lunch, Gwrhyr and Faolan followed the river southwest to see if it was possible to set up a camp just out of sight of the path and the river's ford. They had yet to see any travellers, but why take any chances?

Upon their return they informed the group that a little more than a hundred yards down river, the banks rose to a moderate bluff. They might have to move a few boulders and remove some saplings, but they thought it would make an excellent camping spot because it was more protected than the openness of the ford. It also safeguarded them from any possible flooding or rising dampness from the river itself.

This time everyone happily consumed their crackers and cheese along with some carrot sticks and apples. They were all eager to set up camp and actually spend the night in one place for more than just one night.

Once again, and even knowing that they were all probably safe, the tents were pitched in a rough circle, or more technically, a cross, with Yona and Eluned taking the spot furthest to the west and Gwrhyr and Jabberwock within six feet to their left, and Bonpo within six feet to their right. Eluned could only smile—Gwrhyr was growing increasingly protective of her, and she found it very flattering when once she would have found it extremely annoying. He hadn't tried to kiss her again since that time in Favonia, and she couldn't decide whether to be thankful or bothered.

Faolan and Chokhmah pitched their tent as far to the east as they could and still be a part of the circle. This meant that the horses were tethered in front of their tent at night because the campfire was to be situated nearer the other three tents. It was a sacrifice they were willing to make for a little extra privacy.

Once Bonpo's brawn was no longer needed to help move boulders or pull up saplings, he set off with Chokhmah to see what fresh things they could scavenge for dinner.

Yona and Eluned started collecting and stacking firewood although they were warned by Faolan not to stray too far into the forest.

"At least not until I've checked it out," he told them.

"Maybe you should go do that now," Eluned said. "We don't want anyone getting lost in there tonight."

"Good point." If they were going to be here more than a few days, they would probably need to set aside an area for privy use. There were some drawbacks to camping in one area. They would also need to move the horses around during the day to avoid overgrazing and manure buildup. So much to think about! He went over to Gwrhyr, who was rigging up something to which they could tether the horses at night, to share his concerns.

"That means we need to find a spot for Eluned to wait as soon as possible tomorrow," Gwrhyr said. "Once she's settled in, we'll have plenty of time to work on things like that during the day."

"Will she be safe alone all day?"

"Probably," he replied, "but we will have to come up with a way to check on her. Too bad Mérimée is on the other side of the mountains."

Faolan nodded. "Maybe we'll run into a pixie or faery, or some other creature that can help us out that way. I know Mérimée mentioned that he'd get word to leave us in peace, but we can still hope."

"That's definitely something we will all have to ponder," Gwrhyr agreed. "I understand that she needs to be alone to draw Nyx to her side, but I'm really uncomfortable with leaving her alone in the forest all day. Patience is not one of her virtues, and I'm afraid of what she might do if left to her own devices."

Faolan sighed. "Well, I knew this wasn't going to be easy."

"That just might be the understatement of the century," Gwrhyr laughed, clapping him on the back. "So, what's the most important thing to do next?"

"Let's go scout the woods closest to our camp. As Eluned pointed out, we don't want anyone getting lost in there tonight."

14ᴛʜ Colth

The forest wasn't actually as bad as they'd anticipated, Faolan was happy to discover. There was a lot of growth, yes, but there were numerous deer trails as well. Or were they Nyx tracks? Faolan wondered. Rua had said there were no large predators, so by process of elimination that made the paths that wove through the forest unicorn trails as there would be nothing to prey on deer.

Eluned had told him that Nyx had deserted Avalach more than a century ago. That meant she had probably been in Hardaigh Forest for nearly a century—plenty of time for her wanderings to produce horse-sized byways—and clearly she was a wanderer. And, no doubt, the smaller animals used her pathways, as well, keeping them well tread and free of too much brush.

Faolan suspected if they stuck to Nyx's trails, they wouldn't have to worry about uncertain ground. Surely, the unicorn would avoid boggy areas. She was at as much risk for getting stuck in a bog as any other animal.

He was pleased to report this back to the group. As long as they stuck to the trails and did nothing more, perhaps, than step behind a tree, they were sure to be all right until they could set up something more permanent.

FOLLOWING A DINNER that included fresh greens and some mushrooms, which were all Bonpo and Chokhmah could find without going into the woods, the group had turned in with the promise of a full day spent improving the camp, fishing, and searching for fresh food on the morrow.

Out of habit, they awoke early and as soon as the sun was high enough, Eluned, Gwrhyr and Faolan, in wolf form, began searching for a suitable place for the Princess to spend her days.

When Faolan appeared in his animal form, it was all Eluned and Yona could do not to pet him. Knowing that he was actually Faolan somehow made that inappropriate. But Chokhmah was correct—he was gorgeous—with thick grey and white fur tinged with tan and black. The only thing that looked like Faolan were the grey-blue eyes that shone with an uncharacteristic intelligence.

His eyes seemed to say "Ready?" and he nodded his head towards the forest. Eluned and Gwrhyr nodded, and followed him.

"I feel awkward touching you," Eluned said, "but I will say that you are an extraordinarily magnificent animal."

Faolan looked back over his shoulder with a canine grin, his eyes shining, and Eluned was glad she had said something.

The trio spent the morning exploring various trails, but always reached a dead end, so to speak. There were paths all over the place, but none of them led to a clearing, nor could they find any potential sites just off the trail. They decided to head back for lunch and try again that afternoon.

"YOU DON'T HAVE TO FEEL BAD about touching me when I'm a wolf," Faolan informed her at lunch when he could speak again. "When I am in wolf form, I am a wolf. An intelligent wolf, perhaps, in that I can understand what people are saying, but you can still scratch me behind the ears, or whatever. I'm not even capable of taking that as a sexual overture."

"Seriously? Is that okay with you Chokhmah?" she asked the gypsy.

It did not bother her, but even if it had she would have claimed it was all right. She had missed the bond she had with Eluned, and if she could mend the tear in it by allowing her to pet her beloved Faolan while in wolf form, why not? "Of course you may, my dear," she said. "Canines love to be petted."

"So do humans," Faolan noted.

"Truer words were never spoken, my love," Chokhmah said, taking his hand.

"Really?" Eluned said, turning to Gwrhyr and patting him on the head. "You're such a good boy."

"Funny, Princess," he laughed, and scratched her under the chin. "Whose the sweet little baby?" he cooed.

Everyone laughed before returning to their conversations.

"You're hair is really soft," Eluned said quietly to Gwrhyr. "I had no idea. And I like the way you've kept your beard trimmed since we left Prythew."

"Thank you," he said. "I didn't think you'd noticed."

"Of course I did," she assured him, and stood up. "Time to hit the trail?"

Gwrhyr stood as well. He was still basking in Eluned's attention. He had kept his beard trimmed because she had told him in Prythew that she liked it. "Actually, it's probably safe enough that Faolan doesn't need to come with us this afternoon," Gwrhyr said, anticipating actually getting to spend some time alone with her.

Eluned nodded. The trails had been solid that morning, and they hadn't even run into any animals, fantastical or otherwise. "Just one thing," she said.

"What's that?" he cringed inwardly; worried that she'd want to invite Yona along.

"I think we need to pick a path and stay on it for longer than fifteen minutes. We should walk, I think, a bare minimum of half an hour away from camp, maybe even up to an hour. I don't think we've been getting far enough away from the presence of other people."

"Fair enough," he agreed.

"And," she continued.

"You said one thing," he interrupted.

"I just remembered. I noticed a trail that was blocked by a blow down as we were coming back for lunch. I know it seems silly, but I have a feeling we should try it."

"Let me talk to Faolan, and then I'll be ready."

"No problem," she responded. "I need to refill the water jug, anyway."

About five minutes later, they were both ready and Eluned led the way back into the woods following the path they had taken to return to camp.

"We passed it shortly before we got to camp," she said, "and I only caught a glimpse of a trail twisting back into the woods . . . here it is." She stopped in front of a large ash tree that had fallen, by all indications, quite some time ago. The leaves had long since withered and blown away, and only the stouter branches remained. "I think I can climb over it."

She pulled herself carefully to the top, between two branches, stood atop the trunk for a moment before jumping down to the leaf-littered trail.

Gwrhyr quickly followed suit and then pulled a watch from his trouser pocket. "We no longer have a wolf's sense of time to count on," he explained when he saw the bemused expression on Eluned's face.

"It's not that," she said. "It's just that I didn't even know you had a pocket watch. It's lovely."

"It was my father's, but I haven't needed to use it until now," he paused. "That's not completely true. I used it a number of times while I was with Arawn's army, but you weren't around then."

"May I see?"

He held out his palm, on which it lay. A heavy gold chain attached the watch to a leather loop sewn just above his pocket. "I didn't want to risk losing it," he told her when he saw her notice.

She moved a little closer and lifted the timepiece from his hand. It really was exquisite—also gold with an ornately engraved phoenix on the cover that protected the watch face. "Beautiful. It looks very old."

"It has been in the family for generations," Gwrhyr admitted.

"Well, note the time," she said cheerfully, "and we'll see where we are in half an hour." She began to walk, but her mind was racing. For months she had seen Gwrhyr as nothing more than a well-trained spy for King Uriel. An intelligent and quite handsome spy, perhaps, but just one of Uriel's subjects willing to perform necessary duties for his king. Not unlike, she supposed, Olcan and Faolan in some ways.

But the watch carried the sigil of Aden on its cover, which struck her as odd, and it was clearly old and expensive. Now she had to re-think Gwrhyr. Maybe he was more than just a spy. Could he possibly also be the son of one of Uriel's lords? That would definitely explain a lot of what she knew about him, particularly how well educated he seemed—from his knowledge of languages, to his mastery of weaponry, to his ability to play the harp.

"You're being awfully quiet," he said, and she jumped. "And easily spooked," he added. "What are you thinking?"

"I," she began. "Hmmm. It's just," she stalled for time as she tried to decide how much she should say.

"Just say it, Princess."

"Are you the son of one of Uriel's lords?"

Gwrhyr chuckled. "The pocket watch?"

"It strikes me as . . ." she trailed off.

"Too nice for an ordinary man?"

"Yes," she admitted, cheeks flaming. She was glad he could only see the back of her head.

"Unfortunately, I can't answer that. I meant it when I said I was bound to secrecy." And he would be so grateful when he no longer had to avoid the truth.

"I understand," she replied, but thought—he didn't say that he wasn't—which in all likelihood meant that he was. Interesting. Very interesting. She returned her attention to the trail.

Gwrhyr surveyed the slight form in front of him with amusement. Would this new development change things between them? Would she be more likely to allow herself to become interested in a man who was closer to royalty? Honestly, he hoped so. He knew that she wanted to experience love, but he thought he also knew her well enough to know that it would be very difficult for her to go against her father's wishes. She was the only heir to the throne of Zion. Her first crush on this journey had been a prince, after all. She had also turned down a chance with a king already. He was pretty sure that before Arawn had considered her as a sacrificial offering, he weighed the merits of making Eluned his wife. If she had been a little more enthusiastic about the Crimson King, she might now be the Crimson Queen.

How many more single princes or kings might the Princess run into on this journey, excluding those from enemy kingdoms, which he was certain she'd want to avoid? The answer was zero. He found himself biting his lip to prevent him from breaking into a huge grin. Perhaps he really did stand a chance, after all.

"Now you're being quiet," the Princess suddenly spoke up. "You're not angry that I figured all of that out are you?"

"Figured what out? You still don't know anything for sure."

She glanced at him over her shoulder. She could see a glint in his eyes and the dimple at the corner of his mouth—he always got that look when he found her amusing. "Why is that funny?"

"Funny is not the word I'd use."

"What word would you use?" she pressed him.

"I guess I'd say 'enjoy'. I get enjoyment from your seemingly insatiable curiosity. There's a lot going on behind that beautiful face—you're always thinking, observing. Not necessarily correctly all of the time, but still."

"Hmmm," Eluned grunted. She couldn't decide whether or not that should perturb her. It was both a compliment and not. A sparkle from the left caught her eye, and she stopped without warning.

"Whoa," Gwrhyr said, nearly stumbling into her. "What is it?"

She guided him backwards a step or two. "Look," she said, pointing into the woods. "What's that?" The sunlight was refracting off something they couldn't see. Was it worth the risk of entering the woods to check it out?

She started to step off the path.

"Wait," Gwrhyr put a hand on her shoulder. She stopped, and he pulled a handkerchief from another pocket and tied it to a trailside branch.

Stepping off the trail, she found herself ankle deep in the leaf litter. "This seems awfully deep," she commented. Gwrhyr knelt down and brushed some of the leaves away.

"I think this might be another pathway," he said.

She kicked away the leaves at her feet. "I believe you're right."

Pushing the leaves away with their feet to leave a clearly

marked path, they made their way toward the shimmering light ahead of them. The trail curved between two very large oaks and opened up into a small glade. The sun reflected off a spring-fed pool towards the left side of the clearing, which was bounded by ancient oak, ash, birch, and rowan trees. Amidst the few boulders that dotted the grassy glade, late summer wildflowers bloomed in profusion.

Eluned looked up at Gwrhyr to see if he was taking it all in. "It's beautiful," she breathed.

He nodded. It was just what they were looking for. He pulled his watch from his pocket as Eluned stepped into the glade. "It's been less than half an hour," he remarked. "That means it is only a mile or so distant from camp."

"That seems far enough, doesn't it?" She listened for a moment—just birdsong and a breeze rustling the leaves of the surrounding trees. Even the spring was silent. She walked toward it and Gwrhyr followed.

"Oh look!" she ran the last few steps to the placid pool. Just behind the spring, but out from under the shade of the trees, grew a row of raspberry bushes and they were covered with ripe fruit. "We have to take some back," she enthused. "I love raspberries!" What could they carry them in?

She looked around, mournfully.

"What is it?" There was concern in Gwrhyr's voice.

"What can we carry them in? We can't carry them in our hands. They'll be smashed by the time we get back. She had carried nothing with her but Dyrnwyn.

Gwrhyr thought for a second, then pulled a small leather pack off his back. Reaching inside, he pulled out the water jug—a wide-mouthed clay jar sealed with a cork cap. "What about this?'

Eluned's eyes lit with joy. "Perfect!"

"Sip before I dump it?" They did have a beautiful spring at their feet, but Gwrhyr had lugged the bottle the whole way.

"I wish it were wine, though. I feel like celebrating, but sure," she smiled, reaching out her hand for the jug.

When it was filled with raspberries, Gwrhyr corked it, and they took one last look around the clearing. "Are you sure you're okay with this? You're going to be spending several long days here."

"Well, I already regret not having brought at least one book on this journey, but I do have my journal and Dyrnwyn. That will have to be enough. At least it's lovely and peaceful." A thought struck her. "And hopefully it won't rain."

"We'll play that by ear," he said. "If it looks like it's going to rain, you stay in the camp. If it does rain, I'll come and fetch you."

"Why can't I just run back there alone?"

"I don't even want you alone here all day by yourself, but I understand that it's the only way to lure Nyx. But," and his voice grew stern, "I do not want you, under any circumstances other than fleeing for your life, to go back and forth to this clearing alone. Either I, Faolan or Bonpo will escort you. Understood?"

She lowered her eyes and nodded meekly so he wouldn't see the anger blazing in them. She hated being ordered around.

"I just cannot risk anything happening to you again," he said, thinking of how she had nearly died on that sacrificial altar. That had been far too close for comfort, and Omni definitely had been watching over them that day. "Divinely protected or not, we shouldn't take chances. That reminds me of a story whose moral is: Trust Omni, but always tether your camel."

"I don't understand."

"Basically it means one should have complete trust in Omni, but never count on It to take care of every last detail. Come on, I'll tell you the whole story on the way back to camp."

ELUNED WAS STILL PONDERING Gwrhyr's tale when they reached the camp. She wasn't sure she liked it, but it made sense. All that was required of them was to do everything possible to ensure the success of the Quest, including their own safety, and Omni would take care of the rest. At least, that was the general idea. It unnerved the Princess, though, because she hated not knowing if, and when things would happen; she hated not having any control. It was a constant struggle, and a precarious balance.

Only Bonpo and Chokhmah seemed to have managed the refined art of living in the moment despite the tragedies in their lives. Jabberwock seemed okay most of the time, but she knew that he still experienced nightmares about his flight from the Vale Vixen, and his loss of Kamali in the Devastation of Pelf. What a shock it must have been to him to have to flee paradise, and to lose everything he held dear. And yet, he still survived.

Yona had given up a cushy marriage, and what would have been a life of luxury to join this quest. Faolan, too, had left a settled life of horse farming to help secure the ultimate goal of peace for the Thirteen Kingdoms. That was probably true of Gwrhyr, as well, she thought. A lord's son needn't put his life on the line for a divine quest. Nor the daughter of a king, she added. She may have fallen into gathering the treasures unintentionally—clearly Omni had placed the book entitled Thirteen Royal Treasure of the Thirteen Kingdoms in the small library in Mjijangwa for her to find—but she had made the choice, as well.

And while they all had a part to play, it was she who had been led to Dyrnwyn. She was the only one capable of drawing Nyx to her side, and she was the only one who had a treasure bearing her name—The Ring of Eluned, which allowed her to become invisible when she held the moonstone that came with it in her palm. Eluned unconsciously fingered the pouch that lay hidden beneath her blouse where the moonstone resided.

"You're quiet again," Gwrhyr said as they left the woods.

"It's a hell of a lot of responsibility for an eighteen-year-old, Gwrhyr," she said in a voice choked with emotion.

He put a hand on her arm to stop her, and she turned to face him, eyes brimming with tears. Gwrhyr cupped her face in his hands, a face he loved more every day, and looked her in the eyes. "You are not alone. Every single one of us would gladly give our lives for you."

The Princess laid her head against his chest once again, and allowed the tears to flow. She knew she didn't deserve such devotion after all the times she'd been so horrible to him.

Gwrhyr hugged her tightly to him, and waited for the flow of tears to ebb. He no longer had a handkerchief to offer her. They had decided to leave it tied to the branch so they wouldn't miss the trail the following morning.

She finally drew in a long, shaky sigh, and looked up at him, a smile trembling on her lips. "Thanks again. I'm sorry for making this a pattern."

He kissed her forehead. "I wasn't lying when I told you I felt honored that you feel comfortable enough with me to do this."

"Really? You don't think I'm being silly?"

"You said it first. This quest is a lot of responsibility for an eighteen-year-old. Why the youngest and most inexperienced person in this group was chosen to bear the brunt of that, I'm sure only Omni knows. But, I will say it again. We are all here to help you carry that load, and you can cry on me any time you need to."

"Thank you," she whispered, hugging him. The only problem was that every time she did this, she felt more and more comfortable in his arms. And that made her wonder, yet again, why he hadn't tried to kiss her since that morning in Seemu.

What she didn't know, and what Gwrhyr would never say,

is that he had no intention of kissing her again until he was certain it was something that she wanted as well. He had kissed her twice—once in anger, and once in impassioned jealousy. That wouldn't happen again. And, even though he had felt her begin to respond before Irirangi had dragged him off her, he couldn't risk that it was any more than a response. No, it had to be entirely up to her, and if that meant a long wait then so be it.

Hearing a shout, they broke apart and turned to see Faolan and Yona heading their way.

"Success?" Faolan asked when he was close enough.

"Eluned's hunch proved correct," Gwrhyr said.

"We found the most beautiful little clearing about a mile from camp," she informed them. "It had a spring, and flowers, and most importantly . . . show them Gwrhyr."

Gwrhyr removed the pack from his back again, and pulled out the jug containing the raspberries. Faolan looked unimpressed, but Yona was appreciative.

"I'm sure Bonpo will be happy to add those to our meal tonight," Yona agreed, picking one out of the jar and popping it into her mouth. "Mmmm, scrumptious."

Eluned grabbed a couple for herself. "I love raspberries, but I better get those to Bonpo before I eat them all."

Gwrhyr handed Eluned the jar, and she and Yona went off in search of the giant.

"So, it's a likely spot?" Faolan asked once they were out of range.

"It does seem perfect," Gwrhyr admitted. "I still intend to escort her there and then back again every day. And if I can't for some reason, then either you or Bonpo can do it. I think we've all learned how easily the Princess gets distracted, and while that's honestly been helpful to us for the most part, I just can't risk her getting lost in those woods."

"All it would take is just one will o' the wisp," Faolan agreed.

"She does have a tendency to be distracted by sparkly things," Gwrhyr agreed. "It was the reflection off the spring that caught her eye today—so, a good thing. But despite the fact Mérimée said to ignore will o' the wisps, I'm not sure Eluned is capable of doing so."

"And all it would take is her losing track of time . . ."

"As she often does," Gwrhyr noted.

"And end up walking back to camp in the dark . . ."

"Exactly. So, it is our duty to make sure that doesn't happen, and we don't know how long we're talking."

Faolan nodded. It could be a matter of days. Or weeks. He just hoped it wouldn't roll into months.

24ᵀᴴ COLTH

Ten days. Eluned had spent ten full days waiting for the unicorn. She had watched as the ripe raspberries disappeared, and then stopped producing fruit. The Princess saw the late summer flowers slowly fade away as the early morning chill of the approaching autumn began to turn the green grass golden. The trees were also beginning to display their fall colors although it would be another month before they turned completely.

Would she still be here when the clearing was carpeted with fallen leaves? Changing scenery apart, she was seriously about to go insane with boredom. Only one day of the ten had been spent in camp, and that had been a trial in and of itself, because it had rained steadily for twenty-four hours, and had nearly driven everyone crazy.

She and Yona had spent the entire day confined to their tent. They had played tarok, and talked about their respective childhoods, their dreams for the future, and books they had read . . . and Eluned had been extremely grateful to be able to head back to the clearing the following morning. They had all breathed a huge sigh of relief when the sun had appeared to illuminate an almost cloudless sky. Only Faolan, as a wolf, had faced the torrential rain during that time although even he wasn't out for long.

During the past ten days she had developed a routine for each day: Gwrhyr walked her to the clearing shortly after sunrise. It was a nice time for her because she got to enjoy half an hour in conversation with him before having to be alone with only herself for company for the remainder of the day.

Once she reached the clearing, she spent the hours until noon practicing with Dyrnwyn, writing in her journal and daydreaming. Swordplay came first because it was always chilly when she first arrived, and it was a good way to warm herself up. Then she would write in her journal until her hand cramped, getting down as many details of her journey as she could remember. She was trying to impart every aspect of the Quest up until the current day. She was still working on that. So much had happened since she'd drawn the calendar back in Arberth, and she'd never written down anything that had actually happened to her.

When the sun was high in the sky, she would eat whatever Bonpo had packed her for lunch. They had more access to food now so she never knew what she would find—it could be a mushroom sandwich (he had brought meal with him to make flat bread) or it could be cold fish or hare. It just depended. They were definitely living each day as it came.

A few days into nearly dying of boredom in the afternoon, she had talked Gwrhyr into harp lessons. That way, she could practice what she'd learned the previous evening to help her wile away the afternoons. And while she was getting quite accomplished at wasting time, the boredom and loneliness nearly drove her to tears. By late afternoon, she was fretfully watching the sun's arc toward the western horizon, and anticipating Gwrhyr's impending arrival. Eluned's only consolation was that every day the sun set just a little bit sooner.

Not a single one of them in their wanderings in Hardaigh

Forest during the day, not even Faolan, had happened upon a magical creature of any sort. Apparently Mérimée had kept his word. Other than Gwrhyr when he walked her to and from the clearing, and at this point it had always been him, every one else tried to keep well away from the Princess in order not to scare off Nyx. They had even gone so far as to ford the river and scavenge for food on the opposite side of the Leprican, but still there had been no sign of the gentle beast.

It was late in the afternoon on Eluned's tenth day of waiting in the clearing, while she was strumming the few chords she'd learned from Gwrhyr on his borrowed harp, that she had the peculiar sensation that she was being watched.

She stopped mid strum and looked around the clearing, heart thumping painfully against her ribs. Had Nyx finally found her? But it wasn't a unicorn that she finally picked out at the edge of the clearing, not far from the spring. It was a very large cat. The feline was breathtaking—midnight black except for a white spot on its chest—and it surveyed her with inscrutable lambent green eyes. Had her harp playing, or the water offered by the spring, drawn the creature?

Eluned could easily see that it was larger than a normal cat, maybe three feet long. She wasn't sure, but she desperately wanted to move closer to it. Yet she was also afraid that if she moved, she might chase it away.

"Hello," Eluned finally spoke trying to keep her voice low and friendly. "Did you like my music?" she asked, and started strumming again, though softly. "I'm just learning. I don't really know any songs yet."

The cat continued to watch her, and deciding that nothing ventured was nothing gained, she continued to speak. "You're probably wondering what I'm doing here in the forest all by myself." The cat remained still other than the slight twitching of the tip of its tail. "The truth is," she couldn't keep the sigh out of her voice, "that I'm waiting for Nyx." The cat blinked. "I don't want to capture her," she explained quickly. "I just want the Halter she is wearing.

"I know you might not understand me," Eluned continued, "but if you do, and you know where she is, could you please tell her I need her. We have to find these treasures or we will all be at risk."

The cat stood and approached her slowly. Eluned remained in place. She'd been sitting on one of the boulders, and honestly was ready to move as it was starting to get uncomfortable, but she would not risk frightening the cat. It stopped a couple of feet away from her and scrutinized her again.

"I promise," Eluned said, extending her right hand slowly. "See that ring? That's the Ring of Eluned. I have the moonstone in a pouch underneath my shirt. And see the sword to your right? That's Dyrnwyn. A pwca named Aeron led me to it. I know I'm just guessing, but I suspect you are more than just a cat, and we've already met a faery fox. "And," she sighed, and sent a fervent arrow prayer to Omni, "you might even already know all of this, but if you do understand what I am saying, please help me."

The cat blinked at her again, and then his ears pricked, and he turned his head as if listening.

"That's probably Gwrhyr," Eluned said. "It's about time for him to escort me back to camp."

Returning his gaze to the Princess, the cat extended a paw. Eluned reached out her hand, palm raised, and the cat placed his paw in her hand.

"Thank you," she said, lower lip trembling with emotion. "I owe you the world."

The cat stood and padded its way back across the clearing, stopping by the spring for a quick drink before disappearing into the forest. Eluned was still sitting on the boulder, mouth slightly open in delayed shock, when Gwrhyr entered the clearing.

"Eluned, what is it?" he called out, jogging the last dozen feet or so.

She turned to him, eyes filled with wonder. "I just . . . I just am never going to get used to this." She breathed.

Gwrhyr glanced around the glade, but nothing had changed since that morning. He swallowed hard. He was used to messing things up. "I didn't scare away the unicorn, did I?"

"What?" Eluned was standing, and packing away the harp into the velvet bag that protected it. "Oh, no! Sorry. Honestly, I probably would have been yelling at you had that happened."

"Good point. So, what actually occurred?"

She handed him the harp and picked up the sword. "I think I met a faery cat."

"A faery cat?" They began walking back to camp, and she told him what had transpired with the overly large cat she had encountered.

"That sounds like one of the cait sidhe," Jabberwock said. They were all gathered around the campfire following the evening meal. It had become a nightly ritual—an outdoors version of conversing around the dining room table.

"But it didn't have wings?" Yona sounded disappointed.

"Definitely no wings," Eluned emphasized again. These faeries really differed in their appearances—from human-sized to hand-sized, wings and no wings, mammals and humans. It was hard to keep track. "Yet, it seemed to understand what I was saying. I'm sure of it. The only question is—how long will it take the cat to find Nyx, and how long will it take Nyx to get back to me, assuming she wants to do that?"

Gwrhyr slipped an arm around her shoulders. It was his intention to stay as close to her as possible. Some day it would happen . . . and she never seemed to mind his casual embraces. At least not yet. "I believe it will happen," he said. "I guess it really just depends on how far Nyx is from us at this moment.

How long it takes this faery cat to find her, and convince her to seek Eluned out, I can't say. But, I believe this cat will be convincing."

"Oh, cats are," Chokhmah said. "They are so . . . well, I must admit that we gypsies tend to consider them unclean. But I like to see the wisdom in all animals. And cats, well you cannot argue that there is a certain wisdom there behind those enigmatic eyes." She looked at Faolan and they gazed into each other's eyes for a moment before rubbing noses.

Definitely, offensively in love, Eluned thought with another twinge of jealousy. The Princess longed to be annoyingly in love. Yet, she could feel Gwrhyr's warm body next to hers, his arm still slung casually about her shoulders. It wouldn't take much, she admitted to herself. She'd just have to lean into him. But something prevented her from doing that. It was too public, for one thing. More importantly, she was the daughter of a king betrothed to a king. Eluned had already made a fool of herself with Irirangi. As a princess, she needed to watch herself. But, she wanted to be in love. She wanted some passion. A kiss. Just a kiss. Why was everything so difficult?

THE TWENTY-FIFTH OF COLTH promised to be a perfect late summer day. The sky boasted a few fluffy clouds, but none that threatened rain, and it was still warm enough not to need a coat. Eluned had spent the entire breakfast deep in thought. As she was often silent first thing in the morning, no one paid it much attention. But, when Gwrhyr showed up at her tent to escort her to the clearing, Eluned began to plead.

"Can't I have just one day off? Please. If the faery cat really is going to seek Nyx out for me, then surely it will take more than one day for all that to transpire. It didn't even have wings so it has to walk. And even if it isn't, I'll go crazy if I have to spend yet another day alone. Please?"

As if he could resist those sea green eyes, he thought,

but he tried to look like he was taking it under consideration. "Why, is there something in particular you want to do?"

"Well, I hadn't thought that far," she said. "But it would be nice to do something that didn't involve swords, journals, or harps."

"Hmmm," Gwrhyr pondered. What could he offer that would allow him to spend the day with the Princess? The truth was that despite their morning and afternoon walks, he felt like he almost never saw her anymore. "How about a ride? It's been a while since you've been on a horse, and I'm sure Ronan would love some more exercise. We've been taking turns exercising him, but he could really stand being out for more than an hour."

"That's an excellent idea! Can we ride north on the path since I haven't been that way yet?"

"Of course," Gwrhyr agreed. "We haven't really travelled that way either since you've been in the clearing because we didn't want to risk chasing off Nyx." And then, because he didn't want to give her a chance to say it and risk hurting his feelings, he asked, "Should we ask if anyone else wants to ride with us?"

"I guess that's only fair," she responded although part of her wanted to be alone with him. The truth was that they talked very little on the short walk to the clearing because it was morning, and she was always a little grumpy about spending yet another full day on her own. In the evenings, she had very little information to impart, and just wanted to hear about what had been going on in the camp. She hadn't had a real chance to talk with him since she'd discovered he was probably the son of one of Uriel's lords. Maybe he was a marquess or even a duke.

Gwrhyr had a sudden flash of inspiration. He focused all his thought on Jabberwock and begged: *If you can hear me please ask the others to bow out of taking a ride with the Prin-*

cess when I ask them. Hoping that had worked, he turned to Eluned. "Why don't you go ask Bonpo to pack us up something for lunch, and I'll go see if anyone else is interested," he said to Eluned.

"Sure." Turning toward the campfire, she took a few steps before stopping in her tracks. What if they needed more than two lunches? She turned around, but Gwrhyr had already disappeared. Oh well, she'd just tell Bonpo that there might be more.

But the Bandersnatch had been talking with Bonpo when he received Gwrhyr's message so the giant was already aware of what was going on when Eluned walked up.

"No plobrem, Plincess," he said. "I make more if I 'af to."

She looked around. Yona was nowhere to be seen. In the woods, perhaps? During the past ten days, Gwrhyr and Faolan had built separate latrine areas for the women and the men. They were at opposite ends of the camp, and the best way, they had decided, to avoid potential embarrassment. Gwrhyr was talking to Chokhmah and Faolan, and she walked over to join them.

"Are you guys coming along?" Eluned asked.

"Oh, I am so sorry, my dear," Chokhmah apologized. "Faolan promised to help me collect some herbs and other greens today."

Faolan shrugged, "It sounds fun, but I haven't been able to spend much time with Chokhmah the past few days while I was working on a paddock for the horses, and I promised her." He spread his hands, palms up, as if to say he had little choice in the matter. "Have a nice ride, though. It seems a beautiful day for it."

"Thanks, Faolan. See you guys later then." Chokhmah hugged her before the couple strode away, arms linked. She turned to Gwrhyr. "That leaves Yona."

"She already told me she couldn't go," Gwrhyr informed her. "I think it's her turn to fish or something?"

"So why aren't we saddling the horses?"

"What? You didn't do that already?" he teased.

"I thought you had," she retorted.

"You think our lunch is ready yet?"

"I don't know," she said. "But we can find out on our way to the horses. Let's just make sure he packed us some wine, as well. We might as well make a real picnic of it."

"I'D FORGOTTEN HOW MUCH I MISSED THIS," Eluned admitted as they headed north on the path that led to the Kingdom of Aden. The Seven Sisters towered above them to the right and the trees of Hardaigh Forest to their left. It wasn't long before the trail curved and the Leprican disappeared behind them, and they rode in a companionable quiet for a little while, listening to the birds twittering in the trees, the sound of their horses hooves on the rocky turf, and the rustle of small animals on the forest floor.

"You're never going to tell me anything about yourself?" the Princess finally broke the silence.

"You've probably already figured out more than you were meant to."

"Meant to?" she seemed surprised. "That sounds planned."

"That came out wrong," he admitted. "What I meant was that I was sworn to secrecy."

"You were just supposed to be some average guy exploring the world or something?"

"Yes, something like that," he agreed.

"It was how well-educated you seem to be that always had me flummoxed. I mean, no offense, and I wish it weren't so, but a good education is hard to come by."

"You mean expensive. Well, maybe that's something you could remedy when you are queen," he suggested.

"What do you mean?"

"I mean that as queen, you could look into forming some sort of public education system for Aden."

Now there was a thought. Wouldn't that be amazing? "Do you mean teach those who wish to learn or require them to learn?"

"Good question," he said. "There's something to ponder while your wiling away the hours in the clearing."

"You never cease to amaze me, Gwrhyr."

"Hopefully, I never will," he laughed.

"Definitely something to aspire to," she giggled. "But seriously, there's really nothing you can tell me?"

"Let me think about it. Meanwhile, why don't you tell me what it was like growing up as the only child of King Seraphim and Queen Ceridwen. You've complained a lot, but was it really that bad?"

She sighed. "Yes, and no. In many ways it was wonderful, but I think a lot of that was due to the fact that I had Jabberwock. He was definitely my rock. I love my parents, and I know that they love me. It's just that I keep finding out how little I know of the world, and it hurts that they chose not to educate me in things that would have helped me be a better queen. I was more spoiled than I should have been."

"You're learning now," Gwrhyr said.

"I'll say! Although it's almost like drowning. Sometimes I can barely keep my head above the water."

"I think you're managing quite well," he said. "The girl who walked into that inn in Mjijangwa seven months ago is not the same woman who waits patiently in a clearing everyday for a unicorn to arrive."

That brought tears to her eyes, and she was glad that she was riding in front of him at the moment. The path had narrowed as it passed between some fallen boulders. It was nice that he thought so well of her, and she wasn't about to confess that little patience was involved—just sheer determination.

"Thank you," she said. "It's true that I wanted to be such a grown up back then and clearly wasn't."

"Don't be too hard on yourself. The seed was there and it was already sprouting. They say Omni knows our hearts better than we do ourselves. Clearly Omni knew what was in yours, or you wouldn't be holding Dyrnwyn right now."

She glanced down at the sword that almost never left her side these days. "But that's true of you, and of everyone else, as well. Clearly we all have something that Omni desired for this quest." She lapsed into silence again as the path widened and he nudged Ruari alongside her. She wasn't sure just what to tell him about growing up in Castle Mykerinos—it all seemed so dreadfully boring and unimportant now.

A little while later, he changed the subject and they spent the remainder of the day chatting about music and books and the various poets they admired. They were making progress, and he wasn't going to push it.

7ᵀᴴ Meen

Yet another long and boring day ahead, Eluned thought, surveying the now familiar glade that she was rapidly growing to despise. When she was sure that Gwrhyr must be out of range to hear her, Eluned allowed herself to begin weeping uncontrollably. She had been sitting in this clearing for twenty-one days, and she wasn't sure she could take it much longer. And while she didn't count the two days she'd been stuck in her tent due to the rain because that had been a prison of a different nature, she'd actually sat in this clearing on several occasions during a light drizzle. Gwrhyr had lent her his voluminous cloak so she could stay as dry as possible. She needed to be available just in case Nyx happened to show up. And she would never admit to anyone how incredibly miserable those days had been.

And that wonderful day off when she went riding with Gwrhyr felt like an eternity ago. The guilt was the worst, though. She felt an intense amount of guilt over the plight of her fellow Questers. They had been camping in the same spot for twenty-three days; and if that wasn't bad enough, they were doing all the work while she sat in the clearing slowly going insane with boredom.

That was another thing she couldn't complain about—how could she admit to her friends that she was bored to tears when everyone else was working every day. Although she was becoming quite accomplished on the harp, they spent their time taking care of the horses and making sure the animals had enough food; gathering firewood, which now meant they had to chop up blown down trees; and searching for food for themselves by hunting, fishing and gathering.

Bathing meant dousing one's self in the cold waters of the River Leprican most of the time, and the rare hot "bath," which involved both toting and heating water. Clothes and bedding had to be washed occasionally because, frankly, they stayed mostly dirty. It was hard to keep clean when you were so close to the earth. She'd grown quite accustomed to the reek of body odor, and could only imagine what they smelled like to others. Fortunately, there had been no others. Hardaigh Forest truly was isolated and not a sought out destination or major trade path, and less so as late summer waned toward autumn.

She chafed. It continually grated on her that she wasn't there to help her fellow travellers. It hurt deeply that they were building deep connections that she had no part of because she was stuck off in this clearing by herself. She was extremely aware that she had no idea what went on during the day when she wasn't there. Everything always seemed the same when she returned at night—Bonpo was always his cheery self, Jabberwock either poker-faced or grouchy, Gwrhyr . . . well, Gwrhyr had unfailingly walked her back and forth to the little glade each day, and seemed constant in his devotion to her; and Chokhmah and Faolan seemed as much in love as ever. But Yona, what must it be like for her? Eluned was sure she yearned to be on the way and adventuring again, not stuck in camp while her friend was a mile away sitting in a clearing waiting for a unicorn that might never show up.

Eluned sobbed and keened, rocking back and forth as each paroxysm of grief struck her again and again. She finally had to scrabble in her pack to find a handkerchief to soak up the copious fluids she was emitting. That was the worst thing about really crying, she thought. It hurt enough to cry like this, it felt like her heart was rending itself in two, but it was made even more degrading by the tears, snot and drool that were a part of it. She was a mess, and she was so glad Gwrhyr wouldn't return for hours. She couldn't stand him seeing her like this. She'd cried on him enough as it was.

She was still sniffling—sinuses throbbing from the unexpected abuse, eyes swollen and red from the tears—when she heard something, and looked up, bleary eyed, praying to Omni it wasn't Gwrhyr. Had she cried so loudly they'd heard her back at camp? She was suddenly mortified.

Her breath caught in her throat, and she choked back another sob—this time one of exultation. It was Nyx.

The unicorn stood at the edge of the clearing, just a few steps beyond the path she took each day to enter it. Head cocked, and ears twitching, the beautiful beast seemed to be regarding her with caution, and maybe a little bit of tenderness.

Eluned hiccoughed another sob, and whispered, "I've been waiting so long." Then she shook her head, and almost giggled. Picking up Gwrhyr's harp, she placed her fingers on the correct strings, and said. "It's funny. I wanted to learn this tune because I heard from Ziza, Rua and Mérimée that you had exiled yourself here. It's one of my favorite songs of The Advent. But today I realized that I am the one who exiled myself here to wait for you. We've both been in exile."

And she began to strum, and sing in her beautiful contralto, "O Come, O Come Emanuel, and ransom captive Israel. That mourns in lonely exile here." She stopped, and sang again, a cappella, "That mourns in lonely exile here."

Nyx's little goatee nearly dragged the ground. If unicorns cried, she was weeping.

Eluned extended her hand. "Come," she murmured. "You don't have to be in exile any longer."

The Princess was sitting on the ground, back supported by a boulder. Despite her swollen eyes, she could still watch as the unicorn made its way towards her. Nyx was the most beautiful creature she ever laid eyes on. White as snow but also opalescent. Her horn glimmered like pearl. Her hooves were onyx. But her eyes were her most compelling feature. Jabberwock's eyes reflected whatever he was looking at but the unicorn's eyes were mesmerizing. It was as if her eyes bespoke a dimension one could never know—they were all the colors of the rainbow and yet they weren't. They were compassion and love and peace. That's what color they were.

Nyx was finally standing just a foot away, and the Princess opened her arms as if to say, "Come, let us love one another."

And the unicorn, being a unicorn, but scared nonetheless, could do nothing but oblige.

Kneeling down beside her, the unicorn laid her head in Eluned's lap. The Princess gently stroked her forelock, her muzzle, and pulled a stray leaf from her goatee.

"Nyx," she spoke gently. "I'm not here to capture or even hurt you. I want to remove the Halter from your head; the Halter that sent you into exile." And then she proceeded to tell the unicorn everything—from leaving the castle that had been her home for eighteen years to finding herself in this clearing. "It's time," she continued, "to relieve you of this burden, and allow you to be truly free again. We will continue our journey to acquire the remaining treasures—just five left. The most difficult five, but we can do it if you let me take off this halter. Will you let me?"

Nyx lifted her beautiful head, and her horn seemed to glimmer in anticipation. She looked into Eluned's eyes with something close to adulation, and the Princess nearly wept again. She very slowly began to unbuckle the Halter, which actually seemed rather coarse and common on this magnificent creature.

Once unbuckled, she slowly drew it off Nyx's head, and it was almost as if more than a century of weight had been lifted off the creature's shoulders. The Halter was meant to bring the owner whichever horse he or she wished for. A unicorn was not a horse. As far as Eluned was concerned, they were the most magical of the fantastical beings that populated her world. But those beings were rapidly disappearing.

"Nyx?" she asked, placing her hand under her muzzle and lifting it until they were looking into each other's eyes. "How many unicorns still survive in this world?"

The unicorn's eyes dulled with dysphoria.

"Yes, that's what I thought. Why? Why must we destroy what we don't understand?"

It was a rhetorical question, but Nyx sighed audibly.

"Yes, I know. It's what destroyed our world before and will again. Unless we gather these treasures, and let the Thirteen Kingdoms know that they have no choice. That peace wins."

Nyx whickered at this and Eluned hugged her. "I don't want to let you go, and yet I know that you have to be free. I still cannot believe that people once captured unicorns. My heart hurts. It's so wrong. So, be free Nyx. My friends and I, and once I become queen, the inhabitants of my kingdom, are going to change that too, we will never do anything to hurt the few of you I assume that remain."

Nyx neighed her appreciation, and the Princess had one last request. "Can we spend the rest of the day together? Until Gwrhyr gets here this afternoon?"

The unicorn, now halter-less, and feeling hope for the first time in more than a century, nuzzled her.

"Can we do this, Nyx? Can we bring peace to our world?"

Nyx looked at her as if to say, "We are with you. All of us magical creatures."

"Thank you. Did the faery cat find you?"

"Kellas?" It was such a strong thought that if the boulder hadn't been behind her, she might have fallen backwards.

"Kellas? That was his name?"

Nyx whickered.

"Praise Omni for Kellas. He brought you to me."

Nyx whinnied again. It had taken awhile, but it was little cat feet that had to make their way to the unicorn. He had done it. She may have had to wait all that time, but Nyx was here now. The Halter of Clydno Eiddyn lay by her side, not that she could imagine any horse in it, but she didn't know what might happen. Nyx was free. They had another treasure. She should be ecstatic. She was complacent, true, but why didn't she feel like she should be dancing around the clearing? Anticlimax? Still in the throes of depression? She just knew that she wanted to spend the remainder of the day with the unicorn's head in her lap.

AND SHE DID. SHE WAS PERFECTLY CONTENT to just hold the beautiful animal. She even took out her own brush and coaxed the knots from the unicorn's mane and tail, and even her forelock and goatee. She looked dazzling by the time the Princess had finished with her. Her coat glistened like the morning dew, and she had a new light in her eyes.

"For the first time," she informed Nyx, "I'm going to actually hate for Gwrhyr to arrive."

Nyx whickered.

"Yes, I know," Eluned admitted. "I think he loves me. And to be honest, I really like him. Oh, damn it, I can tell you because you won't tell anyone. I am really attracted to him. I tried to deny it, but he really is gorgeous. I just want to run my hand through his hair. And those lips. The way they felt against mine. And I like being with him. He makes me feel safe and loved. He is always there for me, and he doesn't care if I cry on him, or harass him. He's so loyal. The only problem is that I am betrothed to King Uriel." She paused. Nyx waited patiently for her to continue.

"Let's just assume he's a duke," the Princess finally spoke again. "I know that at the very least he's the son of some lord. He certainly hasn't denied it. Anyway, if I told Uriel that I'm . . . can I say this? Can I tell him that I might be falling in love with one of his dukes? I just. Damn. It seems so wrong, so unfair to him. He's the man I've been betrothed to since I was a child, and someone who will strengthen the alliance between our kingdoms. By Omni, why is life so complicated? Should I care that Uriel might be hurt, or should I follow my heart? I'm so confused." She found herself weeping again into the unicorn's mane.

"Take a deep breath," she heard the voice of the unicorn in her head. "You have plenty of time. Take it slowly. Your heart will tell you what is the right thing to do."

"I love you. Thank you for being here for me," she said, unsure whether Nyx could hear her thoughts.

"And thank you for setting me free," Nyx thought in return. "You cannot even begin to imagine what it is like knowing that someone tried to capture you."

"Ummm, actually I can. I've been betrothed to someone I don't know since I was a child. I'm supposed to marry this man I have never met. That feels like I've been trapped in a cage."

"And you know nothing about him?"

"Nothing substantial. Just rumors," the Princess admitted.

"Good rumors or bad rumors?"

The Princess paused for a moment. "The truth is that I have never heard a single bad thing about King Uriel," she said. "Despite the fact he is only twenty-one, he's known to be incredibly responsible and wise. Perhaps losing both his parents by the age of thirteen had some effect on that. Bad behavior might have cost him his kingdom, and having already been allied to Zion through his betrothal to its princess may have increased the burden of responsibility."

"It is a dilemma," the unicorn's voice resounded in her head. "Fortunately, as I said, you have time. Have faith that the correct solution will present itself."

Eluned leaned her head against the boulder musing on what Nyx had just said. Isn't this always what it came back to? Trust. Faith. Had Omni steered her wrong yet? Her eyes flew open. It had suddenly sunk in that the sun no longer warmed her face. What time was it?

"Time to say our farewells," Nyx thought, lifting her head from Eluned's lap. Nyx stood, slowly. They had been on the ground a long time. She shook herself as Eluned used the rock to propel herself to her feet, grimacing as pins and needles of pain shot through her legs.

The Princess hugged the unicorn, and said, "Do you have to remain here, or can you now seek out others of your kind?"

"If there are others of my kind. I have been in Hardaigh so long that I no longer know. But, yes, I intend to look. It is pleasant enough here, but rather lonely."

"I can vouch for that, and I've only been here for a few weeks," Eluned agreed. "Please just stay away from Annewven, Simoon, and Adamah, at a minimum. I don't trust those kings at all."

"Do not worry, my beloved," Nyx thought, nuzzling her neck. "I intend to search the friendly countries first. Now it is time that I must go."

Eluned bit her lip. She didn't want to cry again. "Thank you, Nyx. I will never forget you."

"Good luck on your quest. May Omni be with you." Like Kellas, Nyx departed the clearing by way of the spring, drinking deeply of the clear cold water before disappearing into the woods beyond.

The Princess watched until she could no longer see the

glowing white form that stood out amongst the greens and browns of the forest. Her stomach grumbled, and she realized that she had never taken the time to eat lunch. Too late now. She felt sure Gwrhyr would arrive any minute. Nyx seemed to be as attuned to that as Kellas had been.

She heard the crunch of leaves underfoot, and turned to greet Gwrhyr. It may have only been the seventh of Meen, but autumn was early this year. A number of leaves had already fallen, and the leaves that were still on the trees were rapidly shedding their bright colors and drying up.

"What happened?" Gwrhyr asked when he entered the clearing.

"What do you mean?

"Your face. It's practically glowing," he paused. "Is that . . .?" His gaze was focused on something that lay at her feet.

Eluned looked down. The Halter. She had completely forgotten about it after she'd removed it from Nyx. It didn't look anything like the Halter in King Arawn's tapestry. The Halter that the Princess Morrighan was sliding over Nyx's muzzle in the tapestry was clearly an artist's rendition. It had been golden and jewel encrusted. The actual halter, which Gwrhyr was now picking up, was constructed of well-worn leather, the metal bits looked like they must be iron because they were thoroughly rusted.

The Princess giggled.

"What's so funny?"

"That is what I have been sitting in this clearing for three weeks for. Look at it."

"I'll admit I was expecting something a little more impressive," he held it up in the fading light.

"Did you see the one in the tapestry?"

"At Castle Pwyll? Yes, briefly, when I was walking past the dining room with Captain Bleddyn one day. I didn't get a chance to study it, but I seem to remember it was gold."

Eluned slung her backpack over a shoulder, picked up the

sword she had never practiced with, and the harp she had only briefly played for Nyx, and started moving toward the trail.

"I'll carry that," Gwrhyr took the harp from her hand.

"Thanks. You know, I guess it's possible that there was a time that the Halter was embossed with gold, and it may have had jewels, as well. Nyx has been wearing it for more than a century."

"But would you use iron buckles and rings on a golden halter?"

"Good point. Well, I think it's a good thing that it's so plain. It certainly doesn't look like the kind of thing one might want to steal. As a matter, of fact, we can hide it in plain sight," Eluned suggested.

"How so?"

"Derry. Who's going to look for a magical halter on a donkey?"

THERE WAS CELEBRATING AT THE CAMP that night, and Bonpo brought out a cask he'd set aside for commemorating this moment.

"What is it?" Eluned asked when he carried it out to the campfire.

"It vely old cognac," he said. "I swipe from Alawn's cellar in Alberth."

"What?" Eluned was shocked, but began laughing hysterically. "You always surprise me, Bonpo. I wish you had taken several after the way he talked about you when you disappeared."

"Not vely kind, 'uh?"

"He called you a traitor because you resettled in Zion," Eluned said.

"Well, we arr know 'e not vely nice king."

"Yes, we do, so let's toast to the fact that we now have eight of the thirteen treasures," Eluned said.

Even knowing that it might take a day or two to transition

the camp back to nature, and begin the next step in the journey, everyone remained in high spirits. Gwrhyr and Faolan parceled out chores for the following day—everything from filling in the latrines to tearing down the fences that had corralled the horses. And they discussed, but only briefly because there really wasn't much choice, where they might travel to next.

It would have to be Naphtali, Eluned thought. It was a neutral kingdom, but they actually had a chance of gaining an audience with Queen Njima. The Crock and Dish of Rhyngenydd the Cleric was said to be in Naphtali. That would be a fun treasure to have, she mused, as the containers would fill with whatever food was wished for.

Whether the queen was in possession of it, none of them knew. What they did know was that the remaining treasures were either in one of the kingdoms in the Awen Alliance, or the Devastation of Pelf. None of which they felt compelled, at this moment, to pursue.

At this point, it was also the easiest kingdom to travel to, as well. They need only take the path northward from the river ford to Aden, and then pass through Aden, which bordered Naphtali to the south.

"I'M SO EXCITED," Yona said, as they got ready for bed. "I may actually get to meet Queen Njima."

"Oh, you'll definitely meet her, or we won't meet her at all," Eluned pulled on her sleep shirt.

"What do you mean?"

"Just that we are a team now," the Princess tried to explain. "And, I know I'm saying this despite the fact I just spent nearly a month sitting in a clearing by myself, but I'm tired of all the games we've had to play, and honestly, we may have to play them again. I imagine we will have to break into smaller groups to find the remainder of the treasures.

"There's no way I can go to Simoon, for example," she continued. "Nor can you. If King Hamartia heard or saw us, we'd be recognized immediately. But, I don't see why we can't go to Queen Njima as who we are, and just state our case."

"What if she refuses?"

"I just have a feeling that she's going to want to meet this group of people who caused so much havoc in Annewven, and the woman who turned down King Hevel and stole his treasure."

Yona laughed. "The Great Deception. I prefer the word 'appropriate' rather than stole, though," she laughed again. "Even though I did steal the thing. It is also true that that is something Queen Njima and I hold in common. Turning down the men we were betrothed to. Maybe that's one of the reasons I am looking forward to meeting her."

9ᵀᴴ Meen

Everyone worked hard on the day after Eluned met Nyx to return the camp as much as possible to its original appearance—difficult because they'd been there nearly a month, but not impossible if they did it right. Once they were on their way, it wouldn't take long for nature to cover the signs of their disturbance as the trees littered the area with their fallen leaves, and the next spring's growth erased what little damage remained.

They started out about mid-morning on the ninth after seeing to last minute details, such as making sure the fire, which had been burning nearly non-stop for weeks, was thoroughly doused and buried. And everything went swimmingly until late afternoon when they were stopped in their tracks by a colossal landslide that completely covered the trail.

Massive boulders and tons of earth had effectively built a wall more than eight feet high across the path and into the woods. It was far too precarious and steep to attempt to climb over, particularly on horseback.

Faolan offered to shift, and survey the option of riding around the damage through the woods as it was clearly out of the question to attempt crossing by ascending the rocky slopes of The Seven Sisters.

So they waited for Faolan to return, murmuring in dismay at this stroke of bad luck.

After pondering the situation for a few minutes, Eluned broke the silence with laughter.

"I know I say this a lot," said Gwrhyr, "but what's so funny?"

"I'm laughing at myself, actually," she replied, "and at my outrage that we've been delayed. But think about it and all we went through to get to Favonia. Now think about all the bad things that have happened since then."

One by one everyone started to nod. The truth was it had been pretty smooth sailing since they reached Seemu in the Phaeton. They had managed to gather three more treasures with nothing more than a few scares for Yona, and a great deal of boredom for the Princess, particularly. That seemed a very small price to pay considering near death had been the price for the Phaeton and Chessboard.

"Maybe this," Chokhmah indicated the landslide, "is a reminder that we should slow down."

"I agree," said Jabberwock. "We do have a tendency to chomp at the bit."

"Can I ask why the three years for the Princess?" Gwrhyr wondered aloud. "I'm aware that she has to marry King Uriel in three years, but why take that entire time out in the world?"

Eluned shook her head. "Don't look at me. I didn't arrange it, and naturally I agreed. It was an adventure."

Everyone turned to look at the Bandersnatch, who shifted uncomfortably in his basket atop Derry's back.

"It was the number I was given," he explained, lamely. "I guess I assumed it would take longer . . ."

"You mean you knew we were supposed to be gathering the treasures?" Eluned interrupted. "You told me you didn't know."

"You needed to discover it on your own," Jabberwock sounded apologetic.

"What if I hadn't?" Eluned asked.

"Then it wouldn't have been meant to be." The Bandersnatch admitted, "but I promise you that I did not put that book in the library at the Trade Route Inn nor did I have anything to do with Aeron seeking you out."

"Did you know we'd run into Bonpo or anyone else?" Eluned continued to press him.

"The barrow wight was not my doing, either," he avoided directly answering her question. "I was only responsible for getting you out of Castle Mykerinos, and making sure your father presented you with the Ring."

"There is one thing we haven't accounted for," Yona said as a chill breeze ruffled manes and hair. "Time-wise, that is."

"What's that?" asked Gwrhyr.

"Which direction are we heading?" she prodded.

"North, of course," he said.

"And what time of year is it?" Yona continued.

A gust of wind rattled loose some of the stones in the landslide where they tumbled to the ground at their horses' feet as if to emphasize where Yona was trying to lead them.

Eluned groaned. "Winter is coming. The autumnal equinox is fast approaching, and it won't be long until it's going to be just too cold to travel." She was remembering the miserable trip to Sheba that had been toward the end of the previous winter.

"You're correct, Yona," Jabberwock confirmed. "We're going to have to come up with a plan. But we still have a good month or so until we have to do that, so I say let's concentrate on getting to Naphtali and finding the Crock and Dish; then we can worry about what we're going to do to wait out winter."

A skittering of rocks caught their attention, and they looked around to see Faolan emerging from the forest, shaking his head.

It was Chokhmah's turn to groan. "What is it, my love?"

"It's possible, but it's going to be slow going, and a little bit hazardous," he said. "The landslide pushed its way maybe a quarter of a mile into the woods, so not too bad, distance-wise. Unfortunately, it ends at a boggy area, and that's going to be somewhat treacherous to make our way through while on horseback. We're going to have to lead the horses, and Jabberwock, along with myself in wolf form, will have to pick out the path. I don't see any other way. Bonpo is also going to have to be particularly careful.

"One more thing," he continued. "Because it's so late in the afternoon, and it's already starting to get hard to see under the trees, I would recommend that we camp here tonight, and attempt to get around the slide tomorrow morning."

Everyone looked at the ground around the landslide. It was pretty rocky. But they all dismounted because riding back the way they'd come wasn't an option as it felt like a step backwards. The group decided to split up chores—Eluned, Chokhmah and Yona scavenged the area for firewood while Bonpo, Gwrhyr and Faolan moved stones so they would have a flat place in which to set up their tents. Tonight the tents would be closer together than usual because they would have to be set up on one side of the fire, and the landslide used as a protective wall on the other. Stones were piled in two lines perpendicular to the wall to form a makeshift stall for the horses. Even Jabberwock did his best to help out by scrounging up enough kindling to start the fire.

As soon as the sun was high enough in the sky to be seen beneath the trees, the Questers began the task of making their way around the landslide.

"Keep an eye out for two sturdy logs," Faolan suggested. "We could use them to help us over particularly bad patches."

"Bog bridges?" Gwrhyr asked.

"Exactly." Faolan said. "Now I need to go shift. Can you take my clothes, Chokhmah?"

She followed him behind some denser brush and soon returned carrying his belongings. "He will not be able to return for them," she explained.

Gwrhyr offered to lead both Ruari and Fiachdubh, but Chokhmah informed him, as Faolan reappeared from the forest in wolf form, that Faolan's stallion had been trained to follow him when he was a wolf.

It was a long and arduous process. The company agreed that Bonpo would go first as his greater stride and strength might be necessary should someone, horse or human, need to be pulled from the muck. Also, it was felt that if he could make it through the fen without getting stuck, the rest could surely follow in his footsteps, particularly the horses whose hooves couldn't cling to the tree trunks Bonpo was carrying.

There were a few close calls—once with Bonpo, himself, when he felt his foot being sucked into the mud and pulled it loose, returning to where he had been standing. Faolan tried a slightly narrower stride with no luck, and then jumped to test one slightly larger, and Bonpo was able to step over the bad patch. But it meant the rest had to use the puncheons, and the horses had to be coaxed into jumping the distance by a sound slap on their flanks. Aine stumbled upon landing, left hind hoof sinking into the swampy ground, but Bonpo was there to grab her reins and physically haul her to a solid spot.

Finally, well after the sun had reached its midpoint, they made it to higher and much more solid ground, as the trail on the northern side of the landslide came into view.

While Bonpo pulled out a quick snack to get them through until dinner, Chokhmah hurried back into the woods to bring Faolan his clothes.

When he returned as human, everyone began to clap.

"We couldn't have done it without you, brother." Gwrhyr shook his friend's hand.

"He's right," Jabberwock said. "My weight wasn't signifi-cant enough to determine just how bad some of those areas were."

Eluned and Yona beamed at him, and Chokhmah kissed his cheek. "See, your hunch that you needed to be a part of this quest has been proven correct yet again."

"Thank you," he said, voice choked. "I hope I'll be able to continue to prove myself."

The rations they had brought along with them were rap-idly diminishing now that they no longer had fresh reserves to draw from. And, as autumn approached, there were less and less fresh foods to gather as well. They snacked on pemmican and prayed to Omni that they would reach the border town of Batum in Aden without too many more delays.

"It's actually more of a hamlet," Gwrhyr warned them, "but we should still be able to pick up some supplies there."

Eluned stood up and stretched. "Let's go. I want to get as far away from this slide as possible before nightfall."

"Seriously," Yona agreed. "We spent most of the day get-ting what, less than half a mile down the road?"

"Maybe even less," Gwrhyr noted, as they got back on their horses and started riding northward again.

Fortunately, they encountered no more obstacles for the remainder of the afternoon, and were able to stop before sunset in an area that had clearly been used before as a camp.

"Been a rong time, do," Bonpo noted.

It was true that the area was flat and boulderless, but the ashes in the fire pit had long since been washed away.

"At least that means there's probably plenty of downed wood." Eluned, choosing to be optimistic, said over her shoul-der as she headed towards the forest. She soon returned with an armload, and good news. "I found a small brook in the woods so at least there's fresh water available."

"Probably the reason this area was chosen as a site," Jabberwock reflected. "Was there a path to it?"

"Yes, I was following a path I found," she said. "Experience says that in Hardaigh Forest that's the safe way to go."

"Can't argue with that," the Bandersnatch agreed.

As she turned to make another trip for firewood, she noticed that once again Gwrhyr was setting up his tent adjacent to hers. It no longer annoyed her that he felt so compelled to protect her even though they hadn't had much time for serious conversation since their horseback ride nearly two weeks ago. But, that was fine, she decided. Nyx had said she had time, that she should follow her heart. So she would take things slowly, and try to listen to what her heart told her. And at the moment, it told her that it was fine that Gwrhyr wanted to protect her. It would be nice, though, if they could spend some time alone again.

THEY STUMBLED INTO BATUM just after sunset two days later. They were ravenous with hunger—their rations consisting only of pemmican at this point. Even Faolan in wolf form had managed to capture little more than a small rodent each day.

"Please, please, please tell me that there is somewhere in this little village that can provide us with some food," Eluned begged.

The little village was as small as Gwrhyr had said it was.

"Wait here," he told them. "Let me go talk to a few people." He dismounted, handed Eluned his reins because he'd been riding next to her, and went off to see what was available. It made sense that he do the asking, she thought. He was the one from the Kingdom of Aden, and was apparently well acquainted with its king.

He returned about ten minutes later, retrieved his reins from the Princess, and said, "Follow me."

It was just a short ride down the hard-packed dirt road

to a long low building where three teenagers, a male and two females, waited to take their horses.

They dismounted, retrieving their bedrolls, and the items they needed from their saddlebags, and followed Gwrhyr into the building.

"It's really more of a gathering place," Gwrhyr explained when they entered the wide, open space, which featured a large central fireplace. Long tables with benches had been pushed back toward the walls so that there was room around the fireplace.

"We're going to have to sleep on the floor tonight," he said, apologetically. "They don't get many travellers here, and can usually offer hospitality in their homes if it is needed. I didn't want to break up the group, nor put an extra burden on them."

Everyone murmured their agreement. Staying together was a priority.

"But they have offered to prepare us a meal, and help us pull together enough food to get us to Ponike. From there we can travel northward on the main road to Naphtali."

Eluned's ears had perked at the mention of Ponike. The coastal capital of Aden was where King Uriel's castle, Bennu, was located. In less than three years she would be living there.

"Will I be able to see Castle Bennu?" she asked him.

"You can't miss it," Gwrhyr informed her. "It's on a high bluff overlooking the harbor in the Gulf of Eudaemon." He studied her for a minute. "Curious about your future home?"

The Princess blushed, but nodded. "It seems fair to know where I might be spending a portion of my life."

"Portion?"

"I assume that when my parents die, King Uriel and I will have to divide our time between Castle Mykerinos and Castle Benno." She paused. Her parents weren't that old. "Although I guess it's always possible that we'll have a child old enough to send there by that point." She looked stricken.

"That hard to imagine?" Gwrhyr asked.

"I just can't imagine being a mother yet. Eighteen seems too young."

"You're not getting married until you're twenty-one," he reminded her. "I wouldn't worry about it until then."

"True," she smiled at him. "I have plenty of time." She looked around. "Now where do I want to put my bedroll?"

"Next to mine," Gwrhyr said sotto voce.

Eluned guffawed, and punched him in the bicep. "You wish!" But, it turned out that was just where she ended up—flanked by Yona to her right and Gwrhyr to her left because apparently he was never going to miss a chance to be by her side.

The Princess had just finished spreading out her blankets when the food appeared. It was modest fare, but at this point she would eat just about anything. Platters of roasted chicken baked in olive oil and spices were served with huge bowls of plain rice, including a simple gravy of olive oil, butter, spices and chicken broth along with crisp green beans with slivered toasted almonds. It was a feast as far as she was concerned, and it didn't take her long to fill her belly. They washed the food down with a chilled, dry white wine. The result was a pleasant drowsiness.

"Feeling better?" Gwrhyr asked after Eluned had pushed her plate away and leaned her head against his left shoulder. He always tried to sit to her right, if possible, because she was left-handed.

"Mmmmhmmm," she murmured as he put his arm around her narrow shoulders. He was often surprised that someone so small could be so strong. She continually amazed him with her fortitude and stamina. "It's exactly what I needed," she yawned. "I might actually survive."

He leaned his cheek against the top of her head. "I think we all may," he said, but he was very aware of the warmth of her body against his. They were all "rode hard and put up wet," as his father used to say, but he reveled in the fact that the Princess Eluned could easily go from the exotic beauty who had brought nearly every man to his knees the night she wore that black velvet gown to King Arawn's dinner party to the dirty-haired and mud-smeared woman wearing trousers at his side. She was no prima donna. The truth was, she was going to make an excellent queen.

What he'd never told her, or anyone else for that matter, is that he had been there that night when she'd been escorted to the party by the young page. It wasn't that he was spying on her, per se, as much as he had an insatiable need to see her in that dress. She had been so distraught about wearing it that he couldn't bear the thought of Arawn and his friends seeing her in a dress that revealing before he did.

And she had taken his breath away that night in Prythew as well. Gwrhyr had been aware of her beauty since the night she, Jabberwock, and Bonpo had stumbled into the inn in Mji-jangwa. But he'd allowed jealousy, among other things, to color his perception of her. When he had seen her walking down that hallway, chin raised in determination, confronting the task ahead of her with courage despite the fact her inherent modesty demanded otherwise, his love for her was sealed. At that point he had resolved that nothing, man or beast, would ever come between him and the Princess.

That's why Irirangi had been such a shock at first, but Chokhmah convinced him that it was nothing more than a passing infatuation. The Princess was too intelligent and inde-pendent, she had told him, not to eventually recognize that the Prince was essentially a misogynist, and that her dedication to the Quest would win out in the end. As per usual, the gypsy had been correct.

Now here they were, all these months later, leaning con-tentedly against each other. When was the last time they had fought? He wasn't sure he could remember. There had been plenty of teasing, but their last real fight might have been the night she'd stomped off into the darkness only to return with Dyrnwyn hours later. No, he corrected himself, it was on Favonia—the last time he kissed her. He was sure they would fight again. It was inevitable. He only hoped that they would recover and move on.

As it was, it was time to settle down for the night. They would, no doubt get a late start the following day because they would have to scrape together enough supplies to make the four-day or so trip to Ponike. Once in the bigger city, they could easily find rooms at an inn and take a couple, or even a few days for a well-deserved break.

The following morning, Faolan put himself in charge of securing feed for the horses. They'd long since run out of oats and hay, and they'd been subsisting mostly on grasses for a little while now. Chokhmah walked with him to the stables, and with Gwrhyr and Bonpo off seeking rations for the humans, Yona and Eluned were left to their own devices.

"I feel like I should be doing something," the Princess groused to the Bandersnatch who was trying to nap by the fire.

"I can think of numerous things you could be doing," Jabberwock said. "Journaling for one. When was the last time the two of you wrote in your journals?"

They surveyed him, guiltily.

"As I suspected. And, of course, you could be practicing the harp before you forget what Gwrhyr's taught you, or you could begin teaching Yona some moves with a sword. Are you trained in swordplay, Yona?"

"I have a dagger," she said. "I bought it in Hagafen. I could practice with it."

"Or you can take a walk around the village," he suggested, "but don't stray too far if you do as we want to leave as soon as we've acquired what we need."

None of the options thrilled her. She wouldn't mind reading but she'd finished the books she'd brought from Favonia on *The Queen of the May*, and had neglected to pick up another in Thírnagall. But Jabberwock was right—there was plenty she could be doing. "Journals?" she asked Yona. Those would be the most difficult to catch up if they left them too long.

"Journaling, it is," Yona agreed with a sigh. They were soon settled quietly at one of the long tables, and Jabberwock returned to his dozing.

THEY MANAGED TO GET OUT OF BATUM shortly after noon, and made decent time the rest of the day, stopping and setting up camp an hour before sunset. They had decided that unless circumstances called for it, they would no longer push themselves to the point of exhaustion.

"As a matter of fact," Gwrhyr said about an hour after they'd left Batum, "after we reach Naphtali it might behoove us to take a little time before we venture into enemy terrain."

"You mean if we stay out of sight for a while, they might lower their defenses a bit?" Eluned asked.

Gwrhyr nodded approvingly. "Exactly."

"So, we'll be spending the winter in Naphtali?" Yona asked.

"That will depend on how soon we can garner the Crock and Dish," Jabberwock spoke up.

"In other words, it depends on how amenable Queen Njima is to helping us?" Yona said.

"That will have a lot to do with it," Gwrhyr admitted.

FOUR DAYS LATER THEY WERE SETTING UP CAMP in their final site before reaching Ponike. If they had pushed on another two to three hours, they would have arrived after the gates were shut for the night.

"It would be a risk to camp any closer," Gwrhyr told them. "I'd like to think that this kingdom, as it's my home, is safe everywhere. But the truth is that no kingdom is without its bad element, and there are those who like to prey on the unlucky travellers who don't make it into the city in time. I prefer to play it safe at this point."

Everyone agreed. Why needlessly put themselves in harm's way when they were sure to face their own share of danger in the future?

17ᵀᴴ Meen

The seven of them passed through the city gates into Ponike about eleven o'clock the next morning.

"You're the expert, Gwrhyr," Eluned turned to look at him, riding to her right. "Where's the best place to lodge for a few days?"

"It depends on what we're looking for," he said. "Lodging runs the gamut from fleatrap to relatively luxurious."

Eluned looked around at her friends. She was aware that they really didn't have any money, but she also knew that they could sure use a little pampering about now. It had been more than forty days since they'd slept in an actual bed or taken a real bath. She glanced at Jabberwock, and he nodded. King Seraphim would take care of this. "I vote for luxury. I think we could all use a few days in real beds, and have the ability to take a decent bath, eat good food, and drink exceptional wine. Am I forgetting anything? I'm sure my father won't begrudge us a few days stay in a nice inn." She turned to Gwrhyr. "That makes sense, doesn't it?"

"Absolutely. The Scarlet Phoenix it is then. Follow me."

They wound through several streets until they reached the eastern edge of the harbor. As they emerged out of the shadows of the several-storied buildings that lined the avenue through which they passed, Eluned drew in her breath. There it was, perched high above Ponike—Castle Bennu—her future home. The polished grey and white granite edifice sparkled in the morning light. Golden banners bearing the Crimson Phoenix that was the sigil of the kingdom hung from each tower and trembled in the slight breeze.

"It's impressive, isn't it," Gwrhyr stated, reining in Ruari when he noticed the Princess stopping.

"It is definitely breathtaking," Eluned agreed.

Castle Mykerinos was beautiful, but not quite as imposing. The castle she grew up in was situated atop a twenty-eight-acre plateau above the River Musk so it was like most castles in that it was visible from the surrounding countryside. The plateau wasn't that high, only about five hundred feet above the valley from which it rose. The castle was constructed of white limestone, which was lovely, but not as impressive as the granite that glittered from the towers of Castle Bennu, which looked to be a good thousand feet or so above the harbor town below it.

"Is Uriel in residence at the moment?" she asked, her stomach twisting in trepidation that the answer would be affirmative.

"Why?" Gwrhyr asked. "Do you want to meet him?"

It occurred to her that Gwrhyr could probably arrange that, and she looked stricken. Did she really want to be introduced to her betrothed by the man with whom she was falling in love? She looked at Gwrhyr, eyes wide. "I'm not sure I'm ready for that," she whispered.

"Fair enough," he said, letting it go without another word. "The inn is on the other side of the harbor. We continue this way." Secretly, he was relieved. That could have been very awkward. "If you're worried about meeting him," he said to Eluned who rode by his side, "perhaps I should make the arrangements at The Scarlet Phoenix. Otherwise, it might come to his attention . . ." He didn't need to finish the sentence. Eluned was already speaking in a rush of gratitude.

"Oh could you? I'd be so grateful. I'm sure my father will see that the bill is paid."

"Not a problem," Gwrhyr smiled. "Besides, I do have some connections. So, rooms? Do you and Yona want to share?"

"I'm fine with it," She looked back over her shoulder. Yona was riding just behind her. "You okay with sharing a room or would you prefer your own?"

"Sharing's fine. It'll be nice to be back in a room where I can sleep on a mattress, and not sleeping in a tent on the ground. It will be like we're back at Castle Prythew."

Eluned grimaced, and Yona hurried to say, "Before we went to Arberth, that is."

"Those were some nice days, weren't they? Eluned smiled, remembering.

"The calm before the storm," Gwrhyr muttered.

"Thank Omni we are far, far from that place now," she reached out a hand to him, and he squeezed it.

It took another quarter of an hour to make it to the western side of the harbor, and a little over five minutes past that to arrive at the inn. Eluned once again held Ruari while Gwrhyr went inside to make arrangements.

He really excelled at it, she thought, remembering how he'd come to their rescue at the Trade Route Inn. She had been exhausted and on the verge of tears at that point, not to mention the fact she had still been a spoiled brat. Between the Mountains of Misericord and meeting Gwrhyr, she'd begun her education of what it was like to be a normal human. Of course, she thought, surveying her friends as they waited, were any of them normal? What was normal anyway? Everyone was who they were, and she loved them for it. The Princess didn't think the Eluned of almost seven months ago would feel that way.

Gwrhyr soon returned with their keys. Keys! When was the last time they had stayed somewhere with keys to their rooms? They grabbed the things they needed from their saddlebags, and handed off their horses and Derry to the inn's groomsmen before trudging up the steps to their lodgings.

It wasn't until she walked inside that the Princess realized what a truly opulent accommodation they were entering. She hoped her father wouldn't be too angry about footing the bill. 'Relatively luxurious', Gwrhyr had said. Was he kidding? What was the word she'd read in her great-grandmother's romance novels? Posh. Yes, this place was definitely posh.

"This is even nicer than the Lord Mayor's home," Yona whispered in her ear.

And it was magnificent—exquisitely carved dark wood walls were covered with beautifully embroidered wall hangings. The walls were offset by a fresco-painted ceiling, sumptuous carpets on the marble floors, crystal chandeliers, shining brass oil lamps, and more. Eluned had a hard time taking it all in, particularly as she was now acutely aware that she smelled, and that she was dressed in mud-spattered leather trousers. For the first time in a while, she longed to put on one of her dresses after she bathed.

The Princess glanced at Yona. She was also aware that Yona had only her riding skirt and blouse in addition to her trousers and cotton sweaters. Eluned immediately began making a mental inventory of what she had with her that Yona might borrow for that evening. Chokhmah, she knew, still had at least one or two skirts and blouses with her so she was taken care of, but they would be expected to be dressed for dinner.

Because of the way in which they were travelling, their wardrobes were limited. Eluned was sure that they were all, including Gwrhyr, ill-prepared for dressing up as it was impossible to carry clothing for every possible contingency in their saddle bags. The Princess decided that she could offer Yona the gypsy skirt and blouse that had belonged to Chokhmah's grandmother as the outfit was just a bit large for her, especially as they had all lost a little weight since leaving Bogaine. The various tones of green would look good on her. She could wear the lavender undershirt and sea green brocade dress that had been fitted to her in Arberth. Otherwise, there was only the white cotton skirt remaining.

The inn had three stories and they were on the second floor—Room 228 the key said. Eluned opened the door and swung it open and they stared in genuine admiration for a full minute before stepping inside. She wanted to cry. Did Gwrhyr somehow know to get this specifically for her? No, he couldn't have.

A large canopied bed filled one wall and the colors of the bedclothes were very similar to those on her bed at home, and she remembered, Castle Pwyll, as well. Everything was in tones of lavender, sea green, and pink—her colors. Opposite the bed, a large fireplace warmed the room, and a small sofa and two armchairs along with a small table were settled in front of it.

The wall opposite from the doorway featured several large windows, light filtered by diaphanous curtains of lavender. The walls were covered in white-flocked rose pink wallpaper. To the left, just past the fireplace, a door led to what was no doubt the bathroom. On the wall to the right, between the bed and the windows, was a large armoire.

By Omni, let my father forgive this expense, Eluned prayed, because this room is sheer perfection.

"It's more beautiful than the room in Castle Pwyll, if that's possible," Yona said.

Eluned stepped into the room, laid her tapestry bag on the floor, and walked to windows. She always had to check out the view before she could settle into her room. Yona joined her and they gazed for a while at the lovely view of the harbor—

ships at anchor, ships out in the Gulf of Eudaemon, people rushing by on the street below. It felt so peculiar to be back in the bustle of city life. It had been months. For a moment she felt incredibly alive, and then her heart quelled. She thought she could make this her home with Gwrhyr, but could it be her home with Uriel?

Yona had already checked out the bathroom, and started running a tub of hot water. "You're first," she told Eluned, "but I figured, why not get things started."

"Why me first?" the Princess asked, genuinely puzzled.

"I love you," Yona hugged her. "You're first because of this," she spread her hands to indicate the room.

Eluned hugged her back. "Okay, but we might want to see if we can get a few things pressed for tonight. Try these on while I'm bathing," she said pulling the green skirt and blouse from her tapestry bag. "If they fit, you can wear them tonight." She withdrew to the bathroom where she gratefully shed her road-begrimed clothes.

Stepping into the hot water of the bath, all her burdens just slipped away. She felt like the cares of the world drifted off her shoulders, and as the water grew cool she allowed them to slide down the drain.

"Your turn," she told Yona as she emerged drying her hair on a towel in a robe provided by the hotel. "My advice. Let your worries go. By Omni, you will feel so much better. But," she giggled, "I had to scrub the dirt ring before I got out of there. I knew I was dirty, but I had no idea I was that filthy!"

Eluned had already started the bath for her, so Yona told her that the skirt and blouse, though a little short, would serve her fine that night. "I held them up to me because I didn't want to soil them," she explained.

"I'm sorry," the Princess apologized. "We'll go out this afternoon or tomorrow and find something that fits perfectly."

"Darling," Yona kissed her on the forehead. "I would die

for you. Do you know how much it means to me that you worry about me?"

Eluned just looked at her, bemused.

"No. You don't. And that's what makes you, mind my vulgarity, so kusemmak wonderful."

"Kusemmak? Is that a pirate word?"

"It's definitely one you hear often on the docks in Seagirt." Yona laughed before traipsing off to the bath shedding dirty clothes as Eluned giggled.

As soon as Yona was settled in the tub, Eluned began to worry. When were they to meet up again? She didn't remember any time being set nor whether they had formed any plans. What room did Gwrhyr say he was in? 208? She hoped so. She'd hate to knock on the wrong door. She called out to Yona that she'd be right back and left the room.

She tread down the hall, wet haired and bath-robed. She knew Gwrhyr would forgive her. He'd certainly seen her a lot worse. After turning the wrong direction first, she finally found 208 and knocked.

Gwrhyr answered the door about thirty seconds later, wet and with a towel around his waist.

"I was expecting Jabberwock," he said, lamely, when he realized it was the Princess standing before him.

"Damn, I . . ." she said before words failed her. But he looked really good, and somehow she'd managed to insinuate with that first word that his nearly naked torso had actually impressed her more than she might care to admit.

"Honestly," he conceded, reaching out a hand to touch her wet curls, "it looks like we're in the same predicament. Come on in."

He, too, had a nice room—a smaller bed and fireplace because he was alone, but more earthy colors—blues and browns.

"Suddenly I can't remember why I'm here." She sat down on the love seat in front of the fireplace. Her knees felt like jelly. It was as if seeing him barely covered had shut down all rational thought in her brain. "Oh yes," she forced herself to remember, "Yona and I were wondering if we were going to meet up again today or just fend for ourselves."

"What do you want?" he said, sitting down beside her.

"I want you to put on a robe, at least," she choked. "Sorry, you just look . . ."

"Yes," he stared into her eyes.

She stared back. She wanted desperately to kiss him. All at once she realized that she wanted him more than she ever dreamed possible.

He leaned toward her. "Yes?"

She couldn't stop herself. She moved towards him, and he pulled her into his arms. And then they were kissing, and she never wanted to stop.

But finally she pulled back with a hand against his chest, murmuring "stop, stop."

And, of course, he did.

"I can't," she said. "I can't be unfaithful to King Uriel. Damn. What am I going to do?"

He pulled her close again. "We'll work this out," is all he could think to say. But at that moment all he wanted was to be one with her. And yet, and yet, he greatly admired her self-control—because she was betrothed, and she would only go so far to dishonor that.

"You do know it's not you," she said, looking into his eyes, "it's just . . ."

"I understand," he said, kissing her again. "I do. It might take a while but we'll figure this out."

Damn, he thought, this was a problem he'd never account-ed for. Something was going to have to change. Meanwhile, he'd have to be content with her kisses. Although he thought he could probably live with that for the time being.

"So," she whispered in a half laugh, "what are the plans?"

"First, you have to promise you won't back away from me," he murmured. "I can control myself, but not if you pull away from me. I don't think I can stand that."

"No, never," she promised. "But I can only risk going so far."

"I understand, but you're not going to act like you hate me tomorrow, are you?"

"No! Never!" she said again. "I just want to be with you."

"Okay," he repeated. "We'll figure this out. It may take a while, but we will. And I forgot to say earlier, you don't have to worry about the king. I learned that the he is not currently in residence. He's on a diplomatic mission to, ummm, Tarshish, I think."

"Good," said Eluned, "then we really don't have to worry yet." She kissed him again because his lips felt so wonderful. "You never told me if there are any plans," she said when she pulled away from him again.

"I thought this was our plan," he tried to kiss her again. He'd waited so long for this.

"That would be nice," she laughed, and forced her self off the sofa, "but Yona must be wondering what happened to me, and I'm getting hungry." It had to be well after noon by this point, she thought, and as if on cue, she heard a church bell somewhere toll the hour of one.

"I can come by your room in . . .?" he waited for her suggestion.

Would their clothes have been pressed yet? Probably not. She'd just have to wear wrinkled clothing. In that case, "Fifteen minutes?"

She turned toward the door. She could easily spend the rest of the day alone with him, but that wouldn't be fair to Yona. With one last kiss, she departed.

He watched her walk away for a second before shutting the door. What he'd desired since he'd met her had finally come true, and with it a host of complications. He would enjoy the victory for the mean time, but at some point he would have to face the problems that had arisen. What was most important was that he loved her, and despite the fact neither of them had spoken the words, he knew the same held true for her.

"Where have you been?" Yona asked when Eluned finally returned to the room.

"I got distracted by Gwrhyr," she admitted.

"Distracted, huh?"

"Oh Yona," she cried, collapsing into an armchair, covering her face with her hands, "he came to the door wearing nothing but a towel."

Yona snorted with laughter. "And you in a bathrobe! How far did things go?"

"We only kissed. I can't go farther until I break my betrothal, and I am still not certain I can do that."

Yona sat down on the couch, and took Eluned's hands. "Let me just say, and don't be embarrassed or angry or taken aback, that we've all been waiting for this to happen. I could tell he was in love with you the first time I met him. I just didn't expect it to take you so long to figure out that you felt the same way."

"Really?" Eluned couldn't help but look mortified. "It was that obvious?"

"Faolan's not the only one who is an open book," she smiled. "I'm going to blame it on inexperience. You had preconceived notions of what love should be, and it took a while to get past that."

Eluned sighed and stood up. "We have to get dressed. He'll be here soon to take us to get some food."

Yona stood as well. She was dressed in her riding skirt and blouse already. "They came by to get our evening wear to press, and took our dirty clothing with them."

Eluned rolled her eyes. Of course they did. She guessed she'd be wearing the white cotton skirt and blouse she'd left Castle Mykerinos with. She hadn't worn them since she'd left Annewven. They were a painful reminder of the past, and she wasn't sure why she'd hung onto them. She'd wear them one last time for old time's sake, and get something newer and more grown up after she ate. That went for shoes, as well. The suede boots she had worn when she and Jabberwock had started on the journey were the suede boots she was still wearing, and they had done a lot of walking since then. They were really decrepit at this point, embarrassingly so.

It didn't stand out when she was on the trail, but it would here. She needed new boots at the very least, and perhaps an inexpensive pair of flats to wear whenever they ventured into a town on the way to Jazeel, where Queen Njima resided. She still had the nice pair that matched her brocade dress, but they were too nice for everyday wear.

She was pulling her hair back into a ponytail when Gwrhyr rapped on the door. Yona opened it, and he stepped inside, and laughed out loud when he saw the Princess.

"What?" she asked, eyes wide, lower lip extended in a faux pout. She was trying really hard not to laugh herself.

"Come here," he said, but he was walking toward her. He pulled her into his arms, shaking his head. "You look so much like the school girl I met seven months ago, and yet," he tipped her chin with his forefinger, "you're not the same at all."

The Princess became serious. "Thank you. That means a lot to me." There's something about taking a human life that changes you forever, she thought.

He kissed her forehead. "Now you're Fy Drysor."

Eluned pulled away from him to look up into his face. "What does that mean?"

"It means you're my treasure." He kissed the tip of her nose. "It's the language of the Hallowed Treasures."

He leaned down to kiss her lips and was interrupted by Yona.

"Okay, lovey doveys, are we meeting anyone else for lunch or . . .?"

"No," Gwrhyr smiled at her. "It's just the three of us, and if you're in the mood for a little adventure . . .?"

HE LED THEM DOWN A COUPLE OF STREETS before turning off into a little alley. "I know it looks iffy," he said, "but trust me, the food here is amazing." He stopped in front of a turquoise blue door. "These people are from a small corner of my, uh, Aden. They're the last remnants of their people," he spoke quietly. "They were nearly devastated by the apocalypse. But, they're survivors, and their food is incredible."

He opened the door, and they followed him in. It was dark inside because the alley didn't allow for much light, but it was fragrant and as soon as they opened the door, an older woman rushed forward and greeted them warmly. At least Eluned assumed she did. She was speaking in a language Eluned had never heard before. She was pretty sure it didn't even belong to the Thirteen Kingdoms. It was like that time Chokhmah had cursed in the library—completely unfamiliar.

But she took Eluned's hand and bowed over it, and grasped Yona's warmly. She had the feeling that Gwrhyr had informed her that Eluned was the Princess and Yona was her best friend or something along those lines.

The woman led them to a booth in a dark corner of the room, and after Yona and Eluned had slid in on opposite sides, Gwrhyr sat on the bench next to the Princess.

"So, what are they serving today?" Eluned asked, surreptitiously finding Gwrhyr's hand under the table.

"I'll explain when it arrives," he squeezed her hand, and let it rest against his thigh, "but meanwhile I've ordered a pitcher of their fruited wine. It's refreshing. You'll enjoy it."

A young boy soon arrived at their table with the pitcher

and three glasses. Gwrhyr started to thank him, and Eluned interrupted. "The least you can do is teach us the word for thanks."

He did so, and she and Yona thanked the boy, who, beaming, quickly disappeared into the darkness.

"Such wonderful people," the Princess said. "Genuinely hospitable. You don't see that much anymore."

"No, you don't," Gwrhyr said, lifting his glass. "To us, and to this quest. May it be blessed by Omni."

"Amen," Eluned and Yona agreed and the three clinked their glasses together before taking a sip of the wine.

"Mmmm," Eluned enthused. "This is really good." Slices of lemon and orange floated in the chilled light red wine, which fizzed with carbonation. The beverage had been lightly sweetened, which made it even more palatable.

"The food is even better," Gwrhyr said. If Yona hadn't been there, he would have been tempted to give the Princess a kiss. Instead, he just squeezed her hand again.

While they waited for the food, they made small talk, and Eluned admitted that she and Yona were in desperate need of clothing.

"Not much," Eluned said, "because we can only carry so much, but we each need at least another formal outfit and I don't know about Yona, but these," and she pulled a leg out from under the table and lifted it so they could see, "are the only walking shoes I own. And you have to admit that they're pretty disreputable." Neither Gwrhyr nor Yona could argue with that as Yona's were newly purchased as part of her costume when she stole the treasure, and not quite as travel worn.

"You do need to take into account," Eluned informed Yona, "that I wore these to hike over the Mountains of Misericord in a blizzard. They've got snow wear as well."

Yona laughed. "Yes, Eluned. Don't feel guilty. We agree that you need new boots. Right, Gwrhyr?"

"Absolutely." He ran his hand from her knee down to

where her boots reached at mid calf. "Those are . . . well, honestly, I'm amazed you can still walk in them."

They were still bantering along these lines when the food arrived—a steaming platter of meat covered in a thick brown sauce with rice and beans.

"Smells like chocolate," the Princess inhaled again. "I hope it tastes as good as it smells."

"Oh, it does," Gwrhyr said and began piling their plates with food.

Several mouthfuls later, Eluned said, "Now, I was happy with the chicken in Batum, but that doesn't even come close to what we're eating now. Thanks, my . . . Gwrhyr. Wonderful recommendation." Her cheeks were pink as she quickly took a bite. She'd almost called him 'my heart' as it was what Rowena called Ivanhoe in one of her favorite books, *The Gunslinger's Troth*. By Omni, could she do that? What was the line she couldn't cross? This was all so confusing, especially when every molecule of her wanted to stop resisting; to just let it be.

Yet, she was eating with both Yona and Gwrhyr rather than alone with him. They had to be on their best behavior not just because of Yona, but also because they were eating in public. Besides, she had begun to notice that everyone seemed to treat Gwrhyr with a certain deference. Clearly he was known in this place, more than just connections as he had called them. If she had to make a wager, she'd be willing to bet that he was the son of the King Uriel's most trusted? Highest? Lord. The way he could talk to anybody, or just walk into the inn and get them incredible rooms. She was sure that Faolan and Chokhmah had been granted the honeymoon suite. Gwrhyr was just that way. He was always looking out for others. No wonder the king trusted him so much. And yet, and yet, if that were true, would he really risk angering Uriel by falling for his betrothed?

It didn't make sense unless he really was truly in love with her and willing to lose everything for her. She took a deep breath and a large gulp of the wine. The implications of that were staggering. Clearly, he had made that choice. He was willing to risk everything for her.

She wasn't sure what to think of that, but she wasn't given time to do so because her thoughts were interrupted by Gwrhyr squeezing her hand and asking her a question.

"I'm sorry," she apologized. "I was a thousand miles away. What did you say?

"I only asked if you were finished."

She looked at her plate. She no longer had any appetite anyway. "I'm finished," she said.

It was as Gwrhyr was saying their goodbyes, and giving their thanks to the older woman who had greeted them at the door, that Eluned realized what must have actually happened. It explained everything. He hadn't told the woman that she was the Princess Eluned. Of course he hadn't. Gwrhyr had introduced her as his girlfriend. He knew she didn't want to be recognized here. She felt a great sense of relief. She was in Ponike incognito. She could touch Gwrhyr in public if she wanted to.

21ST MEEN

Four glorious days later they left Ponike to continue their journey northward.

"I didn't know it was going to be so difficult to leave," Eluned said, gazing mournfully back over her shoulder as they passed through the city gates. The time they'd spent in Ponike had been paradise compared to the past month of waiting for the unicorn to show up.

Gwrhyr had shown them the highlights of the city while they were there. One day, he had taken her and Yona, and Chokhmah and Faolan, sailing in the Gulf of Eudaemon. Eluned smiled, remembering the feel of the warm sun on her head, the wind in her face. The single-sailed catboat was called The Porpoise, which Eluned found very appropriate as it skipped across the waves and circled a couple of the small islands which dotted the harbor. One of the islands, known as Khamsa because of its shape, was home to a pod of seals. The Princess could have spent hours admiring their soulful faces and mournful liquid eyes. But they'd had to return to Ponike because Bonpo had been given permission to help prepare their meal that night, so they couldn't miss it.

That evening they feasted on tender sesame seared ahi

tuna steaks with a watercress, chile and ginger salad alongside fragrant jasmine rice, and washed it all down with a dry but fruity pale pink wine.

They spent an entire day rummaging through Ponike's bazaar where they not only found the clothes they needed, but pretty much anything that could be imagined from herbs, spices and teas to bells, books and candles. Gwrhyr had to physically pull Eluned away from the books, but not before she bought several, so that they could return to their lodgings in time to dress for dinner.

The best part of their stay, as far as she was concerned, was the many, many hours she had spent alone with Gwrhyr exhilarating in their togetherness. It had involved a lot of kissing and touching, yes, and that had been wonderful, but she had truly enjoyed getting to know him better—the time spent in his arms talking about everything from the dreams of their childhoods to their hopes for the future.

Time alone was probably over for the most part. They weren't free spirits like Chokhmah and Faolan. They had to be mindful of what they did in public. But still, she glanced at him because, as usual, he was riding right next to her, she would do anything to feel his kisses again. Eluned wanted more than that, actually, but that would have to wait. And while it was true that too much kissing could be agonizing, she still longed for that closeness. She had to keep the perfect balance.

We're on the road again, she reminded herself. That will make it easier, right? Days filled with travelling, making and breaking camp would keep them very busy. And then she had to laugh at herself because there was a time when she wanted nothing to do with this man. In fact, she was still amazed at the change in their relationship. He had made her so angry early on, and yet now she couldn't imagine being angry with him. He thought of nothing but her. He was smart, funny, caring. His body, his face, his lips, even his hands thrilled her. What more could she want?

The Princess rode on knowing that Gwrhyr was by her side, secure in the knowledge that whatever presented itself that day they would be able to handle it together. They'd managed to escape from King Arawn. They made a prodigious pair.

But, the ride that day turned out to be uneventful, and they camped in a designated site with much less than the usual banter. They weren't quite back in their tents again as the designated site offered them a shelter to use. Still they'd given up their comfortable beds for the hard wooden floors of the three-sided hut. Bonpo prepared an awesome meal, but it couldn't quite compare to what they'd had in Ponike. He just didn't have the resources.

They were back on the road, the Princess chided herself again, and they needed to get accustomed to that. Funny how when they left Favonia they were all eager to do this, and now they had to force themselves. Yes, they wanted to find the next treasure, but why was it that they had to be uncomfortable to do so?

Because, Eluned found herself rationalizing, nothing worth winning is ever easy to get. She also found herself fretting over the forms they would have to fill out when they entered Naphtali. Gwrhyr said there'd be questionnaires—brief but necessary for entry. She sighed. Worrying about it wouldn't make them disappear.

Arriving at a designated campsite that evening, they found themselves alone and were relieved by the fact that they could all fit inside the three-sided shelter, though it was a tight squeeze with Bonpo. Chokhmah and Faolan graciously chose to set up their tent, both so they could be together as well as to allow the others a little more room. Eluned and Gwrhyr used the opportunity as an excuse to sleep next to each other.

The Princess fell asleep, wrapped in her blankets, but with her head against Gwrhyr's chest. And she wouldn't have it any other way. Eluned could spend the rest of her days, she thought, wrapped in Gwrhyr's arms.

But, morning always arrives, and the Questers found themselves once again braving the elements—this time in a frosty rain. There was only a week left in Meen, but Autumn was arriving with a vengeance.

They pushed on with memories of their brief paradise in Ponike rapidly fading as the reality of being back in the out-doors finally sank in. It figured that when they began the Quest again, the weather would conspire against them. It was as if a bell was clanging—they were back on the right track.

"Nothing easy is ever worth winning," Eluned muttered.

"What?" Gwrhyr asked.

The Princess just shook her head, and shivered. Thank Omni, she opted to go ahead and purchase a cloak while in Ponike.

THEY MADE IT TO YET ANOTHER SHELTER after another hard day's ride. After eating, they settled down as quickly as they could. There were a few other travellers, but they had set up tents, so Gwrhyr once again had a reason to share space in the shelter with the Princess.

Morning dawned with the smell of fresh brewed coffee, and they crawled from beneath their blankets and faced the morning chill. Today they would enter Naphtali and make their way toward Jazeel. One step after step closer to the Crock and the Dish, Eluned kept reminding herself. The only prob-lem was that Jazeel was at least a week away, and at some point they would have to cross the Pegasus River. Jazeel was on the western side of the river, which took its name from their sigil—a winged horse. Or was it the other way around? She couldn't remember, but it didn't matter. They were hoping to cross this river before they reached Jazeel as there was a less frequented trail on the western side, which paralleled the river.

The reason crossing the Pegasus River was complicated is that they weren't sure they wanted to be recognized when they entered the capital city. There were several river crossings as one drew nearer to the city, but they also required filling out questionnaires.

Why are you seeking entrance to Jazeel was one of the questions. Because we want the Queen's treasure wasn't a valid answer. They would have to enter Jazeel with as little notice as possible. And that meant they would need to cross the Pegasus River as soon as it seemed viable.

Near the end of the day's trek they arrived at the Naphtali border crossing. They would have reached it sooner but a beautiful autumn day had enticed them to spend a little longer than they needed when they broke for lunch. In other words, they found themselves napping in the warm sun for more than half an hour.

They managed to bluff their way through on the main road, but knew they wouldn't be so lucky when they got closer to the Queen's city. They were such an odd lot that it was easy to pass themselves off as mummers. Their token gypsy was even willing to read fortunes for the guards.

The sooner they found a feasible ford across the river, the better.

That night they camped, with probably half a dozen other travellers, at a well-worn site on the banks of the Pegasus. They were all disgruntled as they were accustomed to their privacy. Not a single one of them opted to sleep in the shelter, but Gwrhyr did manage to convince Jabberwock to share the tent with Yona that night so that he could share a tent with Eluned again.

Jabberwock gathered everyone before they headed off to their tents. "I want everyone to sleep as much as possible," he said, brow furrowed with worry. "I sense that we have a trying time ahead of us."

Gwrhyr considered this for a moment. "It figures," he sighed. "We've had it easy for far too long."

The next day was colder but still sunny, and as they were eating a hurried lunch by the banks of the Pegasus, Jabberwock once again cautioned them to be on the lookout for a place to ford the river.

"I can't stress enough," he said, "how absolutely necessary it is for us to cross the Pegasus before we reach Jazeel."

They nodded at him solemnly. They could see the river below them. It was wide and the current was swift. They just needed to find a spot that was both shallow enough, and where the current was slower, so that they could cross on horseback if possible. Too deep and the horses, particularly the donkey, Derry, would be at jeopardy. That risk would double if they had to lead the animals across. Another motivation to finding a good fording spot was that once they crossed the river they would be mostly alone again, and they were accustomed to their solitude and enjoyed the time they spent together.

The remainder of that day was spent with all of them surveying the river whenever they had a chance. The group felt as if a massive cloud was hanging over them—and not a fluffy white cloud but a dark grey cloud bursting with thunder and lightning.

Towards the end of the day, just a couple of hours before sunset, Bonpo halted them. He pointed to the river which now lay about one hundred feet below them. The Pegasus stretched very broad at this point and it appeared to be shallow as well.

"What you tink, Jabb? Good time to closs?" he asked.

Jabberwock surveyed the river for a moment. The width bothered him but it did seem to be shallow. The current was also still rather swift, but if the river were indeed shallow enough, that wouldn't matter as much. "Unfortunately, we won't know until we get down there. So, the next question: can we get down there?"

A quick search turned up a precarious little path that switch-backed down the steep slope to the river.

The trail was very narrow, and Faolan recommended that they lead their horses. "It will be easier for them to maintain a sure footing," he explained. Following Faolan's lead, they dismounted and began making their way toward the river. At the bottom of the bank, they led their horses out onto a shore composed of fist-sized rounded stones, polished smooth by the current.

"I imagine the river fills up to the bank here following the ice melt in the summer," Gwrhyr said.

"It's probably a lot deeper and swifter then too," Faolan agreed.

Gwrhyr and Bonpo, who were the tallest, walked up to the river and tried to guess its depth. At the edge, you could see the rocks just beneath the surface, but just a few feet from the shore the current was swift enough that the constantly moving water blocked their view.

The Pegasus seemed to be one- to two-feet deep at this point, maybe as much as three. Surely they could risk that on horseback, although Bonpo would have to wade across.

Back on their horses, with Jabberwock still in the basket atop Derry, they began to slowly make their way across the Pegasus, Faolan leading with Gwrhyr bringing up the rear.

They were about two-thirds of the way across when suddenly Faolan's mount, Fiachdubh, stepped into a section of the river that brought the water up to his shoulders. Faolan cursed and gave the horse its head. He could feel the strength of the current against his legs. The stallion pressed forward one small step at a time and within six feet was climbing back up to shallower water.

Chokhmah had stopped when Fiachdubh was struggling to get out of the deep water. Halelu was strong but smaller than Fiachdubh. There really wasn't much choice. She clucked to the horse and the gelding pushed through the deep spot in the river. Ronan and Aine followed, and then it was Derry's turn.

Bonpo stepped into the gully, carved no doubt by the force of the spring runoff, and immediately sunk to his waist.

"Vely cord," he informed them. They knew. All of them were wet to the knees. "I tink too deep fol Derry," he said, pondering whether he should try to carry the animal to higher ground. The water might bear a lot of his weight. But, hearing his name, the little donkey stepped into the hole and was suddenly floundering. Bonpo had hold of his lead, but the swift current grabbed the poor animal and began tugging him down river.

"Hold on tight, Bonpo!" Eluned's voice was filled with fear. "Jabb's on his back! Derry is wearing the Halter!"

Except Jabberwock was no longer on Derry's back. He'd floated out of the basket and was desperately dog paddling trying to remain afloat. Gwrhyr immediately jumped off Ruari, and went after the Bandersnatch while Bonpo fought the current and pull of Derry to reach a shallower spot. Faolan and Fiachdubh were soon a few feet away. Faolan had pulled a rope from one of his saddlebags and was tossing it to Bonpo.

"Grab this and hold on!"

Bonpo caught the rope and twisted it several times around his wrist. With Fiachdubh pulling, Bonpo was better able to fight the current and was soon only knee-deep in water. From there, he was able to pull the donkey from the river with the lead.

Meanwhile, Jabberwock had been carried a couple of dozen feet down river. Gwrhyr used the current to his advantage and soon caught up with him. Grabbing the Janawar with his left hand, Gwrhyr tried to stand and found the river to be neck deep. He was going to have to go back towards the bank from which he started. Holding Jabberwock aloft, Gwrhyr shuffled backwards, one step at a time, and soon the water had dropped to his waist and finally to mid-thigh.

Ruari had returned to the original bank as well, so Gwrhyr

waded to shore, and then made his way to him. He still had to get to the opposite shore. Already, his friends were scavenging for wood to make a much-needed fire. He mounted his stallion, and following the route they had first used, because at least he knew what to expect, he and the shivering Bandersnatch forded the river.

"Bad news," Bonpo said when they finally reached the other side.

"Worse than nearly losing Jabberwock and Derry?" Gwrhyr asked as he handed Jabb to the giant. As soon as he was on the ground, the Bandersnatch shook most of the water from his fur.

"Some o' da gear was washed away." Bonpo said.

"How bad is it exactly?"

"My tent an' bed loll," Bonpo said, and swallowed. "An haf da food."

Gwrhyr scrubbed a hand across his face. When it rained, it poured.

"Well, let's get that fire going, and we can talk about it while we dry off," he said.

With everyone working together, it didn't take them long to gather enough wood to build a roaring fire because if they stood still, they'd start shivering. Most of them were wet to varying degrees, and changed into dry clothing as soon as possible before spreading their things out on the stones to dry in the late afternoon sun.

"You can snuggle up with me if it will make you feel warmer," Eluned offered to Gwrhyr when they were settled down in front of the fire.

"You'd be willing to make that sacrifice?" he asked with great solemnity.

"All for one, and one for all." The Princess groaned, but she failed miserably trying to hide her smile.

As soon as they were all thoroughly warmed, and the

shock of nearly losing their beloved leader and one of the treasures was beginning to wear off, they began to address their losses.

"I sreep outside. Not a probrem," Bonpo said.

"It will be if it's raining," Eluned said, "and I absolutely forbid your sleeping in the rain."

"Her majesty, Queen Eluned, speaks," laughed Gwrhyr.

"I'm not a queen yet," she corrected him, nudging him with her elbow.

"You sounded like one, Fy Drysor," he nuzzled her ear. She was sitting in front of him, pulled tight against his chest to keep him warm although he hadn't actually been cold in quite a while.

"She's right, though," Yona chimed in. "We can figure it out if it rains. I'm sure, for example that Gwrhyr can squeeze into our tent. We have only a week's travel before we reach Jazeel. Surely it won't rain every night?"

"Omni willing, it won't? Right, Chokhmah?" Eluned winked at the gypsy.

"That is right, my dear. Omni willing." She returned her wink.

Chokhmah had taught her to say that every time she worried something might happen, Eluned reminisced while shifting on the uncomfortable stones. "I hate to say it, but I don't think I can sleep on these rocks tonight. We're going to have to climb up that bank and see what we can find before it gets too dark to see."

Everyone agreed, but groaned when they stood. The idea of climbing a steep slope in the dusk was far from inviting.

They made it to the top in the last of the fading light. Fortunately the area on top of the slope was flat and grass-covered, and they quickly threw up their tents and gathered more firewood. Because in the gathering darkness they couldn't fully survey their surroundings, they nestled the tents as close together as possible and tethered the horses in front of them.

Bonpo had carried some water up from the river and set about making a soup with some of their more perishable items. Might as well use those first.

When they were gathered together around the fire eating dinner, Bonpo brought up their lack of rations.

"About haf our food wash away," he informed them again.

"I can think of several options," Gwrhyr offered. "We can cut our portions in half and that should get us to Jazeel under-fed but alive. Or we can stop an hour or two early each day and see what we can scrounge up, but that might add extra time to how long it takes to get there."

"You said several options," Jabberwock reminded him.

"Well, we could always eat normally," Gwrhyr said, "see how far that gets us, and scrounge from that point, but that's risky. We could end up starving."

"Or," Faolan said, "we could reduce our portions, stop an hour early and scrounge—kind of a compromise of the first two."

"Any preference?" Gwrhyr asked.

"I think we should try Faolan's idea first," Eluned said. "If we eat too little, it might be more and more difficult to push ourselves each day."

"And we certainly know how to look for food, don't we?" Yona said. "We did a lot of that while waiting for Nyx to arrive."

"Then we'll try that for a few days, and see if it works," Gwrhyr agreed. "At least we're walking alongside a river. We may be able to fish."

"Ol fine flesh water mussels," Bonpo said. "Liver may get calmer in praces too. Maybe fine clawdads also."

"Mushrooms, nuts and greens," Chokhmah added with a laugh.

"Maybe even apples, pears or some berries," Yona giggled.

"Or rabbits?" Eluned winked at Faolan.

"Who knows?" Faolan smiled. "Maybe even grouse or pheasant."

Yona slapped her head. "For Omni's sake," she said. "Why didn't I think of this before?"

"Think of what?" asked the Princess.

"The Hamper! Why can't we put some of what we have in the Hamper? It will provide us with plenty of food," Yona exclaimed. "I feel like such an idiot. We were practically starving when we reached Ponike."

Silence descended as everyone took in the impact of what Yona had just said.

Finally, Gwrhyr laughed and shook his head. "Don't be too hard on yourself," he said. "Not a single one of us considered it. We all knew you were carrying it."

They all chuckled in disbelief at their addled brains.

"Well, we've thought of it now, or Yona has, rather. I know one thing for certain," Jabberwock's mouth split open in a wide grin revealing his skewed teeth.

"What's that Jabb?" the Princess asked.

"That together we can accomplish whatever we set our minds to. We should try sitting down and discussing problems together more often."

"Amen!" everyone cheered.

"Wait, wait," Bonpo ordered. "Still have cognac." They waited while he found the cask and poured them all a generous dose. "To my bes' fliends," he raised his glass. "May our quest be success!"

"Here! Here!"

2ND GORT

Taking advantage of the Hamper of Gwyddno Long-shank's ability to provide food for a hundred when food for one was placed within it, the group was able to continue to make good time toward Jazeel. They awoke in anticipation of reaching Jazeel sometime during the afternoon following their sixth night camping on the western side of the Pegasus River. They also awakened to find the ground covered in frost.

"Brrrr," Eluned shivered, steam wisping from her mouth as she stepped out of the tent. "Where did this come from?" She pulled her cloak more tightly around her. They were definitely going to have to hunker down for the winter after they found the Crock and Dish. The Princess hated being cold, and she would go out of her way to avoid a repeat of the snow storm she was forced to travel through not long after they crossed the Mountains of Misericord when she left her father's kingdom.

Chokhmah was sitting by the fire, hands extended towards the flames for warmth. She was clad only in her leather trousers and what looked like Faolan's wool sweater. The Princess sat down next to her after Bonpo handed her a mug of coffee.

"You must be freezing, Chokhmah!" Eluned exclaimed. "Don't you have a cloak or a coat?"

"I am afraid I decided to wait until we arrived in Jazeel to purchase something warmer," she explained. "Faolan has kindly lent me his sweater."

"He's enduring the cold for you? That's sweet," Eluned continued, "but don't you have the coat of Padarn with you?"

Chokhmah looked horrified. "I cannot wear that!" she exclaimed. "It is a treasure."

"That's silly," Eluned said. "I wear a treasure all the time." She held up her right hand to show the Ring of Eluned glimmering on her ring finger. "We use the Hamper, I carry Dyrnwyn, and the Halter is on Derry. Besides, if it makes you uncomfortable to wear it, you could still buy another cloak or something in Jazeel."

She looked around for Gwrhyr who was finishing folding up their tent. "Hey, Gwrhyr," she called. "Come tell Chokhmah she can wear Red-Coat's Red Coat."

He strode over to the fire.

"He's wrapped," Faolan muttered under his breath.

"What?" Eluned asked peering around Chokhmah to where Faolan sat at her right side.

"Around your little finger," he smiled.

"You're one to talk!" she teased him. "Seriously, I don't believe that of either of you for even a second."

"Believe what?" Gwrhyr asked, sitting down next to the Princess. He was ready for another cup of coffee, and indicated so to Bonpo.

"I don't believe you're wrapped around my little finger," Eluned said.

"Good," he looked indignant, "because I'm not. Who says I am?"

"The guy who's wrapped around Chokhmah's little finger," the Princess laughed, but it was clear she was teasing Faolan.

"I was just kidding," Faolan held up his hands in surrender. "I only said something because you came scurrying over here so fast when the Princess called you."

"And you're blue with the cold because Chokhmah's wearing your sweater," Gwrhyr kidded him back.

"True enough," he admitted. He kissed Chokhmah's cheek, and she took his hand.

Not to be outdone, Gwrhyr kissed Eluned's cheek.

"Enough. Enough," Eluned said, as Yona joined them by the fire.

"Enough of what?" she asked.

"It's not even worth going into," the Princess told her. "I called Gwrhyr over to see if he agrees that Chokhmah should wear the Red Coat, at least for the day, so that she can be warm and Faolan can have his sweater back."

"Of course she should," Gwrhyr said.

"Have you not seen it?" Chokhmah asked. "It is rather large."

"Does that matter if it keeps you warm?" Yona asked.

"I suppose not," the gypsy agreed.

Faolan stood. "I'll go get it for you."

Eluned snickered, and Faolan pointed at her, "Watch it, Princess."

She giggled. "Yes, Sir Wolfman."

Faolan walked away shaking his head. Sometimes he had to remind himself that the Princess was still only eighteen.

He returned with the Coat, and Chokhmah stood and peeled off Faolan's sweater, which she'd layered over a blouse, and traded it for the large jacket of red wool.

"That is pretty big," the Princess acknowledged as Chokhmah pulled it on. She'd be swimming in it.

As Chokhmah began to button the coat, it rapidly began to shrink and shift to cling to her figure. In moments it fitted her snugly, arms the perfect length and falling to her ankles.

There was a collective gasp as everyone surveyed the gypsy in shocked silence. The once voluminous coat now fit her perfectly. Chokhmah returned their amazed stares, her eyes wide and her head shaking in denial.

"Who are you?" Gwrhyr asked.

Chokhmah was shaking her head.

"That's freaky," Eluned said. "We need to do an experiment. Let me try it on. We know I'm royalty."

Chokhmah removed the Coat while Eluned took off her cloak and handed it to Gwrhyr. Once the Coat was removed, it returned to its former shape. The Princess put it on, and similarly, it constricted to fit her diminutive frame. She pulled the Coat off and handed it to Yona. "You try."

Yona handed her cloak to the Princess, and put on the Coat. It swallowed her. "Definitely not royalty," Yona said. "But, we all knew that."

Yona returned the Coat to Chokhmah, who put it on again, and it once again transformed to fit her physique. "I do not understand," she said. "My aunt is a queen, but only by marriage. She and my mother are Roma. They were raised by gypsies, and I was raised by gypsies. This is true for many generations. We have no royal blood."

Jabberwock who had been contentedly watching the interplay between his fellow travellers all this time finally broke his silence.

"Do you know if Queen Miryam tried the Coat on?" he asked.

"She told me that she had tried it on out of curiosity, and that it was too large for her," Chokhmah said.

"And by that token, the Coat would not fit Queen Miryam unless she is truly your aunt," Jabberwock said.

"Are you saying that she is not my mother's sister?" Chokhmah looked shocked.

"I am saying that your mother is not your true mother," Jabberwock said.

The color drained from the gypsy's face, and Faolan quickly grabbed her, and pushed her gently to the ground. "Put your head between your knees," he said, but she was already doing that.

A minute later, she raised her head and sat up straight. "What about my father? Perhaps he was royal? I truly do not understand. I was never told that I was anything other than the child of Rachel and Yaakov. That Miryam was my aunt, and Moshe, my brother." She looked at Jabberwock who was regarding her eyes alight with secret knowledge. She drew in her breath. "What is it you know?"

"It's highly unlikely your father was your biological father, as well. There is only one rational answer," the Bandersnatch said.

"Which is?" Eluned stomped her foot in frustration. "Just tell us!"

"I believe that Chokhmah is the lost heir to throne of the Kingdom of Pelf," he said. "This is selfish on my part, but it would be nice if we had another affirmed member of the Triquetra Alliance. At the moment, we are evenly matched."

Gwrhyr nodded. If this were true, it might help swing the political balance.

"Yet how could this be? I do not understand. I have no memories outside our camp." Chokhmah said.

"I'll tell you what I know," Jabberwock said, "but it's going to have to wait until we reach Jazeel. If we don't hit the trail soon, we won't make it before the gates are closed for the night."

THEY MADE IT TO JAZEEL MID-AFTERNOON, and passed through the city gates with barely a second glance from the guards. Now that they were safely ensconced in the city, they immediately began searching for suitable lodging.   W h i l e they were willing to stay somewhere less luxurious than The Scarlet Phoenix, they also preferred somewhere with acceptable beds where they could take a warm bath. Gwrhyr spoke Naphtalese (was there a language he didn't speak, the Princess wondered) and asked a woman selling hot chestnuts if she knew of a respectable place. She directed them to The Merkabah, which was located in the heart of the bustling city.

Once again Gwrhyr made the arrangements, and they soon found themselves in simple but comfortable rooms, each with its own brazier to remove the chill from the air. Yona and Eluned shared a room once again, as did Chokhmah and Faolan, and the Princess was quick to note that it was probably too small for all of them to meet in. There weren't even any chairs—just cushions on the floor that could be placed in front of a very low table or moved closer to the brazier if it was warmth that was desired. There was also only one window although it did lead to a balcony overlooking a modest courtyard dominated by a large fig tree, which was rapidly losing it leaves; that is, they seemed to be falling quicker than they could be raked up.

There were no private baths, but there were designated baths for women and men, so they decided who would go first. Eluned suggested doing it by age, oldest to youngest, which meant she would be last, but that seemed fair to her. Allowing the still a wee bit shell-shocked Chokhmah to have the first bath was actually her goal. And while she was anxious to begin the process of removing the road dirt, she could wait another hour if necessary.

When it was Yona's turn for a bath, Eluned went in search of Jabberwock, who was sharing a room with Gwrhyr. He answered the door with wet hair.

"Looks like you got the first bath," Eluned smiled. "I think I prefer you in a towel, though."

Gwrhyr pulled her into his arms, and she tried to pull away.

"I'm still dirty," she explained. "You'll have to take another bath."

"I revel in your dirtiness, Fy Drysor," he kissed her.

"Thanks," she smiled up at him, "but that's not why I'm here."

"It's not?" He seemed disappointed.

"Maybe when I feel human again," she said, glancing around his room. It seemed to have the same proportions as hers. "I was actually looking for Jabb."

"What is it you want, Princess?" the Bandersnatch was curled up on a cushion next to the brazier.

"I know we usually meet in my room," she said, "and I suspect that we'll need some privacy when you tell your tale tonight, but our rooms are just too small for everyone to gather in. I just thought I'd let you know that we may need to seek out another space."

Gwrhyr looked at Jabberwock, "What do you think?"

"Is there a private dining room, perhaps?" the Bandersnatch asked.

"I can check." He held out his arm for the Princess. "I can escort you back to your room."

"Thanks for considering the need for privacy, Eluned," Jabberwock said. "It hadn't yet occurred to me."

"You're welcome," she smiled at her friend. She would never stop thanking Omni that he was still alive, and that was due in large part to Gwrhyr's quick thinking. She leaned her head against his upper arm. "I'm so glad you were able to rescue him," she murmured as they left the room. "I can't imagine this quest without him."

"Me either," he agreed. At her door, he left her with a lingering kiss. "Let's try to find some time alone together soon," he said. "I know it's only been a little over a week, but it feels like forever."

She nodded and let him hold her for a moment before he left to seek out someplace for the group to meet.

"I've never tasted anything like it," Yona enthused about the stewed pomegranate puree that contained ground walnuts, chopped onions, and chunks of poultry.

They were all basking in the aftermath of the glorious meal they'd been served, and waiting for the dishes to be cleared so they could listen to Jabberwock.

"Stewed gleens good too," Bonpo said. "Lemine me get recipes fol we reave." The thick soup of parsley, spinach, leeks, coriander, kidney beans, dried lemons, and turmeric-seasoned lamb along with a spice he was unfamiliar with had been excellent. Both dishes had been served with saffron flavored rice that had been nearly caramelized.

"Do you know what is odd?" Chokhmah said. "I have a sense that I have smelled these odors before today. They seem so familiar. Gwrhyr, will you not ask them if this is native Naphtali food when they return to clear these dishes?"

"I'd be happy to do that," he told her.

Eluned was practically in Gwrhyr's lap, head against his chest, drowsing, and she started awake at the sound of his voice. "I could really fall asleep right now," she murmured.

"But you're not going to, right?" Gwrhyr kissed the top of her head. Her hair was fragrant with the shampoo she had used.

"I wouldn't miss this story for the world," she said. "Just make sure I haven't nodded off before he starts."

"You have my word," he promised.

A few minutes later a young man knocked, and then entered to clear the table. "Excuse me," Gwrhyr said. "Are these Naphtali dishes?"

The youth shook his head. "No sir," he said. "This inn is owned by a family whose ancestors refugeed here from Pelf centuries ago. They have kept their foods and traditions so they will never be forgotten."

Gwrhyr thanked him, and told him that the meal had been wonderful, and then repeated what the young man had told him.

Chokhmah's eyes widened, and filled with tears. Was it true? Was she really heir to the Kingdom of Pelf?

Once the remains of their repast had been cleared away, the group quieted in anticipation.

"It was long ago and far away," Eluned winked at Jabberwock. She had grown up listening to him begin many tales that way.

"Indeed it was Princess," he said. "Indeed it was." He cleared his throat, and began: "More than a millennium ago, as most of you no doubt know, the Kingdom of Pelf was a beautiful nation that bordered the western shores of the Sea of Blood, except then it was known as the Djed Sea. Does anyone remember its sigil?"

"It was a black kraken on red," Eluned said. "You taught me that."

"I'm glad you remembered. The capital of Pelf was on the Anoon Ocean in Buta, and when the royal family was threatened and war imminent, the queen took the children—I believe it was two boys and a girl—and fled across the Djed Sea to Naphtali's capital, Kamea, located on the eastern shore of the Djed Sea.

"This was all perhaps a century or two before my time. After the cataclysm that created the devastation of Pelf, and caused the Djed Sea to become toxic, it was easy for the heirs of Pelf to disappear."

He stopped for a moment to lap at his water, and Chokhmah asked, "If there were three children, surely there must be numerous heirs to the throne of Pelf? It has been centuries since they left their kingdom."

"This is true, but I have learned much in the past five hundred years since I escaped from Dziron. The princes and princess did wind up in Kamea, but were forced to flee from the fallout that eventually destroyed that city, as well. Unfortunately, the youngest prince did not survive the ionizing sickness, and a dozen years later the princess and her child died in childbirth."

"Who did she marry?" Eluned asked. "Was it known that she was an heir to Pelf?"

"And what happened to the remaining heir?" Faolan asked.

"Yes," Jabberwock continued. "They were still in Naphtali at that point, and the Princess was known to be royal. She married one of the younger sons of the royal Naphtali family. As for the remaining heir, he eventually disappeared. From the research I have done over the years, I am convinced he ended up in Sheba. I think he was very aware of his royal status, and fearful of his enemies, he decided to settle in Baharimto where he lived the life of a fisherman."

"What were their names?" Eluned interrupted. "You keep saying he and she and prince and princess. They must have had names."

"Of course they had names." Jabberwock raised his muzzle and rolled his eyes, miffed although he was thoroughly accustomed to her interruptions. "Alborz was the eldest prince, Parisa was the princess, the middle child, and Gaspar is the prince that died. I was going to get to that—the names Alborz and Parisa are essential to this story."

The Princess looked chastened, and pulled Gwrhyr's hand over her mouth. "Don't let me say anything else," she told him.

"But I like hearing your voice." She gently nipped his palm. "Ouch!" he said, pretending that it hurt.

"Are you two quite finished?" Jabberwock asked. Gwrhyr pulled his hand away from Eluned's mouth and nodded.

The Princess pretended to sew her mouth shut.

"Thank you. So, we left Alborz in Baharimto where he is earning his living as a fisherman. But, it doesn't take long for him to realize that he does not wish to intermarry with the people of Sheba. Had he remained in Pelf, he would have been king. Not only does he not want to dilute his royal and Pelfan blood, but he also does not want to lose their traditions, the foods, their songs, their language, and everything that made the Kingdom of Pelf unique.

"He learns that the royal family were not the only Pelfans to resettle in Naphtali, although some had fled to Dziron and Kamartha. But, there was a particular family, well extended, that had settled there—the family of one of his father's lords.

"Alborz returned to Naphtali, sought them out, and convinced them to return with him to Sheba. They found an uninhabited cove about two-dozen miles from Baharimto and set up their own version of Pelf. He even named his little kingdom Buta. They intermarried among each other, refusing to blend their blood with the natives, and everything went splendidly for centuries as each new heir was handed down the story and received the name of either Alborz or Parisa."

Jabberwock paused for a second. Chokhmah's eyes shimmered with impending tears, and he realized that what followed might break the fragile dam of her lids.

"Until about forty-four years ago, that is. It was about that time that a chieftain from a neighboring village of livestock herders named Khalfani, I believe, decided that he didn't like the idea of a town made up of what was, essentially, refugees. He was really quite furious that they had been allowed to exist for so long without becoming part of Sheba.

"He undertook a trip to Mwezi-barafu to complain to the king at the time, King Adeyemi's father, who didn't show the appropriate amount of concern. Khalfani wanted the king to be as outraged as he was and demand that the people of Buta become a part of Sheba or find somewhere else to live. He returned to his village and decided to take matters into his own hands.

"He met with the current Alborz who told him in no uncertain terms that things were not going to change in Buta. Two nights later the hamlet faced a surprise attack by the able men from Khalfani's village. They slaughtered everyone. Everyone, that is, except a nineteen-month-old girl and her nanny."

Jabberwock paused again so Faolan could dry the tears that were now flowing down Chokhmah's cheeks. She took a deep breath, and nodded.

"Parisa's mother had died in childbirth, and Alborz assigned a great aunt to care for her. She was chased by Khalfani's men but managed to escape with the little girl. And then she disappeared."

"There was no word of what became of her?" Chokhmah asked.

Jabberwock shook his head. "But when we stumbled upon your Pomona last Neeon, I started having my suspicions. What is the likelihood, I asked myself, that Omni would set you in our way on the very day you were celebrating your husband's death anniversary? It wasn't just the timing—you and the Princess were drawn to each other like magnets. The way you arrived at the campsite as we were talking about Favonia. There were just too many things setting off my inner alarm bells. But I didn't know, couldn't know for sure. You resembled your brother, and later, Queen Miryam, enough to throw some doubt on my conjectures. And you certainly didn't seem aware of the possibility that you were anything but Roma.

"You would have been so young when you were taken in by the gypsies that you probably have no real memories of anything else. Although it is possible that your aunt knows the truth, or at least some of it. Perhaps that's why she so readily gave you the coat."

"How ironic," Chokhmah half laughed, half sobbed. "All those centuries spent keeping the royal blood of Pelf pure, the trouble my great aunt went through to ensure that I was safe, only to have the line end with me."

"Queen Parisa," Eluned murmured.

"Perhaps," Chokhmah agreed. "But I have no kingdom and I have no heir."

"Does that really matter? Perhaps it will all work out because you have something even better," the Princess told her. "You have us."

3RD GORT

The next morning the group gathered around the table in the private dining room they had used the previous evening. After enjoying a breakfast of flat breads, feta, and other cheeses as well as pastries with butter and jams, they turned to the next step in their quest. As they sipped at their coffee or tea, they deliberated how to go about requesting a meeting with Queen Njima. Yona was in the process of suggesting they send Princess Eluned as an emissary when the innkeeper escorted a messenger into the room.

"Princess Eluned?" he asked.

She stood, brow creased quizzically. Who knew she was here?

He handed her the note with a bow, and she received it with a nod.

She read the brief message and addressed her friends. "Our attendance is requested at Castle Indalo this evening at six o'clock for dinner with Queen Njima." She turned to the messenger, "Please tell the Queen that of course we will be there." He bowed and left the room.

"I guess we won't be seeking that meeting after all," said Faolan.

"I can't say I'm surprised," Gwrhyr said. "I imagine she's been waiting for us. I'd wager most of the Thirteen Kingdoms know we're seeking the treasures at this point."

"Her guards must have been keeping an eye out for us at the city gates," Jabberwock said.

"If they know what they're looking for, we're hard to miss," Faolan said turning toward Bonpo with a frown.

"Solly," Bonpo apologized.

"I was teasing," Faolan winked at him. "You're essential to this quest."

"And how many, um, fox-like," Eluned couldn't bring herself to say dog, "mammals ride on the back of a donkey?"

Bonpo guffawed. "Dat might rook odder dan giant!"

"It never even occurred to me!" Jabberwock chortled.

Soon they were all laughing along with Bonpo and Jabberwock because it is impossible to listen to a dhami dhole and a dzu-tch laugh without joining in.

"Well," Eluned said when the hilarity had subsided to the occasional snicker, "I think I have a dress that needs pressing."

"True," Yona chimed in. "We want to look our best tonight."

The Princess grinned at her. "You mean you want to look your best tonight."

Yona blushed but she didn't deny it. She had been looking forward to meeting Queen Njima since Eluned had first suggested it while they were at Castle Emrys in Arberth. And now that day had finally arrived.

Eluned was studying Yona. It had been more than three months since her friend chopped off her hair to play the part of the nun, and it had now grown back to chin length. It framed her face beautifully and Eluned told her so. "Don't worry," Eluned said. "I'm sure she'll be smitten with you. How could she not be?" She took Yona's hand, and led her from the room. "Let's go see what looks best on you."

When they were gone, Gwrhyr cleared his throat. "I am just going to state that for incredibly selfish reasons I hope Yona and Queen Njima fall madly in love."

Chokhmah smiled, a glint in her eyes. "Then you might have some uninterrupted time alone with your Princess, is that not right?"

"Amen," he agreed. "I have a feeling that it won't be long before we're taking a forced break from each other."

"Meaning you'll return to Aden for the winter, and she'll be returning to Zion?" Faolan asked.

Gwrhyr looked at Jabberwock. "That sounds about right," the Bandersnatch agreed.

THE WOMEN LOOKED SPECTACULAR when they gathered downstairs to wait for the carriages that would escort them to Castle Indalo. While in Ponike, they had all invested in formal dresses. Yona had chosen a gown of deep crimson silk with a sweetheart neckline and gold embroidered bodice. The bell sleeves featured gold embroidery at the elbows before flaring out in a diaphanous red chiffon. Chokhmah's dress was very simple, but looked incredibly regal on her. How could they have not known she was royal, Eluned wondered when the gypsy met them downstairs before they travelled to the castle. The dress was cap-sleeved with a modest V-neck, but it was the fabric that was so remarkable as it was completely covered in glittering gold beads. The gypsy literally sparkled.

Eluned's gown was deceptively innocent with its high neck and cap sleeves. The empire-waist dress fit closely to just below her breasts, where it fell in layers of chiffon and lace in varying tones of peach, cream, and pink. The lace covered bodice managed to conceal that which was meant to be concealed while still revealing a hint of skin beneath. Gwrhyr felt his eyes drawn to her time and again, and thanked Omni more than once for Eluned's love.

Cuhvetena's golden necklace of emeralds and opals was not only too gaudy but would distract from the bodice. Although, Eluned thought, it might have come in handy that evening if it still retained any of its powers of enchantment. On the other hand, she could definitely wear the golden dragon torque she had purchased in Arberth. The small ruby eyes and amber tail complemented the dress.

Gwrhyr and Faolan escorted the Princess and the Gypsy, and climbed into the first of the two carriages. The evening was chilly, and they'd all been forced to wear cloaks or coats once they stepped outside. Chokhmah straightened her shoulders, and with a secret smile, stepped proudly into the courtyard in the Red Coat of Padarn.

Bonpo escorted Yona, who carried Jabberwock up into the carriage.

The ride to the castle took about twenty minutes because they had lodged downtown and Castle Indalo was situated on a bluff overlooking the Pegasus River. When they arrived, a servant escorted them down a broad hallway lined with candles shimmering in cut brass lamps, to an arched doorway leading to a large room that featured a splashing fountain in its center. Colorful tile work covered the walls, and the room was lit with more cut brass lamps.

As they entered the room, a woman rose from one of the low sofas that nestled with several others in a corner on the left side of the room. She stepped out from behind a carved brass table, and Eluned could hear Yona behind her draw in her breath. Astounding didn't even begin to describe Queen Njima. She was tall, perhaps six feet, which was startling in itself. But she was also slender and her skin, the color of dark chocolate, seemed to glow in the candlelight. Her perfectly oval face featured high cheekbones, almond shaped brown eyes, full lips and a small nose. She wore her curly hair in a close-cropped cap. An extraordinary dress of flowing silk in shades of saffron orange and royal purple clung to her slender frame. Below the deep V of the neck, the fabric cross-hatched across her ribs and down to her hips before trailing to the floor.

"Princess Eluned," her voice was mellifluous. The Queen was extending her hand, and Eluned stepped forward to clasp it.

"Queen Njima," she said. "It is an honor to meet you."

"And it is equally an honor to meet the future queen of Aden and Zion." Queen Njima smiled revealing straight and pearly teeth.

"Shall I introduce the rest of my friends?" Eluned asked. The Queen nodded, and following the introductions, they were invited to seat themselves on the low sofas, which were strewn with silk and velvet throw pillows. Eluned and Yona were invited to sit with Queen Njima, and Gwrhyr bit his cheek to check his anger, and sat graciously with Chokhmah and Faolan even though he really resented not being able to sit with Eluned.

Yona admired the hand-painted gold leaf ceiling while the Princess looked longingly at Gwrhyr. She bit her lip and widened her eyes in attempt to look distraught when he glanced her way again, and he smiled, which made her happy. She liked making him smile. It deepened the dimple next to his mouth. She'd fallen in love with that dimple the night she first met him even if it had taken longer to come around to the rest of him.

Njima was asking her a question about the Crock and Dish, and she turned to answer it.

"Naphtali is said to be home to The Crock and Dish of Rhyngenydd the Cleric," she informed her. "Are you aware of the location of these items?"

"Yes, I have heard about these treasures," Njima said. "Whatever food one wishes for is supposed to appear in the Crock or on the Dish? Is that correct?" Eluned nodded her assent, and Queen Njima continued. "But I do not believe they are here in Jazeel. They are most certainly not in Castle Indalo."

The Princess was about to respond when servers laden with trays of food interrupted the conversation—spongy flatbread was placed in front of them along with a variety of spicy meat stews, cooked vegetables and salads. They were then instructed to tear off pieces of bread and scoop up whatever they desired to eat. They washed the food down with their choice of beer or wine, although Eluned fell in love with a potent honey wine, that she had to keep reminding herself to take small sips of in order not to over indulge.

Once the food was removed, the Queen led them to another corner of the room where several low sofas were gathered around a small round table. When they were settled in, she requested to be told the entire story.

"I must know everything that has happened since the Princess Eluned began this journey," she said. "I realize that this has been a dangerous quest for you . . ."

"Spies?" Gwrhyr interrupted.

"A necessary evil considering the threats from the Awen Alliance," she explained. "Regardless, I vow to keep what you say in the strictest confidence. I realize as Naphtali is a neutral kingdom, you might feel the need to withhold some information from me. Yet I feel strongly that unless I know everything, I cannot commit to allowing you to obtain this treasure."

Eluned looked at her fellow Questers. "Does that seem fair?" she asked.

"How do we know that you will keep your promise?" Jabberwock asked as Gwrhyr frowned.

"You don't," Queen Njima said. "Unfortunately, you must accept my vow in good faith. I swear by Omni that what you tell me will not leave this room. That's all I can do."

Chokhmah studied her for a moment before speaking. "I sense that she is telling the truth."

Jabberwock's muzzle split in his peculiar skewed grin. "Yes," he said. "I now believe so as well."

Eluned began the recitation with occasional help from Jabberwock, Bonpo, Gwrhyr, who still looked unsure, and Chokhmah. Yona told her part of the story, and they all took turns sharing what had happened since they reunited and returned to the Quest.

"The lost heir of Pelf," Queen Njima murmured when they had finished their tale. She examined Chokhmah for a moment, taking in the dark-fringed amber eyes. "You do have the look of the Pelfans, Queen Parisa."

"I am afraid I will always be Chokhmah the gypsy," she said.

"But, you'll always be my queen," Faolan said.

Chokhmah turned to him and smiled, taking his hand in hers. "And that is why I love you, my darling."

"Is this awkward having two couples on the Quest?" Njima asked. Clearly she had noted the interplay between Gwrhyr and Eluned. "And are you not betrothed to King Uriel of Aden, Princess Eluned?"

The Princess blushed. "I agree that's awkward. I am probably going to have to break that promise, which I hate doing, but as the betrothal was made for me, not by me, I think it's possible. Otherwise, I imagine the fact that there are two couples might be somewhat difficult for Yona, and I am sorry for that as well."

"I honestly don't mind," Yona told her friend. "It's not as if we were going to end up together, right?"

Eluned nodded, "Although I will always love you as a friend."

"As I will you," Yona said.

"It is late," the Queen stood, "and we must get you back to The Merkabah. I insist that you all return here tomorrow and stay here in Castle Indalo until we figure out where these treasures might be. I will send the carriages for you before noon."

"Thank you," Eluned said. "We truly appreciate your hospitality."

The Queen shook all of their hands, and Jabberwock's paw, and none of them missed the lingering look that Njima shared with Yona.

As promised, the carriages arrived shortly after ten o'clock the following morning, and they climbed aboard and made their second trip to Castle Indalo. Once there, they were escorted to their rooms, and the Princess was secretly thrilled to find out she wasn't going to have to share a room with Yona. She'd had hardly a second alone with Gwrhyr since Ponike.

Befitting her status as a princess, and perhaps the eventual Queen of Zion (though not Aden if she cancelled the marriage with Uriel), her room was both large and well appointed.

An exquisite bed composed of dark wood and hand-tooled silver studded with gemstones occupied the wall to the right of the arched door. A richly embroidered duvet in tones of vibrant pink, blue, and purple covered the bed along with numerous toss pillows in similar shades.

A large sofa composed of similarly hand-tooled silver occupied the space in front of the four arched windows that took up most of the opposite wall. A barrel table sat next to each pillowed armrest. Braziers were scattered about the tiled floor as were numerous throw rugs. Hanging lanterns with intricate cut work and colored glass along with a couple of mirrors in ornately carved and hand-painted frames completed the room. An arched doorway to the left led to a private bathroom.

Eluned walked over to the windows and opened the shutters. Her room looked out on a courtyard where a fountain splashed into a fishpond, and even though it was late in the year, there were numerous flowers blooming.

The Princess hung up her dresses in the large ornately carved armoire that stood against the wall to the left of the door before she went to check out the bathroom. The sunken tub looked really inviting, but she could bathe later. Eluned was about to take a seat on the couch and enjoy the view for a moment before catching up her journal when there was a knock at her door. She wasn't surprised to find Gwrhyr standing there when she opened it.

"That was fast," she acknowledged.

"Fast?" he said, stepping into the room and shutting the door before taking her into his arms. "I made myself wait five minutes."

To continue to afford the group their privacy, lunch was served in the same dining area they had feasted in the previous evening. Although Queen Njima wasn't present, she sent a message that she would join them again for dinner.

"It's fortunate that she isn't here," Jabberwock said, nibbling at his spiced fish and lentils, "because we must discuss what we want her relationship to this quest to be."

"What do you mean?" Yona returned the piece of bread she'd been raising to her mouth to her plate.

"The treasure is in her kingdom, and she probably has some idea as to where it might be . . . " Jabberwock began to answer.

"Ol at reast a good idea," Bonpo finished his sentence before scooping up some more lentils. "Vely good, dis food," he added.

"Anyway," Jabberwock rolled his eyes and sighed. "I sincerely doubt that she will allow us to ramble about her kingdom unattended. She's shown far too much interest in what we are doing."

"And now she knows everything," Eluned added. "Everything."

"Are you saying that you think she wants to join the Quest?" Yona asked.

"I think it's a very strong possibility," Jabberwock agreed.

"Or, she might insist that we travel with a guard," Gwrhyr said.

"Another possibility," said Jabberwock.

"I don't want to travel with a guard." Eluned frowned. "It was bad enough having to be around other travellers, but to have someone watching our every move . . ."

"But, what if she wants to help us search for the treasures?" asked Yona.

"Then she must commit fully to the Quest, as we all have," Jabberwock said. "This isn't a jaunt, and should we find the Crock and Dish, and I think we will, we still have four more treasures to recover."

"And they're all in dangerous places." Faolan's brow creased as he considered the implications.

"And as you noted recently," Jabberwock continued, "as a group we really stand out."

"That means that we will have to break up into smaller groups," Chokhmah said.

"It is definitely something we will have to consider," the Bandersnatch said. "But, meanwhile, the Queen is our current dilemma."

"Well, obviously I don't have a problem with it," Yona said, "if that's something she really wants to do. It would round out our numbers for one."

"If she does join us," Eluned pondered aloud, "shouldn't she ally her kingdom with Zion, Aden and the other kingdoms in the Triquetra Alliance?"

"It would definitely swing the balance of power in our favor," Gwrhyr said.

"And you are more than welcome to claim the alliance of the Kingdom of Pelf," Chokhmah said, "if indeed I am the last surviving heir."

"Actually, that's not insignificant." Gwrhyr said with all seriousness.

Jabberwock cleared his throat. "I hadn't even considered it, but if Chokhmah is Queen Parisa, and I have every reason to believe she is, then she has every right to ally her kingdom with whomever she chooses."

"Hmmm," Chokhmah mused. "My kingdom may be populated by Aberrations, but they are descended from humans. Perhaps it is time to start treating them as such."

Jabberwock eyes widened in horror. "You haven't seen them! And I'm not sure you want to!" He was silent for a moment remembering the suppurating flesh and the fetid, rotting, putrid odor of the beast that had killed his mate, Kamali.

"Much can change in five hundred years," Chokhmah said. "We have no idea how they might have mutated since you last saw them. But, I agree that now is neither the time nor the place. The Quest is all important."

"Another thought," Gwrhyr said. "If Queen Njima joins the Quest and allies herself with us, we could make quite the delegation to Tarshish. It might convince them to join us as well."

"I thought you said that King Uriel was on a diplomatic visit to Tarshish? When we were in Ponike. Remember?" Eluned said.

"I did say that," Gwrhyr admitted, "but I am saying now that it would be much more effective if representatives from all the allied nations paid King Dodi and Queen Chahindra a visit."

"But their son is betrothed to a Dzironian princess," Eluned objected.

"Neither of whom are first in line for either of the thrones," Jabberwock interjected. "Perhaps that can allow for a little manipulation, as well."

"I don't know. Queen Njima really embarrassed them by cancelling the betrothal with Prince Aahil," Eluned reminded them.

"All right, all right." Gwrhyr raised his hands in surrender. "That is obviously a complication to be addressed at another time. As Chokhmah said, the Quest really is all important at this point, and we don't know what will happen once we gather all the treasures."

"But to return to the subject at hand," Eluned said, "I have no objections to Queen Njima joining the Quest if she agrees to fully joining the Quest, which in turn would mean allying her kingdom with the Triquetra Alliance."

"Anyone else have any objections or thoughts?" Jabberwock asked. There were murmurs of 'no' and shaking heads. "Then we shall speak to her about this tonight."

THE PRINCESS WAS NOW ACCUSTOMED TO THE FOOD of Naphtali, and it was much easier that evening for her not to over consume. She'd gone to bed the previous evening with a painfully full belly, and she didn't want that to happen again. As they had the night before, they made small talk during dinner but turned to business once the dishes had been cleared.

"I have been thinking about this," Queen Njima said, "and I am convinced that the treasures must still remain in the former capital."

"Kamea." Jabberwock stated.

"Correct," Njima said. "It is said that everyone had to flee so quickly that only what was absolutely necessary was carried with them."

"And it would have been very easy to leave behind a pot and a dish," Jabberwock said. "By the time it was safe to return, they were long forgotten."

"It is also my understanding that by the time it was safe to return, no one wished to do so," the Queen said. "Jazeel was fully established by that point, and the Djed Sea was still too toxic, and remains so to this day."

"But it is safe enough to travel there and search?" Gwrhyr asked.

"I believe so, yes." Njima replied. "This is something I am very interested in." She was greeted by silence. "I think I am missing something," she finally pierced their muteness.

"It's difficult to explain." Jabberwock cleared his throat. "This is a very special quest. What one might call a Divinely-inspired search for the Thirteen Hallowed Treasures. Each one of us has felt called to be a part of this mission, and each of us has fully committed to continuing the Quest despite the inherent dangers."

The Queen studied Jabberwock for a moment taking in the import of what he had said.

"I guess what he's trying to say, Queen Njima," Yona began.

"Just Njima, please."

"Njima," Yona blushed. Just looking at the Queen made her heart race and her hands tremble. Speaking to her on a first name basis felt so intimate. "He wants to know if you feel led to search for the treasures or if it's just idle curiosity or a desire for adventure."

"And if it's the latter?" the Queen asked.

"Then we would have to respectfully ask you to decline from taking part," Princess Eluned spoke. "We work as a team, and it would be essential for you to be a part of that team and not just an onlooker."

"As you know there are rumblings of war from Annewven, Simoon and Adamah," Gwrhyr said. "Gathering these treasures together might give us a chance to prevent that."

"I apologize in advance, Queen Njima," Faolan spoke up, "but the hell with diplomacy. What they are beating around the bush about is that if you join the Quest, you would have to continue it. There are four more treasures to find not including the Crock and Dish—all of them are located in non-allied countries."

"Except for Pelf," Chokhmah couldn't help but add.

Faolan grinned at her and squeezed her leg. "Queen Parisa has kindly offered the alliance of the Kingdom of Pelf, which means . . ."

"You would require the alliance of the Kingdom of Naphtali if I were to join the Quest?" Njima finished for him.

Everyone nodded, faces solemn.

"That is a lot for me to think about," she said. "First of all, I just met you, and from what you have related to me, you became acquainted with each other while travelling." She paused, studying their faces for a moment. "Apparently I am not to be allowed that luxury?"

"It wasn't until we reached Mjijangwa that I realized we were on a quest," Eluned reminded her. "By that time, Bonpo and Gwrhyr were already a part of the journey. Bonpo felt called immediately, and Gwrhyr . . ."

"I realized that it was meant to be when I saw Eluned reading the book about the treasures," he said. "It was as if all the puzzle pieces fit perfectly."

"Chokhmah felt called almost immediately," Eluned continued, "but I have to admit that it took me a while to get to know Yona and trust her with the knowledge of what we were doing."

Yona had begun nodding while the Princess spoke. "When Eluned and Chokhmah took me aside and told me, I realized that it was meant to be. It felt so wrong being with Hevel and Arawn and their cronies, and so right being with Eluned and her friends. And once I agreed to steal Adamah's treasure, I was all in."

"And once I heard that the treasures were being gathered, I knew that I had to be a part of it," Faolan said. "And travelling with Yona from Hagafen to Favonia only confirmed that."

"As soon as we met him, we know it true," Bonpo spoke. "I felt as stlongry as I did when I met Hiurau and 'Leened at my inn."

"Perhaps, I must get to know you each personally," the Queen said. "I have Council meetings scheduled all of next week, but I can meet each of you singly for dinner. I can give you a final answer the evening of the 12th of Gort. Will that work? Will a little over a week be detrimental, time-wise, to your quest?"

"I think we can spare a week," Jabberwock said.

"Wonderful," Njima replied. "In that case, I will dine with you in the order that you joined the Quest. I assume that Jabberwock is the leader."

"Definitely," Eluned frowned at the Bandersnatch. She was still a little miffed that he'd known that the ring her father had given her was one of the Hallowed Treasures; that he had been steering her toward seeking the treasures when they first started the journey.

"Until then," the Queen continued, "you have free reign of Castle Indalo. Feel free to use the library or practice your weaponry. I even have an indoor swimming pool."

"Library!" Eluned's eyes lit up. "I can't wait until tomorrow. I just finished the books I bought in Ponike."

"It would also be a good idea to practice your swordplay," Gwrhyr told Eluned as he walked her and Yona back to their rooms. "Yona, you could probably use some instruction as well."

"That's very true," Yona agreed. "Why don't we do that first thing then we can go to the library in the afternoon?

The Princess reluctantly agreed. She hadn't practiced with her sword, Dyrnwyn, since they'd camped next to the River Leprican in Dyfed.

"I think I want to try that," Yona said, pointing to the far end of the practice grounds where arrows were being shot into bosses outfitted with circular targets.

"Have you ever used a bow before?" Gwrhyr asked.

"No, but it looks fascinating," Yona said. "Can I at least try it once?"

"I don't see why not," he said. "Let's walk over there."

The Princess wasn't interested, but as Yona had waited patiently for her to finish practice, she accompanied them without complaint.

After getting her set up with a bow, some arrows, and a

glove, Gwrhyr offered her some brief instruction. "Now, I just have to set the target up," he said, "and you can shoot."

Yona carefully nocked her arrow as she'd been instructed, drew the bowstring and loosed the arrow. Her aim was just slightly below right of center.

"You may have the knack." Gwrhyr said, eyebrows raised in surprise. "Try again, but try to correct your aim."

Yona did, and this time was even closer to center.

"Go again," Gwrhyr said. "I think all you need is practice. You've definitely got a gift."

Yona's face was beaming. "Maybe I'll finally have something more to offer than my pretty face," she laughed.

"I'm definitely impressed," Eluned said. "If this continues, we'll have to outfit you with your own bow and arrows."

"And a quiver to put them in," Yona giggled, excited about this unforeseen talent of hers.

"Absolutely," Eluned promised. She was just relieved to see her friend so happy for a change. Not that Yona ever let on that she wasn't completely happy, but the Quest since they'd left for Bogaine had supplied her with little opportunity for proving her worth. The Princess hoped that Yona's meeting with Queen Njima also went well. She had wanted them to get together for months, and she hadn't missed the way they looked at each other.

12ᵀᴴ GORT

It was finally the day that they would learn of the Queen's decision. And, Eluned thought, to be completely honest she hoped the answer would be yes if for no other reason than they'd just spent an entire week waiting to hear. That, and the fact Yona was clearly smitten with the woman. All Eluned had to do was mention the queen's name and Yona's cheeks would flame and her eyes sparkle. She was also giggling a lot more than normal.

The Princess had tried to get her to confide to her how their meeting had gone, but Yona would say only that it went well—for more than an hour she had refused to say anything to Eluned.

"I can't take it anymore," she finally relented. "The hurt look on your face—I can't take it anymore. It went really well. And I mean really."

"Yes? Oh Yona, you don't know how happy that makes me!"

"Actually, I do," she admitted. "You told me back in Arberth that you thought we should meet. I'm not sure how you knew that we were such a perfect fit, but you were right. She is an amazing woman. She's beautiful, she's funny, she's strong, she's intelligent. Her people seem to adore her." Yona sighed. "I can't even begin to tell you how much I admire her."

Eluned threw her arms around her friend. "I am so, so glad. I just had a feeling that it would be true; it's nothing I can explain, but it was very strong. By Omni, I hope she says yes to joining us."

WHILE THEY WAITED, Gwrhyr and Eluned had spent many hours practicing their weaponry while Yona improved her archery skills. Chokhmah and Faolan wandered into Jazeel in search of the herbs and spices the gypsy needed for her special teas.

"I have absolutely nothing remaining," she told the Princess at breakfast their first full day in Castle Indalo. "I could not make a healing tea or potion if I so desired."

"I hope you find what you need," Eluned said, "and let me know if the market is worth venturing to as it looks like we're going to have plenty of time on our hands. Besides," she winked at her, this gives you more time alone with Faolan, right?"

"And you with Gwrhyr, I would suspect?"

The Princess nodded, blushing. "I would never have believed it if you told me this would happen before you did the tarot reading for me. But he really is wonderful, isn't he?"

"That, if you recall," she smiled her Chokhmah smile, "I did tell you then, and you adamantly did not believe me."

Eluned hugged her. "I am so happy that you agreed to be a part of this quest."

"My dear, I cannot tell you what it means to me that I trusted my instincts on such short notice and accompanied you and your fellows," she bit her lip to prevent the tears from filling her eyes. "I never thought I would find love again, for one, but I also feel like we are doing something important for our world."

IT SOON BECAME THEIR PATTERN to discuss the previous evening's meeting with Queen Njima during their dinners. In general, all were greatly impressed with the queen, but she was extremely adept at what Eluned said was called a "poker face."

"I read about it in one of my great grandmother's books, one of my favorites," she explained. "It was about someone who was a gunslinger, and they played a card game called poker."

"What's a gunslinger?" Yona asked

"Someone who wields a weapon called a gun, which shot something called bullets," she explained.

"I don't understand," Yona said.

"It was something they held in their hand," Eluned attempted to explain. "The bullets are the projectiles that were propelled from the gun."

"So not unlike a bow and arrows?" Yona asked.

"I don't think so. They struck me as much more deadly," Eluned said, "because the weapon could easily fit in one's hand. The bullets are pointed and made of metal and make a very loud noise like a small explosion when they are fired from the gun. Oh, and they carried them in belts on their hips. Definitely more compact than having a sword banging against your leg."

"And a poker face?" Gwrhyr asked.

"It was a face devoid of expression," she said, "so that the other card players couldn't tell what cards you had drawn."

"Poker face," Faolan nodded. "I like it."

"Well, you'll see when you meet with her," Eluned said as at this point only she and Jabberwock had met with the Queen, and Bonpo was with her that night. "But don't you agree, Jabb?"

"Indubitably," he said. "I imagine that neutral expression comes in very handy when she has to make judgments. It also shows that she's taking all of this very seriously."

The week passed with meals together, trips to the market, hours spent in the library reading and playing cards. Gwrhyr and Eluned also managed to spend numerous hours alone together—usually between dinner and bedtime curled up in each other's arms on the sofa in her room. Gwrhyr finally relented and told some stories from his childhood, but he still refused to talk about King Uriel.

"But you do know him?" Eluned pressed.

"Of course, but I can't say anything," he said. "When the time is right, I'll tell you everything, I promise, but I just can't yet."

"Okay, I'll trust you," she said, running a finger lightly over the crease between his brows. "Don't worry."

"I won't," he said, but he still looked worried.

"Where's Yona?" Eluned asked as they gathered in the dining room on the 12th of Gort. "Surely, she's anxious to hear the Queen's answer."

There was the sound of laughter and a murmur of voices, and Queen Njima and Yona entered the room holding hands.

"I guess that's our answer," Eluned whispered to Gwrhyr, who nodded.

Njima's poker face had disappeared, and she suddenly looked much younger than her twenty-eight years.

Everyone was watching the Queen in anticipation, and she laughed merrily. "You should see your faces," she said. "Obviously the answer is that I am willing to fully commit to this," she squeezed Yona's hand, and tears welled in her eyes. "I cannot even begin to tell you how wonderful this week has been for me. I feel as if in seven days, I have found seven good friends. I have never had the chance to experience friendship. My parents were very untrusting; they were certain everyone was looking to gain something from them, and they feared that I would be used as a pawn by someone to get what they wanted from them."

Eluned was crying by this point. "I know exactly what you mean," she said as tears slid down her cheeks. "Until I started on this journey, I had only Jabberwock. I didn't know what it was like to have real friends."

Gwrhyr hugged her close. He couldn't say it, but he also understood what she was talking about.

"Where's the champagne?" Yona giggled. "It's time to celebrate!"

Njima nodded to a servant, and then she and Yona squeezed in next to Gwrhyr and Eluned on the couch.

"Ready?" Gwrhyr turned to look at Njima, who sat astride her buckskin mare, Makeda. She, like Yona, Eluned and Chokhmah, had gladly acquired a pair of leather trousers for the journey to Kamea.

She nodded and gave him a thumb's up sign, grinning broadly.

Yona now had a quiver of arrows slung across her back and a bow easily within reach behind Aine's saddle. Both Gwrhyr and Eluned carried their swords in scabbards hanging from their waists, and Njima had a small throwing axe at her side. Only Chokhmah preferred not to carry a weapon, but Faolan insisted that she at the very least carry a small dagger. Yona was more than willing to offer her the dagger she'd purchased in Hagafen.

No one had ventured to Kamea in centuries that any one was aware of, Njima had said, and they did not know what they were riding toward. It could be nothing more than ruins, but the land beyond the wall also could have become home to Aberrations. They needed to be prepared for whatever they might have to face.

Knowing that, they had spent the next three days following Njima's decision to join them preparing for the next part of the journey. While Bonpo, Chokhmah and Faolan rounded up supplies for the trip, Eluned, Gwrhyr, Yona and Njima had practiced their weaponry.

"You've really mastered that throwing axe," Gwrhyr told

Njima one day after he and Eluned had taken a break from practicing and had wandered over to watch her. "I assume you don't have any problem with tents and camping?"

"I look forward to it actually," the Queen replied before sauntering off to see how Yona's practice was proceeding.

The Princess turned to Gwrhyr with a grin. "Does this mean we get to share a tent now?"

"This will shake things up a bit, won't it?" he said. "I take it you'd like to share a tent with me?"

"Any excuse to be in your arms," Eluned said.

"Oh, you don't need an excuse, Fy Drysor." He pulled her into his arms. "But will Jabberwock allow it? We'll have to ask."

"We have once before," she said. "But he is like that, what was that story? Some little insect or rodent sitting on one's shoulder constantly whispering in your ear when you made the wrong choice?"

"Was it a mouse? I don't remember. At any rate, somehow I think that night might have been an exception," Gwrhyr mused. "I have a very strong suspicion that he might insist on being our chaperone."

"That's fine with me," the Princess said. At this point, she just wanted as much time with him as possible. She suspected she'd be spending a long, cold winter without him. In addition, she knew she couldn't request him to be there when she broke her betrothal to King Uriel. That was something she was going to have to do on her own. "I'll ask, and he's more than welcome to curl up with us. It's not like I haven't camped with him before this. We were alone when I first left Castle Mykerinos."

A DAY'S TRAVEL OUT OF JAZEEL brought them to the turnpike that travelled northward to Kamartha. Another, smaller road headed southward towards Aden. Their pathway lay straight ahead, and it was here that a massive fortification had been set up to prevent the ingress of any Aberrations.

Fortunately, more than a couple of centuries had passed since it had last seen any upkeep, and it had long since been overgrown by the forest. Unfortunately, this suggested that the road beyond the wall had succumbed to nature as well, which would mean forging their own path, and perhaps slowing down their journey to the ruins of Kamea.

Rather than admit defeat, despite the fact it was late in the day, the group decided to find a way across the barricade and at the very least, camp on the opposite side of the bulwark. They had prepared for this in advance, perusing ancient maps from the Queen's archives that outlined how the barrier had been constructed. While the wall extended approximately a mile to either side of the roadblock, somewhere within the overgrowth straight ahead was a gate that allowed the sentries at the time access to the other side. They hadn't had to make the wall too deep because the Aberrations were somewhat zombie-like in their ability to reason. If the straggler made it through, they were easily picked off and they tended to travel in packs on easily accessible terrain.

Njima had even discovered that the key that had unlocked the gate was actually a series of numerals that had been input electronically. It had been a very long time since electricity had been available. So long in fact, that there was only the vaguest understanding of how it was created, but that it seemed to hold a power not unlike lightning. That, in itself, was scary, and people were still too fearful of what electricity, among other methods of power, had resulted in. It was just too dangerous. They had agreed that once they reached the wall that it would probably just take brute force and hand labor to clear away the growth and find the gate.

Once the Questers reached the wall, they dismounted, and with great caution pulled back the growth until they discovered the door through the barricade. Jabberwock insisted that the group leave the front of the barricade as unmolested as possible in order to prevent any possible spies from tracking them. They had been too incautious when they entered Jazeel, and as the Questers had learned upon meeting Faolan—spies were everywhere.

They found the gate, and discovered that it had, unprotected as it was from the elements, corroded until it had resettled back into the earth. The travellers could easily remove by hand what little remained protruding from the wall.

Naturally, a tree now fully blocked the gateway on the opposite side of the rampart though, and Bonpo set to work with an axe. The group had to have a big enough space to get their horses through.

The forest was also dense on the other side of the palisade, and using the machetes Derry had carried for them from Castle Indalo, they began to whack away at the plants and saplings that covered the area. They spent the next hour clearing enough ground to allow them to set up their tents for the night. The sun was rapidly fading as a fire was started and Bonpo began to prepare a hastily made meal.

"Is it always like this?" Njima asked, spooning some stew into her mouth.

"Depends on what you mean by 'this,'" Eluned said. "Do we have to carve our way through the forest all the time? Not usually. We've had to clear ground to camp, but we've never had to make our own trail. Do we often barely get camp set up before dark? More often that not, I'm afraid."

"It's kind of exciting," she admitted. "It is as if we really must work to survive. I'm not used to that, but I like it. It makes me feel alive." She kissed Yona's cheek and Yona leaned into her.

"I agree. It's like when I escaped with the Hamper. It's almost as if you're super aware all the time," Yona agreed.

"I think it's because we always feel the need to push on as far as possible before stopping for the day," Gwrhyr explained.

"If we make a concerted effort, we can stop early, but it is rare. Like tonight, we often eat by campfire light."

Njima nodded. "On the bright side, there is nothing like some hard labor to whet the appetite."

"Absolutely," agreed Faolan.

"And once again," added the Princess, "thank you, Bonpo, for a wonderful meal."

There was a round of "hear, hears" before the group returned to sating their hunger in an exhausted silence.

They retired to their tents for the evening, Eluned smiling inside because Jabberwock had agreed that he would share a tent with herself and Gwrhyr.

THE FOLLOWING MORNING, as everyone complained of sore muscles, the Questers got back to work clearing away the foliage as they searched for the remains of the road that led to Kamea. Even if it had long since become overgrown, there had to be a trace. The throughway had been a major trade route for centuries before the fleeing residents of Kamea had cordoned it off.

"I found it!" Jabberwock called out about half an hour later. He was small enough that it was easy for him to slip through the dense foliage and find the depression that had once been a paved road more than seventy-feet wide. Clearly, the road had first become overgrown by grasses before being invaded by small shrubs, brambles and other plants, and finally by trees.

Somehow, the forest that covered the road wasn't quite as dense as that on either side of it, and it was easier to make their way through it. Occasionally, they would have to stop and chop away some thicker briars or shrubbery, but for the most part they made decent time. They had travelled about ten miles when the road began to open up even more.

It only took a quarter of a mile of this newly open forest road before Faolan, who was leading, reined in Fiachdubh.

"This just feels wrong," he said. Everyone else quickly stopped as well.

"I agree, my love," said Chokhmah who was riding behind him. She turned to Gwrhyr, who was behind her. "What do you think?"

"Why is it so clear?" he wondered aloud. "It looks as if it has been receiving controlled burns."

"Yes," Faolan nodded, brow creased, "as opposed to forest fires caused by lightning."

"We'll continue," Gwrhyr called over his shoulder so that everyone could hear after considering this new development for a moment, "but keep alert."

The road remained easy to travel for the remainder of the day as there was no longer any major brush to cut their way through, and although they all felt that something was amiss, nothing else occurred to set them on edge.

An hour before nightfall, they stopped once again to set up camp. Faolan and Gwrhyr stood in conference for several minutes before they decided how to set the camp. This time they were even more careful about where and how they set up their tents and tethered their horses.

Before they began dinner, they even discussed briefly whether it was wise to start a campfire. But the fact that it was so chilly at night now, and frosty first thing in the morning decided them in favor of taking a chance.

"So where are they?" Eluned finally broke the silence.

"Who?" Gwrhyr, who was sitting next to her as usual asked, but he shifted uncomfortably on the cleared ground.

"Someone is maintaining this forest," she explained, although she knew he knew what she was talking about. "Why are they maintaining it, and where are they?"

"Here's my best guess," Faolan answered her. "They are keeping this section of the forest as free from wildfires as possible because they are protecting something else."

"Something," Chokhmah added, "that we will, no doubt, discover tomorrow."

"Yes," Bonpo agreed. "Dey don' want lisk something."

"I just hope they're friendly," Eluned murmured. "I'm not sure I'm ready to kill anyone again."

Gwrhyr hugged her closer. He didn't want that for her either.

"Well, that's it," Jabberwock said. "We continue, but we keep on the look out. And, we act friendly until we know otherwise."

They all agreed that was the right maneuver. There were moans and groans as they stood up because now they were really sore after another day of clearing brush.

"Perhaps a good night's sleep will help," Eluned said, massaging her left bicep as they made their way toward the tents.

18ᵀᴴ Gort

The next day, the travellers had barely ridden half a mile following a quick lunch when the landscape changed from the controlled burn forest they had camped in to fenced-in pastures to the right side of the road, and fields planted with corn and barley to the left.

They reined in their horses, surveying the open land around them in silence.

"Somebody lives here," Eluned stated the obvious.

"I take it you know nothing about this?" Jabberwock asked Njima.

She was shaking her head. "I had no idea. No one has dared venture this way in centuries. Who could be living here?"

"I assume we'll find out," Gwrhyr said, "because we really have no choice but to go on. Let's just hope they're friendly."

They rode on, weapons at the ready. Within a mile, they began to see scattered flocks of sheep on the right side of the road.

"Sheep usually mean shepherds," Faolan said, "or at the very least, sheep dogs."

He wasn't wrong. Three black and white dogs began barking and racing in their direction. They drew up their horses.

The dogs took position on the road in front of them and continued to bark.

Eluned started breathing deeply in the hope of stilling her thudding heart. She noted that both Gwrhyr and Njima had tightened their grips on their weapons, and her hand reflexively sought her sword. Faolan's eyes squinted into the sun as he scanned the pasture for the shepherd that was probably heading their way.

A minute or so later, a little boy of about eight years of age, scrambled over the fence and skidded to a halt just behind the dogs. His mouth dropped open in wonder and his large amber eyes regarded them with amazement.

Weapon hands relaxed, and Faolan called out a greeting in the Common Tongue. The little boy shook his head to indicate that he didn't understand. Chokhmah dismounted and approached him very slowly. The boy's thick and wavy, nearly black hair and golden brown eyes with thick black lashes mirrored her own.

He stared at her in awe, as well. He said something in a language none of them could understand and pointed to himself and then to her.

"Jabberwock," Chokhmah croaked, cleared her throat and tried again. "Jabberwock, could this boy possibly be a Pelfan?" The innkeepers in Jazeel had intermarried enough that they shared only vague similarities with Chokhmah, although they had the thick-lashed eyes like she and this boy.

"Very possibly," Jabberwock spoke from his basket atop Derry, and the little boy gasped.

A middle-aged man hurried down the road, shaking his head in wonder. They waited for him to arrive.

"Horses," he said. "I'd forgotten they still exist."

"You speak the Common Tongue," Gwrhyr said.

"We always knew this day would come," he explained. "Most of us have learned the Common Tongue just because of the eventuality."

The youth said something and pointed to Chokhmah.

"He says you look like us," the man said.

"Do I?" Chokhmah asked.

The man regarded her for a moment. "Eerily so."

"There's a reason for that," Eluned said.

"Princess," Chokhmah said, shaking her head.

"No, he should know," Eluned said, and continued despite the fact Gwrhyr was glaring at her and also shaking his head. She turned back to the man and boy. "I hate secrets. This is Queen Parisa," she said quickly before Chokhmah could attempt to dissuade her again. "I'm the Princess Eluned of Zion, and that," she pointed to Njima, "is Queen Njima of Naphtali."

Gwrhyr groaned audibly. He was going to have to have a talk with her later. There were just some things that were better left unsaid.

"This is just . . . " the man began. "I'm speechless. I think I need to take you to see our imperator. She will want to hear all of this. I am Cyrus," he added, "and this is Jahan, my son," he lay his hand on the boy's shoulder.

"How far must we go?" Faolan asked. There were only pastures and fields as far as the eye could see.

"It's only a few miles," Cyrus said.

"Then you should ride with us," Faolan reached a hand down to help swing him up. "It won't be comfortable," he indicated the tent strapped behind his saddle, "but it will be faster."

"Jahan can ride with me," Chokhmah said. Gwrhyr dismounted, and lifted the boy onto Chokhmah's lap.

His father said something to him, and the boy laughed, eyes sparkling. "I told him that now he'd really have something to brag to his friends about," he explained. Chokhmah smiled. The little body in her lap was practically thrumming with excitement.

About half an hour or so later, they reached a huge complex of barns, outbuildings, and numerous little cottages.

"We live in community," Cyrus said, "but I will let Nahid explain all that to you." As they rode into the compound, numerous children and adults gathered around them, staring at them in awe. "As I said," Cyrus continued, "we don't have horses. They are legendary to us."

A woman who looked strikingly like Chokhmah though a bit shorter, and a little more curvy, stepped forward as Cyrus and the others dismounted.

"Welcome to Kuna," she said.

"This is our Imperator, Nahid," he introduced her. She was now looking at Chokhmah in dismay.

"You appear to be a pure bred Pelfan," Nahid said. "How is this possible?"

"She introduced herself as Queen Parisa," Cyrus informed her.

"Actually, Eluned introduced me as such," Chokhmah corrected him. "I am still not entirely sure that it is true."

Nahid's eyes widened. "It was our understanding that the royal family didn't survive."

"It is a long story," Chokhmah said. "Perhaps we should sit before we tell the tale? But first, our horses. Is there someplace we could tether them?"

Nahid spoke to the gathered youth in Pelfan, and several young men and women rushed forward, eager to help. She explained to them what needed doing and as they were handed the horses' reins, the teens began leading the beasts toward a barn.

"The largest animals we have around here are sheep," Nahid apologized, but I am sure your horses will be well taken care of."

"I don't doubt that at all," Eluned watched the horses and donkey being led away. The kids looked in awe of the huge animals.

The Imperator led them to a square building. Inside, a

raised stage at the front held a long table. "This is where we hold our weekly community meetings," she explained, as they walked down a center aisle between rows of chairs until they reached the stage. Nahid invited them to sit, and Bonpo, looking at the small chairs, offered to stand.

"You could use the stage itself as a chair," Eluned pointed. The stage was several feet above floor level. Bonpo nodded.

"Dat make sense. Tanks, Plincess," he said, sitting on the edge of the platform. Nahid took a seat at the center of the table and Gwrhyr, Eluned, Chokhmah, and Faolan sat to her left with Njima, Yona, and Jabberwock sitting to her right. Interested adults and youth filled in the seats in front of the stage.

When everyone was seated and quiet, Nahid said, "Perhaps we should begin with introductions. The room grew more and more still as those whose skills with the Common Tongue were less than adequate struggled to understand what was going on. After Gwrhyr introduced himself, Cyrus raised his hand.

"Yes, Cyrus?" Nahid asked.

"Maybe I should translate," he suggested. "I'm pretty sure that not everyone understood that." He spoke in Pelfan and looked around to see a few of the people, mostly youth, nodding.

"Yes, go ahead," Nahid agreed, and thereafter as each person introduced themselves, they would pause so that Cyrus could translate. After Bonpo finished introducing himself, Nahid sat thoughtfully for a moment before speaking. "I have so many questions, but I think the most important at this point is the reason behind such a distinguished, not to mention unusual, group of people travelling together?"

"That's a long story, particularly if we must translate as we go," Eluned said. "Do you have the time?"

Nahid spoke in Pelfan and then informed the group that she had given those gathered allowance to leave if and when it was necessary.

The Princess nodded and launched into what was fast becoming a well-worn story. As was usual with the group, they took turns telling their parts though Gwrhyr was rather terse as he explained his portion.

They were well into the tale when Nahid paused them, and called out a number of names—Sanaz, Ziba, Laleh, Shahin, Kaveh, and Kir. Three woman and three men stood. She spoke to them briefly in Pelfan, and they bowed before turning and leaving the building.

"I have asked them to go and prepare our evening meal," Nahid said. "Please continue."

"AND NOW WE ARE ON OUR WAY TO KAMEA to search for the lost Crock and Dish," Queen Njima finished the story a couple of hours later. "Does anyone live there, do you know?"

"It had been destroyed by fire by the time our ancestors arrived," Nahid said. "They pushed on to this location and began creating a self sufficient community."

"That is a tale that I would like to hear," Chokhmah said.

"I will be happy to tell it," Nahid replied, "but I think that we should move over to the dining hall at this point, and I can talk with you there. In the meantime, the chairs in this room will be moved so you all may sleep in this building tonight."

Eluned and the others thanked Nahid, and followed her out of the meeting room toward the dining hall. This was a long rectangular building outfitted with numerous long tables and benches. A long buffet-style table was set up at the rear of the building. Through the open door behind it, the Princess could see a detached building that was clearly used for cooking.

It wasn't long before trays of steaming food were placed on the table. The Questers, who were clearly honored guests at this point, were encouraged to fill their plates.

The food varied from spicy vegetable stews to grilled lamb and chicken to fresh fruits and cheeses, the latter supplied by sheep's and goat's milk, they were told. Chokhmah seated herself next to Nahid, and within a couple of minutes Jahan had wiggled himself in between her and Faolan. Cyrus strode over, and apologized, but Chokhmah informed him that she was happy for Jahan to sit with her.

"His mother?" she asked. Cyrus shook his head. "I'm sorry for your loss." Her voice was filled with compassion. "I, too, lost my mother."

"Thank you," he said, pointing to where he'd be sitting. "Please send him over to me if he becomes a problem."

"I promise," she smiled, and ruffled the boy's thick hair.

After they had enjoyed their meal for a few minutes, the imperator began her tale.

Prior to the confluence of events that caused the Devastation, she told them, a group of scientists, about a dozen women and men, had created an underground laboratory on the outskirts of Buta where they could work in secret on human enhancement through genetic modification.

"It's not so much that they were trying to create something new," she explained, "but rather that they were trying to breed for human mutations that already existed."

Jabberwock was the only one nodding in understanding. Everyone else looked nonplussed.

"For example," Nahid continued. "Pelfans already had a natural and not that uncommon mutation—Distichiasis—or double eyelashes."

"Well that explains it," Faolan grinned. "Chokhmah used her mutation to entrance me."

"You're one to talk," Yona, who was sitting to the right of Faolan, laughed, and said the word "Wolfman" under her breath.

"I'm not sure that's a mutation you can 'breed' for as it isn't a choice," he countered quietly.

Nahid smiled. "Double eyelashes are a dominant trait although they are not always as lush as ours tend to be." She returned to her story. "What they were breeding for through direct manipulation with eggs and sperm were the mutations of super endurance, hyper photographic memory and the ability to eat anything without it hurting the digestive system."

"Those mutations were already in existence in Pelf?" Chokhmah's voice echoed with astonishment.

"To a minor degree, but these scientists were certain that Pelf, and maybe other kingdoms were heading toward some major catastrophe, and they were trying to prepare for surviving beyond that."

"It turned out that only Pelf was destroyed," Jabberwock said, "although the Djed Sea was poisoned, and of course, Kamea was devastated as well."

"It was really only the unanticipated acceleration of climate change, and the wars which ensued that drastically reduced the world's population," Gwrhyr added.

"And why most of the planet is under water or ice now," Eluned concluded.

"Were they successful with this genetic modification?" Chokhmah wanted to know. Jahan had scrambled onto her lap, and she gave him a hug.

"They were," Nahid conceded, "but not everyone had all the mutations. We have at least one, and sometimes two, but rarely all three. Unfortunately, they did not discover that these modifications left them with one serious drawback until they had already fled Pelf and the Aberrations."

They waited in silence, and she continued. "They had already settled here in what they came to refer to as Kuna, and had begun the work to make the land arable. When they left Pelf, it was from the remains of Buta. They did not have boats and would have been forced to cross the outlet of the Djed Sea into the South Ocean but by this time the sea was cut off."

"A plate shift caused by explosives, I believe," Jabberwock said.

Nahid nodded. "It allowed them to cross by land and make

their way up to Kamea, which they found in ruins. Not only were their children on this overland trek, but they also brought with them sheep, goats and chickens as well as the seed they would need. And by the time they arrived here, they had even begun to call themselves by a new name—as far as they knew Pelf no longer existed and they were nothing like the Aberrations. They designated themselves the Preternaturals."

"Sounds appropriate," Chokhmah murmured. Jahan's eyelids were beginning to droop and he laid his head on Chokhmah's shoulder.

"What they discovered once here," Nahid continued, "is that they had also carried with them, in the bodies of those who had been genetically modified, a mutation for a new form of progeria, a mutation that could be carried by the host without affecting it, but passed on to the child."

"Progeria?" Eluned interjected.

"It's a form of rapid aging," Nahid explained. "And in this new mutation those who exhibit the symptoms rarely live beyond the age of eight."

"And therefore can't reproduce," Jabberwock said. "Which explains, if I understand correctly, why your population numbers remain so low."

Nahid shook her head, sadly. "That, in addition to things like accidents, infections, dying in childbirth, and that type of thing. Otherwise, we remain relatively healthy. But, we have a very high incidence of progeria."

"I am sorry," Chokhmah' eyes glistened with tears, and she gently kissed the cheek of the sleeping child on her lap. "May I ask what the symptoms are?"

"Jahan does not display any of the symptoms," Nahid replied hastily. "The symptoms appear in the first year of the child's life—their growth slows, they lose their hair, and one can see that their face is narrow with a small jaw and a beaked nose, and it gets progressively worse from there."

Jahan was clearly one of the lucky ones, Chokhmah thought. "It is never easy to lose a child," she said, "but to have that eventuality as a normal part of one's existence is difficult to imagine."

"I wish I could say that it is something we have come to terms with," Nahid said, "but death is never easy to accept and progeria, itself, is neither an easy life nor easy death."

"How many children with progeria do you have here at the moment?" Jabberwock asked.

Nahid shifted uncomfortably in her seat.

"At what age?" Jabberwock asked.

"As soon as it's certain," Nahid admitted. "The community decided centuries ago that it was cruel to both the parents and the child to watch them disintegrate like that, particularly as it does not affect brain function. Perhaps if the mutation was rare, things might have gone differently. It was, still is, a difficult choice but as there is no treatment, it seemed the only humane one."

"Are you saying?" Eluned was aghast.

"Euthanasia," Jabberwock stated.

"There is no physical pain," Nahid explained. "The child goes to sleep and never awakes. The parents grieve, naturally, but they would be doing so eventually. What am I saying? There is no way to compensate for the grief caused by our ancestors' attempts to improve us as humans. And yet we have no choice but to live with the consequences."

"It is certainly a moral and ethical dilemma," Chokhmah concurred. "And one that I cannot speak to as not only have I never had a child, but I have also never seen a child with this condition."

"Believe me," Nahid sighed. "You don't want to."

"You sound as if you speak from experience," Jabberwock said.

"I'd say that about once every few generations, we forget

what it is like, and we allow these children to live," Nahid's voice trembled. She took a deep breath, and spoke again. "One of those children was my first child. A daughter. My husband and I were so happy. We called her Arezoo, and all was well until she was nearly a year old. Then we realized she had the mutation. Her growth slowed, her hair fell out. And yet we just couldn't submit to the plan for euthanizing her. We begged the imperator and council at the time, and were granted her life. It was horrendous watching her age so quickly, and then die when she was seven. And it is difficult to explain to a child what is happening to them."

She was silent for a moment. "My husband's grief was intolerable. He sank into a deep depression and within a year of her death, he had taken his own life. Needless to say, when that happens, the entire community grieves, and we don't allow it to happen again. At least, for a while."

There was an extended moment of silence as they digested Nahid's story.

"So you continue to isolate yourselves to prevent the spread of this mutation?" Jabberwock's question was more of a statement.

"Yes, and we would request of you, Queen Njima, that we continue to be allowed to do so," Nahid said to the woman who sat opposite her.

"I see no reason not to grant your request," Njima said, "but I have one caveat."

"Yes?" Nahid's brow creased.

"We are going to great lengths to collect these treasures in an effort to prevent the war threatening the Awen Alliance," she explained. "But should war come to pass, I would ask that you lend your support in whatever way possible."

"I can't confirm that until I talk with my council and my people." Nahid looked around her at the smiling and chattering people who occupied the other tables.

"Understood," Njima said. "We leave early tomorrow for Kamea. But, we shall return this way. I will expect an answer then."

"That seems more than fair." Nahid bit her lip. "Will there be repercussions if we say no?"

"Of course," the Queen said, "but what form that might take I have yet to determine. Obviously, you lived in Naphtali for centuries without ever paying taxes or offering any other support. I will not punish you because we were ignorant of your presence, but should you choose not to join with us on occasion of war, we will have to work out some form of recompense. I do not mean that as a threat but rather as a way to be a part of the Kingdom of Naphtali."

"That, too, seems more than gracious." She turned to look at Chokhmah. "I wish you could stay longer. It is so nice to meet a Pelfan who isn't harnessed with these mutations."

"I would really like to spend some time with this community," Chokhmah agreed, "even though there is no first hand experience of Pelf among us, you did say that everyone here is familiar with the history of Pelf and your exodus from that Kingdom?"

"We have a written history in our library," Nahid said. "Perhaps someday you might have a chance to read it."

Chokhmah's eyes glowed with anticipation. "I would love that opportunity. Perhaps when this quest is over, I can return?"

"You are always more than welcome, Queen Parisa," Nahid smiled and stood. "It has been a long day, and I wish you all a good night. We have breakfast here at dawn before we all head to our various duties. You will, I hope, join us."

"Thank you," Chokhmah caught Cyrus' eye, and he walked over to collect his sleeping child as Nahid walked away to say goodnight to her fellow Preternaturals.

"Thank you," he told her. "He fell for you the moment he saw you."

"Don't we all," Faolan muttered under his breath while helping Chokhmah to her feet.

The gypsy grinned, and ruffled the boy's hair again. "He is very sweet, and I look forward to seeing him again upon our return."

The others stood as well and followed Nahid out of the building, thanking everyone for the food and hospitality as they left.

19ᵀᴴ Gort

Following a quick breakfast in the dining hall, the Questers said their goodbyes to those of the Kuna community who were still eating. Then, riding double file, they returned to the road to Kamea.

"What are you thinking?" Gwrhyr asked Eluned after she had ridden in silence for more than half an hour.

She was still chafing a little from his little speech the previous night as they were getting ready for bed—explaining why she needed to be more cautious when imparting information. She had felt strongly that telling Cyrus and the other Preternaturals their story was important to the Quest. And, she thought she been had been proven correct. Yet, Gwrhyr was also right, she admitted to herself. It would not have hurt to know a little more about their situation before saying anything. She would try to be careful in the future. "Probably too much," she responded.

"What do you mean?"

"I keep being amazed at how complicated life is—nothing is black and white, everything is grey. It's funny," she trailed off.

"What is?"

"When I was young, everything was black and white for me," she explained. "Even my clothes—white for spring and summer, black for fall and winter. Breakfast was at eight o'clock, lunch at noon, and dinner at seven. I studied with Jabberwock in the morning, and with Brother whoever-it-was-at-the-time in the afternoon. Everything was so scheduled and orderly. History was just that—history. But it's not that simple, and I will never see it that way again."

"I love you."

"What?" She wasn't expecting that.

"You're just not the same person I met last winter," he said.

"I don't understand. Are you saying that you love me or that you love love me?"

"Love love," he grinned. "I like that. Yes, I love love you."

She smiled back at him while considering what he'd just said. It was true that her feelings had changed for him over the course of the past several months, but did she really love him? She thought she did. At least, that's what she imagined love was supposed to feel like. "I think I love love you too, Gwrhyr."

"Excuse me!" Faolan called back at them. "We're drowning in sap up here."

There was laughter from the couples ahead of and behind them.

"Wat goin' on?" Bonpo, who was at the end of the cavalcade, called out. Eluned and Gwrhyr had been talking quietly, but had still been overheard by Faolan and Chokhmah ahead of them, and Yona and Njima behind them.

"It's nothing, Bonpo," Yona giggled, looking over her shoulder, at the giant. "Gwrhyr and Eluned are just in love love with each other."

Bonpo chuckled. "It 'bout time."

The Princess found herself blushing once again, but this time she didn't mind.

ACCORDING TO CYRUS, WHOM THEY'D ASKED before they left Kuna that morning, it would take the group about one and a half days to reach the outskirts of Kamea.

"About a day's ride from here," he had told them, "the road will once again become more difficult to travel because we haven't kept it clear all the way to Kamea."

"Maybe we should sharpen the machetes before we leave." Yona had said, rubbing her right bicep, which was still a little sore.

"We can do that for you while you eat breakfast," Cyrus had offered, and they'd been handed the now razor sharp knives when they left.

TOWARD THE END OF THE DAY, when it looked as if the brush was beginning to get thicker, they stopped and made camp. It was a little earlier than they usually stopped but none of them could face clearing a camping spot and having to clear the road the following day.

The early sojourn did give Bonpo a little more than usual to prepare a decent meal, which included some vegetables and goat presented to them as they left. He stewed the chunks of goat meat and the eggplants, peppers, onions and squashes with some jarred tomatoes, spices and wine, and in a little over an hour they were sitting around the campfire enjoying their evening meal.

"Gosh Yona," Eluned suddenly spoke from her reverie, "I just realized that it's only two weeks until your twenty-first birthday. Guess you won't be setting a wedding date with King Hevel now, huh?"

Yona laughed. "And I can't tell you how glad I am that's not going to happen."

"I am happy as well," Njima kissed her cheek.

"It's only ten days until my birthday," Gwrhyr interjected.

Eluned quickly did some addition in her head. "You were

born on the First of Hetal? How old will you be?" She realized she had never asked.

"It's my twenty-second birthday."

She was silent for a moment. "You know, the longer we're all together, the more I realize how little I know about everyone." She stood up. "I'll be back in a second. A minute later she returned, journal and pencil in hand. She opened the book, pencil poised, "Now tell my your birthdays everyone."

"Chokhmah," she cried when the gypsy confessed her birthday had been on the 17th of Saitheh, "why didn't you tell me?"

"I'm sorry, my love," Chokhmah said, "but it was May Day, and not only was there a lot going on for the celebration, but do you not remember how miserable you were that day?"

The Princess looked crestfallen. She did remember. She'd been awful to be around that day from the horror of having to spend time with King Arawn to the anxiety of waiting for Yona to return from her visit with her pirate friend, Libni. "I am so sorry," she apologized. "I was horrible that day. Just horrible."

"It is quite all right, my dear," Chokhmah soothed her. "I will have many more birthdays, I hope."

"I hope so too," Faolan pulled her closer.

"Well, I am still deeply sorry, and I promise it won't happen again," the Princess assured her. "So what about you, Bonpo?"

"I no know birfday. Some time in winter. Lees or Beth," he told her.

"Can I make up one for you?"

"If it make you happy, yes," he agreed.

"Yes, it will make me happy," Eluned smiled. "Well," she mused, "as Faolan was born in Beth, why don't we say you were born in Rees. How about the 28th? That's the last day of Rees so almost Beth?"

"Sound good to me, Plincess," Bonpo chuckled. It amused him that the Princess was worried about something that was insignificant to him. He didn't even know how old he was; he'd lost track many years ago.

"And what about you, Jabberwock? You're the only one who hasn't said," she turned to look at him. He was curled up close to the fire.

"I have absolutely no idea when I was born," he admitted.

"Does that mean I can pick a birthday for you too?"

"Be my guest," he yawned.

"What's your favorite season?"

"Summer," he responded. "I like being warm."

"Hmmmm," she pondered. "How about the twenty-fifth of Teeneh?"

"That strikes me as very random. Is there a reason?"

"It's the day Queen Fuchsia was born," she replied.

"Ah yes," Jabberwock remembered. "Your great grand-mother used to love celebrating her birthday. Actually, she loved celebrating everything. She was forever coming up with excuses to jubilate," he chortled. "She loved a good party."

"So, the twenty-fifth of Teeneh is fine with you?"

"Absolutely," he grinned. "Queen Fuchsia and I can share a birthday."

"Good," she shut her journal. "From now on, we celebrate everyone's birthday."

"I'm first," Gwrhyr slung an arm around her shoulders. "Do I get to pick my birthday present?" he whispered in her ear.

"I'm afraid to ask," Eluned leaned into him.

"Just teasing," Gwrhyr tipped her chin, looking into her eyes. "I would never ask you to do anything you weren't com-fortable with."

"How do you know if I'm not comfortable with it unless you ask?" she teased back.

"Mmmmm," he pressed his forehead against hers, "then I might just have to risk it."

"Yeah?" the Princess pulled back to look at him.

He gazed into her eyes for a moment. "It's sorely tempting, I'll tell you that." She shivered as a cool breeze tousled her curls, and he pulled her into the crook of his arm. Leaning her head against his shoulder, she watched the dancing flames of the fire—they were almost mesmerizing. Combined with the warmth of his body, and the murmur of her friends talking quietly around her, it wasn't long before she felt her eyelids drooping.

"Time to call it a night, Fy Drysor?" Gwrhyr murmured.

Eluned yawned and stretched before reluctantly standing. "Yes," she admitted. "I have a feeling it's going to be a tough day tomorrow."

THEY HADN'T RIDDEN A QUARTER OF A MILE the next morning before they were forced to dismount and begin hacking their way down the road. They took turns throughout the day—Faolan and Chokhmah, Eluned and Gwrhyr, Yona and Njima, and Bonpo—alternating who was doing the cutting each time their arms got tired. By the end of the day, not only were they exhausted, but they also had absolutely no idea how much further it was before they reached Kamea.

They cleared out a camping spot, gathered wood for a fire, and set up tents automatically, bodies numb with exhaustion. Even Bonpo was tired, and it was all he could do to scrounge together some bread, cheese, hard sausage and some dried fruit. As the evening was bordering on cold, they mulled some wine and stared blearily into the fire waiting for the alcohol to numb the pain a bit.

Eluned was particularly miserable—not only were her arms sore, but she had also wielded the machete enough to raise blisters on her palms, which had later burst and were now raw and slightly bleeding. Yet, she didn't want to say anything or complain because no one else seemed to be suffering similarly.

She finally hiccoughed back a slight sob, and broke the

silence. "Will we even know when we reach Kamea? I mean, other than because we're standing on the shore of the Sea of Blood?"

"I'm sure we'll know," Gwrhyr attempted to assure her, reaching for her hand to squeeze it. She flinched, and his eyes narrowed. He took her wrist and forced her to turn over her palm.

"By Omni, Eluned," he was aghast. "Damn it, why didn't you say anything?"

A tear slid from her eye, and she sniffed. "I didn't want to be a bother."

"What is it?" Chokhmah asked.

"Broken and bleeding blisters," Gwrhyr told her.

Groaning a little, the gypsy stood. "I have some balm and bandages. I will go and get them."

Faolan jumped to his feet. "I don't want you heading off into the dark alone." He picked up a lantern and they moved toward their tent, returning a couple of minutes later with the items she needed to treat Eluned's wounds.

"No magic tea for this, huh?" Eluned tried to joke as Chokhmah spread the balm over the blisters.

The gypsy smiled. "No, but this ointment has something in it that should take away some of the pain." She wrapped her palms in linen bandages and ordered her not to do any more brush cutting until the wounds were healed.

"See, that's why I didn't say anything," Eluned cried. "I'll feel so useless."

"I am sure you can make it up to us later," Chokhmah was using her soothing voice again. It often worked on the Princess.

"But . . ."

"But nothing," Gwrhyr said. "What you can do instead is rest tomorrow, and then do the bulk of the wood gathering and other camp preparation tomorrow night."

The Princess considered what he said for a second. Hopefully, by the following evening they would be in Kamea, but they would still need to camp. She nodded. "Yes, that seems fair. I'm willing to do that." She paused. "But, I still think I'm going to need another mug of wine before I can sleep tonight."

"You're not the only one, honey," Njima said.

"Absolutely!" Faolan agreed. "Ladle it up, Bonpo."

"Sure ting," the giant said with a grin, "but me first!"

Later, when they were walking to the tent they were sharing with Jabberwock, Gwrhyr stopped Eluned and drew her into a hug before taking her chin in his hand. "The entire burden of this quest is not on your shoulders. We are a team for a reason, and that is so we can share responsibilities and help each other when it is needed. Never, ever hide something like that from us again, okay? We could have prevented it altogether if you had only told someone."

"I'm so sorry," she choked back her tears. "I just worry so much that you still think of me as a pampered princess and I keep feeling like I have to prove that I'm not that person anymore."

"Fy Drysor," he said. "I know better than anyone just how much you've changed. I, no we, just want you to be you. We love who you are not who you think you should be."

The Princess wiped away a tear. "Thank you. I promise not to do anything like that again," she grinned. "Although you may come to regret that."

"I doubt it." He pressed his lips to hers forcing himself to pull away a minute later. "And I never will if you continue to kiss me like that."

HAD THEY PUSHED ON another twenty minutes, they could have camped on the plain the previous night and not been forced to clear a campsite. They rode out of the forest to find that the road opened up onto a high plain within a couple of hundred yards of their campsite. The path was wide and distinctly visible as it made its way westward across the plain with only the occasional cactus or scrub brush to disturb the short grass that covered the terrain.

They had ridden a couple of miles when Faolan reined in Fiachdubh and pointed to the north.

"What are they?" Yona asked, squinting. "They look too small to be deer."

"Not to mention the fact that deer don't tend to herd in groups that large," Faolan added.

"Antelope or gazelles, perhaps" Jabberwock suggested.

Faolan looked at Jabberwock and they both nodded. Where there was prey there were predators. Clucking to Fiach-dubh, Faolan continued on, but he was careful to continually scan the plain on either side of the road.

"We must be getting close," he said after they had ridden a few more miles. The plateau was ending and the road slowly began to descend and it wasn't long before they could see the still waters of the Sea of Blood in the distance.

As they made their way down off the plateau toward the former Djed Sea, Eluned found her heart accelerating in anticipation of her first glimpse of the ruins of Kamea. While most castles occupied high points on the landscape, the palace in Kamea was said to have taken up most of a peninsula that protruded into the Djed Sea. If they could find that peninsula, assuming it hadn't sunk beneath the waters of the Sea of Blood, they might be able to find the Crock and the Dish.

'It just has to be, it just has to be,' Eluned found herself repeating over and over in her head. Because otherwise, what would be the point of the Quest? It might take some search-ing but surely they could find them. She glanced over to see Gwrhyr watching her. "What?"

"You were muttering something."

She laughed out loud. "So much for my internal mono-logue! I really thought I was thinking that."

"Thinking what?"

"That we have to find the Crock and Dish," she sighed. "It just has to be."

"Indeed." His nod was perfunctory. "Otherwise why would we be here?"

"In other words, stop worrying about it?" She smiled.

"Exactly."

The next curve in the road finally brought them the view they'd been waiting for—the ruins of the former capital sprawled northwards and southwards along the coast of the Sea of Blood covered mostly by sand. They reined in their horses to survey the vista for a moment. It was quite sobering. Here and there rock or brick walls or a broken archway protruded through the debris that covered the city, but the centuries had done their work and very little of the old buildings could be seen.

The occasional gust of wind wending its way down from the plain sent little dervishes of sand whirling through the ruins like gritty ghosts.

"Looks like we'll be exchanging our machetes for shovels," the Princess noted.

There were a few grunts in response but mostly silence as they studied the coastline below them trying to pick out the peninsula that would have been home to Kamea's palace.

Gwrhyr pointed to a spot to the northwest of where they were standing. It seemed a likely spot, particularly if you took into account the fact that the sea's level looked as if it had dropped at least a thousand feet in the meantime.

"It makes sense," Jabberwock agreed. "With the outlet to the sea closed, sea levels would become dependent on how much water flows into it."

"In which case, the level probably rises a little during the spring melt," Gwrhyr agreed. "I imagine the sea is now hypersaline, though."

"Does that make water a problem for us then?" Faolan wanted to know.

"Good question," Gwrhyr admitted. "I'm sure any wells have long since been filled or caved in, and while I don't doubt that there are springs down there, I don't know how long it will take us to find one."

"Time to pull out the magic hamper, Yona," Eluned said. "Do you still have water in it?"

"Water, wine and olive oil," she informed them.

"Good," Gwrhyr nudged Ruari with his feet, "then it's time to make our way to Palace . . ."

"Shamash," Njima said. "It's the Shamash Palace. It was said to be quite beautiful—lots of arches, and columns, and bas relief artwork of the Kingdom of Naphtali's history on both the inside and outside of the palace walls. "

"Just one more thing," Gwrhyr noted as they continued their descent into the city. "Keep an eye out for anything we might use as a shovel."

They reached the outskirts of the city about noon, and stopped for a quick lunch of sheep jerky and oatcakes. Now that they were off the windy plain, the road was no longer visible. They were going to have to carefully pick their way across the city toward the shores of the sea.

"We're going to have to lead the horses," Faolan told them when they were ready to move on. "Without a clear path, they could easily step into a pit or hole. That is, we just don't know what's underneath the sand."

"Should you not then shift?" Chokhmah asked. "It would seem safer if you led us through the city as a wolf."

"Yes, you and Jabb," Eluned agreed. "He can communicate, you can find the way."

Faolan looked around. They were pretty exposed at the moment, and he didn't feel comfortable stripping in front of his friends.

"Chokhmah and I can hold up a blanket," Gwrhyr said.

Faolan nodded and dismounted while Chokhmah detached one of the blankets that was rolled up behind her saddle. He then helped her off Halelu. Within minutes, the process was over and they continued their trek across the city with Gwrhyr leading Fiachdubh as well as his own horse, Ruari.

It took them the remainder of the day to finally reach the peninsula and the ruins of Shamash Palace. As they searched for a solid area in which to set up camp, Bonpo suddenly groaned.

"What is it?" Eluned asked. It was rare for Bonpo to be anything but jolly.

"We no haf wood," he told her. "No wood, no fire."

No fire meant they would have neither hot food nor heat to dine by that night. "We have oil lamps for light," she said, "but we're going to have to figure this out tomorrow." If only they had put some charcoal into Yona's hamper. They had used it for heat in Jazeel. If only they had brought a briquette or two with them on the journey. She wanted to kick herself for not thinking of it.

"What is it?" Njima, and the others, hurried over to them. "You two look worried."

"We don't have any wood," Eluned moaned. "Please tell me that one of you had enough foresight to carry along some charcoal."

"Of course," Njima assured her. "I always carry charcoal with me."

The Princess hugged the Queen. "Oh, Praise Omni! If we put a few pieces in the Hamper then we'll have a steady supply while we're here."

"And," Faolan noted, "if this city was reduced to ashes as some point, I imagine we'll come across some charred wood when we start digging."

"I would have been willing to keep you warm Princess," Gwrhyr teased her.

"Don't worry," she laughed, now greatly relieved. "I still expect you to."

"I suggest that we forego the coal fire tonight," Jabberwock added. "It will soon be dark, and I imagine that tomorrow we will be setting up a more permanent camp elsewhere. Excavating the palace is going to take a while as we have absolutely no idea where the Crock and Dish were kept. We have to assume the king and queen were aware that they possessed them or we wouldn't have been sent to gather the treasures. So cold rations tonight, Bonpo, and early to bed for us all. We have a lot of work ahead of us."

"In that case, we're going to have to take turns watching the horses," Faolan noted. "Without a fire to scare away possible predators, we could be leaving ourselves open to attack."

"Do you think there are predators out there?" Njima asked.

"Honestly, I think they would confine themselves to the plateau," Faolan admitted, "but just because we didn't see anything today doesn't mean there isn't anything out there. We can't risk losing the horses, though. If we each take an hour, it shouldn't be a problem, though. Who wants the first watch?"

"I'll take it," Njima offered.

22ND GORT

The group decided that the first order of business was to find a more permanent spot to camp. A quick search of their immediate surroundings revealed to them that some areas had collected more sand than others.

"Which," Gwrhyr noted, "means the areas with less sand are more protected from the wind."

"If we can find an enclosed area with little sand it would make a good camping spot," Jabberwock agreed.

They divided into the obvious groups of twos with Jabberwock accompanying Eluned and Gwrhyr, leaving Bonpo behind to keep the horses safe and to make lunch. They set out in different directions to look for likely campsites with the agreement to meet back at the current site at noon.

"Yona, come look." Njima was peering through an arched doorway.

Yona joined her, and started nodding her head in approval. "There's very little sand in there."

"It looks as if it was once an inner courtyard." In the center of the wall on each side was an arched doorway with a couple of narrow arched windows up high and to either side of the door. Yona and Njima were standing in one of these arched doorways. Along all four sides of the enclosure, a portico supported by narrow columns shaded the wall. In the center of the sand-covered courtyard was a piece of sculpture that probably once served as a fountain.

Yona stepped down into the portico, and Njima followed. "That's odd," she pointed. "Are those bones?" She took a few more steps, leaving the portico and entering into the courtyard where she leaned over and picked up a skull. She held it up to show to Njima, who stood by her left side. The skull rattled, and upon inspection she saw that some of the teeth from the jaw had fallen into the brain cavity. "Why is it so pitted?"

"Shhh," hissed Njima, suddenly painfully gripping Yona's left forearm.

Yona was opening her mouth to protest when she felt fear instantly suck the air from her lungs. Her throat was so dry she couldn't swallow. They were surrounded.

There had to be at least half a dozen or so that she could see, and probably more behind her. Cobras the color of sand had reared up around them and leaned towards them, tongues flicking. Their heads seemed a little larger than normal, and scales covered the area in which there should have been eyes.

Njima and Yona stared into each other's eyes barely daring to breathe. Was it motion or sound that had attracted them? How long before they attacked?

Clearly they hunted in a, what was the word? Yona tried to remember. The cobra was the sigil of Adamah's neighboring Kingdom of Tarshish. She should know this. The memory returned, and she smiled despite herself. A quiver. How ironic. But the quiver full of arrows on her back wouldn't do her any good now as it would involve too much movement to get at them and her bow. She glanced down at the skull in her hand. What if she threw it? Would they follow after it? Could they make it through whatever gap occurred if they did?

She looked back up at Njima and then down at the skull again, making a slight nod to indicate, she hoped, what she planned to do. Njima nodded, preparing to make a mad dash back to the doorway through which they had entered the courtyard.

Yona slowly raised the skull until it was at shoulder level, cocked her arm back and tossed it as hard as she could toward the opposite side of the courtyard. As the skull left her hand, they were already turning and running toward the portico. Most of the snakes had flung themselves after the skull but there were still a couple to maneuver through, and as she sprinted past them, Yona felt a sting on the back of her thigh.

Njima also gasped in pain, as a sharp pain bolted up her right calf. But they continued to run until they were sure none of the cobras were chasing them. Only then did they finally skid to a halt and tug down their leather breeches to inspect the damage. But it wasn't bite marks they found on their legs but rather small but splotchy burns.

"It's like acid," Njima said. "I think that they must be spitting cobras, not biters."

The acid was strong, though. It had burned tiny holes through their pants, and the wounds stung, but clearly had they not been running away, it would have been their eyes the snakes were aiming for. What better way to incapacitate your quarry?

"They were hoping to make us as blind as they are, no doubt" Yona said, pulling her trousers back up.

"I imagine their prey is usually much smaller." Njima tied the laces on her pants. "That was quick thinking with the skull, by the way. I'm not sure I would have thought of it." She smiled and drew Yona into a hug, kissing her on the tip of her nose. "Every day you surprise me. Every day you make me realize just how blessed I am to have found you."

"I feel the same way." Yona returned the kiss. "We must

thank Eluned. If not for her, we wouldn't be here." She giggled. "If not for her . . ."

"We wouldn't be fighting cobras?" Njima laughed, sliding her arm around Yona's waist as they began to walk back toward the campsite.

"Or have solved the mystery of the pitted skull," she grinned. "I still think it's the perfect place to camp, though," Yona said.

"I do wonder where those other doors led," Njima mused. "Ours was clearly off a hallway of some sort, but were one or more of the other rooms bedrooms, a dining or sitting room?"

"Perhaps we need to recommend a possible 'Battle of the Courtyard' to the rest of the gang?" Yona suggested. "The Questers versus The Spitting Cobras. Or can I somehow fit 'quiver' in there?"

"Ah yes, I'd forgotten," Njima smiled broadly. "A quiver of cobras."

"Yes," Yona grinned. "How apropos, huh?"

"Very. The Questers versus The Quiver. I like it."

THEY WERE THE FIRST TO ARRIVE BACK in the courtyard.

"'Ello dere!" Bonpo greeted them. "You find someting?"

Yona rolled her eyes. "You have no idea what we just went through, but we'll wait until everyone gets back to tell the story. The answer is yes, though. We think we found an excellent spot."

During the next half hour or so, the remainder of the group trickled back into the campsite—Faolan and Chokhmah about twenty minutes later followed by Gwrhyr, Eluned and Jabberwock in another fifteen, the latter having pushed their search as long as possible.

"We thought you'd never get back," Yona jumped up and ran toward Eluned when she first spied them.

"Why? What is it?" Eluned thought Yona sounded truly distressed.

Yona took her arm and led her toward the others, Gwrhyr and Jabb following behind them.

Once everyone was seated, Yona and Njima related the morning's adventure.

"Interesting," Faolan mused. "I wonder if the fountain was spring fed."

"You're thinking about the fountain?" Yona shook her head in dismay.

"Actually," Chokhmah patted Faolan on the arm, "he has been worrying about the horses all morning."

"I'm even more confused, if possible," Yona's brow creased in frustration. She'd been expecting wonder, fear or even excitement, but the horses?

"Don't get me wrong, Yona," Faolan tried to smooth things over. "It really is an incredible story—not only being attacked by what seem to be mutant cobras, but figuring out a way to escape with little injury. I can't say I'm surprised by your resourcefulness. If it weren't for your ingenuity, we would never have crossed paths. But, I've had the horses on my mind all morning because I realized last night that there is nothing but sand here."

"And horses can't eat sand," Gwrhyr nodded in understanding, "and we haven't carried enough feed with us, particularly as we don't know how long this is going to take."

"And," Faolan continued, "water is also a problem. We desperately need to find a supply of water."

"What do you propose?" Jabberwock asked.

"Until we find another source of food, I suggest that we take turns—me and Chokhmah, Gwrhyr and Eluned, and Yona and Njima—taking the horses up to the plateau and allowing them to graze all day. We can return to the palace at the end of the day. We can probably find water up there, and hopefully do a bit of hunting. There's antelope so there may be other creatures as well. We're not on the banks of the Leprican anymore, so we need to figure out some other way to maintain our stores of food."

Everyone was nodding—nothing to argue there. They needed to drink and eat to survive.

"Unfortunately," Njima responded to Faolan's original thought, "we didn't have a chance to check out the fountain. I guess the real question is whether or not anyone found something better or is it worth trying to kill the cobras and take over that courtyard as a campsite?"

"It does sound like it would be easier to guard than any open area," Gwrhyr noted. "We still don't know what else might be lurking around here—big predators that feed on antelope are a possibility as are Aberrations. There may be other mutated creatures here as well."

"You didn't happen to come up with a plan for killing the cobras, did you?" Eluned wondered.

"I have a couple of options," Yona said. "I could be the bait, and we could kill them when they reveal themselves to attack me. If we're all armed with machetes and swords, you could station yourselves around the portico nearest to where I stand and surround them yourselves. I'm assuming chopping off their heads will work best."

"Why you?" Eluned looked distressed.

"Because I've already experience the way they attack," Yona explained. "I could find something to protect my face—a cooking pot? Leather?"

"Wat da udder option?" Bonpo asked.

"We could throw something into the midst of them and attack them from behind," Yona admitted. "It sounds less risky, but I think they'd be distracted as soon as they realized that whatever was tossed into the courtyard isn't alive. We don't know what or how they can sense . . ."

Njima interrupted. "I just want to add that it is a fact that the tongues of snakes are like super noses so they should be able to smell pretty rapidly that whatever we've thrown, unless we can find a live animal, is an inanimate object. And as these snakes are blind, they can also probably sense movement and maybe even heat. We don't know why they don't have eyes, but I do know that the eyes are usually not a snake's best feature. These snakes have clearly evolved to find their prey and kill it efficiently. And the amount of pitting on the skull Yona picked up seems to indicate that they use the acid for more than just blinding their prey."

"That makes sense," Faolan nodded. "If they kill in a pack . . ."

"A quiver," Njima interjected.

Faolan raised an eyebrow. "In a quiver, then. If they kill their prey together then they would need to be able to eat it together."

"Seem too risky trow someting," Bonpo said. "I tink I shoul' be da bait."

"Bonpo has a point," Gwrhyr said. "His height and his weight are the two main factors. If these cobras spit acid, I doubt they could reach his eyes, for one. But, we don't even have to risk that because we could find something to cover his face just as easily as Yona's. He could also help kill them because of the length of his reach."

"We could roll blankets around Bonpo's legs on top of his pants to add another layer of protection," Chokhmah suggested.

"If we plepare, ack fast, I tink we can do," Bonpo said. "But firs'—runch."

"And some of Chokhmah's magic balm," Yona agreed. "Both Njima and I have small burns on the back of our legs."

"Thank you, Bonpo," Eluned said, as he handed her a plate. "I appreciate the sacrifice, but if it looks too dangerous when we get there, I'll insist that we look for another spot to camp."

"Tank you, 'Leened. I plomise I be caleful."

When they were fully prepared—machetes and swords in hand, Bonpo's legs wrapped with blankets, and the rectangular piece of wood he used as a cutting board to hold over his face—the group, minus Jabberwock, set off for the courtyard. Eluned had briefly considered using her ring to become invisible, but decided against it. Why hold the moonstone in her hand and risk losing it when the cobras couldn't see her anyway?

"Here it is," Njima stopped at an arched doorway. "Honestly, I'm almost afraid to step back in there. But you can see there is less sand here, and you can even see bits of the tile in the portico." She stepped down into the courtyard and the others followed her.

"We have no idea what's through those other doors," Yona told them. "Hopefully not more snakes."

"First things first," Gwrhyr drew his sword. "Let's get rid of the immediate danger. Is that where you stood?" He indicated a spot where the disturbance of the sand by their feet ended.

"Yes, we didn't get any farther than that," Njima agreed.

"So we just need to spread out on this side of the fountain," he continued, "and remember to keep your eyes safe, as well. Use a hand or arm to block them, if necessary."

They spread out, Yona and Njima heading to the right, Faolan and Chokhmah to the left. Gwrhyr and Eluned remaining in the portico where they entered the courtyard.

"Are you ready, Bonpo?" Gwrhyr asked.

Bonpo nodded and stepped into the courtyard, board in one hand and machete in the other. He took a few steps and stopped. The cobras' response was almost immediate. Some were hidden in the sand, but others slithered disturbingly fast from the opposite side of the fountain as if the sand were oily as opposed to being gritty.

"By Omni, that's so kusemmak creepy," Yona grimaced, raising her machete. "Let's go!" She shouted, stepping into the courtyard.

It all happened quickly, but it felt like slow motion to those who were doing the chopping. Bonpo managed to kill the most snakes because his reaction was immediate, and with one great swing of his machete, four cobras were decapitated. Chokhmah killed one while Faolan managed another two, Yona, Njima and Gwrhyr each sliced through a couple, and Eluned, with the magic Dyrnwyn in hand, exterminated another three.

"Dinna," Bonpo laughed, retrieving a headless body from the sand.

"Seriously?" Eluned was horrified.

"Snake meat betta dan no meat," he explained. "In stew, tase rike chicken."

"I'll take your word for it," The Princess twisted her mouth in disgust. "And try not to think about it. I'm not touching them, though."

"No need, Plincess. "'Member—waste not, want not."

"Okay, Bonpo, I know you're right. The more important question, at the moment," she turned to Gwrhyr, "is did we get them all?"

"We need to check the other side of the fountain, but I think so." He began to walk in that direction and the others followed slowly.

But there were no more, and Gwrhyr suspected that sixteen snakes were probably pushing the courtyard's ability to keep them fed.

"I imagine that fountain is spring fed," he walked over to inspect it. "A water source would be an excellent draw for prey."

They began to scoop the sand out with their hands while Bonpo rounded up the snakes. It didn't take long for the sand to go from dry to wet. And with enough of the wet sand removed, the water began to rise up into the bowl of the fountain again.

"Praise Omni," Faolan breathed a sigh of relief. "Now we

have a way to water the horses, and water for ourselves as well."

"Now, if we can just use those rooms," Yona turned to face the nearest door. "Njima and I will check this one." The women walked toward the door cautiously.

"We'll take that one," Gwrhyr looked at Faolan and pointed to another door, "if you and Chokhmah search the last one."

The general consensus seemed to be that the rooms were in pretty good shape. In addition to the arched doorways and windows leading out to the courtyard, there were also doorways and windows leading out to what once must have been corridors, but were now blocked by sand and debris.

"I'm guessing," Gwrhyr informed them, "that this must once have been the royal quarters because the door in the room we checked was covered in bronze, which probably prevented the wood inside from rotting."

"Same here," Faolan said, "but it could just be hollow now. I didn't think to check but we couldn't open it."

"This section must have been somewhat protected from the fire," Njima conjectured. "I'd guess that doors out into the courtyard were shut behind them when they fled, and that protected the rooms." The courtyard doors were also bronze but had been easy to push open. "It does makes me wonder what happened to the door that led from the corridor into the courtyard, though," she added.

"Maybe it was left open and so it burned too?" Yona suggested.

There were also two smaller rooms to either side of the room furthest from the main corridor, and entrances from each room into those rooms, but no entrance into the corridors, just high narrow arched windows overlooking the hallway.

"Perhaps a privy room of some sort?" Chokhmah surmised.

"I don't see any reason why we can't clean up the courtyard and rooms, and figure out a way to use them to sleep in," Gwrhyr decided.

"It would certainly be helpful if we uncovered some sort of pit toilet in those smaller rooms," Chokhmah observed, "otherwise we will be forced to figure out something else that is preferably snake free."

Faolan nodded. "There may be more snakes not to mention other creatures we have yet to encounter. But how do we split up? There are only three rooms."

"I could share with Yona and Njima if they don't mind," Eluned offered, "and Gwrhyr could be with Bonpo and Jabb."

"I sreep out hea, Plincess." Bonpo had settled down and was using his cutting board to skin the snakes. "Set tent flont dat doah," he pointed to the archway that led to the main corridor. "Dat way, keep guard, and keep blazier goin'"

"What if it rains?" Eluned worried.

"Sreep in tent, Plincess, but if make you feer betta', sreep unda porch when rain." He smiled at her and she returned it.

"Thank you, Bonpo. That does make me feel better. Are you sure that's what you want to do?"

"Vely shooa, Plincess," he returned to the cobras.

Eluned wrinkled her nose in disgust, and turned to the others. "Let's go get Jabberwock, the horses and our gear, and get to work!"

1ˢᵗ Hetal

A week had passed since they had set up camp in the courtyard, and life was quickly becoming habitual.

They had managed to clean up enough the afternoon after finding the courtyard that they were relatively settled in by
nightfall. The following day a new routine began: while one
couple led the horses and the donkey up to the plateau to spend
the day grazing, the other two couples along with Jabberwock
began excavating around the palace. Bonpo remained in the
courtyard cleaning, preparing meals and digging trenches in
the two smaller rooms to be used as the necessary facilities.

Faolan and Chokhmah took the first shift watching over
the animals, and in wolf form it didn't take Faolan long to find
a decent water source on the plateau; the same spring, in fact,
that had attracted the antelope. Hunting was another job required of whoever was shepherding that day, and that proceeded with varying degrees of success.

It didn't take long for Gwrhyr and Eluned to realize they
were hampered by the fact they had only swords. Their first
day on the plateau, Eluned pulled Dyrnwyn from its scabbard
and pointed to the antelope in the distance, "How close do you

think I can get before they stampede?" She paused, watching the blue fire swirl up her arm. "Away from us."

Gwrhyr had laughed. "We're going to have to think of something else."

They arrived back in camp empty-handed, and with profuse apologies. There was bound to be a stream from which they could fish somewhere in Kamea but they continued to search the plain as it seemed more likely to find something there. The first time they returned to the plateau, they had ridden southward with no success, and on this first day of Hetel, the plan was to ride northward.

Because of Yona's proficiency with the bow, she had managed to shoot a couple of prairie chickens on her first trip to the plateau, and a few hares on the second. Faolan had taken down an antelope, and later, a deer.

Back at the palace, the excavators had managed to scavenge a growing pile of charred wood, but very little else. Apparently, the palace had been pillaged as soon as the royal family had escaped eastwards. Using their mugs to dig, they tossed sand out the nearest window. They had yet to find a single dish much less a crock, which meant they had yet to find the kitchens.

"What is it?" Gwrhyr asked Eluned as they rode northward. They had been riding for about an hour with Makeda and Aine attached to either side Ronan's saddle by leads. Gwrhyr, on Ruari, was leading Halelu, Fiachdubh and Derry.

"I'm sorry," she said. "I didn't want to be down on your birthday. I want this to be a good day."

"But?"

"It's like waiting for Nyx," she explained. "There is nothing we can do to make finding the treasure any easier or quicker."

"We will find them, though. I'm sure of it." He sighed. "This quest can be exciting, but it has also definitely been a practice in patience for all of us."

The Princess suddenly laughed—one of her patented tinkling-of-bells trills that Gwrhyr had come to know as genuine amusement on her part.

"What?' he couldn't help smiling.

"I was just remembering how desperate I was to leave Castle Mykerinos and get out and experience the world, and here I am doing exactly what I thought I wanted, and I'm champing at the bit again. Seriously! Why can't I learn to enjoy each day on it's own?" She mulled over all the times since she'd started this adventure that she'd been eager to move on.

"Life is kind of like hurry up and wait," Gwrhyr said.

"You read my mind," she smiled at him. "It's like a wave—sometimes you're on the crest and sometimes you're in the trough and there's a lot of waiting in between. And every time I'm in the trough and think I can't stand it another moment, I begin to crawl out of it again."

Gwrhyr was nodding. "That pretty much sums it up. So are you in the trough now?"

"I think I was when we started out this morning, but the tide has turned," she laughed.

"Good," Gwrhyr chuckled, "I prefer to spend my birthday with a happy Princess."

They continued to ride northward, the plan being to ride until noon, eat lunch and then head back to the palace. A little over an hour later, sometime between nine and ten o'clock, Eluned reined in Ronan.

"Listen," she told Gwrhyr who was coming to a halt with the other horses. They had eventually retreated back into silence, but the mood was definitely cheerier. She waited a few seconds before asking, "Do you hear it?"

His brow creased in concentration. "A dull roar?"

"Waterfall, perhaps? Or rapids?"

"Let's find out," he clucked to Ruari, who began walking again.

"They hear it too." Eluned pointed out the horses' ears, which had begun to twitch. Water also meant greener plants than the dry prairie grass to which the horses were becoming accustomed.

A quarter of an hour later, they could make out the gleam of sun on water. The roar was louder, but the plain was still flat.

"I'm going to go with rapids," Gwrhyr said.

"Probably a rapids leading up to a cascade," Eluned ventured. "Maybe the plateau begins to drop off further eastward this far north."

"Good point," Gwrhyr grinned. "Now who's the know-it-all?"

Eluned laughed, gaily. She didn't often outsmart Gwrhyr. "Happy Birthday!" She threw back her head and laughed some more.

He chuckled. "Laughing at my expense is going to cost you."

"What's it going to cost me?" she giggled.

"Perhaps a swim. Rivers are usually calm just before a rapids."

Her eyes widened. "It'll be cold!"

He was counting on that. It would prevent him from getting into too much trouble. "We'll have plenty of time to dry off. We're still a couple hours shy of noon, and we have a couple of blankets to dry off with." The blankets were to sit on during lunch, but they could be used as towels.

"I don't know," she waffled.

"I do. And I have yet to ask for a birthday present. Besides, I won't ask you to take off all your clothes."

She guessed he could see her in her underclothes. After all, didn't she hope to be naked with him someday? Was there really any harm in it? Not to mention the fact that she was feeling kind of filthy—they'd been reduced to mostly cloth baths since they'd left Castle Indalo, and the washing of hair and clothes was a major undertaking. She felt as if every pore on her body was clogged with sand, and it would be a good way to get her small clothes cleaned. "How about a tentative 'yes'? I'd like to see the river first."

"Absolutely," he agreed.

A few more minutes brought them to the shore of a wide and shallow river, which narrowed and became extremely rocky about one hundred yards down stream where the river began to descend through the rapids.

They'd barely dismounted before the horses and Derry were chomping greedily at the greener grass on the river's bank. Twenty feet or so upstream, the river began a slow curve to the north, and in the curve a small sandy beach could be seen.

"Let's check that out," Gwrhyr pointed to the beach.

It seemed perfect. Standing on the beach the water that lapped the shore was crystal clear and they could see that at least for a few feet it was pretty shallow. Eluned sat down in the sand and unlaced one of the boots she'd bought in Ponike. She pulled off her sock and walked over to the water where she dipped her foot into the river.

"Brrr," she shivered. "It's cold, Gwrhyr."

"You could have used your hand," he reached into the water. It was kind of chilly, but he was determined. "We'll get used to it pretty quickly, and we don't have to stay in long."

"Well, it would be really nice to feel clean for a change."

"I'll go get the blankets," he started walking back toward the horses, "since you've already removed one boot."

She sat down on the sand and unlaced the other boot. She removed it, but she wasn't going to take off the remainder of her clothing until he did.

"Can we get undressed at the same time?" she asked when he returned.

"Of course."

She waited for him to remove his shoes, and then pulled off her sweater because she had another shirt underneath. Which to remove first—shirt or pants? He was already bare-chested, but that wasn't a surprise. She'd seen him shirtless numerous times.

Pants, then shirt were slowly removed, and she stood there shivering in the still chilly mid-morning air. He was removing his pants, and when he looked up and saw her standing before him, pale skin covered in goose bumps, he was torn between pulling her into his arms and making a mad dash for the water so she wouldn't see how much he desired her.

But it was too late.

"That didn't take long," she snickered.

"If you could see yourself you'd understand why." His cheeks colored despite himself. Sometimes it was difficult being a man.

"Well, I'm flattered," she smiled at him. "Ready for the proverbial cold shower?" She nodded to the river.

"Unless there's another option."

She laughed. "At this point—only in your dreams." She reached out a hand. "Let's get clean."

The river began to slope downwards about six feet out and soon the water was waist deep on Gwrhyr, and chest deep on the Princess.

"This is far enough for me." Eluned stopped and quickly immersed herself. She emerged from the icy water gasping for breath. "That knocked the wind out of me," she told Gwrhyr when he reemerged.

"It's bracing, isn't it?" he laughed.

"If by bracing you mean freezing," she couldn't help but giggle even though she was shivering violently.

He pulled her into his arms. "Let's get you out of here, and warm again. You ready?"

She nodded and he scooped her up and carried her back

to shore where he immediately enfolded her in a blanket before wrapping himself in one.

"Better?" he asked. She was still shivering despite the blanket.

"I would be if you held me."

He spread out his blanket, and she joined him on top of it.

"I hate to suggest this, but maybe you should remove your wet underthings. I'll spread them out to dry, and I promise I won't look when you take them off. I'm just afraid that you won't be able to warm up with something that cold and wet against your skin."

She couldn't stop shivering. "Turn around." He did and she quickly removed her under garments and wrapped herself in the blanket again. "I'm ready." She handed them to him, and he walked over to the grassy bank above the beach and placed them in a sunny patch before rejoining her on the blanket. He didn't seem to be as affected by the cold as she was.

"Here," He spread his arms, "let me give you some of my body heat."

He held her blanket-encased body for the next fifteen minutes or so until her shivering had subsided completely.

"Someday, I won't have to get cold for us to do this, right?" she murmured against his neck.

He smiled. That day couldn't arrive too soon for him. He kissed the top of her head where it lay nuzzled beneath his chin. Her hair was still damp, but no longer soaked. "And any time you want to," he promised her. He'd currently hold her any time she desired if the temptation to go further than just a kiss wasn't becoming more and more difficult to battle. "Have you decided how you intend to rescind your betrothal?"

"Well, I'm certainly not looking forward to the bedlam that it will no doubt cause so I'm going to get it over with as soon as possible," she admitted.

"That's probably a good idea," he agreed.

"As soon as I get back to Zion, I'm going to request a face-to-face meeting with Uriel. Hopefully, he'll be willing to make the trip from Aden. You know him, what do you think?" She propped herself up on one elbow so she could see his face.

"I doubt he'll be able to refuse you." He pushed a raven curl off of her face. "I know I can't."

Eluned chuckled. "But, I know that's not true. That's one of the reasons I love you—you have no problem letting me know when I am being unreasonable." She pulled his head down for a kiss.

Jabberwock had suggested they needed to return to their Kingdoms for the winter, and he could see the wisdom in that. But, they hadn't even gone their separate ways and he was already looking forward to the day they could be together unhindered by any other obligations.

They basked in the sun for another half hour or so before Gwrhyr went to retrieve their lunch basket. Following a leisurely lunch, they gathered up the horses and made the trek back to Shamash Palace.

"Hopefully," Eluned said, "this is the last time we'll return empty handed. Now that we've found a river, next time we'll have to figure out a way to fish in it."

THEY ARRIVED BACK AT THE PALACE to discover their fellow Questers had spent yet another fruitless day in search of the treasures.

Another four days passed as usual, although they now were able to add fish to their diet, when Faolan awakened them in the middle of the night.

Bonpo, a very light sleeper, had grown accustomed to Faolan's nightly forays into the city in the form of a wolf. He would usually return from scouting the town an hour or so after he left.

This night, the sixth of Hetal, he'd been gone longer than

usual because they had celebrated Yona's twenty-first birthday the previous evening by consuming too much cognac. Just one small bottle in the Hamper provided more than enough to fete their friend. Faolan had already spent some time that day in wolf form during his stint with Chokhmah on the plateau. He had managed to run down another antelope for their dinner. That exercise, combined with the cognac, meant that he slept soundly that night.

Tonight, on the other hand, he was restless and had ventured further south than usual, tracking the scent of something that smelled putrid. He was curious—had something died or had something been killed. It was worth finding out. What he didn't expect was surprising a pack of Aberrations foraging for food. There were a half dozen of them, and he stopped, staring at them in shock. He had heard they existed. Jabberwock certainly vouched for it, but he still wasn't prepared.

Their movements were very ape-like. Faolan was reminded of a gorilla he had once seen in a travelling show in Thírnagall. The great beast had been taught to do tricks and dance. But their movement—crouched and loose-limbed—was all that was reminiscent of the gorilla. Their eyes bulged and oozed, and running sores covered their naked bodies. Their feet looked human but their hands were mutated into lobster claws—the index finger and thumb fused together to form one side and the other three fingers to form the second. And they were the source of the smell—it was as if they were decaying even as they lived and breathed.

Faolan was so busy studying these monsters of human mutation that he realized nearly too late that he'd been spotted as well. A wordless grunt of recognition erupted from one of the creature's lipless mouths, and Faolan realized that as far as they were concerned he was their next meal.

As they lumbered after him, he turned and bolted northward as fast as his four feet could take him. It wasn't until he reached the palace that he realized he might have inadvertently led the Aberrations to their camp.

He skidded past Bonpo's tent and howled a warning. Bonpo, along with Gwrhyr and Jabberwock were out in the courtyard in a flash followed shortly by Eluned, Njima, and Yona and then Chokhmah in various states of undress.

So much easier, Eluned, who was still half asleep, was thinking, if women could go around bare chested like men without causing a stir. Unfortunately thousands of years of evolution would probably never change that, particularly as it had not changed yet.

"What's going on?" Gwrhyr asked the Bandersnatch as Faolan remained in wolf form.

"He says that he spotted some Aberrations south of here and they may be tracking him back to the Palace." Jabberwock was grim.

"Oh no!" Eluned paled. "Are they as awful as Jabberwock claims?"

Faolan looked at her with what could only be sincere contrition in his eyes.

"Kusemmak," Yona cursed.

"I take it we're going to have to fight these things?" Njima asked.

"Vely rikery," Bonpo agreed.

"Everybody get fully dressed and grab your weapons," Gwrhyr ordered them. "Except for you, Chokhmah. We may need you to be ready to treat any wounds we might receive. And be quick. We don't know how long it will take them to get here."

"Fortunately," Jabberwock called after them as they returned to their rooms, "Faolan says there are only six of them so at least we have them outnumbered."

Eluned turned around. "Not if you and Chokhmah aren't fighting."

"Kusemmak," Yona repeated before disappearing into her room.

Gwrhyr and Eluned rushed back to their room. Her hands were trembling as she pulled on her socks and boots.

"Are you up to this?" he asked, pulling his leather jerkin over a sweater—a little more protection for his chest.

"I'm sorry," Eluned apologized for her quaking hands. "I grew up with tales of how horrible these monsters are, and then I found out that Jabberwock's mate was killed by one of them."

"Is that a yes or a no?"

Her hands continued to tremble as she laced her boots. She took a deep breath and exhaled slowly, attempting to calm herself. She lifted her chin and looked Gwrhyr in the eyes. "Yes. Yes I can do this."

"If you're sure?"

"Well," she laughed but it sounded forced, "if I could handle being nearly sacrificed alive, surely I can do this. Right?" Then she had a thought. "Gwrhyr?"

"Yes?"

"It just occurred to me," she admitted, "this might be the perfect time to use my ring. We know they can see. Won't it be to our advantage if I can attack them without them being able to see me."

Gwrhyr studied her for a moment, brows creased and biting his lower lip as if he was struggling with something.

"What is it? Is it not a good idea?"

He shook his head. "No, it's an excellent idea. It's not that, it's just . . ."

"What?" she took a step closer to him.

"I have a confession to make," he admitted.

"What is it?" For a minute her heart beat wildly—was he going to give her a reason he couldn't be with her?

He walked over to the bag that held his clothing and toiletries and removed a moth eaten cloak.

"I don't understand," she shook her head in confusion.

He swung it around his shoulders and disappeared.

"Kusemmak," she breathed. It was the only word that seemed to fit. "The Mantle of Arthur."

He removed it, and she could see him again. "Did King Uriel give that to you to take on the Quest? Surely, you didn't steal it?"

He didn't know whether or not to be relieved. "Yes," he confirmed. "I'm allowed to have it."

Eluned laughed. "That's amazing! With two of us invisible, we should be able to defeat them." She leaned over and picked up Dyrnwyn, which lay next to her bedroll. It was time to return to the courtyard.

It really was an unfair fight, a massacre, in fact. The first Aberration to enter the courtyard was quickly dispatched when Njima's axe appeared out of the dark and lodged firmly in its brain. The next creature received an arrow to the heart. There was a pause of about ninety seconds before the next two creatures launched themselves through the arched doorway only to be met by Faolan and Bonpo.

While Faolan lunged for the Aberration's throat, Bonpo's sheer size stopped the second in its tracks. It scampered backwards. It was impossible to determine gender in the mostly dark courtyard, but the giant seized it with his left hand while using his machete to slice its throat with his right.

"Da udder two escapin'," he shouted, and the invisible Gwrhyr and Eluned sprinted after them, Eluned clutching the moonstone in her right hand so hard that it left an impression in the center of her palm that she could still see the next day.

The Aberrations literally did not see them coming even though Dyrnwyn's blue light flickered momentarily as the sword found its way through the creature's heart. Gwrhyr slayed the other beast, and they stood for a moment surveying their handiwork.

"I really don't like it," Eluned sobbed, tears sliding down her cheeks as she slipped the moonstone back into her leather pouch. "I'm tired of being forced to kill."

Gwrhyr removed his cape before pulling the Princess into his arms. "I'm so sorry, Fy Drysor." He kissed her forehead. "But, we had no choice. They were clearly here to make a meal of Faolan. Obviously they didn't, or perhaps they even couldn't, count on an ambush."

She nodded, leaning her head against his chest for a moment, then sighed deeply. "Okay, I'm ready to go back and see how the others are doing. What about?" she pointed to the bodies at their feet.

"Leave them for now. I have a hunch we'll be burying them soon."

The others were feeling just as dismayed and depressed by the massacre as Eluned.

"And yet," Jabberwock said, "we had no choice. They were clearly attacking. What we don't know is whether it was a hunting party and there are more of them out there, or if we've wiped out a band of Aberrations."

"We also don't know what their capabilities are," Gwrhyr added. "How intelligent they are or whether any of their senses are especially sharp."

"Good point," Njima nodded. "If there are others, they might be able to find their way here by smell, for example."

"Which why we mus' bury soon," Bonpo said.

"Now." Jabberwock agreed.

"Are you all right, Chokhmah?" Eluned queried. "You've been awfully quiet tonight."

"I am just saddened that this," she indicated the pile of bodies near the doorway, "is all that remains of my people."

"That's not completely true," Yona argued. "What about the Preternaturals? Perhaps you could convince them to return to Pelf and re-settle there."

"I do not think that is a good idea," Chokhmah said. "They

have done a lot of work to be where they are, and, of course, they have the need to keep the progeria gene contained. As long as Njima does not mind them being there, I see no need to change that."

"We also need to keep in mind that we don't actually know what it's like in Pelf now," Eluned was thoughtful. "Those Aberrations were here in Naphtali. Why? We don't know if some other group found a way to save itself or even protect itself to begin with, and maybe they have since chased off the Aberrations. We just don't know."

"This is true, my dear," Chokhmah frowned, forehead creased in thought. "We do not know, and there is always hope." She was silent for a second. "If nothing else then, can we not give these poor creatures a proper burial?" She turned to Yona, "I believe you have some experience with that, my dear, do you not?"

Yona laughed, ruefully. "That I do. Too bad Olcan's not here. He has even more experience with burial services, but I think I can say something meaningful."

"Well, let's get started," Faolan, who was back in human form, wrinkled his nose, "because they reek to high heaven."

It took them the remainder of the night to bury the Aberrations, and they fell into an exhausted sleep as the sun was rising. Gwrhyr and Eluned didn't get the horses to the plateau until noon, which meant they didn't have time to get to the river that day. Despite the previous evening's disruption, the Questers made an effort to slip back into the daily routine—finding the treasures being of paramount importance as winter hastened their way.

11ᵀᴴ HETAL

Faolan and Chokhmah were taking their turn on the plateau again, and the rest of the group had moved to the southwest corner of the palace to continue digging up the ubiquitous sand.

"Seems like just yesterday that I was saying that this is getting incredibly boring," Eluned groaned.

Gwrhyr laughed. "It might as well have been. It was the day before yesterday."

"And the day before that," chimed in Jabberwock.

"And the day before that," Yona laughed.

Eluned was giggling by this point. "All right, all right. I get it. I say it every single time. But, that's because it's true every single time. If for just once we could find something a little more interesting than a piece of charred wood or pottery . . ."

They dug for a few minutes in silence before Eluned spoke again. "I have a question, Jabberwock."

"Yes?" He stopped digging and shook some grains of sand from his nose.

"I've been thinking about the Aberrations." She handed her tankard full of sand to Gwrhyr who was holding his hand out for it. "Doesn't it seem odd that they haven't changed in centuries?"

"I imagine it has to do with the fact that they are extremely inbred," the Bandersnatch mused.

"Seriously!" Njima agreed. "Who on earth would want to mate with a creature like that?"

Both Eluned's and Yona's face twisted in disgust.

"Except," Gwrhyr handed Eluned her tankard, "for another creature like that."

"Their smell alone is noxious enough to scare most animals away," Eluned said. "I'm amazed that they can even find anything to eat."

"The Aberration that killed Kamali was hiding beneath the sand," Jabberwock reminded Eluned. "They have probably come up with ways to hunt that mask their smell. I'm sure they weren't prepared to run into Faolan that night."

"It does make sense that they can only exist here and in the Devastation," Yona mulled it over. "Otherwise, surely they would have all been exterminated by now."

"That's both sad and true," Eluned frowned. "It's not their fault they're so monstrous. No human would ask to become what they've become."

"So does that make killing them a kindness?" Gwrhyr asked.

"That's a good question," Eluned crouched down to scoop up some more sand. "Not unlike trying to decide whether to euthanize the children born with progeria. Do we get to decide which is the greater good? In this case, we don't know enough about the Aberrations to decide. We know they breed. Did the Aberrations we killed have children? Were they being watched by other Aberrations?"

"I'm not sure I want to know the answers to those questions." Yona walked over to the window to toss out her sand.

The implications were devastating. When they buried

the bodies, it had clearly been three men and three women. It was entirely possible that their were little Aberrations waiting somewhere, for nearly five days now, for their parents to return with food. It was also possible that there had been no children or that they were old enough to forage on their own. One thing was certain and that was that they really had no way of finding out without risking their own lives or winding up needing to kill more Aberrations.

"Best to just let it go," Eluned spoke softly. "I just hope we find the treasures soon. I'm not sure I want to be here any-more."

The others nodded their heads in agreement. Winter was fast approaching and the weight of the responsibility to find the treasures was getting heavier by the day.

It was still an hour or so until noon when they heard Bonpo lumbering their way calling, "Plincess! Jabb!"

"We're here!" Eluned shouted turning to face the sound of his approach. "What's wrong?"

Bonpo appeared around the corner tears streaming down his face, and carrying a large clay pot in his outstretched arms.

"Is that?" The Princess ran toward him. "By Omni, Bonpo, how did you find them?"

Eluned was beginning to wonder if they would ever find the Cleric's Crock and Dish with their magic ability to be filled with whatever food was wished for. She peered into the pot and broke into hysterical laughter. "Is that?" she howled with laughter, nearly hysterical with relief. "Oh Bonpo, that's too funny. Is that the stuffed dumpling soup you fed me the first time I met you?"

Bonpo was bellowing with laughter by this point causing the aforementioned soup to slosh around in the pot.

The others were crowding around him.

"Do you have the dish?" Jabberwock queried.

"Back in courtyard." Bonpo indicated with a nod of his head.

"Where were they all this time?" Gwrhyr asked.

"Come," Bonpo turned around. "I show you." He led them back to the courtyard, Crock grasped firmly in his large hands, Eluned practically skipping beside him.

Entering the courtyard, Bonpo placed the Crock next to a pottery dish at the edge of the portico. He then led them across the courtyard to the portico that ran alongside the room shared by the Princess, Gwrhyr and Jabberwock.

"See dat roose tile?" Bonpo pointed to a tile just to left of their arched doorway.

"I've tripped over it many a time," Eluned confirmed.

"I tink it 'bout time to fix dat so I lemove tile to fratten sand an' reset."

"And?" The Princess prompted.

"An someting not feer right. I scoop 'way some a da sand and find box 'neath it."

"Which naturally you had to remove," Jabberwock agreed.

"'Course! Fine tleasures inside."

"How long did it take you to think of filling the Crock with the soup?" Eluned wanted to know.

Bonpo grinned broadly. "'Mediately!"

"Well, we shouldn't let it go to waste," Eluned turned to walk back across the courtyard. "As I remember it was excellent, and it's only getting colder by the second."

"This is quite good, Bonpo." Njima praised him after he'd ladled the soup into bowls for each of them, and she'd taken her first bite of dumpling. "You said you've had this before Eluned?"

"The day I was attacked by the barrow wight, we stopped early at Bonpo's inn, and this soup was one of the things he served us for dinner." Eluned suddenly bit her lip and with a mischievous grin picked up the pottery plate. "And this is what he gave me for breakfast! It was so good!" Before their eyes a flaky apple turnover appeared. "Yes!" she exulted. She cut it into four pieces and handed a steamy slice to Gwrhyr, Yona, and Njima. "Try it if you don't believe me!"

"Very good," Gwrhyr agreed. "Now I really want to know whether or not Rhyngenydd the Cleric was fat."

Jabberwock chortled. "Perhaps he used them as a way to resist temptation; to remain abstemious in his diet."

"You mean his weight would be a tell tale sign?" Yona asked. "If he stayed lean, he was using the treasures correctly . . ."

"And if he was overweight, he was being gluttonous?" Njima finished her sentence.

"Or," Eluned suggested, "maybe he didn't use the treasures for himself at all, but to help the poor and sick?"

Bonpo grinned at her. "I rike da way you tink, Plincess."

"Thank you, Bonpo." She smiled at him affectionately. "At least now, among the Hamper, Crock and Dish, we won't want for food on the way back to Jazeel. And, even better, we can have whatever we want."

"That could be fun in the short term," Gwrhyr said, "but it could get taxing after a while."

The Princess nodded. "True. Sometimes I don't know what I want to eat, I just want to be fed."

"Either way," Yona agreed. "We won't starve. And, more importantly, it will cut our travel time because we can push a little farther each day if Bonpo doesn't have to prepare and cook a meal."

"Hmmm." Bonpo looked surprised. "Hadn't tought of dat."

"And with it getting colder each night, we can use the time to get in a good supply of fuel for the fire before we go to bed," Jabberwock added.

"So," Eluned handed the plate back to Bonpo and stood. "Should we walk up to the plateau to let Faolan and Chokhmah know that the treasures have been found? It seems unfair to wait until they return this evening to tell them."

"Let's walk up there," Gwrhyr said, "but if we don't see them right away, we'll come back. Otherwise, there is no telling which direction they went."

"Do you want to come with us?" Eluned asked Njima and Yona.

"No, you two go ahead," Yona replied. "We'll stay and help with getting things ready to leave in the morning. Right, Jabberwock? We'll be leaving tomorrow?"

"Unless anyone sees a reason not to do so." He agreed.

"I know I'm ready to get out of here," Eluned shuddered. "We still don't know if there are any more Aberrations living in Kamea."

"Can't argue with that," Yona agreed.

ELUNED WAS ALMOST BOUNCING ALONGSIDE GWRHYR as they made their way through Kamea toward the road to the plateau. Hand clasped in his, she swung it back and forth and chattered her happiness to him.

"I don't know why it makes me this absurdly happy that we've found the Crock and the Dish," she said. "Maybe it's because I was beginning to despair of ever finding them. Or maybe it's because Bonpo was so happy that he found them."

"I imagine some of both," Gwrhyr smiled down at her. Her enthusiasm was contagious. "I'll bet there's part of him congratulating himself on even noticing that something was amiss beneath the tile."

Eluned's eyes widened as she considered this. "I hadn't thought of that! What if he had just smoothed the sand, and replaced the tile?"

Gwrhyr squeezed her hand. "Exactly. Would it have ever occurred to any of us to check beneath the tiles?"

She shook her head. "Omni was definitely guiding his intuition."

As they began to climb the switch-backing road up to the plateau, the Princess continued speaking in a joy tinged rush, bouncing from one subject to another. "I'm so glad we can head back toward Jazeel tomorrow. I am ready for a proper bed and bath. I hope Faolan and Chokhmah are within sight because I really want them to know that the treasures have been found! They'll be so happy! I know we have to stop in Kuna for at least a day, but I think we'll make it back to Jazeel a lot more quickly than it took us to get here." She paused for a moment. "Although it will be strange not sharing a room with you." She paused again. "How long do you suppose we can stay there before we have to return to our kingdoms?"

It had dawned on her that Jazeel also represented the last days they would spend together until she informed Uriel of her wish to break the betrothal.

"I don't know," he answered. "On the bright side, the sooner you get back to Zion, the sooner you can be in touch with Uriel, right?"

She bit her lip and nodded as it was both a moment she was dreading and looking forward to. She was definitely going to have Dyrnwyn strapped to her side when she told her father. She unconsciously gripped the scabbard and felt that familiar jolt of electricity and heat. Yes, she always felt strong and capable with her sword at the ready.

Gwrhyr laughed and she looked up to see him looking at her knowingly. "Taking Dyrnwyn with you when you talk to Uriel?"

"I was thinking of telling my father, actually, but yes it gives me confidence." She smiled back. "It would probably be rude to have my sword by my side when I speak to King Uriel, right?"

"Yes," he agreed. "That might be misconstrued."

She stopped. They were nearly at the top. The next turn would take them to the plateau.

"Promise me that I'm doing the right thing." She peered earnestly into his eyes. "

Gwrhyr wrapped his arms around her and bent down to kiss her before saying: "I vow that I, Gwrhyr, will never intentionally hurt you."

She gazed deeply into his hazel eyes. There were little flecks of green in there—the same sea green as hers. He didn't break her gaze. "But you might unintentionally?"

"It's impossible not to do so," he admitted.

She nodded. She supposed that was true.

"But that being said," Gwrhyr continued, "always remember that I truly believe that together we can accomplish anything." He placed his finger on his heart and then pointed to hers, tapping her chest with the tip of his index finger. "Do you believe me?"

"What was that? I don't understand?" Eluned's brow creased in confusion.

"Whenever I do that know that my heart is your heart," he said.

Eluned laughed. He had been so pragmatic when they first met that she forgot that he was really a romantic at heart. She pointed to her heart and then tapped his chest as well. "I do believe you. And my heart is yours."

"Then let's get this show on the road," he took her hand again, and they began the final ascent to the plateau.

The Princess smiled to herself as they climbed because sometimes they really did seem like more of a group of performers in a travelling show than an assemblage of Divinely gathered Questers.

They reached the top of the plateau and scanned the horizon for a sign of horses or Faolan and Chokhmah.

"What's that?" Eluned pointed to the south where dust

was rising in the air. They began to move in that direction and it didn't take them long to realize that the commotion was heading their way.

"They look too big to be antelope," Gwrhyr said. "I think it's the horses. Why would they be running this way?"

The Princess started running toward the oncoming animals, waving her hands and shouting their names—"Ronan! Ruari! Stop! Halelu! Fiachdubh! Stop! Aine! Makeda! Derry! Stop!"

Gwrhyr ran after her, screaming her name. Grabbing her arm when he caught up with her, he turned her to face him. "What are you doing? They're not going to stop!" He began hurrying her away from the oncoming horses.

The horses thundered past them trailing their leads. "I imagine they are heading back to the palace where they feel safe," he said as they watched them race back to the road, slowing slightly to begin the descent to Kamea.

"I didn't see Derry," Eluned said. "And where are Chokhmah and Faolan?"

"Come on," Gwrhyr said, beginning to jog in the direction from which the horses had approached them. "Let's find out."

It was another ten minutes before they could see Faolan and Chokhmah standing over the prostrate body of what was clearly Derry.

"What happened?" Gwrhyr demanded as they skidded to a stop in front of the dying donkey.

"Some kind of wild cat." Faolan refused to meet Gwrhyr's eyes.

Eluned had already flung herself to ground, hugging the poor animal's head to her breast. Frothy blood stained her sweater as Derry struggled for air. She placed his head in her lap and began stroking his muzzle. He didn't fight much longer. With one final wheeze, his head went limp against her legs and Eluned began to wail.

That was too much for Gwrhyr. He grabbed Faolan by the bicep and shook the smaller man. "Look at me! How did wild cats even get close enough to attack without your scaring them away?"

Eluned looked up at Chokhmah, tears still streaming down her face. "I promised him," she cried. "I promised him that he wouldn't end up like Hayduke." It was then that she noticed that the gypsy's hair was down and that her clothing was in disarray. She began shaking her head as if by denying what she was seeing, it would make it not be true. "You didn't! You weren't!" She couldn't bring herself to voice the truth, but Gwrhyr had just realized what had happened.

"Tell me it's not true." Eluned had never seen him so angry. She hoped that she never had cause to see that face aimed at her. "You two were up here rutting like antelopes and you put our horses in danger? You had one job—graze the horses, keep them safe and return them to the palace in the evening. You're the one who said it needed doing, Faolan. What were you thinking?"

He pointed to the road. "Go back to the palace," he ordered them. "I don't even want to see your faces right now."

Eluned watched them leave, Derry's head still in her lap. She looked up at Gwrhyr, shaking her head. When they were out of earshot, she said, "Even when we went swimming, one of us was constantly checking on the horses. I don't understand what they were thinking."

"Apparently they weren't thinking." He knelt down next to her. "Do you want to try and bury him?"

Eluned began unbuckling the Halter she'd once removed from Nyx. Perhaps she should just carry it in her saddlebags from now on. It certainly seemed to bring bad luck to whoever was wearing it. "No," she finally said. "Why swipe a meal from animals that were only doing what they were created to do? It's not the wild cat's fault, and they may even have cubs somewhere."

The Princess pulled the Halter off Derry before gently laying his head on the ground. Gwrhyr stood and offered her a hand to help her up.

"Let's go back," she sighed. "We have some decisions to make."

When they got back to the palace they found Jabberwock, Bonpo, Njima, and Yona gathered around the brazier speaking in hushed tones.

Bonpo stood and rushed towards them. "Wat happen? Where Delly?" Because the others took turns caring for the horses during the day, it had become Bonpo's duty to make sure they were bedded down for the night. He had become particularly attached to Derry ever since the sweet little donkey had been nearly swept away in the Pegasus River.

The Princess saw him take in her tear-swollen eyes and the blood on her sweater, and his eyes filled with tears. "Wat happen?" he said, voice choked with emotion.

The Bandersnatch, Yona, and Njima had joined them by now. "The horses returned on their own," Yona whispered, "and nearly an hour later, Faolan and Chokhmah showed up and went straight to their room without a word."

Gwrhyr thought one word at Jabberwock, and his eyes glanced knowingly in the direction of the couple's room.

"While Faolan and Chokhmah were distracted by other things, some wild cats managed to creep close enough to attack the horses," Eluned explained.

Yona and Njima looked aghast, and Bonpo's face turned from sad to stony. Eluned now saw what the poacher had seen before he died. There was no pity in that face. No pity, no mercy.

"I gonna hurt," he said, full lips flattened into a frightening scowl as he turned to look at their doorway.

Gwrhyr put a restraining hand on his arm, and shook his head. "Of course you want to right this second," he said, "but you'd regret it a second later, and you know it." The anger left Bonpo's face to be replaced by sadness once again. "We're a team for a reason," Gwrhyr continued, "and we will work this out."

"Can you go talk to them, Jabberwock?" Eluned asked. "At this point, you're probably the most diplomatic among us. I feel like they've been banished to their room like naughty children."

"Which is what they're acting like," Yona interjected.

"True," Eluned agreed, "but they're the oldest humans among us and they need to face what they've done even if it's only facing their shame."

"Fortunately for them," Gwrhyr noted, "this happened near the end of the current quest. They will have an entire winter to decide what they want."

"I'll go talk to them," Jabberwock agreed, beginning to move in that direction.

"Tell them we expect them to join us for dinner," Eluned called after him, before turning back to the remainder of the group. "They still don't know why Gwrhyr and I were up on the plateau. I assume, despite everything, we're going to have a celebratory dinner tonight, Bonpo?" Though she wasn't sure her heart was in it anymore.

"Yes, Plincess," Bonpo sighed. "Wat you rike?"

It was hard to think about food with Derry's blood staining her clothing. "I'll leave that to you. I know you'll choose the right thing. Meanwhile, I need to change," she grimaced, "and wash this blood out of my sweater."

CHOKHMAH BURST INTO TEARS when she saw what Bonpo had conjured up for their evening meal. The veal-stuffed pancakes and sautéed mushrooms had been served the night of her Pomona.

"I am so sorry," she wept. Her eyes were already red and

swollen from all the crying she had done. "There is absolutely no excuse for what we have done."

Faolan's head was still bowed in shame, and he was pale except for two red spots glowing high on his cheeks as if marked by a permanent blush.

Gwrhyr handed him a tankard of wine. He looked as if he desperately needed it. "Remember when we were back in Bogaine," he said, "and I asked you if you were willing to sacrifice in order to give one hundred percent of your attention to this quest? Did I not say, at the time, that bad things could happen if you didn't?"

Faolan nodded and tears slipped from his eyes, sliding down his cheeks. "I can't even begin to apologize enough," he choked.

"How can we trust you to go off on your own and retrieve a treasure if we can't even trust you to look after the horses?" Eluned scolded them before releasing a sardonic laugh.

Faolan and Chokhmah looked at her, stricken. Everyone but Jabberwock looked taken aback. The Bandersnatch just watched the Princess silently.

"I'm sorry," the Princess apologized, "but isn't this ridiculous. Both of you are old enough to be my parents and I sound just like my parents. I'm the teenager here. I'm the one who's supposed to have the raging hormones."

"Eluned," Gwrhyr took her hand in his and squeezed it, "it might help to know that I'm pretty sure that I've never met someone with willpower as strong as yours. Just being near you makes mine stronger."

The Princess looked surprised. "Really?"

Everyone, including Chokhmah and Faolan, nodded.

"You force to be leckon wid," Bonpo agreed.

"Which may explain why you're the only virgin here!" Yona said.

Gwrhyr's cheeks colored but he didn't correct her.

Eluned bit her lip and blushed. She'd had no idea. She had always thought that everyone could be strong that way. "Regardless," she continued, "there is nothing Faolan and Chokhmah can do to bring back Derry, and hopefully," she couldn't help but sniff, "the cougars or panthers or whatever they are are enjoying a hearty meal right now. We just need to decide what we're going to do when we leave tomorrow."

"Leave?" Faolan was confused.

"Did you not think that there might be a reason we were up on the plateau this afternoon?" Gwrhyr asked him.

Chokhmah sat up straighter. Her thoughts had been so clouded by her own shame that it had not occurred to her that Bonpo had no place from which to get fresh veal, or mushrooms, for that matter. "The treasures."

"Yes," Jabberwock said. "Bonpo found the treasures."

"Bonpo?" Chokhmah looked surprised.

"He found them when he went to fix the loose tile near Eluned's door," Njima explained.

"And so we start the return trip to Jazeel tomorrow?" Now Faolan understood. They had lost the animal that carried a lot of their gear.

"Which means," Gwrhyr added, mouth full, then swallowed before continuing. "I'd forgotten how good these were. Good choice, Bonpo. Anyway, either Halelu or Fiachdubh needs to become our pack animal. And, you two will need to ride together. That is, unless Faolan wants to follow along as a wolf. We'll leave those choices up to you."

"Meanwhile," Jabberwock said, "we need to eat up and then pack up. We need to get out of here early."

"Wait a second," Eluned said. Everyone looked at her. "The Halter. We have the Halter. Do you suppose it really has to be attached to the foot of the bed to work?"

Gwrhyr's brow furrowed as he considered this. "I'm not sure, but it seems pretty specific. Does a bedroll have a foot?"

The Princess jumped up. "I'll be right back." She rushed to her room, placed the Halter's lead on the end of her bedroll and wished for a donkey like Hayduke. Nothing happened. She returned to the courtyard shaking her head.

"I suspect it has something to do with tethering the horse being wished for," Jabberwock told her.

"Oh! Horse!" she groaned. "I wished for a donkey." She hurried away again but was back a minute later, sighing. "I guess it really does mean that it has to be tied to the foot of a bed." She collapsed to the ground and picked up her wine." She raised her tankard to her mouth and took a big gulp. She knew she needed to get ready to leave the following morning, but numbing the memory of Derry dying in her lap seemed to outweigh any other consideration.

Jabberwock nodded to Bonpo to leave the pitcher of wine before curling up next to her side as she stared morosely in the charcoal and wood fire. He had spent the past eleven years watching the Princess fall apart over the death of a palace pet, a wild songbird, or even a trapped rat or mouse. Gwrhyr could get their things ready. He'd wait with her until she had enough wine to help ease her into sleep.

14ᴛʜ Hᴇᴛᴀʟ

A very subdued group of comrades arrived in Kuna short-ly before noon just two and a half days after leaving the Shamash Palace. They had left early the morning after Bonpo discovered the treasures in a chill and misty rain that had turned into a downpour several hours later.

It was too cold and wet to stop for lunch and they pushed on until nightfall where they hastily set up camp, tethered the horses, and crawled inside their damp tents for the night.

Omni be praised for the magical Crock and Hamper, Eluned thought, because Bonpo was able to visit each tent and provide the inhabitants with hot soup and later, mulled wine, and she had desperately needed both.

The rain didn't subside until well into the following day, but it was replaced by a penetrating cold that chilled them to the marrow. Eluned had shivered so much during the day that it felt like every muscle in her body hurt, and once again the mulled wine became a precious commodity.

It was with great relief that they turned into Kuna shortly before noon the following day.

While they were all cold and miserable when they arrived at the settlement, Chokhmah had developed a wet cough over night that had them all wincing every time she had suffered a coughing spasm.

Cyrus, whose son had been eagerly anticipating the group's return, quickly hustled Faolan and Chokhmah into his own home. And Jahan, who was ecstatic to see her, waited on her hand and foot plying her with hot soups and teas, and making sure the braziers were always well supplied with charcoal.

Arrangements were made for the others as well because there was some doubt as to how long it would take for Chokhmah to recover. Eluned and Gwrhyr were taken into Nahid's home, Njima and Yona into the home of Sanaz, Nahid's second-in-command. Because of Bonpo's bulk, he happily shared the meeting hall with Jabberwock.

"Those two sleep separately," the latter warned Nahid, indicating Gwrhyr and Eluned, before he trotted off.

"Phooey on you, Jabb," the Princess called after him. She turned to Gwrhyr and Nahid with a frown. "If something was going to happen, it would have already. Does he not trust me?"

"I don't think it has anything to do with either you or me," Gwrhyr assured her. "I think he's still reacting to Derry."

"The donkey?" Nahid asked. "I just realized he's not here."

Eluned shivered visibly, her entire body quaking. "Can we go somewhere warmer? Then I'll be happy to tell you what happened."

"Well that explains it," Nahid noted as Eluned and Gwrhyr finished telling her everything that had occurred since they left Kuna.

"Explains what?" Gwrhyr asked.

"The change in the group dynamic," she explained. "You left here joyous and hopeful, and despite the fact you found the treasures you were seeking, you returned somewhat chastened and restrained as if it were more than just the weather that had dampened your spirits."

"The past few days have been difficult for all of us," Eluned told Nahid. "Because I loved and trusted Chokhmah so much, I've struggled with condemning her for her actions. I could place the entire blame on Faolan, but I really don't believe he's completely responsible."

"They've both been equally amorous since they met," Gwrhyr agreed, as Nahid excused herself to see to having rooms made up for them.

Eluned sighed. "When she's feeling up to it, I will go and have a talk with her. We've spent a lot of time together since we met at the River Mab. And despite everything, I can't imagine a quest without her. But whether or not she and Faolan want to continue will be entirely up to them, and she needs to know that I do forgive her. She's not the only one who has made mistakes."

"Irirangi," Gwrhyr coughed the name of the Favonian prince, and Eluned laughed. There was that. She'd definitely been naïve enough at the time to confuse lust with love. Gwrhyr paused, then said: "And I probably should not have spent so much time with Arawn's army. I almost didn't make it back in time."

"Is that it?" Eluned asked, "Because I feel like there's something you're not telling me. Did you fall for someone while I was in Arberth?"

"What? No!" Gwrhyr's voice was vehement. "I fell for you the moment you approached me at the inn in Mjijangwa. You were so adorable the way you reacted to my assumption Bonpo was your husband."

The Princess laughed, remembering. "Seriously, though! It doesn't even seem possible. He's three feet taller than me and weighs half a ton!"

"I was actually teasing you," he smiled. "You were so easy to annoy back then."

"Well, everything is different now," Eluned said, and

changed the subject. Clearly he had no intention of telling her what he was hiding at this point, and now was neither the time nor the place. "At least all of us are alive. I hate that we seem to lose a lot of animals—Hayduke and Derry, Heiduc and Honeysuckle. Hopefully, Faolan will let me take Ronan back to Zion so that I can ride him again when we set out again next spring."

"Good point," Gwrhyr agreed. "Ruari has been really dependable, and gets along well with Ronan. It would be a shame to lose him."

THAT EVENING BEFORE SHE SETTLED INTO BED, Eluned walked over to Cyrus' house, and knocked on the door. Faolan answered it.

"I'm here to check on Chokhmah," she informed him. "How is she doing?"

"She's feverish," he told her feet, "but Jahan is watching her like an eagle."

The Princess frowned. Why wouldn't he look at her? "You will let me know if that changes, right?"

He nodded, still looking at the ground.

"Faolan?" He was acting like a baby and it was really starting to annoy her.

"Yes, I'll let you know."

She could barely hear him, and she snapped. A resounding clap filled the air and Faolan's head rocked back at the force of Eluned's slap.

He finally lifted his head, and stared at her in shock, his hand rising to cover the bright red mark her palm had left on his pale right cheek. He blinked back the tears that rose in his right eye. "What?"

"Get the kusemmak over it," she commanded. "This is absolutely ridiculous. You made a mistake. Deal with it. We've all made mistakes. When I fell for Irirangi, it was a really stupid blunder. I ended up hurting him in addition to the people I love. Ask any one of us, and we will all tell you we made a wrong choice at some point. I also forgot Hayduke, and am probably responsible for his death. Yes, Derry is dead because you and Chokhmah made a poor decision, but nothing is going to change that. So, just deal with it and move on. Be the man I know you are."

"We will not leave this place until Chokhmah is well and the two of you have decided that you want to be a part of the group. Do you understand?" She finished.

"Yes," he said.

"Now, what you two decide to do once spring arrives is something you can decide this winter, but until then you are a part of this quest. Get it?"

Faolan nodded.

"I love Chokhmah," Eluned continued. "I've known her longer than you, and I can't imagine a quest without her. And, while I don't know you as well, you've become an essential part of our group. Do you believe me?"

"I do believe you, Princess."

"Good, because we can get past this," Eluned smiled and took his right hand in both of hers. "In the grand scheme of things, it's a drop of water in an ocean, right? If nothing else, you'll be more aware of your decisions from now on. Making mistakes is what made it possible for me to sit in that clearing for a month—knowing that if I wandered away or got distracted it might keep me from seeing Nyx kept me focused. At the beginning of this quest I wouldn't have been capable of making a decision like that. Does that make sense?"

Faolan nodded again.

"So, any change for the worse tonight, you'll make sure I know?"

"Yes, I promise," he met her gaze. Chokhmah wasn't the only one with beautiful eyes, he realized.

"Then give me a hug."

They held each other for a while before the Princess stepped back, and looked at him. "Thank you, Faolan, I think I finally have a big brother."

He couldn't help but return her smile. "I always wanted a little sister."

She hugged him again, turned and began to walk back to Nahid's. "Tell Chokhmah I love her, and that I'm hoping she's much better by the time I come to see her tomorrow," she said over her shoulder.

"I will," he waved. "Good night, Eluned."

FAOLAN RETURNED TO THE ROOM where Jahan was caring for Chokhmah. He reclined on the bed by her side and held her for a moment, and then took her hand in his.

"How are you doing, my love?" he whispered in her ear. The dark hair next to that ear was damp with the sweat of her fever. Her cheeks were pink with the heat of her fever and she struggled for breath.

She didn't answer and he continued. "I just had a visit from our Princess." He touched his right cheek. "She reminded me that we are meant to be together and that we all make mistakes. And she told me she truly feels that I am an older brother to her and she hugged me, Chokhmah. And I could feel it. She really forgives us."

Chokhmah's eyes trembled open. "She hugged you?"

"Yes." He had to blink back the tears once again. "And she said she loves you and hopes that you'll be better by tomorrow when she comes to visit. And she wants us to be a part of this quest."

Tears seeped from Chokhmah's eyes once again. "She forgives us?" Her voice was but a whisper.

"She loves us, Chokhmah, and she wants us to be a part of this quest. Don't you understand? We're forgiven," he repeated.

Tears slid down her face for a little while longer before she drifted back into sleep. But this time, there was a slight smile upon her face.

Back at Nahid's, the Princess knocked on Gwrhyr's door. She informed him of what had just transpired with Faolan before broaching the subject of the harness.

"I want to try attaching the harness to my bed just to see if it works," she explained, "but I realized that if it did . . . "

"You'd suddenly be saddled with a horse or donkey to take care of?" he interrupted her.

"Exactly," she agreed, "and then I had another idea."

"What's that?"

"What if we left the Preternaturals with a male and female horse? The book says whatever horse is wished for. Obviously, we could ask Nahid, first, but doesn't that seem like a nice way to return their hospitality?" She gazed appealingly up at Gwrhyr.

He pulled her into his arms, cupping her chin in his hand. "You continually astound me, Princess." He kissed her. "Yes, I think it's an excellent idea."

Nahid was overjoyed when Eluned informed her of her revised plan the following morning—two mares and one stallion. She decided it would be easier to breed more horses with two mares rather than one.

"But Faolan's the expert," she said. "Let me talk to him first." She hurried over to Cyrus' home and once again knocked on the door.

"Good morning, Cyrus!" she greeted him when he opened the door. "How is our patient doing?"

"The fever broke last night," he smiled. "We believe she's on the mend."

"No doubt the ministrations of one very special lad were instrumental in that."

"Chokhmah told him he was a natural healer, and has been teaching him about herbs and medicinal teas this morning. With my help, of course." He indicated that she was welcome to come in, but she shook her head.

"Actually, I'm here for Faolan," she said. "Could you get him for me? I need his advice."

Cyrus disappeared down the hallway, and Faolan appeared at the door a minute later.

"Do you have a minute?" Eluned asked when he arrived.

"Yes, what is it?"

"I need your expertise." She extended her hand, and he took it, brow creased with curiosity. "Come on, I'll explain on the way to the barn."

She told him the plan, and added, "So, we need you to do two things—fashion some makeshift halters that can be used until some real ones are made, and help Nahid decide which type of horse will be best for their needs."

"What if it doesn't work?" Faolan asked.

"Oh ye of little faith," Eluned teased him. "It simply has to work."

Faolan laughed. "Can I borrow some of that optimism?"

"Absolutely," she said. "As much as you need."

They stepped into the barn where a number of people were already waiting, including Gwrhyr, Yona, and Njima.

"We assumed rope could be used for halters at first," Gwrhyr approached them with a large coil of cordage in his arms about the width of a thumb and soft to the touch. "They say they use this to rope their sheep and goats when necessary."

"That's perfect," Faolan took the rope from him. "As a matter of fact, if knotted correctly, this is all you need. Leather's nice but not necessary. Who is going to be caring for the horses?"

Three teens, two boys and a girl of about fifteen years of age, stepped forward and introduced themselves—Firuz, Bahadur, and Azar.

"Tell me you have the hyper photographic memory mutation," Faolan said to them.

"Yes, we do," said Bahadur, the taller of the two males, "and we speak the Common Tongue. The Imperator said that we need to remember everything you teach us."

"Good." He started measuring out four lengths of rope. "First we're going to learn how to make a rope halter."

Gwrhyr handed him a knife with which to cut the rope, and then handing each teen one of the pieces, Faolan spent the next fifteen minutes slowly taking them through the process of learning where and how to tie the knots that would make the halter.

"Got it?" he asked when they were each holding a rope halter in their hands.

"Definitely," said Azar as she tossed her braided ponytail back over her shoulder. It had a habit of swinging forward every time she moved.

Faolan turned to the Princess. "Shall we try the treasure?"

Bonpo had since carried a bed into the barn as it seemed a more likely place for horses to appear.

She handed the Halter to Faolan. "You do it. I don't want to risk bringing forth the wrong horse." Derry was still on her mind and she worried that a donkey might appear before Faolan had a chance to wish for the right horse.

Faolan nodded and crouched down to attach the lead to the foot of the bed. He closed his eyes for a moment, and had barely had a chance to complete his thought when the people around him gasped.

He opened his eyes as the muzzle of a horse whiffled his hair with its warm exhalation. He stood, biting his lip in wonder. The Princess was right; the Halter worked. And the stallion was exquisite—a dappled grey with a straight profile, broad forehead, large eyes and small ears. His chest was deep and wide and his legs, heavily muscled. A perfect draught horse.

Faolan indicated that Firuz should approach—while the boy was shorter than Bahadur, he was much stockier, and showed signs that he might one day be as muscular as the stallion.

Removing the lead from the bed and the Halter from the horse, Faolan showed Firuz how to put the rope halter over his head. "You can attach another piece of rope here," he pointed, "to use as a lead. Now just hold him for a minute and let him get accustomed to you."

Turning toward Azar and Bahadur, and the others who were watching, Faolan explained that he had chosen what he called a Diligence horse, because not only were they powerful, but they were known to be intelligent and willing workers with good dispositions.

"They are also easy to keep, which means they don't need a lot of food to stay alive. Although," he paused, "I would advise you to start growing hay for them to store for winter. Too late, this year, I know, but you'll be fine if you graze them daily. Also," he concluded, "these horses adapt well to different conditions and climates. You should be able to use them for everything from riding to hauling."

Twice more Faolan repeated the process of attaching the Halter and its lead to the bed producing first a beautiful dappled grey mare, which he handed over to Firuz, followed by a midnight black mare with a star of white on her forehead that Azar fell in love with at first sight.

He was handing the Halter back to Eluned when she stopped him. "We need to decide whether or not we need another donkey or mule before we return to Jazeel. I know I'll need one when Jabb and Bonpo and I return to Zion, but which do you prefer—to conjure one now or continue using Fiachdubh?"

Thinking for a minute, Faolan finally admitted, "Honestly, I'm fine either way. What do you want?"

She bit her lip—it was a tough decision—did she want to replace Hayduke or Derry. What was she thinking—she couldn't replace either of them! She shook her head and looked imploringly at Faolan.

"Do you trust me to decide for you?" he asked.

"Please," she assured him.

So, for the final time, Faolan attached the Halter to the bed, and Eluned had to bite her tongue to keep from shrieking in delight like a little girl. The over-sized donkey had a long and shaggy brown coat with a white nose and white rings around her eyes and very large and shaggy ears. She flung herself into Faolan's arms and gave him a big hug.

"She's perfect!" Eluned cried. Most importantly, she looked absolutely nothing like either Hayduke or Derry. The Princess looked up and grinned at Gwrhyr who gave her a thumbs up.

Njima, who was standing next to him, said under her breath, "Now that was a brilliant bit of diplomacy—getting Faolan to handle all of that."

Gwrhyr nodded, clearly the Princess was learning how to treat people as humans and not subjects. Faolan was definitely himself again. "Now if she can just work the same magic with Chokhmah," he said quietly to Njima.

Eluned was leading her new donkey over to Gwrhyr and the others. "Now, I just have to come up with a name for her," she said when she arrived in front of them.

"I have to admit that I've never seen anything like her," Gwrhyr said.

"Faolan said it's a rare breed," Eluned explained, scratching her behind the ears. "Look how sturdy her legs are. I won't feel so bad about her having to carry our things." She reluctantly handed the lead to Bonpo, who would be the one to lead her once they started travelling again. "It's time I had a talk with Chokhmah. She needs to know that she's loved and forgiven. I can also let her know that Faolan's going to be busy for another hour or so," she told the group.

Cyrus led Eluned to Chokhmah's room where she was delighted to find her sitting up in bed and conversing with Jahan. The boy stood next to a window and pointed to the curtains.

"He is teaching me Pelfan, and I am teaching him the Common Tongue," she explained when Eluned entered.

"Jahan, do you mind if I have a few minutes alone with Chokhmah? It won't take long, I promise."

Cyrus translated and the two of them left the room.

Eluned turned to face Chokhmah once they were gone. "First and most importantly," she said, approaching the bed, "Faolan is training three teens to take care of their new horses. He should be back in an hour or so."

Chokhmah raised her eyebrows.

"We decided that it would be nice to leave them with a stallion and a couple of brood mares," the Princess explained.

"And that was your idea?" Chokhmah patted the bed next to her right side, and moved over a bit to give Eluned enough room to sit next to her.

The Princess nodded, climbing onto the bed, and relaxing against the headboard. She placed her head on Chokhmah's shoulder, and took the woman's right hand in hers. They sat in a genial silence for a while before Chokhmah finally spoke again. "Was it your idea to get Faolan to help with that?"

"He is the expert." Eluned's reply was simple.

"I thank you," Chokhmah said. "I have no doubt that it meant a lot to him to be needed by you."

The Princess smiled. "It makes me happy to see him being himself again." She laughed. "I can't wait for you to see the donkey he thought of for me. She's beautiful."

Chokhmah chuckled. "You and your donkeys."

"I still have to name her, " she mused and was silent again for a moment. "I miss this," she added a minute later. "It feels like a long time since we were able to spend time like this together."

"I apologize," Chokhmah said. "I promise that I did not intend for Faolan to come between us."

"Faolan! It wasn't Faolan. It was me. I'm the one who drove the wedge between us to begin with." Eluned was adamant. "If I hadn't been so smitten with Irirangi . . ."

"Then, perhaps, I would have never met Faolan," the gypsy countered, "and also, perhaps, you and Gwrhyr would not be where you are now."

"I hadn't thought of it that way," Eluned admitted. "I'm still amazed at how that crept up on me. Remember how much I disliked him when we first met?"

Chokhmah laughed, which induced a coughing spell. "I am sorry. I am better but not completely out of the woods."

The Princess made a sound of negation. "You were running a fever last night," she reminded her. "I think one of your super powers must be self healing."

"Perhaps so," she agreed. "I get sick so seldom."

"Everyone's health has been incredible on this journey," Eluned reflected. "I'm sorry that what happened in Kamea lowered your resistance so much."

"And now we see where the road of self-pity leads," Chokhmah smiled. "What I was going to say before I started coughing is that I remember the way you and Gwrhyr wanted to rip each other's throats out the day after my Pomona."

The Princess giggled. "He certainly knows which buttons to push. Fortunately, he no longer wishes to do so."

"It was clear at the time, my dear, that he only had eyes for you. You were the only one who could not see that. I imagine that is why he spent so much time away from us when we first arrived in Prythew, and later why he agreed to go out with the army. I do not think that he could bear to see you with King Arawn."

"But I stopped liking him almost immediately," Eluned argued.

"Perhaps so, my love, but you were still spending much time with him. And then Yona came along."

Thinking back to that time was something she usually avoided, but Chokhmah was correct. That was about the time Gwrhyr disappeared—heading off on training exercises and recruitment with Captain Bleddyn. She sighed.

"I would not fret about it too much," Chokhmah counseled her. "Omni uses everything for Its purposes. Choose to believe that what happened helped you learn to appreciate Gwrhyr more."

The Princess kissed Chokhmah's cheek. "See, this is exactly what I miss. You always make me think about things. And I have something you need to think about."

"What is that?"

"Faolan has agreed that he will at least be a part of this quest until we reach Jazeel. And, I've asked him to seriously consider returning to the Quest in the spring. I'd like to ask the same thing of you."

"Of course, my dear! I would not wish otherwise." She paused for a moment. "I cannot speak for Faolan, but I cannot imagine that we will not be joining you again. Omni would have to give me a very clear sign that I should remain behind."

"Even if Faolan chooses to stay in Bogaine?" Eluned pressed.

"If he reaches that decision, I might have to believe that we are not meant to be together. I made a mistake in Kamea. I allowed my passion to overrule my common sense. That will not happen again. The one thing that I do know for sure at this point is that Omni wants me to be a part of this." By the time she finished, Chokhmah's voice was growing hoarse and she leaned her head against the pillows and closed her eyes for a moment.

"I'm glad to hear that," Eluned said, "and it looks like you need to rest." She slid off the bed. "Just one more silly thing."

"Yes," Chokhmah whispered, eyes still closed.

"I was wondering if you could do a huge favor for me."

The alleged Queen of Pelf's amber eyes opened to stare at the Princess. "What? Of course, if I am capable. What is it?"

Eluned blushed, and bit her lip. "I'd like you to name my new donkey."

Chokhmah closed her eyes again, smiling. "I love you, Eluned. Of course I will name your donkey for you. I would be honored."

"Thank you. It's just that she reminds me of you—those big brown eyes and she seems so strong and wise."

The gypsy's smile deepened, and she chuckled. "I think I know exactly what we should call her—Tikvah."

"Tikvah?"

"It means 'hope.'"

"Hope," Eluned said. "I like it. Perhaps this donkey will live."

Chokhmah chuckled quietly. "That is my hope."

Eluned smiled. "I'm going to miss being able to see you this winter. You'll be so far away."

"I will miss you too," Chokhmah sighed, eyelids drooping again.

Eluned tread lightly to the door. "I'm going to miss every one," she said when she reached it, looking back over her shoulder, but Chokhmah was already asleep. She left the room, finger to her lips, and informed Jahan and Cyrus in a whisper that Chokhmah was napping. "I'd wait for a while before I checked on her. She needs to sleep."

18ᵀᴴ HETAL

The Questers arrived back in Jazeel late on the second day after they left Kuna. The Preternaturals sent them away with many thanks and the promise to do whatever Naphtali would have them do should it come to war.

"But let's hope it doesn't come to that," Nahid had said.

Queen Njima agreed. "If we can find all the treasures then we have a chance of keeping the peace."

"May Omni go with you," Nahid said, "and may we meet again."

They set off for Jazeel confident that the path they had hacked into existence a month previously had not grown enough to inhibit their progress.

When they reached Castle Indalo, Eluned begged for one final week together before they split up for the winter.

Naturally, the Queen had things she needed to see to that had been waiting for her return, but Eluned and Yona were fine with that as it gave them a little more time to spend together before Eluned, Jabberwock, and Bonpo travelled back to Zion. It was Yona's intention to stay in Jazeel despite the fact she knew she was more than welcome to stay at Castle Mykerinos.

"It's just too early in our relationship for Njima and I to be apart for that long," she explained to the Princess. "I think we would both worry that out of sight would mean out of mind."

"I understand," Eluned said. "But you will travel to Zion come spring, right?"

"Absolutely! Njima and I wouldn't miss it for the world," Yona assured her.

The week following their arrival was spent as much in each other's company as possible with the only exception being that Gwrhyr and Eluned were offered a little more time alone. Unlike Yona and Njima and Chokhmah and Faolan, they would soon be parting ways.

"You can do this," Gwrhyr reassured the Princess every time she quailed at the thought of informing her father, and then Uriel, of her wish to break the betrothal.

It was a good three weeks ride from Castle Indalo to Castle Mykerinos, the Princess began to calculate in her head. Then, once she informed her father, she'd have to send an official courier to Castle Bennu. It would take another three to four weeks for the courier to arrive there, and another three to four weeks before she got an answer. It might be twelve weeks before she even knew anything definitive. She might not even see Gwrhyr again until they met in Zion at the vernal equinox.

Eluned didn't want to dwell on it. No point in succumbing to depression when she had Gwrhyr and all her friends with her—she'd just take it one day at a time. She had to trust that this would all work out for the good. Omni had guided her so far—surely Gwrhyr was a part of Its plan as well.

Jabberwock, on the other hand, spent the week "interviewing" each of the Questers, interested in sussing out what their true intent might be—were they honestly in this for the good of humankind or was it just the adventure? The most dramatic changes over the course of the past nine months had taken place in the Princess, he thought. To some degree, he knew, it was because she was also the youngest member of the group. Regardless, she had not only matured, but had become more caring of others and had on more than one occasion stepped forward as a leader. He might be the unofficial leader of the group when it came to determining where they went next, but it was often the Princess they turned to for more personal matters.

He was particularly interested in querying Chokhmah and Faolan following the "debacle" on the day the treasures were discovered in Shamash Palace. By the time he was finished talking to them, though, he was convinced that they were thoroughly committed to the Quest, and deeply regretted their faux pas.

After talking with Yona, he could see that she was deeply devoted both to Eluned and the cause. It had opened up a new and better life for her, and she would die, she told Jabberwock, before she would betray the Quest. And, it was true that she had not allowed her relationship with Njima to destroy that.

So, the Bandersnatch thought—Njima. Was she on this quest for Yona and the adventure or was she willing to give her life for continued peace in the Thirteen Kingdoms? It was highly unlikely, he thought. No, he corrected himself, it was absolutely certain that one or more of them would not make it through this quest alive. Sacrifice is often the cost of doing something for greater good, he mused, frowning. Unfortunately, who would make that sacrifice had not been revealed to him.

Pushing those thoughts to the side, he went to meet the Queen. Njima, he discovered, was now as truly bound to the Quest as Yona and the others.

"You cannot even begin to imagine what a difference all of you have made in my life," she told Jabberwock. "Whereas before I ruled almost as if by rote. It was my duty, nothing more. Now I see how deeply interconnected we all are."

The rumblings of war had become a low growl, and while Jabberwock and Gwrhyr were positive that Kings Arawn, Hamartia and Hevel weren't ready to throw down the gauntlet, so to speak, they were definitely heading in that direction.

"How many people in these non-allied Kingdoms are dreading the thought of war?" Njima said, and Jabberwock understood the question was rhetorical as the Queen continued almost without pause. "I firmly believe that most humans only want to live in peace—that their major concern is simply to survive; that although they might fight for that, they don't actually want to have to go that far. The only ones who gain in war are the kings, and perhaps, queens, who are the victors."

Despite the fact they had little to do but take it easy, the week flew by. And when the evening prior to their departure finally rolled around, Eluned didn't think she'd be able to sleep a wink that night. Jabberwock had been accommodating and had allowed them to share a bed although he insisted on being there as well to act as a damper on their desire.

Fair enough, Eluned thought, because it was getting more and more difficult to be satisfied with the kisses and hugs snatched when no one was around to see them.

On their final evening together, though, he left the room with the admonition that he would return in an hour so that they might say their goodbyes in private.

"I trust that when I return neither of you will have embarrassed your kingdoms," he said before trotting out.

"Does that mean he doesn't want to give King Uriel a reason to kill you?" the Princess was puzzled.

"I suppose so," Gwrhyr mumbled, lips pressed against the hollow of her throat, distracting her from any other questions she might have.

The following day the Questers said their farewells with many tears, hugs, and kisses. Gwrhyr was travelling south as far as Ponike with Faolan and Chokhmah who would continue on to Bogaine. Eluned, Jabberwock, and Bonpo would travel northeast to Zion. The only difference this time is that they would be able to use the main trade routes rather than the slower back roads. They could stay in inns rather than camp as they would be journeying through the now allied country of Naphtali before reaching Zion on its eastern border and Aden to the south. Waving goodbye to Njima and Yona, they rode into Jazeel and crossed the bridge over the Pegasus River to the main north-south trade route.

After a final lingering kiss from Gwrhyr, Eluned watched as Gwrhyr, Chokhmah, and Faolan began riding southward. She turned her horse, with some reluctance, northward, and had only travelled a few feet before reining in Ronan. The Princess looked longingly over her shoulder until the man she loved and her two friends were out of sight. When she turned back around she saw Jabberwock watching her from his basket atop Tikvah.

"Do you truly love him?" he asked her.

"Yes, Jabb, I do," she assured him.

"Don't forget that," the Bandersnatch replied.

The Princess shook her head in confusion. "We won't be apart that long. How could I forget that I love him when I already miss him?"

"Things happen." His reply was simple.

"Do you know something I don't know?"

Yes, he thought, praying to Omni that when the Princess found out, the Quest would not have to be forfeited. Instead he said, "Nothing like that. I am only saying that it is good to remind yourself daily, as he travels farther and farther away from you, of how it feels when you are together."

She nodded. "I guess that makes sense, but sometimes you say really strange things, Jabb."

The Bandersnatch chuckled and turned to face the road ahead again.

Because they were travelling the main trade route through

Naphtali to Zion, Njima had sent pigeons ahead to secure their daily lodging. The Princess also sent a courier ahead to warn her parents of their impending arrival.

A LITTLE MORE THAN THREE WEEKS LATER—about midday on the 22nd of Rees—the walls of Castle Mykerinos finally materialized in the distance. They would make it home well before dark.

Eluned was both excited and anxious, and desperately wished to have Gwrhyr by her side when she told her father that she must break her betrothal to King Uriel. As Jabberwock had suggested, and because she had many hours in which to do so, she replayed in her head every moment she could remember from when they first met at the Trade Route Inn until they parted ways in Jazeel. He was already back in Ponike, as it took less than two weeks to travel there by the main trade route. And, if Faolan and Chokhmah weren't at Rose Cottage yet, they would be soon as it took about three weeks to travel to Bogaine from Jazeel, as well.

She loved Jabberwock and Bonpo, but it was going to be a long winter without her friends. Bonpo would be returning to his inn. She had tried to talk him into remaining at Castle Mykerinos for a week once they arrived there because she wanted to celebrate his birthday with him. But, he was anxious to see the Crossroads Inn again, so they had compromised. He would stay an extra day, which now meant they would observe his birthday on the 23rd of Rees instead. As she had arbitrarily assigned him a birth date, she supposed it would have to do.

Then, once again, she would be alone with her parents and Jabberwock. She supposed she needed to tell her father about Gwrhyr as soon as possible because that would get King Uriel to the castle sooner, she hoped, and that meant she could see Gwrhyr sooner.

They passed over the bridge and into the castle grounds

about a couple of hours before sunset, and were greeted by both King Seraphim and Queen Ceridwen.

Eluned found herself crying as she dismounted Ronan and handed him off to a stable hand. Rushing into her parents arms, she cried, "Papa, Mother, I've missed you so much." She hadn't realized until that moment how true that was.

When she had set out for a three-year adventure with Jabberwock nigh on a year ago, she hadn't expected to see her parents again so soon. Nor had she dreamed that the journey would lead her through so many adventures in such a short time or that she would gather around her an amazing group of friends. Her real hope had been that she might fall in love, and even that hadn't occurred as she expected.

And that barely scratches the surface, she thought as she accompanied her parents back into her home of eighteen years, right hand gripping her father's left. She'd survived everything from a snowstorm to an attack by Aberrations and even nearly being sacrificed. Not only that, in less than a year they had managed to gather together nine of the Thirteen Hallowed Treasures.

Only four more to gather, she mused, and a shiver of fear traced an icy finger down her spine. Four treasures in the four most dangerous Kingdoms, and this time they wouldn't have their collective spirit and energy to help see them through.

THE THIRTEEN KINGDOMS

THE TRIQUETRA ALLIANCE

I. The Kingdom of Zion
Sigil: Golden Gryphon on Black

Ruled by: King Seraphim and Queen Ceridwen

Children:1 daughter—the Princess Eluned

Capitol: Castle Mykerinos is located in Goshen

The River Musk flows southward through Zion and Castle Mykerinos is located on a plateau above the river. Other towns and landmarks include Roodspire and Muskroe, the Mountains of Misericord and the Misrule Pass.

II. The Kingdom of Aden

Sigil:
Scarlet Phoenix on Gold

Ruled by:
King Uriel (son of King Gavreel
and Queen Angharad, both deceased)

Children:
Not married but betrothed to Princess Eluned of Zion

Capitol:
Castle Bennu is located in Ponike,
which is a harbor town on the Gulf of Eudaemon

Other towns and landmarks include Batum.

III. The Kingdom of Sheba

Sigil:
Red Hawk on Green

Ruled by:
King Adeyemi and Queen Yobachi

Children:
Three sons—Daud, Paul, and Uwem;
Two daughters—Nala and Prisce

Capitol: Salama Palace is located in Mwezi-barafu

Sheba is bordered to the east by the River Mab. Other towns and landmarks include the Desert of Serket, and Baharimoto, a port town at the River Mab delta into the Anoon Ocean.

IV. The Kingdom of Favonia

Sigil:
Copper Sea Turtle on Blue

Ruled by:
Queen Miryam (King Rangatira is deceased)

Children:
Prince Mauri. He is married to Princess Elili,
and they have three children—one son, Prince Irirangi,
and twin daughters, Leleua and Talei

Capitol:
Whanga Palace is located in Seemu on the island of Favonia.

The other Favonian Islands include Hakinaipo, Hemamoku, Tapurora and Paliaina. Vailima is the main town on Paliaina, which is the smallest and most remote of the islands.

V. The Kingdom of Dyfed

Sigil:
Silver Unicorn on Purple

Ruled by:
King Cian and Queen Chelli

Children:
Eldest child a daughter, Gittan, and a younger son, Bryan.

Capitol:
Castle Abbert is located in Portuma on the Anoon Ocean

The River Leprican flows out of The Seven Sisters, a mountain range in the west of Dyfed and into Hardaigh Forest. The harbor town of Thírnagall is just west of Adamah's western border. Bogaine is a small village to the northwest of Thírnagall.

The Awen Alliance

VI. The Kingdom of Annewven

Sigil: Crimson Dragon on White

Ruled by:
King Arawn (aka The Crimson King)

Children:
King Arawn is not married although he does
have a number of illegitimate children

Capitol:
Castle Pwyll is located in Prythew; King Arawn winters at
Castle Emrys in Arberth on the Anoon Ocean

The River Mab forms the western border of Annewven, and the River Duir flows through the Prythew valley. Ruisidho is a village near the western border of Annewven that is home to Standing Stones atop a hillock. Avalach Forest, near Arberth, was once home to the unicorn, Nyx.

VII. The Kingdom of Simoon

Sigil:
Grey Wolf on Forest Green

Ruled by:
King Hamartia and Queen Foehn

Children:
4 sons: Kaiser, Jarvis, Bemot and Raynor

Capitol:
Castle Rodolf is located in Sigwald

The River Duir flows southward through Simoon and into Annewven before reaching the Anoon.

VIII. The Kingdom of Adamah

Sigil:
Gold Lion rampant on Silver

Ruled by:
King Hevel

Children:
King Hevel is betrothed to Yona

Capitol:
Castle Lavieven is in Stonehelm

The mountain range of Panavhadesh runs through the center of the kingdom, north to south. It towers over Adam's Way, a trade route running from Hashirim southward to Markheshvan. Other towns on Adam's Way include Tobermory and Hagafen. The major port of Seagirt is located on Adamah's eastern border on the Anoon Ocean.

IX. The Kingdom of Kamartha

Sigil:
Black Satyr on Pale Blue

Ruled by:
King Janak and Queen Lakshmi

Children:
3 sons: Amit, Baldev, Chetan;
4 daughters: Amala, Bala, Chandra, Divya;
Amit and Amala are twins

Capitol:
Lamaxana Palace is located in Kaumari

Queen Fuchsia, the Princess Eluned of Zion's great grandmother, is from Kamartha and grew up in the Wilds of Discord near the Kingdom's southern border with the lost Kingdom of Pelf. Later, she returned to Kamartha to become an actress on The Masala, the theater district in Kaumari.

X. The Kingdom of Dziron

Sigil:
Golden Dragon on Crimson

Ruled by:
King Zhang and Queen Ling

Children:
3 sons: Qiang, Chao and Huang.
One daughter: Xiang. Princess Xiang, who is 16, is betrothed
to Prince Aahil of Tarshish who is 22 years her elder.

Capitol:
Tsering Palace is in Jungnay

The Vale Vixen in the Peaks of Vulpecula was once home to the Janawar. The Peaks of Vulpecula is home to the Yeti.

THE NEUTRAL KINGDOMS

XI. The Kingdom of Naphtali

Sigil:
White Winged Horse on Red

Ruled by:
Queen Njima

Children:
She is single, having broken her betrothal
to Prince Aahil of Tarshish.

Capitol:
Castle Indalo is located in Jazeel on the
western side of the Pegasus River.

The former capitol—Shamash Palace in Kamea on the Djed Sea—was deserted after the events that caused the Devastation of Pelf and formed the Sea of Blood.

XII. The Kingdom of Tarshish

Sigil:
Black Cobra on Tan

Ruled by:
King Dodi and Queen Chahindra

Children:
2 sons—Boutros (the eldest) and Aahil (the youngest child)
and one daughter, Huda

Capitol:
Iqbal Palace is in Tartessos, a port town
on the western border with the Anoon Ocean.

Tarshish is the southernmost kingdom. Smuggler's Bay is located to the east, and is a favorite hiding place for pirates.

XIII. The Kingdom of Pelf *aka* The Devastation of Pelf

Sigil:
Black Kraken on Red

Ruled by: No current rulers.
King Alborz and Queen Jazmin ruled before the Devastation.

Children:
2 sons—Alborz and Gaspar;
1 daughter—Parisa. Only Alborz survived.

Capitol:
Zhaleh Palace was located in Buta on Pelf's southern border
with the Anoon Ocean.

Currently the Devastation of Pelf is inhabited by what are
known as the Aberrations.

Pronunciation Guide

Princess Eluned: E-leen-ed
Gwrhyr: Goor-heer
Chokhmah: (ch as in loch) Hock-mah
King Arawn: Aroun as in around
Queen Foehn: Fern
Captain Bleddyn: Blethin (th as in the)
Lord High Steward Hywel: Hoo-well
Lady Celyn: Kay-lin

Animals

Heiduc: Hi-duke

Other

Prythew: Prith-yew
Dyrnwyn: Doorn-win
Castle Pwyl: Poo-ull

Days of the Week

Monday: Deethyeen
Tuesday: Deethmarth
Wednesday: Deethmerker
Thursday: Deethyai
Friday: Deethgwener
Saturday: Deethsadoorn
Sunday: Deethseel

Months

Beth (December 24 to January 20)
Luees (January 21 to February 17)

Neeon (February 18 to March 17)
Feharn (March 18 to April 14)
Saitheh (April 15 to May 12)
Eeahth (May 13 to June 9)
Deer (June 10 to July 7)
Teeneh (July 8 to August 4)
Colth (August 5 to September 1)
Meen (September 2 to September 29)
Gort (September 30 to October 27)
Hetal (October 28 to November 24)
Rees (November 25 to December 23)

Read an excerpt from

Death's Dark Shadows
Book Three of the Hallowed Treasures Saga

18ᵀᴴ LUEES

Eluned's heart was beating wildly in her chest as she hurried down the hallway toward the staircase that would take her downstairs to confront King Uriel. She barely noticed the portraits of former kings and queens of Zion that lined the walls of the corridor. The Princess had seen them nearly every day for eighteen years, had studied them numerous times over the years, but now her eyes were fixed on the marble floor as she rehearsed what she was going to say to the King.

Descending the main stairway to the castle's entrance hall, she tried to swallow the lump in her throat. It felt as if her heart had broken the bounds of her ribcage and lodged itself there.

Shortly after she'd returned to her tower bedroom, she had received word of King Uriel's arrival. She had been floored—his unannounced appearance had been both sooner than she'd calculated and completely unexpected. Why the surprise? Why hadn't they been warned of his approach?

When the page had delivered the message, the Princess had stared at him in horror for a full ten seconds as the shock ricocheted around her brain before she finally pulled herself together enough to dismiss him. And that was odd too.

Why hadn't it been her mother, or at the very least, Jabber-wock, to have brought the message? The Bandersnatch had asked her every day for the past seven weeks or so if she still loved Gwrhyr. And everyday she had replied in the affirma-tive. Eluned missed him desperately—his touch, his kisses, but most importantly, she missed his companionship. She hadn't realized how much she'd come to depend on his being there whether it was just to make a silly observation or to have a serious discussion or even sit in amicable silence.

Now if she wanted to talk to someone she had to seek out Jabberwock or her former tutor, Brother Columcille. It just wasn't the same.

Once the shock of Uriel's arrival began to subside, she hurried to her armoire to change into something a little more appropriate. She was still in the leather breeches and wool sweater she'd been wearing that morning during sword prac-tice. Gwrhyr liked her in pants, but she couldn't assume that the King would. Not that she actually cared what he thought, but she didn't want to outrage her parents. They would see her manner of dress as an insult to the King of Aden if she wore pants.

Eluned decided to go for modest and pulled from the ar-moire a dove grey tulle skirt and lavender sweater made of soft rabbit's fur. After she had changed, Eluned braided her hair in a long ponytail although it took her several tries before her hands stopped trembling enough to do so. The Princess frowned. It was occurring to her that perhaps the imminent arrival had been purposefully withheld from her. Perhaps not a bad idea considering her shaking hands and the butterflies in her stomach, she thought, but it still irritated her.

Walking over to her window seat, she sat down and spent the next ten minutes with eyes closed deliberately trying to calm herself in the way in which Brother Columcille had taught her. Long breath in, long exhalation, as she repeated

"Omni Within, Omni Without". She'd been dreading this day for months, and now it was finally time to face it, and she needed to be in control when she did so.

Eventually she felt her strength and resolve return, and with determination she walked to the door and began her walk down the long hallway to the top of the staircase. It only took a couple of steps before her heart was once again hammering against her ribs.

She reached the stair, took a few deep breaths, and began the descent. As the staircase curved to the right, she risked a peek over the marble bannister. His back was turned toward her, but she'd know that stance anywhere. She stopped, confused. He wore a simple gold crown, and it glinted in the winter sunlight that poured through one of the tall and narrow windows in the entry hall. The dark brown hair that fell in waves to just above his shoulders was as familiar to her as her own ebony curls.

What was Gwrhyr doing here, she thought, mind racing to fit the pieces of this puzzle into something that made sense? Why was he wearing a crown and dressed in the finery of a king? He was supposed to wait until . . . and then the realization struck her like a blow to her gut, and she grunted audibly. The blood drained from her face and black dots swam before her eyes, and she felt herself sway dangerously forward. Her hand reached blindly for the stair rail to steady herself.

The shock was quickly replaced by anger and the blood rushed to her head as tears filled her eyes. What a fool she had been! At her gasp Gwrhyr, or, more appropriately, King Uriel, had turned toward the staircase taking a step in that direction as she reeled forward. By the time he reached the bottom step, she had recovered her balance and was running headlong back up the stairs toward her tower room. Her only consolation was the deeply pained expression on his face, the gleam of tears in his blue-green eyes.

Slamming the door and locking it behind her, she threw herself across the rose pink counterpane that topped her bed, sobbing. She was so embarrassed. How could she have been so blind? Had anyone else figured it out? Had they been laughing behind her back all this time?

There was a knock on the door.

"Go away!" she cried. "Leave me alone!"

"Darling?" It was her mother's voice.

Eluned slipped off the bed and padded to the door. "Did you know?" she asked from behind the closed door.

"Sweetheart." Her mother's voice was placating.

"Mother! How could you?" Eluned began weeping again.

"Please open the door, Eluned."

"No!" She turned her back on the door and walked over to her window seat and stared bleakly out the leaded glass. The Mountains of Misericord to the east were blanketed in snow, and under the overcast sky looked as cold and desolate as her heart felt.

Is this why Jabberwock insisted that I remind myself each day how much I love him, she wondered? It was impossible that he wasn't a part of this. Could she still love Gwrhyr knowing that he had purposefully deceived her from the moment they first met? The joke's on me, she thought, another sob hiccoughing from her. I fell in love with the man I'm supposed to marry. How could she still love him and feel so betrayed at the same time?

She walked over to her bed and retrieved Eira, her stuffed unicorn, before returning to the padded window seat and curling up on it. She hugged Eira to her chest before burying her face in its soft to the touch rainbow-dyed mane. Nyx's mane had been white but opalescent so perhaps Eira's mane was not far off.

"You're avoiding the obvious," she murmured to herself, sitting up straight and taking a deep breath. It was true. It was much easier to muse on the meaningless than to try to decide what to do about Gwrhyr.

There was another knock at her door—this one loud enough to cause her to jump.

"Eluned!" This time it was her father.

"I'm sure you were in on this too!" Her voice was petulant.

"Jabberwock convinced us it was for the best," he explained.

Jabberwock. She should have known. The conniving little beast. She remembered the smirk on his face when she'd been asking Gwrhyr for help that night at the inn in Mjijangwa. "Arghh," she shouted. "I'm going to kill him!

She propelled herself from the window seat and stomped over to her armoire where she'd placed Dyrnwyn. There was a rasping sound as she pulled the sword from its scabbard.

She flung open the door. "I'm going to kill them both," she told her father, the blue light racing up and down her left arm.

Her father frowned and placed a conciliatory hand on her shoulder. "Don't you think that's a little extreme?"

"Not for Jabberwock," she glared at her father, who chuckled.

"I have to admit that there are times I might agree with that, as would have my father."

"Hmpf," she snorted. Jabberwock had been part of the reason his father, King Simeon had grown up without a mother. The Bandersnatch had helped her run away from the castle and back to the Kingdom of Kamartha.

"And yet," King Seraphim said.

"And yet he claims that everything he does is because he has been led to do so by Omni," the Princess concluded for him.

She lowered her sword. "Then why do I feel so betrayed Papa?"

The king pulled his daughter close, and she placed her head against his chest just as she had when she was a little girl crying over some imagined injustice. He let her tears flow silently for a moment, stroking her black hair just as he had when she was a child, before saying, "Do you think you'll be able to join us for dinner."

She looked up at him, eyes still red and swollen, dabbing at her nose with a handkerchief that was clenched in her right hand. "Absolutely not."

The king nodded, grimly. "I'll have something sent up."

"Don't bother," she sighed, stepping back into her room. "I'm not hungry anyway."

"Regardless," he looked at her sternly. "I will have something sent up. I take it you have no wish to see Uriel?"

"Gwrhyr, you mean?" She shook her head. "No, I have to face Jabberwock first. He needs to convince me that this was absolutely necessary." She sighed again. "I'll let you know when I'm ready to face him."

"I love you, Eluned." His eyes were a shade greener than hers, the green of the fjord to her tropic sea, but it was clear whom she'd inherited them from.

"I love you too, Papa," she gave him a tentative smile before closing her door. But this time she didn't lock it.

The Princess returned to her window seat, removed the cushion and then opened it and peered into the compartment. Some of her favorite books and treasures lay within, but she wanted one of her extra special books, one of the novels that had belonged to Queen Fuchsia. She removed the board that revealed the secret compartment and withdrew a small stack of paperbacks, well worn and pages yellowed with age. She inhaled the distinctive musty scent. Eluned wished she could create an incense that smelled like old books, she thought as she perused the stack before selecting *The Gunslinger's Troth*. She had discussed this book with her friends while they were at Castle Indalo. Maybe by the time she finished it, she might be ready to speak to Jabberwock. Eluned had to do something to distract herself—her mind kept flitting back to all the times she embarrassed herself in front of her future husband early in their relationship and her cheeks would flame again and the tears would well in her eyes. There seemed to be a never-ending supply of them.

THE PRINCESS WAS DEEP IN THE HIGH DESERT WORLD of the gunslinger, Ivanhoe, and his beloved Rowena, when there was a knock at the door. She reluctantly put down the book, and walked over to the door to open it to the servant carrying a tray containing a bowl of soup, a slice of bread and butter. Simple fare. Her father was a wise man.

The young woman holding the tray was unfamiliar to her—a sweet-faced young woman with hair the color of corn silk and eyes the pale blue of a cloudless summer sky. "I haven't seen you before, have I?"

"No, yer highness," it was clear the girl wanted to curtsey but was prevented from doing so because she might upset the tray. "Me mum jus' hed a bebby, and I'm fillin' in fer her."

"Please call me Eluned." The Princess indicated that the girl could place the tray on her desk. Any distraction was a good one at this point. She wasn't sure she could look King Uriel in the eyes ever again, and the thought of facing Jabberwock filled her with rage. "And you are?"

"Eleanor, yer highness, tho mos' folks call me Ellie."

"Eluned, Ellie."

"Eluned," Ellie repeated, eyes lowered and the color rising to her cheeks.

The Princess glanced at the window seat where *The Gunslinger's Troth* lay spread-eagled on the cushion, and had a sudden thought. "Can you read, Ellie?"

Eleanor's eyes widened in surprise. "O'course not, yer highness, er, Eluned."

"Would you like to be able to read and write?"

"That's not fer the likes of us," Ellie stared at her feet, clearly uncomfortable.

"Malarkey!" Eluned snapped, and then apologized. "I'm sorry, but I never want to hear you say anything like that again. Now answer in truth. Would you like to be able to read and write?" She'd had a lot of time to think about the idea of teaching reading and writing to those who wished to learn while travelling back to the Kingdom of Zion from Naphtali.

The girl stared into the Eluned's eyes for a moment trying to determine if she really meant what she was saying.

"Yes, I am serious," the Princess assured her.

Ellie's eyes widened as the truth of what the Princess was saying began to sink in, and Eluned smiled. "I will take that as a yes. I intend to talk to Brother Columcille to see if we can arrange classes for those who are interested. I will let you know as soon as something is settled. Does that sound good?"

The girl nodded, and curtsied, but a grin split her face and joy lit her eyes. Eluned dismissed her, and Ellie drifted from the room in a trance-like daze. The theory had been that to teach the servant classes to read and write might lead to an overthrow of the current system. Whether or not that was true remained to be seen. It just seemed so wrong to Eluned. As far as she was concerned denying education to those who sought it was the greater injustice, and she had the power to change it. She would speak to Brother Columcille in the morning. Meanwhile, she had soup to eat and a book to finish, and that would hold off a meeting with Jabberwock a while longer.

She retrieved her book and sat down at her desk. She was lifting a spoonful of warm broth to her mouth when she realized that it was Gwrhyr who had encouraged her to educate the people. She wondered if he had similar programs available in Aden. Her heart was still aching, but she just couldn't find it within herself to be angry with him. She knew how manipulative Jabberwock could be, and she blamed the Bandersnatch completely for the ruse Uriel had been forced into.

When she was finished with her dinner, Eluned placed her tray outside her door so that she wouldn't be bothered again. She was halfway through the book now, and intended to finish it before she fell asleep, but first she'd get ready for bed. She'd kept a fire roaring in the fireplace all evening, but as the hours crept closer and closer to midnight, the winter's chill began to make itself felt. She wanted to don her flannel nightgown and snuggle up in her down comforter for the remainder of the book.

It was well after midnight when she finally closed the book, tears streaming down her cheeks. Sometimes it seemed like she cried earlier and harder each time she read it although the current situation no doubt added to the flow of tears. The strangeness of the world portrayed, and the passionate romance between Ivanhoe and Rowena despite the fact their love ended tragically made the book a compelling read to the Princess. It had, she reflected, probably been the reason she had left the castle a year ago searching for love and adventure.

Eluned was about to extinguish the candle on her bedside table when she realized she'd left another burning on her desk. Cursing silently to herself, she slid out of bed and into her slippers, as the floor was cold, and walked over to her desk. She was just leaning over to blow out the guttering flame when there was a light knock at her door.

Who could be rapping on her door this late at night? She felt an ancient poem rise unbidden to her conscious, one she'd learned as a child and adored for its macabre flavor. "Suddenly there came a tapping, as of someone gently rapping—rapping at my chamber door." Should she ignore it? The tap came again, this time slightly louder, and curiosity got the better of her as it had the protagonist in the poem. She opened the door to find Gwrhyr standing there, his six feet of height nearly blocking the doorway.

"How did you know I was awake?" she glared at him.

"I saw light flickering beneath your door," he explained.

"And you just happened to be passing by?" Her brow wrinkled in perplexity.

"I couldn't sleep, and I just wanted to be near you." He looked at her more closely, and his hand rose to brush away a stray tear. "Are you still crying?"

"What?" She raised her hand to remove his as he was still cupping her cheek. She took another step backwards releasing his hand. "Oh. No! No. I just finished reading *The Gunslinger's Troth*. It always makes me cry."

Despite the fact she seemed wary and her voice was emotionless, Gwrhyr attempted a smile. Wasn't that just like her—to get so caught up in a book? "I love you, Fy Drysor" he said using his pet name for her that meant "My Treasure" in the tongue of the Hallowed Treasures. Then he touched his chest over his heart using his forefinger before touching hers in the gesture the two of them shared.

"I know that *Gwrhyr* does." She took yet another step backward into the room, breaking the contact with his finger. "I don't know if King Uriel does." She paused, and frowned. "You might as well come in. We're letting all the warm air out."

The Princess walked over to the window seat and sat down, and he joined her there.

"Gwrhyr and Uriel are one and the same," he said.

"Are they? Is there anything you would have done in the past year as King Uriel that you wouldn't have done as Gwrhyr?"

"I would have killed King Arawn, I can promise you that," Gwrhyr frowned, remembering. "But the real answer is no. The person you fell in love with is the same person you see in front of you now."

Eluned bit her lip, wanting to trust him, wanting to believe him. Could she? She had forgotten what it felt like to be near him. What she once had identified as annoyance had turned out to be desire.

"I wanted to tell you so many times." His voice was choked with emotion. "If you had ever acted like you even suspected..."

"I can see it now in hindsight. I think I just wanted something more exciting than being married off to a man I didn't know. So I deluded myself into believing that you were someone you weren't when clearly all the signs were there." She tilted her head and stared off into the distance, remembering. It had irritated her to no end that he had known so much about everything, that he wouldn't give her an inch in the beginning. Always harassing her while expecting the best of her.

"I tried to give you clues," Gwrhyr murmured, taking her hand in his. She tried to remove it and he gripped it tighter.

"The pocket watch should have been a dead giveaway," she admitted. "Did Jabberwock know that you were trying to clue me in?"

The King laughed. "Are you kidding? Why do you think he insisted on being our chaperone?"

The Princess couldn't help but smile though it didn't quite reach her eyes. "Ah, it now makes more sense. He was more afraid of what you might say than what we might do."

"I'm sure the thought of us being alone up on the plateau unnerved him completely."

Eluned giggled before clapping a hand over her mouth in horror. How did he make it so easy to be with him? "We were very good though," she admitted, "or restrained should I say? Even after the time we went swimming. And to your credit, as far as Jabb is concerned, you never said anything to make me suspect that you were anyone other than the son of one of King Uriel's lords."

Gwrhyr chuckled. "None of my lords have sons my age, actually. It would have been nice to have a peer to grow up with."

"I know what you mean," Eluned mused. "Njima said she had the same problem. I wonder if that's unusual or just the plight of the only child?"

"I hadn't considered that," he said. "As far as I know, Faolan is the only one in our group who has a sibling."

"Chokhmah did grow up with someone she believed to be her brother."

"We'll have to ask Bonpo whether he had any siblings." Gwrhyr was thoughtful. "Despite the fact we've spent so much time together, there is a lot we don't know about the others on our Quest."

"Or each other," Eluned reminded him, her voice dry. "You know more about me than I know about you."

"Well now you can ask me anything, and I will answer truthfully," he promised.

Eluned was silent for a moment as a thought occurred to her. She took Gwrhyr's other hand in hers, and looked into his eyes. "I am deeply sorry about Irirangi, Gwrhyr. I can't even begin to imagine how much that must have hurt you."

He looked down at their joined hands then back into her eyes. "It hurt," he admitted, "but as I said at the time, it was a wound that could heal."

"There's significantly more meaning to that now."

"What's most important at this moment is that I've missed this—just being together. I've missed you." Gwrhyr cupped her chin in his hand and gazed into her eyes. "Please tell me you feel the same way."

"Every single moment of every single day," she whispered. Damn it, why couldn't she stay angry at him, she thought as he leaned in to kiss her.

"We should go ahead and get married," she whispered into his ear a few minutes later. She also desired him as much as she had that last night in Jazeel.

He sat back so he could look at her more fully. "Are you serious? Why?"

"A number of reasons," she explained, "but the most important reason right now is that I don't want to have to wait any longer. Do you?"

He kissed her again. "Of course I don't." He chuckled. "Are you sure you're ready to give up unicorns?"

Eluned paused, clearly considering.

"What?"

"I'm thinking. This is a difficult decision."

Gwrhyr stood. "Well, if you need me to come back tomorrow and ask again . . ." He feinted toward the door.

"It's already tomorrow. I think I have a better idea."

She stood, and indicated he should come closer. He leaned forward and she whispered something in his ear.

He laughed and pulled her into his arms, kissing her gently on the lips. "I'd be honored to be your unicorn." Lifting her into his arms, he carried her to her bed.

Acknowledgements

A special thanks goes to my writers' group who have made the journey with me—Lois, Lauren, Ginger, Gail, and Katie. I am also grateful to Frank, Margaret, Melissa, and Belinda who read the first full draft of this book. And finally to Olive, who really had my back as I completed the edits on this second novel in the trilogy.

www.ingramcontent.com/pod-product-compliance
Lightning Source LLC
Chambersburg PA
CBHW060816120726
47909CB00006B/1942